MEG HUTCHINSON

Ties of Love

Hodder & Stoughton

Copyright © 2004 by Meg Hutchinson

First published in Great Britain in 2004 by Hodder & Stoughton
A division of Hodder Headline

The right of Meg Hutchinson to be identified as the Author
of the Work has been asserted by her in accordance with the
Copyright, Designs and Patents Act 1988.

2 4 6 8 10 9 7 5 3 1

A CIP catalogue record for this title is available from the British Library

ISBN 0 340 82996 6

Typeset in Plantin Light by
Phoenix Typesetting, Burley-in-Wharfedale, West Yorkshire

Printed and bound in Great Britain by
Mackays of Chatham plc, Chatham, Kent

Hodder Headline's policy is to use papers that are natural, renewable and recyclable
products and made from wood grown in sustainable forests. The logging and
manufacturing processes are expected to conform to the environmental
regulations of the country of origin.

Hodder & Stoughton
A division of Hodder Headline
338 Euston Road
London NW1 3BH

Ties of Love

I

'I told you the first time you came here, your sister died of pneumonia and the brat of a brother up and ran away.'

'I can't believe . . .'

'Who gives a damn whether you believe!' Uriah Buckley slammed a closed fist against a glass-fronted bookcase, shattering several small diamond-shaped panes, and as the shards fell about his feet rounded on the young woman he had kept standing before his large ornate walnut desk. 'What difference does your believing or not believing make?' He snarled. '*I* say it were sickness of the lungs, *I* say it and what Uriah Buckley says be what matters and not what you believes.'

Nerves fluttering like falling leaves, Amber Neale stared calmly at the red angry face.

'No,' she said quietly. 'That is not all which matters. My brother was no more than a child when I left him and my sister in the care of this house and though he was no doubt heartbroken at the death of Bethany he was no coward; Denny would never have run away, he would have waited for my return.'

Across the desk heavy-lidded eyes glinted cold and menacing as dark ice, thin lips drawing back in a vulpine snarl; the voice which a second before had been loud and harsh fell to a sibilant hiss. 'Are you calling me a liar?'

Was she? Amber's heart somersaulted in her chest. Was she calling him a liar? Uriah Buckley was a powerful man in

Darlaston, powerful enough to reduce her life to ashes, to
make it so it wasn't worth living should she cross him; but then
Bethany, that beautiful wide-eyed ten-year-old girl, was not
living and it appeared the Lord alone knew whether Denny
lived or not. But the Lord was not alone in that knowledge,
every fibre of her body, every beat of her heart told her so, told
her the man glaring at her also knew.

Breath quivering in her chest, Amber met the venom
poisoning that remorseless gaze, her veins throbbing as if the
fangs of death had already bitten into them. She should leave
now, go before she angered this man further; but even as the
warning sounded in her brain she answered quietly.

'Yes . . . yes, I am calling you a liar!'

Candles and oil lamp forgotten and unlit Amber Neale sat
staring into the darkness of her bedroom. Why had she agreed
to go, why had she agreed to leave her brother and her sister
and why had she trusted Uriah Buckley?

Across the deep silence of night the past reached out,
touching her, drawing her back into itself, whispering of things
she could not change.

'*Don't go please . . .*' The frightened words of a ten-year-old
girl cried in her soul. '*Don't leave Denny an' me. I don't like this
house, it fears me.*'

She had laughed at that. Trembling now with the memory
she could almost feel the thin shaking body of her sister as she
had gathered her in her arms.

Had they not been comfortable here at Bescot Lodge? She
had said, stroking that almost golden hair. Hadn't they got
food and a warm bed, were not the other servants friendly to
them, hadn't they been kind? There was no need to be fearful;
within a year, likely less, she would be back and the three of
them would be together as they had always been.

A year! Amber felt the air choke in her throat. If only that was all it had been!

She had assured them both constantly through the month of preparations. It was a big step from upstairs maid to becoming the personal maid of Joanna Buckley, the grand-daughter of the master of Bescot Lodge; it would mean a rise in salary, maybe even twelve pounds a year, think how they could live on that. But all her comforting had made no impact on Bethany's fear and the dread which showed in her lovely golden eyes grew more visible with every passing day.

Why had she not heeded that fear? Fingers twisting together, she stared into the darkness. Why had she not refused to accompany Joanna Buckley on that journey? The answer to that was simple, easier to understand than was the reason for her sister's distress. To say no would be to forfeit her place at Bescot Lodge, to be put out on the streets with a younger brother and sister to care for. There were no relatives to whom she could turn for assistance, no place she could find them shelter . . . hard as the decision to leave them was it was not possible to tell the master he must find some other person to travel with his granddaughter.

Joanna had been returned from finishing school less than two months when the letter arrived. The girl had been so excited, dancing and whirling about the huge bedroom flinging gowns and lingerie onto the ornate four-poster bed, blue eyes glistening and fair hair flowing out like a gauze mantle from her shoulders. Her parents had sent for her; she had sung the words, her clear voice sending them ringing around the room: they wanted her to join them to India.

'*Think of it,*' she had trilled, '*all those handsome officers in their regimental uniforms, afternoon teas on the terrace and those wonderful balls . . . Oh Amber, won't it be absolutely perfect!*'

Absolutely perfect. Tears squeezing onto her cheeks,

Amber let the past replay. That was how it had seemed, but only for Joanna Buckley. She had thrown herself into a mad round of fittings for morning dresses, afternoon tea gowns, ball gowns that were clouds of pink, white, lemon, blue . . . a rainbow of delicate silks, lace and tulle; dressmakers coming and going like so many twittering sparrows. Then of course she had needed bonnets, and this had meant hours at milliners' shops followed by visits to the glovemaker, bootmaker and of course a parasol-maker. It had left her exhausted but whilst the granddaughter of the house had flopped onto her bed with a refreshing tray of tea to rest and restore her strength in time for dinner, she, the lady's maid, had to carry on with her duties.

But all of this would not have been nearly so hard had it not been for the increasing fears of her sister. Every night as she plaited the child's hair for bed came the same heartrending plea, '*Don't go, Amber, don't leave Denny an' me alone, I be feared of this house.*'

She had not thought to ask why Bethany was so afraid.

'Why did I not ask?' Fingers twisted so tightly they ached, Amber left the thought whisper into the darkness. 'Oh my God, why did I not ask?'

There had been no sound of footsteps; only the delicate perfume accompanying the slight figure of the Indian girl betrayed her presence. Now she moved closer, a gentle hand reaching to those of Amber knitted together in her lap.

'You have been there again, you have been to the house of him who was once your master?'

'Yes.' Amber's answer was a murmur in her throat.

'But you have learned no more of your sister and brother?'

'He told me only what he said on my first visit, that Bethany had been taken with a summer chill which had rapidly turned to pneumonia and that Denny had run away the day she was buried and had not been seen at Bescot Lodge since.'

'But that is not what you believe?'

No, she did not believe the words of Uriah Buckley. He had looked directly into her eyes as he had spoken them but beneath that ice-bound menace something else had gleamed. She had been shown into his study to be kept standing throughout the brief moments he had suffered her to stay and not in any one of those moments had he expressed regret for her loss nor shown an atom of sympathy for the child who had died beneath his roof. No, there had been no word of condolence, no sign of compassion, but behind the venom spitting from that cold glare, despite the threat in the demand hurled across the desk, she had seen the shadow flit across his eyes, seen the quick working of that thin mouth.

Uriah Buckley had shown no sign of pity for her sister or concern for her brother; contempt and intimidation had been his answer to her questions but underlying that had been that something else, something his anger could not hide or the malevolence of his glare disguise; the something she now recognised. Uriah Buckley was a man in fear! Was it a shadow of his past? And was that shadow cast by her brother and sister?

Movements as sure in the half-light as in daytime, the girl crossed the room to light the lamp and as the lambent glow filtered through the shadows turned to look at the seated figure of the young woman who had saved her life, a life she would gladly give now if it would lift the sorrow from those shoulders, wipe the sadness from that pale face. But it would not; she could only try to give comfort.

'You have seen where she who was your sister lies, the words on the stone that covers her; do they not say, as he did, that she died of pneumonia? The Church of your faith, would it permit a lie, would it allow a non-truth?' Soft cloth whispered with each movement as the slight figure returned to kneel beside Amber's chair. 'Man and stone say the same thing so why do you not believe?'

She could not give voice to the doubt inside, she could not put reason to the feeling; she only knew its certainty.

'Stone cannot lie.' Amber's eyes closed but opened quickly against the sight of eyes that could have been chiselled from ice. 'But the words carved upon it are the words of man and not every man speaks the truth either with his tongue or his hand.'

'But you believe your sister lies in the ground!'

'Yes.' The answer sighed in the quiet room. 'Yes, I believe Bethany is buried in that churchyard but that is all I believe except Uriah Buckley is a liar. His eyes tell he is hiding a secret, that his heart knows a truth too terrible to tell.'

Rani had helped her to bed, sitting beside her until she thought her asleep, then had slipped silently from the room. But sleep was far away. Her glance going to the window, the curtains open to the beauty of the silvered night, Amber's mind crossed the boundary of time. India! How she had romanced the thought of that country during the long weeks of the voyage, lived out a fairy tale of imaginings. It would be bright and colourful; warm days in the shade of an awning chatting to others like herself, companions to officers' wives and daughters; exotic nights when the perfume of a thousand flowers turned the air to heady scent and young men paid her compliments. But dreams were all they had ever been. Helen Buckley, Joanna's mother, had taken the fever, dying before ever they had reached Meerut. The girl had been distraught, lying in her bed days and nights on end until her father had said she must return to England. That and only that had snapped her from her misery. She would not return to England; she would stay where she belonged, with her father, and Amber must stay with her.

She had tried to reason with Joanna. Amber watched the memories take on shape, emerging from the shadows like living phantoms. *There was no earthly reason for her to return home.* The girl had been adamant. *Were her family not in the care of her grandfather . . . would he not care for them, keep them safe?* Her father too had thought the same: his daughter needed a companion. There could be no further argument and without money of her own to buy passage back to England she had been trapped. She had written home explaining to Bethany and Denny what had happened, promising them she would return as soon as possible. Days had become weeks and weeks turned to months and still her promise had not been kept. With the attention of a handsome lieutenant Joanna had gradually returned to the smiling girl she had been in England. Though she visited her mother's grave regularly the sorrow of her loss seemed to fade a little more each day until she had finally felt ready to visit the local bazaar.

Colonel Buckley had smiled when, dragging Amber behind her, Joanna had gone to where he sat taking tiffin, the afternoon refreshment, on the low white-painted veranda.

'*Sit down, Joanna,*' he had said, flicking a raffia fan, '*your energy is too much for an old man!*'

Landing a kiss on his cheek before curling herself at his feet she had laughed. '*Age would never dare attack my father.*'

'*But youth would attempt to charm him.*'

Memory showed Amber the grey-streaked head turning towards herself, the blue eyes smiling.

'*Tell me, Amber, what is it this time?*'

'*The storyteller, Father,*' Joanna had answered first, excitement dancing in her voice, '*the storyteller has come to the bazaar, please may we go to listen to him?*'

'*And who is it says the storyteller has come to the bazaar?*'

'*Everybody says so, the servants . . . Narinder . . . just every-body.*'

Joanna had half risen, placing her hand on his knee like an adoring dog. '*Can we go, Father . . . please?*'

His eyes had shown any thought of rejection was lost yet he had tried to retain some modicum of restraint. '*Is this so, Narinder?*' he had asked the Indian nurse stood apart from them, her sari curling with the touch of a slight breeze. '*Has the storyteller come to the bazaar?*'

The figure Amber knew was simply a projection of her mind nodded its head, the woman's voice sounding softly in her ears. '*It is so, sahib.*'

'*And does he stay?*'

Amber watched the chestnut eyes rest momentarily on those of the colonel then dropped before she replied. '*Only for this day, sahib.*'

'*And tomorrow?*'

'*He goes, sahib, to who knows where.*'

'*I see.*' Jervis Buckley touched his fingers to the head of the girl crouched at his feet. Hair and eyes the colour of her mother's, the face upturned to him so like Helen's. '*If this wonderful storyteller is staying in Meerut for only one day then I suppose I must let the both of you go and hear his tales. But remember,*' he had looked from Joanna's face to Amber's, '*the bazaar gets very crowded and with the storyteller being there then this evening it will be more so; everyone will come from the villages to listen, you don't need me to tell you how fond these people are of their stories, so be sure you stay close to Narinder and when she says it is time to return here you obey her!*'

If only there had been the chance to obey! Amber closed her

eyes, pressing the lids with her fingers to wipe out the pictures. If only she had listened to Narinder; Joanna's ayah, the Indian nurse assigned to look after Jervis Buckley's daughter, had attempted to dissuade the girl. The heat . . . the flies . . . the beggars . . . she had tried each argument in turn, her use of English giving way more and more to her native tongue. The bazaar was not the place for an English memsahib, it was unseemly, there would be the charmer of snakes with his basket of cobras, did they want to see such creatures . . . then there would be the donkeys, the smell of dung, did they want the stink of that in their nostrils?

She could have done more to help Narinder, she could have added her voice to those pleas, said she found the idea of a trip to the bazaar frightening, that she had no wish to go there. Joanna would have listened. She would have been disappointed but she would have listened.

But she had said none of those things! Amber's breath trembled on a sob. She had said nothing and Joanna Buckley had lost her life!

2

Uriah Buckley stared out of the window of the room he grandly called his study. Study, pah! He snorted through his nostrils. He'd never studied anything more than a pick and shovel in his life. His hands were what had earned him his living, bloody hard graft for twelve hours at a stretch digging coal from the entrails of the earth. Neither hands nor brain had brought Uriah Buckley up from the regions of the damned, the mines in which hundreds were doomed to spend their lives to make a few men rich. Yet he had used his brain . . . but the plan had needed no studying.

Across the expanse of lawn interspersed with beds of flowers a border of tall sorbus trees nodded in the warm breeze, their leaves a constant ripple of silver green.

It had been at Sunday Service he had first noticed. Verity Deinol, the only child of Samuel Deinol, the owner of the New Hope deep seam coal mine running beneath Darlaston, Old Park and King's Hill and on into Wednesbury had smiled at him over her prayer book; but the prayer she murmured had been not for salvation but for satisfaction. And he had given her that! The smiling had gone on, the invitation deepening in the eyes that peeped above the hymn book, all cunningly hidden from her parents but the offer nonetheless there. It had needed no one to explain to him what was being presented and definitely no explanation of what could be the result could he but take up the offer.

It had come the following May Day. Carts decked in flowers and drawn by heavy dray horses, their manes and tails plaited with coloured ribbons and horse brasses gleaming like new gold in the spring sun, had taken the New Hope miners and their families on the yearly picnic provided by Samuel Deinol.

She had been there, pretty as a picture in white organdie, her smile innocent as an angel's; but it was no angel smile flashed in her eyes whenever they caught his and it was no angel eventually slipped beneath him in that copse of trees. She was hungry, she had whispered as they ran, hungry, but not for sandwiches and cake; she hungered for him. They had found a place, the open mouth of a disused drift mine now covered with fern and foxgloves. He might have been shocked by the way she had run her hands over his body, pressing her fingers to the hard bulge in his breeches, except his mind was too besieged by the passion now driving all else before it, surmounting every sense bar that of quenching the fire burning in his veins, of slaking the thirst that threatened to choke him, of taking what he wanted. And she had given it, the fever of desire as strong in her as in himself. 'Now!' she had cried the word as she snatched open the buttons of his clothing, 'Now!' as he had lifted her skirts, 'Now!' as they fell together on that bed of soft sweet-smelling fern. Twice more his flesh had hardened responding to the touch of her lips against it, the brush of a moist tongue over its throbbing head, and each time he had thrust it deep into her, answering the desire of his imprudent partner in lust. But, his own lust satiated, he had performed the second and third time with a purpose fuelled by a different lust, a very different desire. A child in her belly, his child, that would bring him the New Hope mine! And so it had. Samuel Deinol had possessed the good sense to realise his daughter's proclivity; what she had done once she might well do again and short of locking her away in a convent he might be unable to prevent it; and a daughter given to the Church would mean no grandson to inherit.

He stared at the patterns of sunlight dripping through the trees sprinkling the lawn with speckles of gold. Verity had delivered that grandson and in the agony of doing so had lost all appetite for lovemaking. But that had given him no grief, he had what he wanted, the New Hope mine . . . and a bedfellow? Those had been bought easily enough.

And the son? The product of that May Day afternoon? He had been provided with the best education his grandfather's money could buy, an education which had turned him into a dreamer. But dreaming could not run a coal mine, it would not build the empire Uriah Buckley intended to construct. So he had purchased him a commission in the Army; let him study Victoria's Empire, find out the hard way how they were come by, then Jervis would be only too willing to devote himself to helping build one for himself. But it had not gone that way. Jervis had liked the military life; as a major it was not strenuous, he had no tiresome parade-ground duties. In fact it seemed it afforded him every opportunity to dream. Even marriage to Helen and the birth of a child had not cured him of that. Yes, Jervis had sired a child, but that child had been a daughter. A daughter! Uriah felt the anger he had felt on hearing the news. A girl! What bloody good was that, a girl couldn't manage a coal mine, much less the iron foundry! He had told Jervis as much, urged him time out of number to get himself more children, get himself a son . . . but there had been no son, no other children, and now Jervis was gone with his company to India . . . India which had killed his wife and daughter.

Why! Uriah felt his jaw harden. Why had his fool of a son gone to that accursed country? Why had there been no more children and why had it been Joanna killed in that bazaar and not that bitch Neale? But it was not too late; Jervis would see he had to return to Darlaston, take over the New Hope mine and the iron foundry, beget a son to carry on the name.

Turning back to the desk Uriah snatched open a drawer. He would write to Jervis . . . yes, he would write and Jervis would come home.

She would have to find some way of supplementing the money Greville had left her. Amber stared at the household accounts she had already checked several times. It had seemed a large enough amount when she had first been told of it by the solicitor at his office in Waverley Road, but it would not last indefinitely, a deal of it having been spent buying this house, small though it was; then there had been the need to furnish it and though all but beds and bedlinen had been bought second-hand the money spent meant a considerable drop in the four hundred pounds which had been Greville's life savings.

Her head tipping backwards to rest against the high-backed chair, Amber let her lids close while her inner vision looked into a pair of blue eyes, their colour heightened by the bronze of years spent in the sun. Sergeant Major Greville Neale had taken her from that crowd, rescued her from a life of nightmare and eventually had married her.

It had not been a marriage born of love yet there had been love in it. She had been allowed to live on the regimental site based at Delhi, the thought of Meerut and what had happened to Joanna being as painful to her as all that had followed that savage attack; but the other European women, the officers' wives and their companions, had shunned her turning their backs whenever she appeared, making it infinitely clear they wanted no dealings with a woman 'gone native'; and the men, some privates and no doubt a few of their betters who would normally have seen her as a prime target, kept their hands to themselves and a civil tongue when having to speak to her. In their eyes she was Greville Neale's 'bit o' fancy' and no one crossed Sergeant Major Greville Neale.

But she had been no 'bit o' fancy'. Though Greville had seen her housed and fed, though he had sometimes called to enquire after her welfare, he had never spoken in any but the most polite of terms and not once had he attempted to touch her. He had listened to her story, piecing together the sobbed broken sentences, the whispered sketchy narratives that told the saga of those lost years; and there had been no con- demnation in his eyes. Then, a few months after bringing her to Delhi, he had told her he was leaving India, he was being returned to England. The news had devastated her. She had come so much to value his friendship; how would she ever manage without it?

Tears lumping in her throat, Amber seemed to see again the bronzed face watching her, the sadness in the blue eyes holding her own, the quiet voice saying she could return home with him: as his wife the Army would have to repatriate her.

His wife! Amber remembered the incredulity which had swept over her, the disbelief which had turned to tears in her own eyes.

'*I cannot be the husband you would want,*' he had said when she had sobbed her acceptance, '*the husband a wife could expect. I can care for you, I can love you as indeed I do now, but never in the physical sense of the word; I am impotent . . . understand, Amber, it is beyond my capabilities to be the lover you deserve.*'

He had apologised to her! Even now the memory of his sadness tore at her heart. As if that could affect what she felt for him. But Greville was wiser than herself. Life had equipped him with knowledge as yet not given to her and he had feared that one day she would desire more than a husband in name only. But time had not allowed for that. A week out at sea Greville had developed an acute pain in the stomach, a pain which deepened over the next long hours, and in two days her husband of a month was dead. The surgeon attached to the ship had tried all he knew, had carried out an operation to remove what he had called the appendix, but it had not saved Greville. Things had gone too far, the doctor had said when informing her of Greville's passing, her husband had been beyond help.

Dear, kind Greville. Amber swallowed the gathering tears. Nothing to show for a life of fifty years, not even a stone to mark his grave, only the deep ocean to hold his body; yet his memory would live as long as she did.

'I have brought tea, memsahib.'

Like quiet music the softly spoken words drifted into Amber's mind and for a moment she was back in the hot sultry garden of that tiny bungalow with the scent of roses and jasmine, of delicious Indian pinks and the gentler carnation, a little world of flowers, and over the heady perfume of them all the fragrance of the beautiful lotus.

'Will I pour for memsahib?'

It was quiet and musical as before but it snapped the invisible cord holding Amber to the past and her eyelids flew open.

'There is no memsahib here, Rani.' Amber smiled but her tone was firm. 'We left that behind in India. Here in this house we are not mistress and servant; have I not yet made that clear for all the many times I have told you? We are friends, you and I, equals in all ways, and that is what we will always be.'

Large brown eyes smiled from a pale coffee-coloured face. 'You have told me many times but my mind is dull, it does not accept.'

'Your mind is not dull, Rani, it is just so very used to

accepting a European as your master. That was only one of the things I saw as wrong in your country and one I pray heaven will soon be changed; but here at least it is already changed.'

'In this house, yes, here I am treated as an equal, but out there in the streets of the town I am . . . how do you say it? . . . a freak . . . a fairground attraction. Women stare and whisper behind their hands, men let their eyes say what their tongues dare not, while young children run away in fear. No, Amber, the Asian and the European are not yet equals and I think your heaven will remain deaf to your prayers.'

Had she done right in bringing this gentle girl to England? Amber watched the delicate hands lift the china teapot. Greville had advised she have a maid for the voyage home but he had not insisted. She could have said no, some other officer's wife would have given the girl a place in her household, but wisely or not she had wanted Rani with her, thinking that to bring her to this country would somehow repay the debt she owed her. Had that been so wrong, was it a mistake? But then she was bound to feel strange; it took time to settle in a foreign place.

'Darlaston is a very small town, Rani.' Amber took the cup passed to her. 'People here are not like those we encountered in London, they are not accustomed to seeing the people of other countries, but they are not unkind; you will find that for yourself once they become used to you.'

'I shall pray that is so.'

And I shall add my own to them. The thought silent in her mind, Amber sipped the hot liquid before speaking.

'I was looking over the accounts; we shall need to find a way of supporting ourselves and before you say you are a liability I say that you are not. We will find a way and we will find it together.'

★   ★   ★

Washing teacups and pots, handing them one by one to Rani
who dried them, Amber thought again of their conversation
about finding a way together. Words! She stared at a cup, its
border of blue flowers bright against the white china body.
They were always so easy to say but how easy would it be to
implement them? Darlaston was a town built on coal; iron was
its bones and steel its flesh and she had no knowledge of either.
All she had ever known had been the tiny cottage set in one of
the fields belonging to Selman's farm. She and her mother had
been allowed to continue living there after the death of her
dairyman father, her mother earning a living as laundry
woman at Wallington House, Bay Tree House and The Hills,
the large important houses of Bloxwich. The work had been
hard and her mother was often exhausted despite the willing
help of a six-year-old daughter. Then had come the day her
mother had told her she was to marry again. She had gone with
her mother to the Church of All Saints at Elmore Green,
listened to the priest saying words she did not understand,
watched the tall fair-haired man kiss her mother then turn to
smile at her. She had not seen him from that day. Strange she
had not thought of that before. But then a child as young as
she had been did not think of asking questions; her new father
was a travelling salesman whose employment took him all over
the country and on the rare occasions he came to the house
she was fast asleep in bed. In the mornings he was gone, only
a toy or a bag of sweets to say he had been.

A little over a year later Bethany had been born and in two
more years had come Denny. There had been more money
which had meant her mother need not work so hard but there
had also been a shadow over that much-loved face, a shadow
which later she, Amber, had come to recognise as the mark of
deep unhappiness. Why had her mother been so unhappy?

Could it have been her marriage . . . was that somehow the cause, was her new husband not what she hoped for? But it was too late for questions. The teacups finished, she carried the bowl of water into the yard. It had long been too late. Four years after Denny's birth her mother was dead.

In the weeks which had followed she had looked for the man she had never learned to think of as her father, waited for every day to bring him, but he had not come. The people of the village had rallied to help her but they had families of their own to keep; it was impossible to feed three more. Then one Sunday following evensong she had overheard the master of Wallington speaking with the vicar.

Slivers of sunlight gleamed on the surface of the water in the bowl, turning it into a mirror which seemed to Amber's tired mind to show that quiet churchyard bathed in the glow of a setting sun.

'. . . *the older girl* . . .' The words of so long ago echoed in her brain. '*The one called Amber, she we can settle in one of the houses hereabouts, maybe my wife can find her a post as scullery maid, but the others, the younger girl and the boy, well I fear they are too young, the workhouse is the only place for them.*'

The workhouse! It had terrified her. Folk in the village had sometimes talked of a place by that name, crossing their forehead and chest as they asked the Lord to keep them from it. They had spoken of it as a house of sorrow; death would be better than going there.

All that night fears of what it would mean for Bethany and Denny had plagued her mind until, well before dawn, she had wakened her sister, helping her dress, then bundling up the sleeping boy had slipped with them into the night. Somehow she had managed to feed them, begging a piece of bread or a cup of milk at every farm they passed, sleeping with them clutched tight against her in a barn or under a hedge, but always together. Then she had called at Bescot Lodge and there had been taken in. Her hands shaking with the memory of it all disturbed the water and the illusion faded. It had all been so long ago and now both sister and brother were lost to her. Tipping the water into the open drain which ran across the yard Amber watched it disappear, slip away as those two children had slipped from her life leaving her with nothing but memories, memories and regret.

3

'I tell you it be impossible, how *could* her know? You've said yourself her were in India along of your granddaughter so lessen her be bloody psychic then there ain't no way her could know.'

Sitting opposite his florid-faced guest, Uriah watched him tip brandy into his mouth. He had invited him to Bescot Lodge to talk business but somehow the talk had turned from the forging of iron to the matter of the young woman who had enquired after her sister and brother.

'Maybe there be no way her can be sure that her's got a bloody fair idea that all were not as I told it.'

'An' how did you tell it?' Small eyes suddenly alert watched over the brim of a recharged glass.

'Like we agreed, the girl took pneumonia and it seen her off . . . but you could see in that wench's face her had no belief in that, her even went so far as to call me a liar.'

'And you let her walk from this house!' The glass lowered slowly. 'You let some chit of a girl, a bloody housemaid, call you a liar an' you let her walk away! I can't believe what I be hearing, why? Why let her get away with speaking to you like that when you should have flogged the skin from her back?'

Was that not exactly what he had wanted to do? In Uriah's mind flashed a sudden picture of a small heart-shaped face; gold-flecked eyes full of challenge as they stared at him, and again a faint touch of alarm tickled along his nerves.

'You can take a whip to a servant,' he said, forcing his mind back to the moment, 'even a housemaid, and nobody's like to ask the reason, but try doing so to a woman with money of her own and you find the constables on your doorstep.'

'Money!' Sharp little eyes narrowed, receding behind folds of flesh. 'I thought you said them kids were destitute, that you allowed your housekeeper to take 'em in when by rights they should have gone into the workhouse, and the eldest of 'em, you said her were maid to your granddaughter. That don't talk to me o' money!'

Why had he bothered asking Elton here; all that interested him was a glass in his hand and his flesh in a woman. Irritation turning to anger, Uriah's answer snapped. 'What I told you was the truth. That wench went to India without a penny in her hand but it seems her came back with her pockets full.'

Almost invisible behind their fleshy barrier the keenly watching eyes hid a mind every bit as wary. 'So how do you account for that, your son . . . ?'

His heavy cut glass crashed onto a side table and Uriah was on his feet, his face wreathed in thunder. 'My son had no part in it! The wench disappeared the same time as . . . as Joanna was killed. His letter telling me of what had happened said they searched for her companion but she weren't found, the nurse woman, my granddaughter, they were recovered and identified but not the English girl who was with them. Her body was never found.

The irate outburst left little impression but the words – Edward Elton swallowed a mouthful of brandy, feeling the trail of it hot in his chest – the words had definitely made an impact. If he needed a sword to hold over Uriah Buckley's head then this was it. 'Well, somebody found it.' He spoke softly and despite the brandy each word was distinct and the insinuation contained in them clear as the sounding of a bell.

'Somebody recovered it an' seemingly made good use o' it.'

Lips drawing back in a snarl, his own eyes narrowing, Uriah glared at the florid face. 'Meanin' what?'

Yes, this would prove a sharp enough sword. Edward Elton smiled to himself. 'Meanin' the wench hadn't a penny in her hand when leaving England yet here her is back in Darlaston wi' her pockets full. Seems there be only one way forra wench to come by money like that an' that be by openin' her legs.'

'For who?' Uriah's foot banged against the delicate spindle-legged table, smashing it across the room. 'Be you sayin' my son . . .'

'I don't be sayin' anything.' Soft and insidious, Elton's answer contrasted vividly with the fury of the man glaring at him. 'But others might; they might think it strange, that girl not being found among the victims of that massacre, they might even ask did her go to that bazaar at all and if not, why not?'

Uriah's fists curled, the breath rasping in his throat. 'Take care, Elton, take very great care afore you says any more! If you be thinkin' what I suspects you be thinkin' then you best keep it in your head or you might find you 'ave no bloody head!'

Sudden as the striking of a snake Edward Elton's answer shot out and this time it was neither soft nor sibilant but cold, vicious and heavy with warning. 'An' you best find a way o' shutting that wench's mouth for good as well as keepin' a still tongue about what occurred in this house. You protect your name and I'll protect mine . . . any way it takes.'

It couldn't be made more clear were it painted on a sign. Uriah felt his anger churn inside him as the other man rose from the chair. Should any breath of the truth about that girl's death be loosed then Elton would see to it Jervis were accused of arranging that business at Meerut, arranging it to cover his carrying on with the older girl and in the process becoming responsible for the murder of his own daughter.

Uriah turned away as the portly figure took its leave, then aimed a savage kick at the empty chair. He had never much liked the man who was his partner; now he positively detested him; but he must not cross him . . . at least not yet.

Why had she come here? Walking back along the narrow lane which led to a small cottage standing by itself in a field, Amber asked herself the question which had played in her mind the whole of her journey to Bloxwich. What had she hoped to find? Denny, her heart answered, she had hoped to find Denny. But even as the hope found its echo her mind rejected it. Her brother had been just four years old when they had left this house, little more than a baby. What would he know of this place, what could he possibly remember after so long? Yet still she had hoped, hoped that somehow he had found his way back to this house; but like so many hopes she had once held this too had proved false. The stretch of Little Bloxwich Lane bordered on each side by fields heavy with crops was quiet and sleepy with no cart or wagon disturbing the somnolent peace. This was how afternoons in Meerut had been: nothing but the hum of insects or the call of a bird in the hot sun-filled gardens of Colonel Buckley's spacious bungalow to break the breathless hush that seemed to herald every approach of evening. Meerut! Amber walked on towards the High Street. It had seemed such a perfect place, but there as here misery had awaited. Was that to be all life held for her?

The screech of a steam whistle rudely snatching her back to the present Amber glanced towards the Church of All Saints. Her mother lay here. Turning quickly through the age-darkened wooden lych gate she walked between the stone-marked ranks of graves all neatly kept, most with a tribute of flowers brought each Sunday afternoon by loving relatives. But until today there had been no flowers for her mother, until today no visit had been possible; free time had not been given willingly by Bescot Lodge and certainly not enough for travelling to another town. But now no one could tell her no; that was something else Greville Neale had given her, freedom from any master, and as long as she could feed herself that was how it would remain.

'Excuse me, may I help you?'

'What!' Startled, Amber stepped backwards, stumbling as her heel caught against the stone border of a grave.

'Hey, it's too soon for you to go in there, besides it's not yours . . .'

A smile lighting his face, a man reached for her elbow, steadying her.

'I didn't mean to startle you,' he said as she regained her footing. 'Forgive me, I wouldn't have spoken at all except you looked somewhat lost.'

'I admit I am a little. I have not been here for some years, not since I was a child. I thought I would remember but . . .'

'Places change.'

Had he said that to ease her conscience or was it a quiet snub? People were unused to the dead being neglected. It was a ritual their resting place be visited every week and the flowers spread all about this churchyard attested to the fact that here in Bloxwich the ritual was carefully observed.

'I have been abroad for some years.' Apology or explanation? She didn't know which and knew even less why she had made it unless it was because of the smile now relegated to deeply blue eyes.

'Even the keenest of memories can sometimes go a little off key after a few years of absence, but if you wish maybe I can help find the spot you are looking for.'

She did not want to tell him her mother's grave was unmarked, that no headstone bore her name. But how to refuse his assistance without appearing rude? Feeling the heat of embarrassment creeping into her cheeks she stared at the flowers she had bought earlier from a ruddy-faced old man sitting outside his cottage door puffing smoke from a yellowed clay pipe.

'Many folk like yourself gets their Sunday flowers from along o' Woodbine Cottage,' he had said, cutting a generous bunch of carnations and sweet peas, tying their stalks with a length of twine then protesting, 'A shilling be more'n twice what they be worth.' But she had thanked him, easing his protests by saying beauty such as those blossoms possessed was above price.

'But here is someone who can help more than I.'

The quietly spoken words chasing her thoughts, Amber glanced up, but the man was already walking away while the dark-robed figure of the vicar came smilingly towards her.

'Ah yes, I remember. It is this way.'

He had recognised the name she had given though his glance had held no recognition of who it was asked after the grave. Following him to the further side of the small cemetery Amber stared at the plot he pointed to. Not a weed, not a single blade of grass marred its surface. Dark and rich, the earth enclosed by a border of narrow flinted stone was smooth and even and at its head a simple cross of wood bearing the painted lettering of her mother's name rose above the bunch of meadow flowers.

'Who?' she choked. 'Who did this?'

A slight frown settling between his eyebrows, the vicar turned to her. 'Why, her son. He comes each week to tidy and replace the flowers.'

Amber's mind reeled. Denny! Denny came here every week.

Struggling against happiness which sat like a lump in her throat she almost laughed. 'Can . . . can you tell me where I can find him?'

His frown deepening, the clergyman hesitated a moment before replying. 'But you have just been talking to him. The man who was here with you, he is the woman's son.'

'Why did I not recognise him . . . why did I not know my own brother?'

The question had sobbed in her brain the whole time of her journey back to Darlaston. Now in her own house Amber cried it aloud.

'It has been long since you saw him.' Rani wrung out a cloth, the perfume of the scented water fragrant with camomile.

'Not long enough to forget him, his face was printed on my heart.' Amber accepted the cloth, placing it over her forehead.

A smile of sympathy touching her mouth, the Indian girl answered. 'Did the man not say even the most keen of memories can sometimes let us down? Your heart carries the image of a child but children grow and their faces change. You have not forgotten the face of your brother; it is just that you do not know the face of the man who was once a child.'

Was Rani right? Could it be that Denny had changed so much he was no longer recognisable to her? But she herself . . . had she too changed beyond recognition? Had the ordeals she had suffered after that terrible evening in Meerut taken away all trace of the girl who had kissed a brother and sister goodbye at Bescot Lodge?

'But wouldn't there have been something: a feeling, a sensing of his being who he was? Why did I feel nothing?'

Carrying the bowl from the small sitting room Rani paused, looking back from the doorway which gave immediately onto an even smaller kitchen.

'You were startled, you had almost fallen, that was enough to disturb your senses.'

Perhaps. Leaning her head against her chair, Amber closed her eyes. Perhaps that was the reason there had been no sense of familiarity when he had spoken to her, but she could not accept it. Faces changed, bodies grew but the bond between brother and sister was not easily forgotten. 'I should have known,' she whispered, 'I should have known!'

Returning from the kitchen the other girl heard the whisper and replied. 'You must not blame yourself. When the veil is ready to be lifted from your eyes then fate will slide it gently away but until that time you have to be strong.'

'And if it should be I do not find him again or if it should prove not to be Denny?'

Coming back to kneel beside the chair Rani took Amber's hand. 'Hold fast to that which is in the heart, let the flame be of love for your brother and not that of the funeral pyre. Faith is beloved of the gods, yours as well as mine, and they give truth of the heart the reward of its desire.'

Opening her eyes, Amber's glance rested on the gentle face upturned to hers. 'If only I could have caught up with him. I did try but he was gone.'

'There will be other times.'

'I asked the priest to tell me where the man I had talked with lived but he did not know. But he did say it was the son of the woman buried in that grave and who else but Denny would keep it so well; it had to be him, didn't it, Rani, it had to be my brother.'

Rani rested her forehead against the hand in her own to hide the doubt clouding her beautiful eyes. Priests were wise men and the English priest no doubt too was wise; but they were only priests, men in the service of God, they were not God Himself . . . and who but He was all-knowing? But well-meaning as the priest intended to be, what he had told Amber could not be so. And her friend? She had been too overwhelmed by hope to have thought clearly on those words. But now she must; she must be made to see the error caused by her own heart.

'Amber,' she said quietly, 'the one who offered to help you find the grave of your mother, was he man or boy?'

Wide chocolate-brown eyes looking into hers held an intensity Amber had not seen in them since leaving India. Now, caught in the profound stare, her mind cleared instantly.

'Think.' Rani's eyes portrayed the strength of her feelings.

Think of what? Amber frowned. What was she meant to think of? The girl had simply asked was the person she had spoken to prior to talking with the priest a man or . . .

Understanding crashing like thunder in her mind, Amber sagged in her chair. Of course! How stupid she had been, how unbelievably stupid! Denny had been eight years old when she had left Darlaston; no more than thirteen now, and the man in Bloxwich churchyard . . . he was not thirteen years old and he was not Denny!

4

Spring was not yet ripened into summer. The gentle girlhood of the year was still young and pretty but soon the blasting heat of summer would strip the beauty from all but the most carefully tended gardens; already the heat of the coming season blazed down upon Meerut as if wishing to burn it from the face of the earth.

Seated in the shade of the long low veranda circling his bungalow, Colonel Jervis Buckley drew in a long breath of the sultry over-warm air, letting his gaze lift towards where he knew the outlying hills of the Himalayas rose beyond his vision. Within a week or two the European women would leave, taking the train journey to the cooler hill country, remaining in Simla throughout the hottest months and returning after the monsoon had dampened the fiery passion of the year and slaked the thirst of this parched land.

India! He sipped the glass of gin spiced with fresh lime and a touch of ginger. The summer could be purgatory for the most hardened, men like himself who had spent years here, but for women not born to such a climate then it was unthinkable.

'*You must let us take Joanna with us . . . the heat in Meerut will be too much for the child.*'

How many times had memory thrown those words at him! Eyelids closing, pressed hard against his eyeballs, he tried shutting off the conversation he knew word for word.

'Believe me, Jervis, Simla will be much more suitable. Your daughter has taken no hurt in coming to Meerut but she made the journey in the winter, but summer, well that is very different . . . very different indeed.'

Georgina Hale, wife of his first officer, had meant well; with four daughters of her own she was convinced she knew what was best for every other girl on the post.

'My own girls have taken no harm by going to Simla and God willing neither will yours . . .'

Eyelids lifting, Jervis returned his gaze towards the far hills. God's will! He swallowed hard. Had that massacre been God's will! But he must not go there again, he must not let himself fall into that dark pit of misery, for next time there would be no climbing out. Self-condemnation would always be with him but to give way would be the end; he would not have the will to drag himself back a second time.

Bringing his glance from the horizon he let it trace a path to the furthest end of the long garden to where the tall neem trees drooped heavily leafed branches, their tips caressing a pair of low rectangular structures of white marble.

Helen and Joanna. His wife and his daughter. They had shared a love for the beautiful spot; now they would share its cool peace for all eternity.

Helen. He would often join her there when his duties allowed and he would tell her of the happenings of the day; how on occasion villagers came to ask for the doctor sahib's medicine or how some squabble had been settled by the District Commissioner, and she in turn would tell him of how she had occupied her day making shopping lists of items she wanted a houseboy to have brought from the bazaar or else receiving a visit from one of the officer's wives, unimportant things, things which at the time he thought so trivial but now would give anything to share again.

Helen, beloved wife of Jervis Buckley. His gaze rested on the stone shaded as always by the whispering greenery. He could not see the words inscribed on it yet they danced before him, burning deep into his conscience. Helen and her daughter were at rest in their tree-shaded haven; they would never know their shame . . . his shame!

Georgina and her husband together with others of their friends had tried to dissuade him from placing Helen's grave in the garden where it could only be a constant reminder of his loss. It was too painful, they had said, and to lay Joanna beside it was only to add to that pain. But some had not been so kind; they had condemned what they saw as a heathen action. What sort of man would deny his wife the right to lie in hallowed ground!

But they didn't understand, none of them did; the ground where Helen lay was hallowed, hallowed by her gentleness, by her love; a love he had betrayed. Had she ever guessed, had she ever suspected the truth behind those withdrawn moods which had so often settled over him at Bescot Lodge? If so she had never by word or deed hinted that she did. Then had come the posting to India. Relief had shone in those quiet eyes.

Leaning deeper into the cane chair he tried to fight off the spectre of his thoughts but the memories were too strong. She had been so happy at the prospect of leaving Darlaston and somehow he knew that happiness was not solely due to saying goodbye to soot-blackened buildings and smoke-laden air, there had been more . . . more to the smile which had played over her lips. But as always she had said nothing, asked nothing; only smiled.

His heart twisting, he watched the scene his mind conjured. A slender soft-eyed woman, her voice trembling as she parted with her only child. A wife and a daughter who would be with him yet had he not brought them to . . .

Suddenly impatient with himself he slapped the fan of woven rattan grass held in one hand hard on the bamboo table beside his chair, upsetting the solitary glass. The veranda was cool yet beads of perspiration oozed the length of his bronzed face. He was angry with his thoughts, angry for allowing them. Helen had been happy here in Meerut, it had made up for the years in Darlaston. She had turned this house into a home, filling it with her own quiet presence until he had almost forgotten . . . but deep inside he had never forgotten. Had her happiness also been a sham, a cover to her true feelings as his own had been? Had she, as well as himself, lived a lie? Why had he ever brought her here, why had he agreed their daughter come out to join them? Hadn't he seen India kill enough women and children? But it was not only in India the hand that had taken Helen struck. It was no stranger in many countries, many continents; it recognised no barriers and entered where it chose, in the home of rich or poor alike. Fever took whomsoever it would and his wife had proved no exception. But it was not fever had taken his daughter! That had been his fault.

Aiming a vicious swipe at the score of flies hovering over the spilled drink, Jervis called irritably for a servant to come and clear it away.

'Sahib.' The answer was immediate as if the manservant waited at his elbow. It wouldn't have been much further for whenever he was at home Ram Dutt was never far from his side.

'Sorry to put you to this trouble, Ram.' Jervis spoke with the respect afforded to all servants in his household.

'Will I to be bringing the colonel sahib a fresh drink?' Ram Dutt missed none of the misery underlying the Englishman's anger. He had been alone too long; why did he not take another wife? Surely the way of the English was wrong, it was not good for a man to be so long without the comforts of a woman. But Ram Dutt's thoughts remained just thoughts as he sponged away the spilled drink. Loneliness wearied the Englishman; it had touched his temples with wings of silver, painted lines about eyes become deeply set and beneath the colouring the sun had given his skin pallor spoke of exhaustion, a tiredness of the body; but it was the eyes, the lacklustre eyes, which told of a less tangible cause, for they whispered the weariness of the soul. The almost imperceptible shake of the head which refused the offer of another drink made Ram Dutt turn away, silent feet belying the sympathy loud in his heart.

Alone once more Jervis returned his gaze to the gleaming white marble structures, his mind tormented by memories, memories he did not wish but could not relinquish. Helen, her hair spread like a cloud over a pillow damp with perspiration, her gentle eyes brilliant with the fever burning through her. She had tried to smile, looking up at him, her soft words branding themselves into his brain.

'*Love her, Jervis,*' she had whispered, tears a glittering mist in her eyes. '*Love her for me, tell our daughter I love her, keep . . . keep her with you, Jervis . . . keep her with you always.*'

She had tried to rise then, agitation heightening the flare of colour blazing in her cheeks, and he had taken her in his arms trying to soothe, but still the words had come.

'*Never send her away from you . . . love her . . . love her as I have loved you.*'

Those had been her last words; she had died as he kissed his promise on her lips.

Love her as I have loved you. Lips pressed hard together, Jervis stifled the cry in his throat. Helen, dear gentle Helen, yes she had loved him and he? He had betrayed that love.

And their daughter?

'Keep her with you . . . never send her away from you.'

Unable to hold the tears, Jervis let them run unchecked.

Joanna would never be sent away. The daughter he adored, the woman he should have loved more, they both would remain in Meerut forever, joined in the quiet peace of a garden.

The flowers were there again today. Amber walked slowly along the path leading towards the spot set in a corner of the churchyard. A pretty collection of deep blue interspersed with white. Set in a plain crock pot, the beauty of their colours against the dark earth had caught her eye as she had walked between the rows of headstones towards that shadowed corner. She had not thought to bring a container in which to place her own bunch of brilliantly coloured snapdragons. Holding them a moment, she read the simple painted words then laid them beside the crock pot at the base of the wooden cross. Perhaps whoever it was tended her mother's grave was there still. She looked around as the thought came, searching visibly for any sign of that dark head. Dark hair! That should have told her the person she looked for today, the one she had talked with last week, had not been Denny, Denny had fair hair. But she could be forgiven for thinking as she had; wanting so badly to find her brother had blinded her to all but that one desire.

'You ain't bin 'ere afore, 've you?'

She had not noticed the thin figure come to stand at her side and the quiet voice startled her.

'Once,' she answered quickly, 'I . . . I have been here once before.'

'Were that on a Sunday an' all?'

Why would this woman want to know what day she had visited this cemetery? Hesitant to reply, Amber looked at her questioner. A black bonnet perched on hair that might once have been brown but was now the colour of ash, a worn shawl tied beneath her flat breasts with a cumbersome knot. The woman watched her out of dull mud brown eyes.

'No.' She answered the unwavering stare. 'No, I came on Wednesday.'

'Could explain why I ain't see you afore.' The woman nodded. 'I wouldn't 'ave seen you if'n you come on a Wednesday 'cos I don't come on no day barrin' Sunday. Be the onny day I gets a minute or two to meself, do Sunday . . . the little 'uns be in at Sunday school an' the old man be sleepin', that gives me time to run down 'ere to see to them as is gone. I can't go bringin' flowers such as I sees you bring but then money don't be elastic, it don't stretch, so I picks a few bits from the hedge or the cornfield.'

Amber glanced at the scarlet field poppies and yellow kingcups nestled in fronds of green meadow fern, their short stems pushed into a cream coloured pottery jar emblazoned with bold lettering announcing 'Pritchard's Potted Meats'.

'Your flowers are as beautiful as any I have seen.' She smiled.

'Ar.' The woman sighed, pulling the shawl more firmly about her thin frame. 'That were one thing the Lord done fair, He med all flowers beautiful, them as grows in the open field as well as them tended in glass houses. He seen them equal, more so than folk, for them He separated, He med rich an' He med poor. I asked Him why when he took my babbies, when money could like 'ave saved them, I asked why rich an' poor, but He give no answer then nor does He give any now no matter the times of askin'. We shouldn't question the ways of the Lord, so my mother always taught, p'raps that be the reason I be ignored.'

She wanted to say heaven never ignored a prayer, that sooner or later they were answered though that answer might not be the one hoped for; that she had prayed a thousand times to be reunited with her sister and brother. But she would have to tell the answer to those prayers, the blessing which was no blessing; she would have to tell that her sister was dead and her brother . . . probably he too was dead.

'You d'ain't bring no jar.' The woman turned her glance once more to the brilliant splash of colour that was the snapdragons. 'Nor no water neither I sees, you should oughta 'ave brought water, them there flowers won't go lastin' no more'n a day or two wi'out it. ''Ere,' she pushed a bottle half-filled with water into Amber's hand, 'put 'em into this, it be better'n lettin' 'em die, there be enough dead afore their time in this place wi'out killin' off them there flowers.'

Thanking her, Amber knelt, easing each of the lovely blooms into the mouth of the bottle then firming the base into the earth.

'I said as 'ow the Lord med all flowers equal,' the woman said as Amber stood up, 'but seems it ain't so, not in everythin' it aint. Them flowers o' your'n 'ave a scent that don't be in poppy nor kingcup.'

Amber glanced at the snapdragons. Sequins of sunlight filtering between the leafed branches draped above them glittered like jewels – the jewels of that man's clothing! Breath catching in her throat, colours swirling together twisting into a brilliant whirlpool, she swayed.

''Ere.' A thin hand caught her arm, steadying her. 'Be you all right . . . do you be tumbled?'

Breathing deeply, her own hand clutching at the woman now looking at her with concern, Amber strove to regain her senses.

'Be you carryin'?'

Still half choked on the fear those gleams of glinting colour had brought instantly to her mind, Amber shook her head.

'Then if it don't be no babby 'ad you near to passin' out.'

'I . . . it is just tiredness,' Amber answered quickly.

'Ar, well, I can understand that,' the woman returned, though the glance she cast at Amber's clothing said she did not understand at all. This wench were dressed like no nail-maker's wife or daughter and her hands, they were not marked and stained from the polishing of awl blades, the instrument used to pierce holes in wood or leather; she had toiled over no anvil nor pumped the bellows of a forge housed in a tiny brew-house converted to the use of the industry followed everywhere in Bloxwich.

Removing her hand from the woman's arm Amber caught the look of doubt in those dull eyes. 'I have only recently completed a long journey,' she explained. 'It was very tiring; India is a great distance from England.'

'India!' Mud-brown eyes sparked with a brief interest. 'Well, I can't be sayin' I knows where in the word that be but if it be like you says, a great distance, then o' course the travellin' be a drain. P'raps you should tek y'self a sit down, there be a bench along of the church porch.'

Across the little cemetery busy now with people bringing their weekly floral offerings the bell of All Saints' clock chimed three.

Feeling slightly guilty for the relief those chimes brought Amber smiled at the woman she knew was merely being friendly. 'I have no time,' she said, drawing on gloves she had removed before setting her flowers in the bottle. 'There is only one train to Darlaston on Sundays and it leaves at three thirty.'

Darlaston! So her guess had been right. This wench were no awl-maker's nor no nailer's kin, nor did her bide in Bloxwich. Satisfied and more than a little pleased with her own deduction, the woman fell into step beside Amber.

'Them snapdragons,' she said as they retraced steps they

had both made in coming to the furthest corner of the church
burial ground, 'be they were growed in that India you said of
. . . be they special like?'

What strange questions this woman asked. Had she been to
this cemetery on Sunday . . . were the flowers she had brought
grown in India? In any other part of the country it might be
looked upon as rudeness to ask what she had but here in
Bloxwich it was not. Most people meant no more than to be
neighbourly.

'No.' Amber hid the smile the woman's interest had brought
to her eyes. 'They were not grown in India and so far as I am
aware they are not special. I bought them from a man in
Darlaston whose garden was full of them and he gave no indi-
cation of them being other than they are, plain ordinary
snapdragons.'

'Ordinary they might be to look at but not to smell. They
'ave a scent like I ain't smelled in no snapdragon afore, no nor
no spiderwort or dropwort which were in that pot alongside.
In fact I smells it now . . . must be left on your 'ands from the
carryin' of 'em. I swears I ain't smelled naught so pleasant in
many a long day; I says could it be bottled then it would bring
a pleasure to women no matter they be queens.'

Sitting in the third-class carriage of the train she had needed
to run to catch, Amber thought of the tired-looking woman
who had given her that bottle half-filled with water. Why had
she not asked? Why had she let such an opportunity slip away?
The woman had been talkative and obviously friendly; she
would surely have answered the question. But she had not
asked it. Turning her face to the window, Amber stared at the
crop-filled fields rushing past but her eyes saw only a face . . .
the face of a boy she could have enquired after yet had not.

5

Greville had been fond of Indian foods. So many years in that country had educated his palate to the spices, herbs and seasonings that were the flavourings of so many of their dishes.

Glancing about her small kitchen, breathing the fragrant aroma of lamb with its marinade of mint and garlic, of red chilli, paprika, cardamon and garam masala, she was whisked back to another time, another place.

A small cluster of mud-brick houses encircled by a few scorched fields filled her mind while the raucous shriek of a woman filled her ears and the sting of a bamboo switch cut across her shoulders.

'Lazy bitch!' She had not understood the language composing the words but the look of intense dislike in the woman's eyes made them clear enough. The switch had fallen again, driving her to the dusty ground, but scrawny fingers had twisted into her hair, dragging her to her feet.

She must work! There was no place here for idleness, no place for the despised memsahib. The cane had proclaimed what words could not, following her every step, every movement of her hands, lashing across them whenever they did not follow each incomprehensible command. They had brought her here, those horsemen who had ridden into the bazaar, carried behind the one who appeared to be their leader, clinging to him for what had seemed forever, stopping only to rest the horses and feed themselves, flinging her scraps she

could not bring herself to eat. They had slept several nights
on the ground but always two of them had kept guard, the
light of their camp fire illuminating their figures, throwing massively enlarged silhouettes across the boulders of
encircling hills until they looked like the grotesque djinn
Narinder had been so fond of warning Joanna and herself
would come in the night and carry them away if they were not
careful to observe her instructions. Then, the final night of
their camping, one of them had crept to where she lay shivering from the fresh breeze cold after the heat of the day.

A shiver running through her now as the vividness of the
memory increased, Amber's fingers tightened about the spoon
held in her hand.

The thin covering they had given for sleeping had begun to
slip slowly from her body. At first her brain was seized with
terror. She had tried not to move, tried not to think of the
stories she had heard from young officers invited for afternoon
tea at the colonel's house, tales of hunting wild animals, of
being turned on by their prey, of cobras rearing to strike.

Blood freezing in her veins, the ability to move lost from her
limbs, her brain had screamed: panther, tiger, hyena, cobra!

Then she had felt it; warm against her trembling flesh, it
crept slowly upwards, sliding over her legs, touching the base
of her stomach.

'Amber . . .'

The touch against her shoulder, like the shock of a burning
brand, jerked the spoon from her hand. Lost in the trauma of
that terrible night Amber saw again the leering grin of a man's
face as his body slid across her own, then watched the glint of
a blade in the dancing firelight, the silver line of it descend,
watched the face turn to stare upwards, the gap-toothed
mouth opening in a wild cry . . . watched the turbaned head
fall from the neck to roll away into the darkness.

'Are you sure you are not ill?'

Sitting in the chair to which Rani had half dragged her Amber breathed hard, stilling the waves of nausea sweeping through her. It had been so strong . . . so real. She had hoped that, being home in down-to-earth no-nonsense Darlaston, the nightmares of her days in India would stop, but they had not. They were as terrifying as they had ever been, leaving her stunned with fear, her lungs tight for want of air.

'I was so afraid. I am still afraid . . . please, you should rest more, it is not good you search so much.'

'It was just a touch of dizziness, this will soon see it gone.' Amber tried to smile.

'No. Chair will not take away what troubles you,' Rani said as Amber sipped the tea she had made for her. 'It can soothe a tired body but it cannot heal a sickness.'

'I'm not sick.'

'Your heart is sick,' the girl returned quietly. 'It cries for rest as your body also cries; you must listen to those cries, they will not warn forever.'

Rani meant well. She was only concerned for her wellbeing but she didn't understand. Amber sipped the sweet tea. But there could be no rest until she knew one way or the other, until she knew whether Denny lived or whether he was dead.

'Your friendship helps so much.' Catching the girl's hand Amber looked into eyes soft and gentle as those of a newborn calf. 'It helped so much when—'

'We shall not think of those times,' Rani said sharply. 'They are gone, finished, and their ghosts must not be called. Now this time I am the ayah and you the child, you shall do as I say or . . .'

'I know, I know,' Amber threw up her hands in defeat. 'I must do as you say or the djinn will come and get me.'

She had not wanted to leave the kitchen; she should not

leave everything to Rani while she rested, but lying on her bed
Amber had to admit the girl had been right in what she had
said . . . though not about the djinn. Despite the belief held by
her friend it was no magician, no genie, which brought fear in
the night, no spirit of magic which plagued folks' days; the only
demon was the one which lived inside them, the one which fed
on unhappiness and fear; and hers would not leave until she
knew of her brother.

Would he be resting now? Guilt pricking like a needle,
Amber got up from the bed. Were their roles reversed, were
he the one searching for a lost loved one, would he give up?
But she had not given up. Smoothing her hair she glanced at
the mirror. A too-thin face, eyes shadowed and heavy-circled,
stared back at her but in their depths she saw the resolution.
She would never give up!

He had written to Jervis, told him of the need for him to resign
his commission, to leave India and return to England. There
had been no answer. Brandy glass in hand, Uriah Buckley
stared across lawns which glowed like green velvet. But no
answer did not mean there would be none. Letters took weeks
to reach India and more weeks to reach his son. He tossed a
mouthful of liquid against his throat, feeling the gag of his
breath as it burned its way to his stomach. Where in the name
of hell was Meerut and why in that same name had Jervis
allowed himself to be sent there? Strings could have been
pulled. He drank again, the brandy liquid fire in his throat.
Money talked; with some men it sounded louder than any
bloody foghorn and many of those men sat on their fat arses
in the War Office and others in the House of Commons itself;
it would have been simple to procure a place of comfort somewhere in this country with no need to follow a regiment
anywhere, much less to a bloody place no man in his right

mind would go to! How many times had he written, how many times had he ordered Jervis to return!

Anger rising, Uriah refilled his glass then turned back to the window. But each time the answer had been the same: Jervis would remain in India.

Fingers tightening until the crystal stem bit into his fingers, Uriah swore viciously, 'Bloody fool, if I had you in this room I'd kick your arse into your neck, I'd show you who was gaffer!' But that was it, he wasn't Jervis's gaffer any longer. The thought halted the anger in its stride. The ordering had stopped when . . . when had it stopped exactly? On learning he was being posted abroad? No . . . no, it had stopped before that. It had not been so noticeable at first, a few days' absence here and there; a few times he had apologised saying he was unable to fulfil some demand or other. Nothing too important, nothing to give rise to real differences between them, yet nevertheless Jervis had for the first time in his life begun to refuse. Perhaps he had found himself a prostitute. Uriah remembered the smile that supposition had afforded him. Let the lad find his pleasure, p'raps like Verity the bearing of a child had left Helen not yet ready to share the delight of the marriage bed, to give the ease a man needed. A few nights with a whore . . . yes, that was the reason behind those times away from Bescot Lodge. But a few nights had become a few weeks and no child grew in his daughter-in-law's belly, no grandson to carry on the line.

'Why?' He had roared the question at Jervis one time he had returned. *'Why is your wife not pregnant with a second child? Is it because you won't or because you can't? Be it on account you be throwin' all you've got between the legs of some common whore? Have you no sense at all, can't you see we need a boy . . . a boy who will one day take over the mine and the iron foundry? Do what I tell you, do it now, put a child in your wife's belly!'*

Brandy held on his tongue, Uriah stared into sunlit space and in it he seemed to see again the look Jervis had given him, a look of utter despising. He had turned away, leaving the house without a word, and when he returned two weeks later it was with a commission purchased with the regiment of South Staffordshires. He had taken Helen from this house and from that time on had set no foot in it.

Beginning its slow descent into evening the sun slanted bronze gold streaks across the perfectly manicured green.

It had been so many years ago, so many years since he had last looked upon the only child he called his own. Oh, he had paid his prostitutes, taken his satisfaction with them, and some had claimed their bastards as his but no child of a whore, even Uriah Buckley's whore, would ever be given Uriah Buckley's possessions. Jervis would answer that letter and this time the reply would be what his father wanted . . . no, what he *needed* to hear. Swallowing another mouthful of brandy, Uriah savoured the blaze of its trail along his gullet. Jervis would know his duty, he would recognise it was imperative he return to Darlaston, to marry again . . . to sire a son.

No one had heard of him. Tired and dispirited, Amber stood at the corner of the Shambles. She had come to Wednesbury with such high hopes, hopes which with the day had sunk lower and lower. She had come by way of Dangerfield Lane so she could enquire of the gatekeeper of Lodge Holes colliery. He had been polite, his brow furrowing as he thought, but after a few moments he had shaken his head. 'There be no lad o' that name workin' this pit, neither fair hair nor dark, but ya could allus ask along of the Old Park or even Hobs Hole, then there be the New Hope pit, they still be bringin' up coal though fer 'ow much longer be anybody's guess fer the seams be runnin' thin.'

She had thanked him, excusing herself as he drew breath to carry on. She had enquired at the New Hope and Old Park mines yesterday as well as those brass and iron foundries she had not managed to visit on the other days she had spent searching Darlaston, but the answers she got were the same. No lad named Denny worked there.

Where could he have gone? If he had truly run away from Bescot Lodge where had he run to, how far could a young child get? Shifting position, she tried to ease the ache of her feet. That question was like asking how far was it to the moon: no one could answer. Denny could have gone the length and breadth of the country; the years would have afforded the time and by travelling just a little each day . . . but to think like that was to destroy any hope she had! She must hold fast to what she told herself every night when her prayers were said: her brother was not far away and soon she would find him. But not, it seemed, in Wednesbury. She had asked at every workplace, in every shop and each of the stalls lining the Market Place as well as enquiring of anyone who would take the time to hear her question. There was nowhere else unless . . .

Pulling her shawl close about her she drew in a short hard breath.

Unless she tried the taverns. They were not places a decent woman entered alone but for her brother she would enter the gates of Hell and Hell, it seemed, was right beside her.

How had she done it? How had she forced herself to enter that hotel? But the Green Dragon, though partly filled with men who fell silent as she entered a large room heavy with tobacco smoke, had not been the hell she envisaged. The landlord had come at once to her side, his presence reassuring and protective. He employed no young lad of her describing, he said, then had asked loudly of his customers did they know of any such. A few minutes was all it had taken but the experience had left her shaking; yet it had to be repeated, she had to do it for as many times as it took.

'You be better put to askin' at the bigger places,' the land-lord of the Green Dragon had advised, escorting her outside. 'They be more like to give work to a lad, especially the George Hotel or the Turk's Head and the Talbot. They caters for carriage trade so could be one of them took your brother on as stable lad but as for the beer houses you should leave them a'be, they don't be places I would advise a woman such as yourself be goin' into, could be as you was misunderstood, begging your pardon for sayin' so.'

She had followed his advice, calling at each of the hotels he had mentioned, and at each she had been given the names of yet other places where her brother might have found work.

Standing again in the Market Place she watched the candle jars being lit at each stall. Evening had stolen up on her silent and unnoticed as that man at the campsite had crept . . . but she must not think of that, she must not give way to the terror which waited its every opportunity to stun her mind, to grip her whole body with fear.

From the hill overlooking the town the clock of the parish church struck seven, breaking the fast-growing paralysis threatening Amber's limbs, freeing the breath already locked in her throat. There were still several hotels she had not visited. Could she go to one more before returning home? The Great Western Hotel? She had been told it stood close to the railroad station and given directions on how to find it. Her mind made up, she walked quickly, following Union Street into Dudley Street, taking a right-hand turn into Great Western Street, breathing a sigh of relief as she saw the station. The hotel was on a corner a little way off from it. Slowing her walk she concentrated on the buildings bordering each side, houses and goods sheds, one facing the other, and part way along the large lanterns adorning the façade of the hotel.

It looked such a grand place. Courage suddenly flagging, she hesitated. Maybe tomorrow . . . but leaving things half done was as useless as not doing them at all! The reprimand sharp in her mind, she stepped forward just as a man dressed in smart dark clothes and high hat came out.

'Excuse me . . .' Flustered by their near collision, Amber stammered her apology.

A slight movement of a silver-topped cane halted the approach of the green and gold liveried doorman and the tall, hatted figure smiled. 'Well now, what a delightful way to seek a man's custom. You fair deserve to earn a florin.'

Earn two shillings! Did this man think . . . did he think her a woman of the streets! Catching her shawl close over her breast she stepped a few paces backwards, her answer quick and low. 'I want no florin.'

The dark-suited figure followed as she retreated further from the gleam of the hotel lanterns. 'Count yourself worth more, do you? Then prove it and we shall see.'

Nerves already trembling, Amber felt the old fear begin its climb along her spine. But this was no campsite in the wilds of India, this was a street in Wednesbury and just a few yards away was a hotel! Holding on to what her brain was telling her, using it to block the scream demanding to be loosed, she answered, 'You have made a mistake.'

His reply was to move forward, pressing her into the shadows until her back came against a wall. 'One of us has,' he said thickly, 'but it certainly is not myself. But before I raise my offer of a florin I need to sample what is on offer.'

'There is nothing on offer!'

'Oh come now, we can drop the play. You are touting your business and I am a willing . . . and very able . . . customer.'

He planted his body square in front of her, the deep shadow of the street enfolding and hiding them as he snatched at the shawl. The quick movement, taking her by surprise, jerked it free from her hands and as she tried to grasp it he had already ripped open her blouse and chemise, the hand not holding the cane fastening over her breast.

'This is how I sample before I buy.'

Hot and smelling of drink his breath fanned her cheek as she twisted her face away from his mouth. It was that moment all over again! The moment a gap-toothed mouth had grinned at her, the moment a hand had touched her flesh, the moment a man had intended to rape her.

Somewhere across the void of reason the flickering flames of a campfire danced in the darkness and a turbanned figure lowered itself, pressing its body against her own.

'No!' It was not so much a scream as a gasp and with it Amber's hands lifted. She scraped her fingernails hard along whisker-framed cheeks; the shock of it caused the man to step sharply back from her as she ran, her boots tapping rapidly on the uneven setts as she raced back along the street towards the railroad station.

6

'You learned no word of him?'

A large white apron covering her pretty pink sari, Rani glanced at Amber, stood the other side of the kitchen table spread now with basins, jugs and several small dark glass bottles.

Wiping the back of one hand across her moist brow, Amber shook her head. She had arrived home the previous night claiming a bad headache as responsible for her being withdrawn and silent, yet she had known the excuse had not deceived the girl who had travelled with her so far across the world. Concern had played in those sensitive berry-brown eyes, it had been obvious in the quiet voice and gentle touch of the hands which had helped her to bed, but it had not formed itself into a question . . . until now.

Placing a handful of leaves and bushy tips of patchouli into a basin she stared at them, her mind's eye showing her a girl, her colourful dress like one of the many gorgeously coloured blossoms which filled Greville's garden, moving between bushes and flower beds. Rani had gathered petals and seeds until she had a sandalwood chest filled with muslin bags in which she put her treasures. Greville had said the girl was collecting memories of her sun-filled homeland and had consented for the chest to be transported with their own boxes, smiling as he added that she would need her memories if England's climate was as bad as he remembered.

Watching her now pour a kettleful of boiling water over the leaves Amber recalled the fearful days of Greville's illness on board the ship. What would she have done without Rani, without the quiet common sense and reassurance which had sustained her then and the friendship which had helped carry her through the dark days in India? Rani had asked nothing of her in all of those times, she had remained at that bungalow only after strong insistence but had earned her keep by working alongside the other household servants.

Steam rising from the basin carried with it a sweet woody aroma. Amber breathed it deep into her lungs. Rani had often used the oil from leaves of the patchouli bush, adding a few drops to bathwater as an aid to relaxation. The leaves, petals and seeds she had brought with her were treasures indeed for in Rani's hands they each became a medicine or a salve. The few European women who had brought themselves to visit Greville's home had sung the praises of the serving girl, each saying she must join the staff once Greville returned to England. But though Rani had her room in the quarters assigned to the servants and though she worked alongside them, Amber had never seen her as anything but a friend . . . a friend who deserved answers.

Stirring the leaves, pressing them gently against the sides of the basin as Rani had taught, she said quietly: 'I asked everyone I saw. I called at every place of business I passed, I even enquired at several foundries and collieries but the gate-keepers said they had heard of no one with the name of Denny.'

Bent over the wooden chest she had brought into the kitchen, Rani studied the compartments comprising its interior. 'Then we ask in other places and of other people while remembering the gods, yours and mine, will reveal what is hidden only once they are ready.'

Once they were ready! Amber stirred the contents of the basin again, breathing in the aroma of the crushed leaves. How long would that be, how much more heartache must she suffer?

Selecting one of the compartments Rani withdrew a goatskin pouch, taking from it a muslin bag. Loosing the string which drew it together she took out a glass phial, the deep plum colour of its contents seeming almost to glow in the light from the window.

'Jasmine!' Amber recognised the phial. 'Surely you are not going to use that, you have so little of it left.'

'The oil of the jasmine flower will take away the stress and fatigue I know your body feels.'

'But jasmine!' Amber protested. 'It is so very precious I would rather you did not use it on my account.'

Holding the phial in her hand the other girl smiled. 'Do not keep unto yourself that which is needed by another. Such is the teaching of my religion; but since the using of it for yourself is worrying to you then as friends it is permitted we share.'

Setting the small glass container on the table she reached a saucer from the dresser, half filling it with water. Uncorking the phial she tipped three drops of the jasmine oil onto its surface and at once a rich exotic scent permeated the room.

'Patchouli and jasmine, they do not fight each other.' She smiled. 'They too are like you and me, they work with each other.' Replacing the phial in the chest Rani set the saucer on the mantel where the warm air of the fire would waft the delicate flower perfume. 'It is beautiful,' she said, her face showing her pleasure in the delightful aroma, 'beautiful as the flower from which it comes; it will soothe the heart as looking at the blossoms once soothed the eye.'

They had soothed. The hours she had sat in those lovely flower-filled gardens had admittedly been restful but that was the past. Watching Rani reach for the brass kettle in which she would distil the patchouli oil from the water in the basin, Amber stifled a sigh. How much of her future would be restful?

Uriah stared at the book-lined walls of the small room Jervis had turned into a library but he was not thinking of his son.

That bitch . . . that bloody snooping bitch had been to the New Hope! She had had the temerity to go asking questions at his colliery . . . of his miners; Christ, if any one of 'em had as much as breathed! But what could they 'ave told her, they knew nothing . . . couldn't possibly know anything. Still, her just going there, her asking after a lad who had lived at Bescot Lodge, that were enough to set tongues wagging and brains to thinking. Not that thinking were any threat to him; there were not a man in Darlaston who didn't have shit for brains. But her! That Neale woman was different. For a start her were not afraid of him; she had faced up to him, had even called him a liar to his face, a thing no man in this town would dare do, and what were more her were no servant of his, he could not threaten to see her on the streets without a penny.

He'd been a fool! Anger hot as bile in his throat, he slammed a fist into his palm. He should 'ave taken a whip to her that day her had showed her face at this house, he should 'ave taught her the consequence of throwin' insinuations at Uriah Buckley. A beating would 'ave set her back in her place: Mrs Greville bloody Neale! He slammed a second blow into his palm. Who the hell did that wench think her were, presentin' herself here then doubting what he'd told? Doubting enough to take herself along to the New Hope mine.

The tail end of the thought catching on his anger slowed it to a halt. That was the danger, the wench had doubts . . . her also had courage and one mixing with the other could act like dynamite. Leave her to gather enough and it could blow his world apart.

Then he must not allow it to grow. Uriah's mind resumed its usual shrewd calculating logic. Mrs Greville Neale must meet with an accident . . . some decidedly tragic accident.

'You be blowing things out of all proportion. So the wench asked a question or two, where be the danger in that?'

'Where?' Uriah glared at his companion. 'You ask where be the danger? Then if you ain't got sense enough to see for yourself where it be I'll tell you: it be to me, it were my house where the deed were done and my bloody corpse will dance from the end of the hangman's noose should it be found out, but I warn you, Elton, it won't dance alone for yours will do the same bloody polka!'

'And that quicker'n we both think lessen you keep your voice down.' Edward Elton's small eyes flicked about the quiet room. None of the men seated with faces behind newspapers or heads bent close in conversation had turned to glance at them but that didn't mean they hadn't heard and though this was a club for gentlemen not every member lived up to the description. There were more than one man here tonight would favour seeing Edward Elton jig to Her Majesty's tune. Raising a finger, he signalled for more drinks to be brought to the table set between deeply upholstered leather wing chairs, then waited until the waiter padded away again on silent feet.

Lifting the glass he twisted it between thick fingers, watching the lights of the overhead gasolière reflect like jewels from the crystal. 'So,' he said quietly, 'this woman is becoming a bother. You think her traipsing about the town asking questions might prove awkward.'

'Huh!' Uriah sniffed scornfully. 'And Edward Elton don't! He thinks there be nobody can put two and two together.'

Still holding the glass in his hands Edward Elton's small eyes glistened above its rim. 'No, he don't think that, what he do be thinking is why does Uriah Buckley be making summat from nothin'? That is what this Neale woman be . . . nothin'! Her be naught but a serving wench, a bloody servant you paid to travel along of your granddaughter to India.'

'And one who come back while Joanna be there still, where her'll be forever lying 'neath a headstone; that be one more reason I'll see that Neale bitch dead, why I'll pay to 'ave her done away with!'

'Now that be a good idea if it be you want the constabulary to come knockin' on your door. *They* be folk who can put two and two together. Uriah Buckley's only grandchild dies in India under mysterious circumstances . . . the girl paid to accompany her returns a while later and calls at Bescot Lodge where she speaks with its owner and a week or so later she is dead. Even I can make them numbers fit. A servant—'

'Her ain't no such now!' Uriah interrupted quickly. 'Her be nobody's servant!'

'Exactly!' His florid face taking on a satisfied smirk, Edward Elton leaned into the depths of the comfortable chair. 'As you say her be no servant – so where did the money her be living on come from? Think, Uriah. It don't 'ave to be you need do the arrangin', could be you don't need 'ave to see to her bein' done away with. It could be the law will swat this little shit fly for you.'

Blowing things out of all proportion . . .

Uriah Buckley snorted at the words returning to his mind. Was it himself being too quick or Elton dragging his heels? Wait and let the police do the job for him. Advice that were all well and good but they had wanted more than a word to go on. It had happened in India, they could not send a man that far, were what they had said. 'We will need to write to your son, he will have to give evidence . . .'

Write to his son! Uriah banged a fist onto the ornate mahogany desk dominating the study of Bescot Lodge. Hadn't he written, hadn't he sent letter after letter only to receive the same answer: nothing! Jervis had replied to none of them so why think he would reply to any they might send? But surely he must have had the same thoughts, thoughts which asked why one wench were spared in that massacre, why that same wench – nobbut a paid servant when her left England – not only returned wi' not a single scratch but with money enough to see her living in her own house? Jervis had always been a fool but he'd have to be an idiot not to ask himself that question. But asking with the mind and asking with the tongue, that were different. Should his son refuse to put one to the other would the Army step in, could they force him to bring an action in the courts?

'Questions!' Uriah banged the desk again, swearing aloud. 'It be nothin' but bloody questions!'

Talk! Pushing angrily to his feet he stamped from the room. That was all it was like to come to in the end. The police talking to him, writing to Jervis, and in the meantime how much talk were goin' on between the servants in this house? And how much of that were being carried about the town?

Gossip. Uriah climbed into the carriage waiting to take him to the New Hope colliery. Gossip were dangerous, it could destroy the life of a man . . . but it were not about to destroy the life of Uriah Buckley. Let the police do their investigating. Leaning against the leather upholstery he watched the streets coming into view. They might find it didn't take as long as they thought; it could be the suspect might just disappear!

Between iron-grey whiskers thin lips clamped. There were more disused mine shafts in Darlaston than there were currants in a bun and he had paid good money to see that one of them hid the body of Mrs bloody Greville Neale.

7

She had stayed at the graveside longer than she had intended. Amber glanced at the sky, dark with the threat of a storm, pewter clouds gathering in great rolling heaps. She had caught the one train from Bloxwich and on reaching Darlaston had meant to go straight home but the desire to sit for a moment beside Bethany had suddenly become a desire she could not forbid herself. That moment had somehow become hours and now it would be dark before she reached the house. Glancing again at the grave she kept so neat she touched a hand to her lips then placed it on the small stone engraved with her sister's name.

'I'm so sorry, Bethany,' she whispered into the gathering darkness. 'Oh my dear sister, how I wish I had listened to you.'

Tears she had told herself sternly she must not shed, rose thickly in her throat as she turned quickly along the path leading from the churchyard. She had vowed she would discover the circumstances of Bethany's death and the reason behind Denny's disappearance but nothing had become of that promise; it might be those children had never existed for no one owned to having seen or heard of them – no one except for Uriah Buckley!

Uriah Buckley! The choking of tears became that of anger. He knew more of her brother and sister than he had said, she felt certain of that, but he was the owner of property, a figure of substance; above all he was a man – and in this world that

fact was all that was needed for his word to be accepted against
hers. Eighteen eighty-two! The thought brought the snap of
contempt to her mind. For women the freedom to act and
often to think for themselves was still no more than a dream.

The quiet of the church grounds was matched by the silence
of empty streets. The sanctity of the Lord's Day was very
much observed in Darlaston; just the walk to church service
and for some a visit to the grave of a loved one being the only
activity Sunday allowed.

Passing along Alma Street she glanced at the tiny tight-
packed houses bordering each side, the soot- and
smoke-grimed walls blending with evening shadows, their tiny
windows lit to a sickly yellow by the glow of an oil lamp.
'Tigers' eyes, they glow like lamps but by the time you see
them you are already halfway through death's door.'

Visiting the home of Colonel Buckley several young officers
had boasted of the dangers of tiger hunts, no doubt to impress
Joanna, but the words, slipping unbeckoned into Amber's
mind, brought a shiver to her spine. There were no tigers
roaming wild in England, no jungles hiding animals waiting to
pounce, but the heath stretching dark and empty from the last
of the houses seemed to breathe its own warning.

Glancing again at the yellowy glow of windows she
hesitated. She could go back to the church and then by way of
King Street and Pinfold Street to Katherine's Cross and from
there follow along Wolverhampton Lane. There were buildings most of that route and that would mean people; but it also
meant at least another hour of walking, another hour in which
Rani would fret, her mind argued, and from the end of
Wolverhampton Lane she would still have to cross a measure
of empty heathland to reach the house she had bought on the
Leys. The house of the overseer of the disused Herberts Park
colliery. Built some distance from the rows of miners' cottages

it stood alone and isolated. Perhaps it was because of the long walk to the town centre and to the foundries which now supplied life blood to Darlaston that no other person had bought Ley Cottage. She had thought of that relative isolation before making the purchase; two women living alone on the heath! But the price had been one she could afford.

To each side of her the glow of windows died as curtains were drawn against the night. The tigers were gone. It should have brought a smile to her heart but as she set off across the heath it brought only fear.

She should have been more aware of the time. Her shawl drawn tight – more against the cold trickle rippling her nerves rather than the cool of approaching night – she chided herself for lack of thought. On leaving the train at Darlaston station she ought to have carried on home and not gone to St Lawrence's churchyard, not given way to impulse. Was that not what she had done that day? She shivered beneath the memories immediately crowding in, refusing to be dismissed. Had she not acted on impulse when asked to support Joanna Buckley in her request to visit the bazaar? Wasn't it her lack of thought had made that terrible disaster possible?

They had swooped from nowhere, fallen upon the small crowd unsuspected as hailstones from a clear sky.

Enclosed in shadowed silence Amber tried to stem the flow of memories but like a herd of water buffalo in flight they rampaged through her mind.

Waves of heat had shimmered up from the road which was little more than a track of beaten earth, every breath of air so hot it seared their lungs as they swallowed the dry acrid dust. But it had not been enough to detract from the excitement which had shimmered inside her. Everywhere fields and open land blistered and shrivelled while crops, what little there was of them, drooped in prayer for rain. But she and Joanna had given no mind to that; nothing could spoil the happiness radiating from the other girl, nothing could spoil this day for her. She had danced out of the bungalow. They would sit beside the storyteller and Narinder would interpret his stories, stories of great battles, she had laughed, of hundreds of war elephants charging the enemy, of brave rajahs and beautiful princesses. In her secret heart Amber had known such stories might not be quite the whole truth but it had not mattered. For an hour or two at least they would be true and she and Joanna would be a part of them. But even in her own eager anticipation she had been aware of the ayah's displeasure. She had made it clear she had no desire to be out walking in the heat, that she preferred the colonel sahib said no to the little mem, why should she want to go anyway . . . She had tutted her irritation with every other step, probably asking herself what interest could a *feringhee* – a foreigner – have in the folk tales told in the market place?

Joanna had ignored the woman's murmurings, crying her own delight and interest at things they passed, even the group of vultures, their hunched bodies etched black against the afternoon brilliance as they squabbled and fought over the carcass of an animal, and moments later stopping to watch a buffalo, its bones threatening to break through its hide, dragging a dead donkey behind it. Slowly it had advanced towards them leaving a trail of flattened millet stalks in its wake. Reaching the point where the sun-scorched field touched the dusty brown track it halted. Giving them no glance the man leading the tired-looking animal cut the rope of twisted grasses, freeing the buffalo of its burden, then without a word turned back the way he had come.

Narinder had shrugged at their horror. 'It is the way of things,' she had said, 'the dead preserving the living. This way the cycle of life continues.'

A little of the joy had evaporated. Catching her foot in a tussock of grass, Amber stumbled but the pictures of the past persisted flashing in rapid succession through her mind.

They had walked on, joined by others. Men in white dhotis, the strip of cloth passed trouser-fashion between the legs then fastened about the hips, their feet sending up tiny clouds of dust with each step while the bright reds and yellows of pagris, the cloth worn about their heads, bobbed like a field of freshly opened flowers, and a few respectful paces behind walked the women and girls, their brilliant saris turning the scene into a cavalcade of colour.

'*Namaste.*' They had greeted Narinder but only glanced shyly at Joanna and herself while the children had skipped and chattered with the vivacity of lively little monkeys.

It was the children who had first caught the sound! Breath tightening her chest, Amber drew the shawl closer, trying to shut out the sounds, the memories, the faint hum which had gradually increased, swelling in volume until it had the vibration of a swarm of angry bees bringing with it the sweet-sharp smell of spices drifting out to meet them on the hot still air.

Narinder had moved closer as they had entered narrow roofless alleyways where sellers of spices sat beside their open sacks of powders and dried fruits, shooing them to hurry, passing along the street of silversmiths, their hammers beating complicated designs into the gleaming metal, and on through the street of silk merchants, their tiny open-fronted booths showing lengths of gorgeous cloth hung in brilliant streamers against the dun brown walls; among the jostle and noise of the milling crowd they had encountered a swami. White paint marking his forehead, a beard straggling to meet a dust-covered loincloth, the holy man had sat cross-legged, eyes closed, giving no acknowledgement of the two annas, the coins

Narinder had placed in the wooden bowl set on the ground before him. Then they had been in the square that lay before a temple. It seemed the building stood before her now, its curved arches and domed cupolas gleaming in the setting sun, a slim minaret rising like a needle into the bowl of the sky.

'In his palace of a thousand singing fountains . . .' The words which had washed over the silent crowd seemed to beat in her brain. Choking on breath she could not expel Amber watched and listened.

'. . . the great rajah sat upon his magnificent throne of purest ivory. In his turban a ruby the size of the egg of a hen glowed with the red fire of a devil's eye, red as blood . . .'

Red as blood! A scream locked with the breath which blocked her throat as Amber saw the crimson colour splash over her dress, merging with cream, staining, marking, red as blood. Red as Joanna Buckley's blood! Paralysed with the same fear that had held her then it seemed she watched the flash of metal above her head, the flash of a sword curving down on her!

The scream forcing its way past her throat she threw herself forwards, stumbling into the gathering darkness.

It was long past the hour of her return. Rani glanced at the sky beyond the kitchen window. She did not need to read a clock for the heavens told her what point the day had reached the same as it had at home in her village, and this sky had lost its sun beyond the horizon.

Amber should have been home by now; the train she travelled on had sounded its whistle hours ago, its screech, never heard when the iron foundries were working, could be caught drifting faintly in the quiet of this one day in a week set aside for the English to worship their God.

Amber had invited her to attend morning service, assuring

her she would be accepted gladly by the congregation. But when she had refused there had been no pressure.

Restricted by the size of the window, Rani's glance moved across a narrow avenue of heath.

Her friend was understanding, to each their own god: Amber would pray to her Christ, visit his house each Sunday morning, and she, Rani, would send her prayers to Rama, paying homage to the god before the tiny shrine kept in her bedroom. She had prayed there minutes ago, imploring the deity to smile upon the *feringhee* girl who was her friend, begging the god safeguard her footsteps, to watch over Amber and bring her home. But would Rama hear pleas made in a foreign land? Would he listen and smile only in India?

Scanning the narrow expanse once more, her keen sight hampered by the deepening shadows, Rani prayed again, the words silent in her heart, words which came to a sharp halt as her eyes caught a movement. Amber? She stared the length of the garden they tended together. No, her friend would have come directly into the house, not gone to stand beside the bushes.

Leaning her face closer against the window, Rani probed the shadowed stillness. Had she been mistaken, was the evening gloom playing tricks with her vision, showing her something that was not there at all? But she had not been mistaken those other times!

Her heart beat in her throat as she stared into the garden. She had seen it there several times half hidden by the line of bushes, something watching the house, something which crouched, hiding itself, whenever she glanced that way crossing the yard and was never there when, armed with a heavy stick, she found the courage to go to the bottom of the garden. Yet it had been there. But was it there now or was worrying over her friend's lateness causing her to see phantoms?

But there was no phantom, no illusion or trick of the mind! Stifling a scream Rani watched the bushes move, watched a shape detach itself from them to stand outlined against the thickening grey, a shape which stood tall against the night: the figure of a man!

What was he doing here? Pulses racing, Rani remained glued to the spot. Was this figure the something she had been unable to define clearly on those other occasions she had glimpsed movement and if so why would a man skulk and hide?

Standing motionless in the gloom-filled garden, the figure watched the window, seeming to sense the frightened girl.

Caught in the trap of fear Rani's body refused to move, but her brain was racing. Why would a man hide himself? Was it so he could enter their house, steal their goods, their money . . . or was he intent on some other crime? Money and goods were not the only thing a man could steal. Had this one come to take what that other one had taken?

Her heart feeling it had stopped in her chest, blood thundering in her ears, Rani's stifled sob echoed in the quiet room.

She had barely entered her twelfth year. Soon she would have been betrothed to a man from the next village and in time would have become his wife. But hopes and girlish dreams had faded on that spring evening.

A fist pressed against her mouth, the gloom beyond the window faded and in its place a glorious blue sky slashed with the red and gold of sunset filled Rani's vision and etched against it a young girl, the first cool breeze of evening teasing playfully at her yellow sari, a water pot balanced on her head, sang as she walked.

The day had been unusually hot and the water she had fetched that morning was almost gone; they would need more for the evening cooking and that of breakfast the next day. It had to be fetched now, her mother had said, for the darkness of night brings many dangers. That is when the tiger prowls in search of prey.

But it had not been the golden eyes of the tiger had watched the girl go down to the river, had watched her fill the waterpot, but the eyes of a man, eyes hot with the craving of the devil in his loins.

With the water pot at her side, she had cupped her hands in the sparkling river, drinking of its cool sweetness, then had splashed her face, laughing at her reflection in the shining depths.

She had been so happy. Tears tracing her cheeks, Rani watched the memories flash in pictures across her mind.

The lowering sun threw shafts of light against gleaming brass, beams which reflected off in red-gold darts as the girl lifted the pot to her head. Her slight body swaying gracefully, one hand steadying her burden, she began to walk back along the track worn between the tall grass. Waiting for her to pass the figure hidden beneath its cover rose silently and catching the girl by the neck threw her to the ground.

There had been no one to help, no one to drag him from her. Eyes pressing tightly shut, Rani tried to stem the run of memory but spectres which the passing years had banished to her times of sleeping ran on unchecked.

The pot had rolled away, the silver line of its contents drawn greedily down into a parched earth. Struggling, the figures rolled together, the young mouth opened in a scream, a scream stopped by a blow that had her stunned. It was then the man had robbed her. Ripping away her sari he had spread her legs wide then, his breathing hard and rapid as his movements, he had pushed himself into her taking that which should be taken by none but a husband.

She had been blameless; the innocent victim of a man's lust, a man who had taken more than her virginity. There could be no marriage, she was no longer a daughter to her father. The day of her rape had been the day of her casting out. No longer acceptable in her village, she had been driven away.

Suddenly as they had come the visions faded and the miasma of fear clutching her body cleared. She had been forced to fend for herself, to use her mind in order to survive, and she must use it now.

8

Stop! She must not run! Even in the tumult of her mind the warning rang clear. Her chest heaving, a pain clipping her side from her mad flight, Amber came to a halt. The heath with its honeycomb of bracken-covered gin pits was hazardous in the full light of day but in the obscuring gloom of night it became positively treacherous; falling down the black throat of one of the pits meant never being found again. She must take care. Gulping in great draughts of air Amber forced herself to calm down. She had allowed her brain to run riot, she had given way to fears she no longer need harbour, had allowed the past to flood the present and in doing so opened up a new and different danger. In her terror she had run blind; even now she might be standing on the brink of a disused mine shaft. One step could find her hurtling into oblivion.

Glancing at the sky she saw with gratitude the sheen of ivory edging a bank of grey. The leaden threat of a storm was passing; wait a few moments and the moon would chase away the darkness, its heaven-sent light showing where the track lay. Find it, stay with it and she would reach Ley Cottage safely.

With the thought the pale alabaster orb cleared its veil of cloud and the heath shimmered silver. Beneath it Amber caught her breath at the sheer luminous beauty. The wide spread of heath had become suddenly transformed into a glittering fairy-tale land. Caught in the spell of it she stared at the heaps of spoil thrown aside by early miners digging for coal, at the clumps of gorse bushes and a few sycamore trees left to grow tall, and which in the magic of the moment became palaces with soaring towers. She might have stared entranced until the gentle moonlight became the pearl of dawn but the squeal of a rabbit clamped in a trap or the jaws of a fox brought her sharply back to reality.

Her mind once more firmly under control she glanced around. The track . . . thank God it was still beneath her feet, and there, no more than a few minutes away, the great winding wheel of Herberts Park colliery rose against the sky. The cottage was not a great distance from the empty mine. Amber breathed a sigh of relief; she was almost home, she was safe, but with the thought came a sound. Not the scream of a rabbit, not the rustle of an animal at her feet, but more the sound of heavy breath rasping as it was drawn.

Her fingers clutched her skirts as she lifted them to run but she choked as the tight clasp of an arm was thrown across her throat and the grasp of fingers dragged her head backwards.

Think! As she stood in the kitchen Rani ordered her mind to obey. The man outside in the garden had come to Ley Cottage for no good reason. How long had he watched; did he know she was alone; was he aware she knew of his presence, his intent? Maybe, but he would not be aware of *her* intent. One man had raped her and lived but a second one would die.

Forcing herself to move naturally though her insides were taut with fear she reached a dish from the dresser and set it on the table on which were the ingredients she had collected in preparation for making the evening meal. Sliding open the drawer of the table she took out a large spoon, making a display of placing it in the dish. Were the man watching he must suspect nothing. Seeming to casually push the drawer back into place she positioned her body between it and the window.

She had not closed it completely and now, reaching for the flour with one hand, she slid the other carefully into the drawer, her fingers closing on a long-bladed knife. Holding it against her thigh, hoping the folds of her sari hid it from view, she tossed her head in exaggerated impatience then walked into the scullery as if in search of some forgotten utensil.

She had given him the perfect opportunity. With her gone from the room he would slip quietly in and wait for her to return and when she did not he would come into the scullery. But she would be waiting. Her back pressed against one wall, the candle blown out, Rani raised the knife above her head.

There had been no sound. Once her sight adjusted to the darkness of the unlit scullery Rani could make out every object. The door! Her throat closing, she stared at it then breathed again, remembering she had locked it after bringing in the bucket of coals from the yard. Why had he not sought her out, what was he waiting for, had he seen the knife? Thoughts flashing like quicksilver, her ears straining to catch the faintest sound, the muscles of her arm ached with the strain of holding the knife above her head. *Why* did he not come? Unless . . . unless it was not herself he waited for!

Amber! Stifling the quick breath of discomfort she lowered her arm. That figure could be waiting for Amber. That was the only answer. The man had watched long enough to realise her friend was not home; he would also have reckoned on her return and that was when he would strike. But she could not let that happen; no matter what harm to herself she had to warn Amber.

Moving soundless as those dangers of the past had taught, she crept toward the kitchen. She gripped the knife firmly in her hand and her heart whispered 'Lord Rama, protect your child.'

The curtain closing off the scullery from the kitchen was at her fingertips. One second more and they would be face to face. Drawing one long breath she held it for a moment. Once past the curtain she must not hesitate. Fingers closing on the thick chenille, she stepped through, then screamed as a heavy boot crashed against the scullery door.

His stiffly braided uniform removed Colonel Jervis Buckley slipped on the cool cotton robe he preferred when in the privacy of his bungalow. It had been a long tiring day followed by an equally tiring reception. He had not wanted to attend; he had foregone the practice since Joanna's death, but with the visit of the viceroy's representative it had been compulsory. The garrison at Meerut was to be reinforced, the trade routes must be protected and the mutinous princes of the north put firmly in their place. It would have been more honest to have said the princes of the north must be firmly *displaced* for it was obvious that was the object of the proposed reinforcement. The government of Britain wanted no opposition to their governing of India.

Taking the robe from his manservant he thanked him quietly. From his first coming to Meerut he had admired the gentle nature of its people, but even the most placid must feel resentment at having their country stolen from them; and that was what it had been. Effected under the guise of overseeing the East India Company, of ensuring there was no malpractice against the native inhabitants, the Army was gradually replacing the Company guards recruited from the villages with its own sepoys, natives trained by the Army. Soon it would be the turn of the East India Company itself to be ousted in favour of the government's own trading company. It would merely be one replacing the other, either way the country would not be relinquished; that and nothing else was responsible for unrest such as that which had taken his daughter's life.

'Will the colonel sahib be wishing a drink?' Ram Dutt turned from hanging the uniform in a cupboard.

'Thank you, Ram.' Jervis nodded. 'Could I have *chai* served on the veranda? It's cooler out there.'

'At once, sahib.' With a slight bow acknowledging the request, the servant padded away.

Fastening the belt of his robe, Jervis glanced at the letter he had thrown down on entering the bedroom. Taking it now from the intricately carved bedside table he stared at the scripted italic lettering. That was the one thing he admired in his father, the ability to write beautifully. But *what* he wrote, the contents of the letters that had come over the years, aroused no admiration. And this one? Carrying the unopened letter out onto the veranda, he looked at it again. Doubtless this also would not revive the respect or esteem which he had once held for the man who was his father.

Drinking the hot tea brought so quickly to the veranda Jervis's thoughts played on the letter he had read. It was his duty to return to Darlaston, to marry again, to produce a future heir to Uriah Buckley's business.

Tiredly he replaced the cup in its saucer. When would his father accept he wanted no part of that business? As for an heir, that would be to live again the lie he had lived so long before.

Resting his head against the curved back of the rattan chair, he looked to where the group of meena trees draped their branches over two white marble headstones. Helen and Joanna, he had deceived them both as he had deceived . . .

Beyond the garden a dog barked and several wide-winged birds lifted into the sky, their shapes dark against the purpling evening. Vultures, feeding on carrion! He swallowed the disgust those particular birds brought to his throat. But dislike them as he did he had to admit they were of use. They helped rid the town and countryside of refuse, their actions were in the open where anyone could see, while his were hidden deep in his heart. Why had they remained so, why had he never divulged his secret? To save Helen distress, to protect the name of Buckley? No. He looked again at the stones gleaming in the semi-darkness. It was lack of courage, cowardice plain and simple!

The temptation had sometimes been there. Then Helen had looked at him with her gentle eyes and he had known he could not add to the pain never truly hidden from them. After Helen was gone a chance had been given again with the coming of Joanna to Meerut but the guilt had stayed locked inside him. Yet was it too late? He glanced again at the letter lying beside the silver tray. Maybe one day he would find the courage.

'Will the colonel sahib take supper in the dining room?'

He had not heard the man come to the veranda but on hearing the softly spoken question Jervis smiled. 'I won't be taking supper tonight, Ram, I ate too much at the buffet put on for the viceroy's representative. Tell the others they can go off duty and you also. I will see myself to bed later.'

'As the colonel sahib is wishing.'

The man moved like a shadow. Jervis watched the tray being carried away. But those others, the men who had swept down from the hills, they had not moved like shadows. They had screamed like the djinn. The people who had escaped the slaughter had trembled as they told of what they had seen. Bewildered by the shrieking clamour they had sat, only scrambling away as horsemen had ridden into the square, their swords flashing, the hooves of their horses trampling any who fell underfoot. But had it been the people of the village those men had come intending to kill. Or was it the *feringhee*, the foreign woman who was a daughter of the English Raj and the one who was with her!

Sending his glance back to the graves lying beneath the brush of heavily leaved trees tears stung his eyes.

'It was my fault,' he whispered, 'it is my fault you lie there, Joanna, I could have forbidden you to go to listen to that story-teller but again I had not the courage of my own convictions and you died as the girl who came here with you will also have died.'

How much suffering he had caused! Eyes closing, Jervis gave way to the grief burning his soul. How much pain! The lives of two young women, the heartache of Helen and the sorrow of . . .

'Oh God!' His cry echoed in the warm darkness and he dropped his head into his hands. 'Oh God, how can you ever forgive!'

Trembling from her recent ordeal Rani looked at the girl she had hauled into the house. The kick to the door had resounded through the quiet rooms, then there had been silence, a menacing hush that had her nerves screaming. She had waited, waited with the knife raised, and then she had heard the soft moan, the moan of a woman. Amber! With a dread she had not felt since the night of that funeral she had thrown open the door, dropping the knife as Amber had stumbled into her arms.

'Who was it, did you recognise him?' Hands shaking as much as her voice, she poured boiling water into the teapot.

'I . . . I did not see who attacked me.' Verging on the brink of fresh tears Amber's reply echoed the terror she had just lived through. 'I heard a sound I realised was no animal but before I could run I . . . I was thrown to the ground.'

'But you were not . . . ?'

'Raped.' Amber gave name to the fear showing so clearly in the lovely brown eyes fixed on her own. 'No. I do not think that was the reason for the assault.'

'Then what?' Rani's brow creased. 'What other reason could there be?'

Amber twisted her fluttering fingers together. 'I . . .' she shuddered, 'I think his intention was to murder me.'

A gasp ripping from her, Rani set the teapot down with a thud. One fear faded from her face only to be replaced by another. 'Murder! But who would wish to murder you?'

'Not me specifically.'

Her legs not yet steady, Rani lowered herself to a chair. 'Amber, please, I am not understanding, what is this "specifically"?'

'I meant whoever attacked me on the heath was not bent on killing me . . .' Amber paused, seeing the frown of puzzlement settle on the other girl's brow. 'Oh dear, I'm not putting this very well. I think the man is most probably escaped from an asylum, that he would have attacked anyone he saw.'

'Then . . . then it will not happen again?'

'No Rani, it will not happen again. The man will be recaptured soon.'

Watching the other girl pour tea with hands which even now were shaking, Amber lost none of the dread weighing heavily inside her. She had told Rani of some possible escapee in order to soothe that girl's worries, but she herself believed no such thing. With his hands about her throat squeezing her into unconsciousness he had muttered her name.

After she had added a few drops of the patchouli oil she had helped Rani to distil to the bowl of water on the washstand, Amber breathed the lovely fragrance deep into her lungs as she washed, trying to cleanse her mind as well as her body. But soothing as the delicate perfumed water was to her body her mind refused to quieten.

'You be bringin' me a tidy bit o' money . . .'

The words she had heard muttered out there on the heath echoed in her brain.

'A tidy bit o' money . . . I thanks you, Mrs Greville Neale.'

She had not included those words when telling Rani of her ordeal. To have done so would achieve nothing apart from causing her friend concern.

'I thank my God and yours you found the strength to run to the house and then to kick the door . . .' The girl's reply implied the rest.

But she had not run to the house! The warm damp flannel held to her face, Amber tried to make sense of her thoughts. Rani had said she had kicked hard at the door, so hard it had resounded through the house, but that did not fit with what she remembered.

Go over it carefully. Try to think only of what you remember exactly. She had told herself the same thing over and over since coming to her bedroom but the advice was not easy to follow when every little sound had her nerves jerking.

Sponging water over her breasts, her mind retraced the events of the last hour. She had allowed memories to flood back: the smell of spices, the gleam of cupolas against a vivid sky, the hypnotic voice weaving its magic . . . then the sound of horses galloping, the screams, the flash of descending blades.

Breath blocking her throat, she dropped the flannel, knocking against the iron bed frame as panic gripped her again.

Blood! There had been so much blood, spraying like crimson rain over her face, splashing in great scarlet patches over her dress, and the people . . . oh God, the people!

Slumped on her knees, her face buried in the bedcover, she sobbed as the horror of that evening played relentlessly.

The people had scattered, falling over each other in the need to escape those gleaming swords, trampling the old and young into the dust in their frenzy and Joanna . . . her eyes had widened with a sort of puzzled look, a look which remained as a glittering blade had sliced through her neck.

9

As she knelt before the small shrine set in her own bedroom, Rani placed her palms together, holding them to her mouth in reverence to the painted figure of Sita.

'My heart tells me my ears did not hear all the words of truth, but those that were not were words of comfort for a friend. Amber's lie was not for herself but for me; they were spoken to keep fear from haunting me, so I pray you, gentle goddess, be not angry that I did not deny them and blame me not for wishing the Christian God also will forgive my friend.'

When her prayer ended Rani rose and stood for several moments listening; but no sound broke through the veil of silence wrapped about the house. The fragrant patchouli oil had done its work, Amber was sleeping.

But would *she* sleep or would she watch the moon die as she had so many times in the years of her casting out, times which had lessened only little since coming to England and this town?

The sergeant major sahib had been kind in allowing she remain at his bungalow and then to be serving maid to his wife on their return home, but all of their kindness had not served to wipe away the pain of denial rape had brought her, the heartbreak of being turned from her home, from her village.

Climbing into bed, her eyes refusing to stay closed, she watched moon-cast shadows move against the walls, shadows which became a young girl with a water pot balanced on her head and, following, a taller darker shadow of a man one arm stretched towards her.

Would she ever forget! Would she ever be free of the horror, the shame! Both hands held fast to her mouth, Rani stifled the rising sobs. She had tried so desperately to tell her mother she was innocent and though her look had told she recognised the truth still her daughter had been sent like a leper from the village.

'Leper' had been the word so often shouted at her. Each time she neared a village, each time she came close enough for the inhabitants to see she travelled alone, that word rang out. Why else would anyone walk from place to place alone? She had the mark of evil, the curse of the devil, she must not be allowed to enter the village, often was driven away by stones or dogs; but some had run to fetch chuppaties or a large leaf holding rice with scraps of vegetables, setting it down well away from their homes before running away and shutting themselves indoors. In the end the call of leper had become her salvation for the alms of food kept her alive. But what seemed a blessing had turned into a nightmare.

The shifting shadows played across the walls of her room, bringing movement to the memories seething in her mind.

The moon had waxed and with its newness had come the red flower of womanhood. How many times it had blossomed since her casting out, how many moons had been reborn? Too many to remember. The sobs stilled, Rani let the past flow unhindered.

The day had been so hot, heat had bounced from rocks that knew no greenery. The earth had seemed barren, empty of life except for a young girl stumbling from the high ground. It seemed she had been alone in the world, that here at last among the foothills of the great mountain she would perish. In her despair she had fallen to the ground praying the gentle consort of Rama to end her life, but Sita had not granted her wish. Instead, with her sweet breath, she had blown across the bare rocks the sound of water rippling and falling and to Rani, half dead from thirst, it had been the voices of the gods singing.

Crying aloud, half from gratitude and half from sorrow her plea had gone unheard, she had scrambled blindly towards the sound, coming eventually to where a curtain of water cascaded down into a small pool. Cool and refreshing, it had relieved her parched throat. She had stared at the ripples widening as they spread across the pool and the stickiness of her body, the feel of the red flower against the inside of her thighs, had cried out to be washed away. She had seen no one since being sent from a village the evening before; she had walked since dawn without meeting a soul and now the sun was sending the scarlet streamers of farewell across the vivid sky. The world indeed was empty and she could bathe without fear of being seen.

The water had received her with gentle beneficence, its velvet touch cooling and soothing. She had stood beneath the falling curtain lifting her face to it, her body rejoicing in its tender touch. She had stayed in the cool shallows, scooping the playful ripples to wash away the stains of her flowering, and only as she turned to clamber out had she seen him.

Etched dark against the sunset, the cloth bound about his head adding many inches to his already tall lean frame, he had watched her.

Watching the flickering shapes imagination turned to people in her mind, Rani recalled lowering herself to her chin, the fear in her eyes bright and clear as the mountain pool. The man had stood a moment longer, then with one foot had pushed her clothing towards her and had turned his back. But she had not moved. Rani remembered the thoughts behind her hesitation. Was his offering her clothes a ploy, a deception aimed at drawing her from the water, to bring her to dry ground where he could take his pleasure of her?

It had taken many moments for the words of her brain to penetrate the terror holding her. The pool was not deep enough to bar him, and the rocks were sharp and high, too high for her to cross quickly; should rape be his intent he could drag her easily from the water . . . yet what rapist offered his victim her dress!

At last she had ventured from the pool, dragging her sari about her wet body. Only then, after she had dressed, had the figure turned. She had been so afraid. Rani drew a long breath but it did not quiver as it had beside that pool. The language he spoke had been similar to her own and gestures had said she was to follow him, she could eat and sleep.

Gopal. Rani smiled at the face seeming to turn to her from the shadows. He had been so kind, so protective of the child he had found in the hills . . . but not so his wife.

'There is no place here for filth,' she screamed whenever Gopal was away from the mud-brick house, *'and that is what you are, filth, why else would you be wandering alone from your own village!'*

She had lied then. Eyes pressed tight shut, Rani tried to push the memory from her. Her village had been struck by the plague, it had taken her parents, her brother and sisters. The whole village had been decimated by its fury, leaving her without family. But lying was evil in the sight of Rama and the god had decreed her punishment. She would remain in the village of Kihar under the protection of Gopal . . . but in the days which followed that protection had not saved her from the hatred of his wife, or the cruelty of her treatment, a cruelty which had not diminished with the arrival of Amber.

Did she also remember the insults, the blows, the slash of a bamboo cane? Her eyes flicking wide once more Rani stared

at the shaft of moonlight coming in at the window, a silver cane
which seemed to strike across her bed. How could Amber
forget? How could either of them ever forget!

Who was it that had grabbed her on the heath, had said her
name as his hands had squeezed about her throat? With a
basket on her arm Amber walked towards the town. Who was
it had tried to kill her and, equally important, who was it had
helped her to Ley Cottage? Whoever the person the arrival
had most certainly saved her life, for no matter what she had
told Rani the attack had been made with the purpose of
murder.

Murder! Amber shivered despite the shawl pulled tight
about her shoulders. But who . . . why? She had thought of
Uriah Buckley but, dislike her as he did, blame her as he might
for his granddaughter's death, surely he would not want her
murdered! But someone had wanted her dead, someone who
stood to make money from killing her. Why then had it not
happened? Had there been two men and had one of them
reneged at the last moment and pulled his accomplice from
her then half carried her home? What other explanation could
there be? And what of the figure Rani said she had seen in the
bushes at the bottom of the garden: was that a third one in
the plot? But her friend had confessed to seeing someone there
before, seeing a shape move quickly in the shadows, a shape
she said was no animal. What reason could someone have for
repeated visits in which they did not make their presence
known, why skulk and hide unless they meant mischief? But
why then had the figure never attempted to enter the cottage,
why no robbery – or worse?

Questions to which she had no answers running in her mind,
Amber followed the cart track which led into Cock Street,
pausing outside of Joseph Barber's draper shop to look at the

pretty pink dress with its deep fuchsia collar and sash she had admired on her last shopping trip. It would suit Rani's dark hair and cream-coffee skin to perfection but to buy it, to offer it to her friend, might be seen to say Rani should no longer wear the dress of her own country. Glancing once more at the gown Amber walked on. Should Rani choose to wear European clothing then the wish to do so must come from her.

Standing in the doorway of the Dartmouth Arms the landlord touched a forefinger to his brow as Amber drew level.

'Mornin.' He beamed. 'It be a fine day.'

'It is indeed.' Amber smiled her reply, seeing the man's bushy brown sidewhiskers lift as his own smile widened. The people of Darlaston were nothing if not friendly; they had a greeting to give as she passed in the streets or a minute to chat as they waited in shops for their turn to be served. Yet somewhere among their number was one ready to snatch her life.

'I tells you it be fact, I 'eard it for meself, fair staggered into the Nag's 'Ead, 'is face white as a winding cloth so Maudie Symons said.'

Several women, dark skirts rustling and black bonnets bobbing, were clustered about another as Amber entered William Blunn's grocer shop.

'Said as they couldn't get a word outta 'im for a five minute.'

'What that meant was it took a pint of ale to wet his whistle, though I never knowed it to tek a five minute nor even a one for Sammy the Screw to down a tankard.'

'Yoh can be as sarcastical as suits yer, William Blunn.' The woman at the centre threw a sharp look at the man behind a long counter. 'But that don't mek no odds, I 'eard what I 'eard and that were Samooel Pickerin' looked nigh scared out of 'is life.'

Scooping sugar into a dark blue paper bag and setting it on his scales, the shopkeeper nodded.

'Probable he got catched in some dirty deal or another. We all knows that man has more twists an' turns than the threads on a screw, that be why he be called as he is. He wouldn't stop at murder if there was enough gain in it for hisself.'

He wouldn't stop at murder. Clanging like a bell in her brain the words caught Amber's breath, holding it in her throat. Could the man they were speaking of be the same one who had attacked her a few nights before?

'So what were it scared 'im?' Another of the women with grey hair caught in a bun on the crown of her head, glared at the shopkeeper, her eyes telling him he interrupted at his peril.

'Said as it come on 'im outta the dark.' Clearly enjoying her moment, the woman telling of the episode lowered her voice dramatically. ''E were crossin' of the 'eath along past of the Leys . . .'

'Now what would Sammy the Screw be doing out there, ain't nothing but the old colliery?'

'Ain't no mind o' nobody's what 'e were doin', William Blunn, a man 'aves the right to walk across the 'eath!' Her answer tart, the woman turned back to her audience intent on finishing her story. 'Well, 'e was crossin' the 'eath . . . tekin' a short cut to Wolverhampton Lane to visit with 'is mother so Maudie Symons tells it.' A note of triumph accompanied the sentence as she glanced at the man folding the edges of the blue package in on themselves. 'Goes to visit every week reglar as clockwork, 'olds respect for 'is mother does Samooel Pickerin' . . .'

'Which be more'n he holds for anybody's property, that man would have the sugar outta yer tea afore you could finish stirrin' it.' Shaping butter between two wooden butter pats, William Blunn grinned at Amber.

'Like as I was a'sayin',' the woman went on, ignoring the remark, 'Samooel Pickerin' were near enough the cottages as belongs to Herberts Park colliery – the owner lets the old miners live in 'em still – he said the moon were fitful, ridin' in an' out of the clouds, so it took all 'is concentrating on where 'e put 'is feet so as to avoid pit shafts, that were the likely reason 'e 'eard no sound as 'e went . . .'

'That or he were too drunk to hear!' Placing the butter on the large brass scale, the grocer grinned again.

A loudness emphasising her irritation, the woman continued to ignore her heckler. 'The 'eath were silent as the grave, Samooel said it fair brought a shiver to the spine an' 'ad it not been for the ground bein' riddled with shafts 'e would 'ave run the rest of the way. Any road up, 'e said 'e could make out the windin' wheel o' the colliery against the sky and knowed he was on the right track when from nowhere it grabbed 'im . . .'

The winding wheel of the colliery – the track! It was all as she herself remembered. Caught as in a trap, Amber listened.

'Catched at 'im round the 'ead and round the throat it did, draggin' 'im to the earth an' there it spoke its evil, like a devil from hell it screeched into 'is ear'

'There you be!' William Blunn nodded again. 'Didn't I say the man were drunk? Sammy the Screw had a taste of the blue devils. That be it pure an' simple, too much ale has a man seeing and hearing what don't be there, it be naught more than his own imagination.'

'Oh ar!' The woman relating the information turned an angry glance at the man now weighing brown peas. 'An' be it imagination leaves weals about a body's neck? Ar, mister clever dick, I said weals, for that were what was about Samooel Pickerin's throat, Maudie Symons seen 'em for 'erself the very night; like the marks of a rope 'er said they looked, that or the fingers of a demon, red and so swelled up they was 'e could scarce speak.'

'But you said as it talked – as it screeched.' Anxious not to be robbed of the rest of the story, several of the woman's listeners spoke in unison.

'So Maudie says.' The woman returned to her narrative. 'Maudie an' Bertha Pickerin' be close as sisters, what one finds out the other one soon becomes privy to. Well, seems Maudie fetched Bertha in to listen to what Samooel were goin' on about when two men from Alfred Stevens' beer parlour brought 'im 'ome. Said 'e were ravin' like a lunatic, did Maudie, that 'is eyes fair stood outta their sockets an' the sweat were pourin' from 'im though 'e were shiverin' like a naked man in a blizzard. It were a demon sent from the regions of the damned, he said, sent to warn 'im the devil be on 'is back and next time 'e would be carried down into the fires of 'ell.' Her tale told, the woman looked again at the shopkeeper. 'Same as yoh'll be should them peas be underweight. Likes his brown peas an' bacon, do my old man, an' it'll be woe betide yoh, William Blunn, should it be there ain't enough to his suitin'.'

It had to be the same man! Amber watched the woman count her change carefully into a black leather purse then leave the shop followed by her still-eager retinue. He had been on the heath, following her or making for Ley Cottage only to seize her as she passed. Either way it made little difference. The man may have been frightened, but frightened enough to stay away from her? Or would he strike again?

10

Uriah Buckley glared angrily at the man standing before him in the study of Bescot Lodge. Why had he thought this one could do the job of seeing the Neale woman to her grave, why hadn't he? But he could go on all night asking himself questions and come morning he still wouldn't have the answer.

'I told you to finish her. I told you I wanted her done for!'

'I . . . I tried, Mr Buckley.'

'You tried!' Uriah's closed fist thumped hard down on the desk, shaking the crystal inkwells set in a heavily figured brass stand. 'You tried . . . and I be supposed to pay for that, am I? I be supposed to give you ten pounds for *trying*! You must think me as bloody hare-brained as y'self. You should know by now that Uriah Buckley don't pay for failure. Now get out afore I 'ave you chucked out!'

He'd known this would be Buckley's answer. On the other side of the wide desk Samuel Pickering twisted a faded dust-stained cap in hands not much cleaner. He had thought of the answer he would get from the man who had offered to pay him for killing that woman on the heath and he had also thought of his own reply. Buckley might be the owner of the New Hope mine, he might have part-ownership of an iron foundry, but scandal could affect rich as well as poor. Ten pounds or have his name in every newspaper for miles around: Buckley had the choice.

As Uriah's hand reached for the bell pull hanging beside a

stone fireplace, Samuel sucked in a deep breath. He had had the fright of his life that night out along of the Leys and it weren't going unpaid for. Fingers tightening even more about the cap, he spoke quickly. 'I should 'ang on a minute afore you 'as me chucked out.'

'What? Who the bloody hell do you think you be talking to! I'll kick you out meself . . . kick your arse up into your neck.'

'You does that an' I goes straight to the *Star*. What you don't pay for that newspaper will. Should mek interesting reading . . . Mine owner in murder plot.'

His hand hovering beside the tapestry cord which would summon his manservant, Uriah's eyes blazed iced fire from a face scarlet with fury. The bloody upstart was threatening him!

Watching temper work visibly across the flushed face Samuel Pickering tried not to show the anxiety playing football in his stomach. Buckley could send for the bobbies, accuse 'im of blackmail, but the hand had not pulled that cord; the man must have realised there's never smoke where there be no fire. Confidence bolstered by the thought rising even higher as Uriah let his hand drop, he smiled inwardly. This was going to be easier than he could have imagined. Buckley was caught in a web and the spider was about to close in.

'I got to thinkin',' he went on, 'that night I were near throttled on that 'eath could only 'ave been set up by somebody as knowed I would be there an' that somebody were you. I told you as I'd found out the Neale woman were living along o' Ley Cottage an' that I would do the job there, but you were not easy wi' leavin' it at that, you wanted the woman *and* her killer both dead so you dreamed up a neat little plan, a nice little disappearance: Samooel Pickerin' would be found in a mine shaft wi' 'is neck broke. Only 'e ain't dead, 'e be 'ere claimin' 'is due, and if you knows what be in the best interests o' Uriah Buckley you'll pay up!'

'Don't talk so bloody crackpotical!' Uriah hissed through clenched teeth.

'Oh it ain't crackpotical,' Samuel returned, 'it be perfect sense. I kills that woman an' you kills me. If I be found then the bobbies thinks I got the wind up an' runs off only to go head first down a shaft, an' Uriah Buckley don't be implicated at all. But try to cross me again, try doin' me down over payment, an' I'll tell the *Star* everythin'.'

'Then do it!' Eyes narrowing to pinpoints, Uriah glared across the desk. 'Go tell that newspaper it were Uriah Buckley out to murder you on that heath. Folk already think your brain be turned what with you declarin' you was attacked by a demon from hell; tell now it were me as almost strangled you and you'll be in an institution for the insane quicker'n you can think.'

One word against another! Samuel's feelings of confidence drained slightly. His word wouldn't go far against that of a man of standing in the town. But then mud sticks on silk as it did on rags and Buckley would want no stain.

'I said as I'd thought it a demon attacked me so as to throw folk off the scent,' he answered quickly. 'Should the Neale woman complain of her attack to the bobbies, two folk on the same night and in the same place . . . they wouldn't suspect me at all.'

No wonder this man was known as Sammy the Screw; he could twist and turn his way out of anything! Watching him now, cap screwed in his hands, Uriah began to think more calmly. An insane asylum? Yes, that was one way, but it would entail talk and that was something best avoided. A little disappearance, the man had used the term himself, and it was a solution would prove adequate: but for the moment it must appear Pickering's dirty little scheme was succeeding.

Uriah kept the look of rage. 'Judging by what I heard the men saying along of the New Hope you were half crazed with fear when you walked into some beer house babbling on about demons and fires of hell; wouldn't take a physician long to certify you insane.' He paused, enjoying the look which had appeared in the other man's eyes; Sammy the Screw wasn't so confident any more. 'So might just be in your own interest to go away and forget we two ever spoke of the Neale woman, and certainly never of any murder.'

The crafty swine was backing out! Slippery as a snake, Buckley was sliding away. But snakes were lethal and this one no less than a viper. How long after he left this house before the constables were knocking on his own door? But a bargain were a bargain and the price agreed should be the price paid! Anger replaced confidence and common sense as Samuel stepped close to the desk.

'I done what you asked,' he said, Uriah Buckley's eyes following his move, 'I kept my side o' the bargain. Now you keep to your'n. Ten pound were the payment you promised.'

'But you didn't do what were asked and I don't be fool enough to pay a man for doing nothing . . . you'll get no payment from me!'

The fingers twisting the flat cap became suddenly still and silence heavy and threatening lay between the two men. Then Samuel Pickering spoke his words, no longer hot with self-righteous anger but dripping from his tongue like ice water.

'You should know, Mr Buckley, there be ways o' payin' other than that med wi' money. Samooel Pickerin' don't shovel no man's shit an' not take payment.'

Pickering shovelled no man's shit! His visitor gone, Uriah sat on in the quiet room. There had been threat in every syllable and threats were easy to carry out in a town riddled with pits. But Uriah Buckley knew for himself how to shovel shit . . . and the first shovelful would land on Samuel Pickering!

'There is no one left to ask. I have been to every place of work in Darlaston and Wednesbury and at none of them has anyone heard of Denny. Should I leave Darlaston, Mother? Should I go to some other town to search for him?'

As she knelt beside her mother's grave replacing faded flowers with fresh ones Amber murmured her thoughts.

'Rani says that would not be the sensible thing to do, she says Denny will return to the place we were last together; but to wait day after day not knowing where he is or what has happened to him makes me feel so guilty. Help me, Mother, help me know what to do.'

The sound of a footfall, soft as it was on the grass, caught Amber's ears; the years in India, of ever listening for the sound of danger, had her hearing honed to the sharpness of a razor edge and in seconds she had scrambled to her feet.

'I beg your pardon, I did not expect to find you here.'

A figure spoke then turned away and in that instant Amber remembered. Vivid blue eyes, dark hair falling over a smooth forehead, face shaven clean of whiskers: the man who had kept her from falling the day of her first visit to this cemetery!

'Wait!' Involuntarily she stretched her hand toward the long-limbed figure, then dropped it with an embarrassed blush as the man turned. 'We . . . we spoke once before, the priest said it was you kept my mother's grave so neat, you brought flowers to her every week. He . . . he also said you were her son.'

The space between them was not enough to hide the tiny frown come to nestle between his brows. 'That is a mis-apprehension of his own making and not of mine,' he said quietly. 'The man obviously thinks that because I bring flowers then I must be a son. I hope his mistake has caused you no offence. I will speak with him when next I see him. Now I will leave you.'

'Were those for my mother?' Amber spoke quickly as the lithe figure made to leave.

Glancing first to the creamy gold roses held in his hand and then to the tall white marguerites Amber had placed beneath the simple wooden cross, he nodded. 'I had intended to place these flowers on the grave but now I see that is an intrusion, I will not do so again.'

'No, they are not an intrusion.' Amber smiled. 'My mother would have liked your bringing her flowers, but since she cannot thank you please allow me to do so for her.'

Heady and strong, the fragrance of the lovely flowers filled her nostrils as she knelt to place them. Roses! Her hands trembling uncontrollably, she was instantly back in the gardens of that bungalow in Meerut a laughing Joanna Buckley gathering handfuls of deep red petals. *Aren't they the most beautiful of flowers?* The girl's voice sang in her mind. *'I will want nothing but roses for my wedding bouquet . . . I even want them for my burial.'*

A cry breaking from her, Amber watched the petals being flung into the air then falling in a shower of scarlet: the scarlet of blood.

'I couldn't help you . . . I couldn't help you . . . they were there before I knew.'

Drawn deep into the horror of that memory Amber did not feel the strong hands lift her or the arms which held her close against a hard chest.

Only long after, alone in her own room, did her brain give back the words it had heard whispered against her hair.

'If tears are all I can have of you then I will take them gladly.'

*   *   *

There be ways o' payin' other than that med wi' money.

Seated in the small room he used as an office at the New Hope colliery Uriah Buckley took the gold hunter pocket watch from his waistcoat pocket. Twelve minutes to eleven o'clock. An acid smile touching the corners of his thin lips, he replaced the watch then reached for a brass handbell standing on an otherwise empty desk. Uriah did not use this room for bookwork.

Twelve minutes. Swiftly his mind ran over the plan he had devised. Two minutes to cross the yard at a run, and that bloody clerk sitting in the outer office would run or get his arse kicked onto the streets, eight minutes for a man to wind his way bent double along the maze of tunnels to the coalface of the deep seam, then one more to call his message to that toad Pickering. Sammy the Screw, the other men called him; Uriah's hand hovered above the bell. Well, it would take more than a screwdriver to get him free if this plan worked. Grasping the bell, the smile gone from his lips, Uriah rang sharply.

''Ave Samuel Pickering sent for,' he barked at the nervous weedy little man who answered his summons, 'I want to see him right away. And tell him there be a constable here, one as wants to ask a few questions.'

'A constable?' The clerk darted a glance about the room.

His face flushing with anger, Uriah banged a fist hard on the desk. 'Do you be bloody deaf! I said tell Pickering there be a constable here . . . you send a lad to run for one afore you crosses the yard. Now bugger off and do as I tells or pick up your tin right now!'

'But . . . but Pickering be pikeman, to fetch him from the coalface will mean delaying the drop.'

'I don't care if he be guard outside of Buckingham Palace I want him here!'

The roar sent the clerk scuttling away; Uriah went to stand at the window which overlooked the yard. He knew the procedure at the pit as well as any man working in it. The first hours of a morning shift were spent undercutting the coal, men lying on the ground using picks to hack a ledge into the face; that done, it was the work of the more highly paid pikeman to scale a ladder some ten, maybe fifteen, feet to the roof of a chamber formed by the constant removal of coal from the deeper seam, and there to hold a metal spike against the hanging coalface and with a perfectly aimed blow of a hammer bring the whole lot tumbling . . . a *perfectly* aimed blow.

Uriah watched the clerk pass the message to a man who disappeared into the mouth of the mine. Precision was the crux of the entire operation, misplace the spike or strike it awkwardly and the roof of the workings came down, burying the pikeman beneath hundreds of tons of coal. To mention a constable would have Pickering shaking in his clogs, have the hands holding the spike and hammer jerk with fear, striking the coal face at a wrong angle.

Touching fingers to the pocket holding the watch, Uriah continued to stare at the black hole that was the entrance to the mine. If he had timed things correctly then word of him being wanted by a policeman should be called up to Pickering at just about the precise moment of striking that hanging curtain of coal!

Withdrawing the timepiece he watched the seconds tick by, watched the minutes reach the hour then smiled as a roar from that dark opening erupted like thunder.

'There be ways of paying, Pickering,' he murmured, dropping the watch back into his pocket, 'there be ways of paying.'

11

'It was the same man I had spoken with once before, the one I thought was Denny.'

How could she ever have made such a mistake? Her brother had fair hair and though his eyes were blue he was of slight build whereas the man in the churchyard . . . But there she went again, forgetting Denny must have changed in the years of their separation.

'And you spoke with him again today?' Cutting lamb she had stripped from the bone into almond-sized pieces, Rani placed them in the heavy-bottomed pan set over the fire.

A sudden flush of pleasure sweeping with the memory bringing a tinge of pink to her cheeks. Amber answered, 'We talked for some time. It seems the priest had simply assumed he was my mother's son. I suppose it was an easy mistake to make seeing as how it was he kept her grave so neat and he was the one placed a cross with her name on it.'

Adding a teaspoonful of ginger to the mortar in which she had already gathered a pinch of mace and another of dried basil, Rani began to grind them together with a pestle. 'But if he is no son to a woman why would a man care for the place where she is being buried?'

Reaching for the parsley she had picked from the garden a few minutes before, Amber hid the smile the quaint phrasing of the question brought, yet it was a smile which contained only admiration. Rani had learned an entirely new language from those whispered conversations they shared under the stars, had repeated words over and again as they had lain huddled together for warmth in the cooler nights of winter when Kewal's acid temper forbade them the shelter of the mud brick house, but though she had tried in her turn to learn that spoken by Rani and the people of the village it had eluded her almost completely.

'I asked that question myself.' The colour still in her cheeks, Amber answered. 'He told me his father had been a seaman and on one visit home had insisted on taking his son to sea with him. He had been nine years old at the time and he did not see his mother again for a number of years, his father always promising that at the end of the next voyage they would return. When during a terrible storm his father was washed overboard and drowned he came home but his mother had moved and it took him almost a year to find her. She was ill with pneumonia when he arrived and died shortly after, but in the days they had together she spoke often of the kindness shown her by my mother. Keeping her grave neat was his way of returning that kindness.'

'Then the gods of the universe will smile upon him.' Rani added a small amount of paprika to the mortar. 'But have they not blessed him already, has he received no naming?'

She had remembered his name; it had lingered in her mind all of the journey home. It played there still but now forced to speak it aloud Amber felt the colour strengthen in her cheeks. 'He . . . he said his name was Zachary Hayden.'

Pouring a little of the butter she had clarified in a separate pan to the mixture in the mortar Rani practised saying the name, the 'r' rolling around her tongue in the way it always did.

'The village to which Zachary Hayden came, was it the same Bloxwich you lived in?'

She could understand the process of thought behind the tiny

frown settling itself between the other girl's eyebrows. How could people of the same village not know each other? Amber scooped up the parsley she had chopped, adding it to the mixture Rani was grinding.

'I knew Mrs Hayden,' she said, turning her attention to a bundle of fat shallots, 'she was often poorly. My mother said it was caused by coming from the steamy heat of the laundry room at Essington Hall, often walking through rain and snow the three miles to her own home. She was a small woman and softly spoken, but what I remember most about her was the sadness in her eyes. The times I ran errands for her she would always smile her thanks but the smile never hid the sadness. I didn't know then it was the pain of parting with her son; she must have been so happy when he finally came home, happy as I would be should Denny return.'

'Your brother will come some day. You should keep that in your heart and not anger the gods by your disbelief.'

Rani and her faith, her belief the deities watched over them ordering their lives. Amber peeled the fine outer skin from the shallots. But neither the Christian Saints nor the gods her friend prayed to seemed to hear for still there was no word of Denny.

A silence fell over the kitchen; Rani glanced at the friend she loved as a sister and her own heart twisted with the sorrow she knew lay heavy in that sister's heart, a sorrow she must try to lighten. Adding the herbs she had ground with the butter to the meat simmering in the pot she asked: 'The man Zachary Hayden, the son of the woman who was friend to your mother, did he bring flowers also today?'

'Yes.' Amber nodded. 'He apologised for doing so.'

Rani turned from stirring the pot, the tiny frown once more appearing between finely marked brows. 'Sorry . . . he say he is sorry for bringing flowers?'

'He thought I would take offence. He said it was an invasion of privacy.' Amber added, seeing the perplexity in the wide brown eyes.

Clearly struggling to understand the complexity of it all, Rani's head moved slowly from side to side, a habit Amber had seen in every Indian she had met and one Rani had not lost.

'I am not understanding,' the girl said slowly, 'how can the bringing of a gift cause this . . . how you said . . . offence?'

Gathering the skins she had removed from the shallots and dropping them in a bucket underneath the shallow brownstone sink Amber tried to explain.

'It is not the same here as in India. In your country it is accepted every person in a village attends the funeral of one who dies and afterwards makes offerings, but here that is not so. Only those who are especially invited attend a funeral and only family make offering at a graveside. It is only they bring flowers each week as a token of remembrance.'

'But others too remember!' Rani frowned again. 'So why can no offering be made by them?'

'It is the custom.'

'But the flowers Zachary Hayden came to give, they marked his respect. Surely you could not refuse to let him make offering, you could not turn away a gift made of love.'

It could not be a gift of love, the man had never known her mother, but a gift of respect . . . yes, it was that.

'No.' Amber smiled. 'I could not turn away such a gift. I took the flowers from him, thanking him for his kindness in tending my mother's grave . . . they were so lovely, the colour so creamy-gold. I knelt to place them beside the marguerites I had already put beneath the cross; I thought how beautifully the colours went together, how they reminded me of the way my mother would describe the angels, their white robes tied with sashes of gold. I bent to arrange them and that was when it happened.'

A look of alarm springing to her eyes echoed in Rani's sharp 'It happened! What happened?'

Shallots half chopped, Amber shook her head. 'I . . . I'm not really sure, one moment I was smiling, breathing in the aroma of those flowers, and the next . . . it was so silly of me to behave as I did, heaven knows what Zachary Hayden must have thought of me.'

'One moment you were smiling and the next you were in India. The fragrance of the flowers touched that which you hoped was banished, it carried you back into the past.'

'The flowers!' Halfway back to the world which had claimed her at the graveside, Amber did not ask how the other girl knew. 'Their scent was so heady,' she went on, 'so like those in the gardens of Colonel Buckley, those huge wonderfully scented roses Joanna loved, but their bouquet . . . surely that was not the cause of my . . . my . . .'

'The mind is a powerful thing.' Rani took up as Amber's words trailed away. 'We think when it does not speak to us that it is sleeping, that the past is lost to it. But that is a deception of our own making, a veil we lay over our pains in order to hide them. We fool ourselves in such belief for the mind does not sleep nor does it forget.' Her fingers ceasing the whipping of a small amount of cream, the girl seemed to stare into a different world and when she spoke again her voice trembled on a knife-edge of emotion. 'It keeps its memories hidden, it robes them in darkness only to use them when we least expect. They are its tools, the instruments by which it brings joy or sorrow, pleasure or pain; they can delight but the happiness is often fleeting, staying but a moment in the heart, then is gone like a feather in a windstorm while sorrow and fear remain a torture in the soul.'

Hearing the undisguised anguish underlying those words Amber caught her breath. Lord, how selfish she had been, how utterly selfish in thinking only she suffered nightmares from the past! How could she not have realised this girl too must remember, that she had also been subjected to humiliation, to pain and suffering! Going to her now she put her arms about her friend, feeling the noiseless sobs trembling through the slight body. Oh, why had she been so thoughtless . . . why had she not seen what must have been there all along, why had she not seen the grief? But she had only seen her own!

Guilt and regret smouldering together she whispered. 'Rani, I'm sorry. I did not think, forgive me. I did not mean to hurt you.'

Rani freed herself, her soft brown eyes glistened through a mist of tears. 'Do not fill your heart with sadness.' She smiled. 'Yours is not the tongue brings me sorrow, your words are not the cause of my tears. That lies, as did your own, in memories.'

Amber glanced at the shallots but did not resume the task of chopping them. 'We share so many of those,' she said quietly, 'so many memories, so much pain.'

'But the gods are kind,' Rani answered, her voice gentle as her eyes. 'They gave us tears with which to ease the pain of the heart, tears which each time they spill dull the ache of the soul and little by little fade the brilliance of memory. Maybe one day they will wash away the last traces, leaving only happiness in their wake.'

Rani's optimism had been their main strength through the dark days of life in that village. Taking up the knife Amber chopped absently at the particles of shallots. Rani had been the one to whisper of freedom, of happiness that would soon be theirs. But lying on the hard earth, bones aching from hours of labour under a scorching sun, body smarting so much from the perpetual slash of a bamboo cane that sleep would not come, she had found that whispered encouragement hard to accept. Yet Rani had never given up; it was her fortitude had kept them both alive, that inner strength which had proved the mainstay of sanity when things got so bad death had seemed preferable to life.

But though against all odds those whispers, the dreams they had conjured, had become reality, Amber only now understood the shadow she had seen sometimes lie across those eyes, a shadow she now knew hid a different heartache, one which struck a shaft of cold along her nerves. Was Rani unhappy here, was she perhaps longing for her own country, her own village and people, as she herself had longed for England, for her brother and sister?

The cold touch numbing her nerves solidifying now to a weight in her heart, Amber dreaded the answer would be yes, that her friend would ask to return to her own home. But the question had to be put. Lifting her glance, her mouth already open to voice the query she had not had the insight to recognise the need of before a moment ago, she paused. Rani had turned from stirring the pan but she was not looking at her, she was staring beyond her to the window, her lips pursed in a sign for silence.

'There,' she whispered, 'there in the bushes, the figure is there again.'

He should not have let his feelings get the better of him. His work finished, Zachary Hayden stared out over the garden he had filled with flowers. He should not have spoken the words he had; the woman wore a wedding ring, she was another man's wife. What if she had heard, what if she had caught those words? But they had been almost soundless, hushed by the silk of her hair.

Amber Neale, she had introduced herself. Amber, he

whispered the name. It suited her; amber was the colour of her eyes, of the tints sunlight highlighted in her hair, gold-flecked amber; a woman and a gem, both were beautiful.

Spread before him the blossoms intertwined their colours like some vast tapestry but Zachary saw only one colour, the shining copper gold of a woman's hair.

Impatient with himself he turned towards the tiny cottage which had been his mother's last home. What on earth was wrong with him! Amber Neale was not the first woman he had seen . . . but she was the first he had not immediately forgotten. He had thought never to see her again after that first time at the cemetery but he had not ceased to see her; her face, her smile, her lovely amber eyes had stayed in his mind throughout the days and plagued his sleep. He had tried to fight the urge to see her again telling himself it would pass, then called himself a fool when it had not. So he had gone to the church-yard but not to the spot where she knelt; instead he had watched from the other side, his whole self wanting to go to her, but without sound reason that would be impolite. Each Sunday he had stood watching her tend the small patch of earth, watched her leave by the lych gate and each time a sting of disappointment had pricked through him. Then last Sunday she had not come. He had waited, screened as usual by a corner of the building. All of the afternoon he had watched for her among the people coming to lay their floral tributes until the last one had gone. The bell ringing for evensong and the shrill blast of a train whistle had finally convinced him it was too late, that she would not be coming, and the sharp touch of dis-appointment had become a stab as he had walked away. Then today, Wednesday, the day he always tended the grave of his own mother and took flowers to that other one, she had been there. Sight of her had stopped him in his tracks. Like a child caught in some misdemeanour he had not known whether to stay or run. Remembering now he felt he would have chosen the latter, that nerves already dancing like leaves on the trees around them would have him leave without speaking; but then the sun had escaped a cloud and his shadow had fallen over her and she had smiled and spoken.

But what had those few minutes with her done except make matters worse for him? Speaking with her had not eased the feeling inside him, had not erased the pictures from his mind but only made them clearer.

Coming into the house, the door closing behind him, he stood with one hand resting on the mantel, his gaze deep in the red heart of the fire.

Flames fanned by the abrupt movement of air danced towards the chimney but Zachary saw only strands of copper-gold hair and the smiling eyes of Amber Neale.

Lord, this had to stop! Resting his brow on the hand touching the mantelshelf he closed his eyes. He had to pull himself out of the pit which was slowly swallowing him. But how? Hadn't he told himself over and again she belonged to another man, that she could never be anything to him? But for all his reasoning the emotions jangling his insides had not lessened.

Drawing in a deep breath he sank into the chair drawn against the hearth. Was such a thing possible? Could that which he had called a momentary fancy be something deeper? Was it a nonsense or could a person truly fall in love at first sight?

That must not be. After all, what would it achieve except to deepen those emotions already churning in his stomach, turn them into a heartache for which there was only one cure? But that cure was banned to him. Amber Neale was another man's wife.

12

It was there, outside by the bushes, the figure Rani had seen before. Amber felt her nerves quicken. Who was it . . . why did he or she continue to come here, what was it was wanted?

'Shh!' Rani breathed as the knife fell from Amber's hand. 'Whoever is there will do no harm to us but only watch.'

'Watch!' Queries a minute before had seen her ready to voice were swamped in the dancing of her nerves. Someone was spying on them, someone who wanted their presence to go unseen!

'Wait.' Her caution no more than a murmur Rani gave the faintest shake of her head, a movement not easily detected from the garden. 'Wait Amber, do not let anger carry you upon its back.'

'How can you say that?' Her own words a whisper, Amber glanced towards the window. 'We have to do something, we cannot let this go on.'

Her glance dropping to the table, her hands moving a dish as though occupied with her cooking, Rani answered quietly. 'Something has already been done, that is how it is known to me that not you or I are in danger from the one who watches.'

Wrenching her own glance from the window, Amber stared at her friend. How could she know that? Unless . . . ! Breath tight in her chest she asked, 'What has been done, has that peeping Tom been here in the house, has he . . . ?'

'No one has been in this house but you and myself. The one who stands now behind the bushes has not come close.'

'Then how do you know he means us no harm, how can you be so sure?'

The demand had been sharp but Rani knew the curtness of it was due to anxiety. Carrying the dish to the fire she spooned a measure of the braised mutton her own people knew as korma sadah into it before facing Amber again. 'Because I went into the garden.' She smiled. 'I went there the night you did not come home at your usual time, I called your name asking where were you . . . were you hurt? Then the bushes moved and I saw the figure running away, I saw it clear against the evening sky – a man's figure.'

'You went outside!' Amber was aghast.

'That evening and others since. I know when he is come even though at first I do not see him. I go down to the bushes yet never am I harmed; that is the reason for my sureness for did he wish to do hurt then he could have done it, but as you see it is not so.'

'But you could have been injured, maybe even killed. Who knows what this man is or where he comes from; he could be a tramp or . . . or a convict escaped from some prison.'

Setting the dish on a plate Rani cut a thick slice of the bread Amber had baked the evening before and together with a spoon put it with the soup. 'You are letting fear into your heart,' she said gently, 'it clothes the senses in shadow and steals wisdom from the mind. Put it from you, allow the light of reason to shine so you may think clearly. When you and I were finally allowed to leave the village of Kihar, once we were freed from the cruelty of Kewal and the threat of the funeral pyre, did we remain to stare from the bushes? No . . . we ran, we ran until the heart in our chest was bursting; should the man who watches us now be escaped from a prison would he not flee as we did? Would he come time upon time to a place where he might easily be caught?'

There was a deal of logic to what Rani said, but even so the risks she had taken, the possible danger she had placed herself in, it could not be allowed to happen again.

'He is no beggar on the road.' Rani was speaking again. 'Beggars ask for alms but this man has asked none, beggars seek a place to shelter from the night air yet he lies himself not in the barn.'

'Then *what* does he want?' It broke from Amber on a note of exasperation.

Taking up the plate, Rani answered softly, 'Perhaps it is friendship.'

Friendship! Amber gasped. Had the girl taken leave of her *own* senses? Friendship did not skulk in bushes, it did not hide from those it wished to embrace.

Glancing again at the window as Rani picked up the plate Amber was at the door before her, both arms stretched to prevent its opening. 'What do you think you are doing? I won't let you go out there!'

Brown eyes soft as velvet met with Amber's. 'What I am doing is making a gift. The mercy the great God showed to us, the kindness of saving us from more sorrow, should be passed to another; that way we show thanks to Him. Because I am safe now in your country should I forget the ways of my own, should the prayers of the heart not be echoed by the action of the hand?'

It was said so quietly, with such sincerity. There had been no accusation, no censure, yet Amber felt a flood of shame wash over her. Dropping her arms she opened the door. Rani could make her gift but it would be with Amber Neale at her side.

He was not a man. Amber looked at the figure Rani had coaxed into coming from the bushes.

Sunlight, spearing the last of its rays defiantly into the gathering night shadows, gleamed on hair the colour of straw and on limbs gangly with youth. The figure which had scared her so was that of a young lad probably of no greater age than Denny. How her heart had leapt when that fair head had appeared from its hiding place, how she had caught her breath thinking it was her brother; but the face had shown her it was not for despite the failing light she had seen the brown mark lying across one cheek. Denny had no mark; he had been born with a clear and perfect skin.

He had taken the dish from Rani, appreciation bright in his eyes, but he would not be talked into eating in the house.

'What is your name?' Amber asked as the food disappeared hastily into his mouth.

'My name?' He paused, alarm halting the spoon halfway to his lips.

He was almost as afraid as she had been. 'We would like to know your name,' she went on, 'friends should call each other by their name. Mine is Amber.'

'I knows that,' he answered, then looked at Rani. 'But I don't know your'n.'

'How do you know my name?' Amber frowned. She had not met this lad before.

'Mother,' he answered, 'Mother talked of an Amber. I guessed you was the one, ain't nobody else in Darlaston be called Amber.'

Holding out her hand for the dish he had already scraped twice, Rani smiled. 'I am Rani.'

'Amber . . . Rani.' He repeated the names, handing back the dish. 'Pretty . . . they be pretty names.'

His mother had spoken of her, but who was his mother?

'We have given our names to you, will you not share your own?' She had asked the question gently, not wishing to add to his nervousness. The light was uncertain, the evening already closing in, but Amber caught the look which darted over the young face – a look of pain.

'You do not have to tell us,' she said quickly, 'Rani and I will just call you friend.'

'You will be my friend?'

'We will both be friend to you,' Rani answered. 'And friends do not need to hide in bushes.'

'I d'ain't mean no 'arm! I ain't never took nothin' nor broke so much as a daisy!'

'We did not suppose you had,' Amber intervened but the lad rushed on.

'I don't never 'urt nobody, I just watches and listens.'

'But why do you watch at this house?'

' 'Cos I don't be so daft as folk says I be. Daft Freddy be the name they calls me. They say I be mutton-'eaded, naught but a juggins, but there be more in this 'ead than there be in many another, more than there be in that of 'im who lives along of Bescot Lodge. I 'eard 'im talkin' to Samooel Pickerin' . . . I 'eard 'im say to do for Amber Neale. Amber were the name my mother spoke of when 'er said you 'ad called to Bescot Lodge an' Freddy can count. He can put two an' two together same as clever folk. Uriah Buckley were feared, that were 'is reason for wantin' you dead. But I reckoned if my mother talked well o' you then I should see no 'urt was done you. That be why I watch; like that night R . . . Rani come into the garden a-callin' o' your name, callin' where was you, I could 'ear the fret an' worry in them shouts so I went back across the 'eath an' I seen 'im, I seen Samooel Pickerin' an' I followed 'im. It were when you passed by I knowed what he was about an' Freddy weren't wrong. I seen 'im grab a'old o' you, to throttle you 'e was, so I grabbed a'old of 'im, took 'im by the throat I did. Oh he d'ain't know it were daft Freddy could 'ave choked the life outta 'im but 'e 'eard what were said an' 'e knowed, 'e knowed next time 'e would be dead.'

So it was Uriah Buckley behind that attack made upon her a few nights before. But why in the world would he want her death? Did he see that as a sort of payment for what had happened to his granddaughter?

Across the quiet expanse of the heath the sound of a church clock striking the hour had the lad turn away.

'Don't go, wait please . . .'

There were so many questions still to ask. He had mentioned Bescot Lodge; could he perhaps have known her sister and brother, might he know of Denny's whereabouts?

'Wait!' Amber called again but the figure had melted away like a mist wraith no sound of his going to tell where, but on the darkness his voice floated.

'You need 'ave no fears o' Samooel Pickerin', 'e won't be botherin' nobody no more.'

Uriah Buckley had wanted her dead just as Kewal had wanted her dead. Uriah had talked a man into murdering her just as Gopal's wife had tried to do.

The moon had risen late but now its feathery gleams darting between clouds danced shadows on her bedroom wall, shadows which flickered like silver flames. Flames! Amber lay with eyes wide open, afraid of the dreams which often came with sleep, but still out of those dancing shadows the nightmare came.

It was evening and beneath the great neem tree Gopal looked around the half circle of sun-baked faces. He had called a *panchayat*, a meeting of the elders of the village.

The present snatched from her, Amber looked on a different time.

'*Men of Kihar.*'

Barred from sitting with others of the village, two huddled figures crouched beside the corner of a house built of mud brick and roofed with reeds, figures which shivered with another unknown fear.

'*Since the* feringhee *was brought to our village I alone have given her food . . .*'

Sitting close to her, Rani's signs and broken English translating Gopal's words were enough for Amber to understand.

'*I alone have provided her with shelter. Now I ask you all to take account of her.*'

For several moments no head moved and no man of the circle spoke. Smoke from dying cooking fires curled languidly up towards where pinpoints of yellow light were swelling into huge yellow-white stars and from a purple horizon a translucent moon began its ascent, bringing the cooling breath of evening.

'*Gopal.*' The man who spoke glanced toward the huddled shapes. '*The girl Rani, maybe a husband might be found for her for she is born of this country, a man might take her even with no dowry, but the* feringhee *. . .*' He broke off, shaking his head while the rest murmured their agreement.

'*Should one of you take the* feringhee *for wife she will not come without dowry. I, Gopal, will provide a marriage portion of two goats, one sack of rice and another of maize.*'

A gasp from the listening women and a screech from Kewal reached the ears of the men but the voice of Gopal overrode them.

'*Men of Kihar,*' he said loudly, '*our countrymen did great wrong in taking the girl from her kin. No doubt they felt sinned against by the white Raj but that does not condone their action. I say to you no child or woman . . . even a* feringhee *. . . should be made to pay for the wrongs done by others yet this happened. But then she was brought here to Kihar and who could have guided her*

*but the Lord of Creation? He has paid us great honour by giving
it to us to smooth a path so painfully twisted and one among us
could show the great god honour by accepting her as wife.'*

Somewhere among the encircling hills a hyena called, its
howl carrying clear on the crystal night; somewhere pain, fear
and death were joined in grisly embrace.

His turban caught by a sudden flare from wood collapsing
into a fire, Gopal's head turned to another man who stood to
speak.

*'We hear what you say, Gopal, but our village is poor. The earth
becomes more barren and the fields give less while each year we
have more mouths to feed. While I honour the great Lord I cannot
take food from the mouth of my little ones or dishonour my blood
by marrying with a* feringhee.'

Each voicing the same rejection, the men rose, drifting away
towards their own homes. Left alone, Gopal had pressed a
hand to his chest, the rasp of his breath loud enough to reach
Kewal who with a scream ran to him.

The sounds heard so long ago, the cries of a frightened
woman, the terse worried voices of her sons, rang loud in
Amber's mind. This was not happening . . . it was over, in the
past. But though she knew what she saw and heard was not
real her mind would not free her and the horror she had once
lived through claimed her yet again.

Men had come running and with the help of Gopal's eldest
son carried him into the house. Beyond its walls the two figures
sat clutching each other's hands. They could run away, take
their chance now while no one watched them, Rani had
whispered, but as they got to their feet a man came for them.

Gopal had sent for her. The small room had been dim and
it seemed the smoke of a lamp filled with oil rendered from
animal fat caught her throat now as it had then. Amber's eyes
closed but still the phantom figures moved. Seated on a crude

bed built of wood and strung with plaited fibre the one man who accepted her waved her to his side. The rattle gone from his throat, his breathing easier, he had taken her hand and when he spoke his voice had held its customary authority.

'From this night, I, Gopal, of Kihar, take this woman for my wife. My sons, greet your sister, wives to my sons greet your sister.' Then turning to meet the blaze of Kewal's eyes he had added, *'Woman of my house, greet your sister.'*

The words had run like a tide passing from men clustered in the low doorway to be grabbed vulture-like by womenfolk eager to know the happenings, but only later had Rani been able to tell her of what Gopal had said.

She was to be wife to Gopal. It should have eased her misery, stopped the beatings, but the opposite had happened. The hatred and vengefulness of the older woman's eyes blazed out of Amber's nightmare.

It had been a week from Gopal's declaration, a week in which Kewal had forced more and more of the work of the house onto her, ensuring it was she who carried the heaviest water jar, she who slapped wet linen against the flat stones on the riverbank as she had seen *dhobi* boys doing a hundred times in Meerut, and all the time the cane switch rose and fell.

But that had not been the worst of it. Amber's eyes opened but memories filled them, blocking out all but the cramped drabness of a house not equal in size to one room of the bungalow at Meerut, her mind hearing only the translations of Rani.

'So you have come at last, feringhee *bitch!'* Kewal's face had screwed up with contempt. *'What has taken you so long? No doubt you have been flaunting yourself before every man you passed, trying to seduce them as you have seduced Gopal, but the marriage he speaks of is not yet celebrated nor will it be!'*

Quick as the spate of words a hand rose, striking hard across the face of the girl standing silent before her.

'*You would dare turn your eyes to my husband, you droppings of a she-donkey! You think to take my place, to become first woman of this house . . . never! Before I allowed that I would make you a gift to Kali. The goddess is ever eager for victims and to see the rumal, the scarf of execution, tighten about your throat would give me such pleasure.*' The hand struck again across the girl's mouth then seized her hair, twisting the red-gold strands.

Seeming to feel the pain of it, Amber's head moved against the pillow as in her mind's eye she saw herself forced to her knees.

'*Beware, wives* of *my sons.*' The voice was dark with hate the eyes blazing with it as Kewal looked at the young women watching her, '*beware this spawn of a hyena for it will steal your husband as that animal steals the food of the tigers!*'

'*Enough!*' Jaspal, the eldest of the sons, entered the room, his rebuke sending his wife and the wives of his brothers scuttling into a corner. Then more gently he had spoken to his mother. '*Make ready the cloth of my father's burying for he is dead.*'

Memories flicked like the pages of a wind-blown book carrying Amber forward past the hours of the following day, bringing her to late afternoon. Constructed beside the river a funeral pyre already held the flower-bedecked body of Gopal.

Dressed in her finest yellow sari Kewal faced her son. '*It is my right . . . you cannot deny that which is the right of a wife.*'

'*But there is no need.*' Jaspal reached a hand towards his mother but she pushed it away.

'*There is every need,*' she snapped. '*It is the custom, a wife honours her husband by accompanying him in death.*'

Jaspal shook his head. '*Suttee, it is no longer an unbreakable custom, you need not go living into the flames.*'

'*All of my life I have honoured the customs of my race, of my religion, and I shall honour them now. Mine is an empty body, the spirit of a woman is merely an extension of that of her husband. No one can exist in happiness without a spirit.*'

The shadow that was Kewal turned towards a younger girl, a girl whose hair flamed copper in the lowering sun, and in the woman's eyes was a vengeance too terrible to read, a smile of pure malice wreathing her lips as she went on. '*And since Gopal's spirit is gone then that of his wife must follow . . . each of his wives, the* feringhee, *too, must enter the flames.*'

'*But that cannot be,*' Jaspel gasped. '*The foreign woman was not wife to my father.*'

Caught deep in the coils of her waking dream, Amber saw the older woman throw back her head in direct challenge.

'*Who says this?*'

The phantom lips drew back in a snarl of accusation. '*Who can say that his solicitude did not become more, that his protecting of the* feringhee *did not bring her to his bed.*'

'*But there has been no marriage ceremony.*'

'*Pah, since when did that prevent a bitch presenting herself to a dog!*' Her face twisted with hatred, Kewal brushed away her son's protest. '*I say I saw her in my husband's bed, I saw the play of man and wife take place there. That makes her wife to Gopal and means she as well as I will lie with him on the funeral pyre.*'

From the window of her room silver moonbeams playing across Amber's bed suddenly became silver-tipped flames; crimson and blue they licked and darted, leaping among the dried scrub set beneath the logs which held the body of Gopal.

'*You wanted to be wife to him,*' Kewal screeched above the roar of flame, '*now you will be with him for all eternity.*'

The contentment which had held her mind, cradling and shielding it from reality, drained as swiftly as the fire had shot into life. Around her the world was bathed in moving dancing sheets of scarlet, the smell of burning cloth filling her nostrils, the acrid stench of smouldering hair clogging her throat and the heat, the terrible searing heat, scorching along her legs, her arms, reaching its great red tongue towards her face . . .

13

'You saw it again, you saw the fire.'

Rani looked at the drawn, ashen face. Amber had said nothing but she had heard the stifled cry from the next room and now in the light of the lamp she had lit could see the evidence for herself.

'Why, that is what I cannot understand.' Fear trembled in Amber's voice and the fingers clutching the sheet were white with tension. 'Why did I step onto that pyre? It was not as though I was unaware of the flames, of the danger.'

Sitting on the side of the bed, Rani covered one of the tense hands with her own. 'Think back . . .'

'No!' Amber shook her head sharply. 'I don't want to think back, I don't want to remember. It is remembering brings the nightmares!'

'And the dreams reawaken the fears which in their turn bring back more horror in the night. This is like a wheel which turns in the mind; it goes round and round bringing the same memories in an unending circle, a circle only you can break. But to do that you must be strong, you must face the fear, not bury it inside you. Only by understanding can you defeat it.'

Defeat it, rid herself of the terror which haunted so many of her nights, the fear which entered her mind at every unguarded moment! If only it were possible.

The light of the lamp shining on Rani's face showed the sympathy bedded in her eyes. 'You are thinking defeat of bad dreams cannot be done, but it can; reach out, Amber, reach out and stop the circling of the wheel.'

'How?' It trembled on a sob. 'How can I stop what I cannot see, cannot touch?'

'But you do see it and it can be touched,' Rani answered quietly. 'When you sleep the memories come, that is your mind trying to cleanse itself of the fears you have stored there. It tries to compel you to face them but in your resistance you do not hear its call and so the fears retreat again into the dark corners to wait for the next time. And there will be a next time, Amber, and a next until you listen, until you hear the cry your senses make while you sleep. You say you cannot touch, but your mind can do what your hand cannot. Look into it now, speak the fears you see there, let the light of reason shine upon them, let its brightness banish the shadows.'

Rani had never said or done anything to hurt her and though the advice she gave now might be of no benefit it would do no harm. Leaning her head against the pillow, Amber allowed her eyes to close.

Pushed back by the glow of the lamp darkness hovered at the window, shreds of itself clinging to the walls as if waiting . . . listening.

'Jaspal said his father was dead.' Moving beneath closed lids, Amber's eyes seemed to watch a moving picture. 'His wife and the others, they began to wail but Kewal did not. She just stared at me; there was so much hatred in that look, so much anger. Then she pushed me from the house. I was not allowed to see Gopal. I was the *feringhee*, the foreigner, and as such could not be allowed near the body of the man who had treated me with kindness. I could not pay my respects. It was the next afternoon when Kewal sent for me. '*The soul of my husband would not journey on unless peace resided in his house,*' she said, '*therefore I offer you the drink of harmony. Share it with me now and let him who is dead travel in tranquillity to the Paradise his soul deserves.*' She took a stone jar from a niche above her sleeping cot, the wives of her sons whispering among themselves as she uncorked the narrow neck, and poured some of the contents into two cups. She gave one to me and she drank the other.'

'The liquid . . . what did it taste like?'

The tip of her tongue touching her lips, it seemed Amber tasted the drink again.

'Sharp,' she said slowly. 'It tasted sharp, bitter on the tongue, almost like aloes.'

'And after swallowing it did you feel differently?' Quiet as the shadows holding to the edges of the room, Rani put her question.

Pausing for a moment, Amber let the pictures run in her mind then, a tiny frown forming between her closed eyes, answered in a tone which seemed to say only now had she realised. 'It was later! I remember feeling . . . feeling nothing! All the unhappiness, the misery, was gone. I was floating on a cloud of contentment that nothing could affect it . . . it was like I had been drugged, like I no longer had the will to do anything.' A drug! Amber's eyes flew open. 'The drink Kewal gave me was a drug, something which took mastery over my brain; it drowned all resistance. That was why I had no fear then, that is the reason I let Kewal lead me onto the pyre. I did not do it of my own volition.'

Pressing the hand she held, Rani smiled. 'Now you have looked into the face of fear and you have understood. Your mind has told you what it had to say, that it was not itself took you into the flames, that control of your will and senses was not your own and you did not go willingly into the fire. Perhaps now the nightmare will end. Memories will still come and for a long time they will stir the pool of sorrow that is within you but maybe the dreams will no longer hold such terror.'

'But why did the drug affect me and not Kewal, why did she have the will to defy Jaspal when he said there was no need to commit suttee, to willingly commit herself to being burned alive?'

Rising to her feet Rani gave a slight shake of her head. 'That is easy to answer. Kewal did not drink the liquid she poured into her own cup . . . that was simply a pretence. Now rest while I make us both some tea.'

That had been Kewal's revenge. Amber stared into the shadows bordering the gleam of the lamp. She had deliberately tried to murder her! She had known Gopal had not taken the foreign girl to his bed but the lie had been accepted. The family, the villagers, they had all stood by, all had been willing to see the *feringhee* suffer a terrible death . . . all except for Jaspal. Fingers of flame had already touched her skirt, devouring the thin cotton like a ravening beast, the tongue of it licking the loosened hair reaching to her waist then reaching upwards in search of her face. It was then Jaspal had caught her arm, dragging her free of Kewal's grasp. Shoving her aside he had reached again for his mother but she had screamed abuse at him, flames filling her open mouth as she drew away, stepping deeper into the heart of the burning mass.

'*My father was* Pradhan *of Kihar, the head man of our village,*' Jaspal had shouted above the roar of the flames. '*You all knew him as a wise man and I knew him as a loving and gentle father, one who would want no hurt or pain to his family and no sacrifice of life. I am not* Pradhan *of Kihar, but I am now head of the family of Gopal and I say from this day no woman of that house nor any that abides in its shelter will commit suttee.*'

The next day Jaspal had given both herself and Rani the

choice of whether to stay or leave Kihar. They had made that choice, leaving the village far behind.

There was talk at the mine, murmurs of Pickering's death being no accident, murmurs which said Uriah Buckley knew well who the pikeman for the deep seam was and knew what time he would be perched atop the ladder. But that was of no concern: not a man at the New Hope would come out with any accusation. Jobs meant a pay tin and without that a family could starve; no, they might mutter among themselves but that was as far as it would go. But the Neale woman was still alive and her questions would be no mutterings in the dark.

Uriah Buckley stared at the newspaper his hands held but his eyes did not see.

There would soon be an answer to his letter. The next few weeks would see Jervis coming home. He would be returning to take his place here in Darlaston, he would be owner of the colliery and of the iron foundry, he would be a man of property, not some silly bugger in a pretty uniform tekin' orders from the government. He would be his own master. Jervis would have learned by now, he would know there was more to life than dreamin', he would be grown in mind as well as body. They had not seen eye to eye in the past; Jervis had objected to bein' tied to the business . . . if truth were known he had objected to bein' tied to a wife. Quiet unassuming Helen! Had she felt as her father-in-law felt, that hers was a marriage of convenience rather than love? One such as his own had been.

The newspaper fell across his chest, and Uriah's mind slipped to the past. Verity Deinol, she had been young and pleasant to look at but that had meant nothing to a young man with his eyes set on a future which wouldn't be spent slaving his guts out in a coal mine or sweatin' his brains away smeltin' iron. The wench had been his passage to freedom and like the son she had borne him he had grabbed it with both hands. But where he had been satisfied with the promise of things to come, satisfied to wait for his wife's inheritance to become his, Jervis had never had that frame of mind; he had professed no interest in mining or the making of iron. There had been constant arguments between them but though Jervis had been a dreamer, a man more interested in art than in iron, he had not relented . . . but the fool *had* run away; gone with the Army to India.

Still the dreaming was over now. Jervis would at last have realised there was no future for him in India. With wife and daughter dead he would know what was stated in his father's letter was the only sensible thing for him to do, to come home, marry and beget a son while he was still able.

The years spent away from his homeland, from the town of his birth, might well have changed Jervis but it would not have rendered him deaf or struck him blind. He could become aware of the innuendo, the veiled accusations flying around the New Hope . . . and then there was the woman. What if Mrs Greville Neale turned up again at Bescot Lodge! Jervis would be certain to recognise her; five years could not have altered her features so much he wouldn't know who she was. Damn bloody Pickerin'! Uriah's fingers gripped the newspaper, crumpling it into concertina folds. The stupid bugger had failed to kill the woman; but she would not be alive when Jervis returned. The next attempt would not fail.

'Maybe I could find work. I can scrub and clean and cook, I can do all things women of the house can do.'

Yes, Rani could do all of those things and do them well, but the people who had the means to employ servants, would they consider a girl whose skin was not the same colour as their own? Darlaston was a small town, it had not the sophistication of London, not yet the experience of people from distant lands. Handing washed dishes to Rani to dry, Amber remained silent. Her friend must not be subjected to the possibility of a snub; they would manage without Rani becoming anyone's servant. But how? Thinking a thing did not magically bring it into being.

'My words, they are not being good . . . is it with disrespect I speak of working for the house of another?'

The pot she had scrubbed dropping back into the bowl of water, Amber turned to the girl. 'Your words are very good and no, it is not disrespectful of you to suggest taking work at one of the houses. It's . . . it's just the vow I made to myself, that once we reached England neither you nor I would ever be servants again.'

Her explanation had not been believed but it had been accepted, and the gentle look in the girl's eyes had said the reason was known and understood. Settled each side of the table in the tiny living room they had made bright with curtains and cushions, Amber ground leaves and flowers of yarrow while Rani pounded seeds of the fennel they had collected from the hedgerows. It had become something of a ritual, the extracting of oils from the flowers of their small garden or plants they found growing wild on the heath, but pleasant as the pastime was it did not relieve the problem pressing ever more often in Amber's mind. The money left her by Greville, though not yet exhausted, could not last. She must find a way of supplementing the little she had left. But the only way she could see of doing so was by taking domestic service – and how to explain that to Rani in face of what had been said in the scullery only minutes ago?

'The very great promise you gave to yourself,' Rani said, not glancing up from her task, 'it forbids you from becoming *nokar* . . . servant to any household, but I made no promise.'

There was no reprimand in the statement, just a simple truth, a truth which caused a quick suffusion of colour to fly in Amber's cheeks. She had presumed too much, taken too much into her own hands; had what she had said earlier not been like a mistress speaking to a domestic, taking away the girl's own choice, had she not treated Rani like a servant!

Regret caused a hastiness in her voice as she rushed to apologise but Rani's shake of her dark head stopped the flow of words.

'You have never spoken to me as a memsahib would.' The girl smiled as their eyes met. 'We have ever had the words of a friend on our tongues and that is the way we will keep it, but even friends must face to the truth. I am not foolish, Amber, it is known to me that money must be earned if life is to be lived honestly.'

'I've thought of that.' Amber laid the pestle she was using aside. 'There is nothing here in Darlaston, nor have I found any who know what happened to Denny, where he went . . . perhaps it would be better to move on.'

'The thoughts of your heart are not hidden from your face.' Her work momentarily forgotten, Rani smiled. 'If you think it best to leave this place then we will go together.'

The hardships and fears that had been theirs since the day of their meeting had resulted in a closeness, a bond that would not be broken, a relationship in which one knew the mind of the other, and she knew the unspoken hesitation in Rani's answer.

Returning the smile she said quietly, 'It is what we both think, we must be of the same opinion before any decision can be taken and my mind tells me yours is not the one I have.'

'You speak with wisdom and you see what I would have hidden from you. I would not keep you from going from this town, to seek your *bhai*, the brother your soul yearns to find, yet neither will I speak untruth, tell you that all journeyings bring us that which we seek, for sometimes we must trust to the God who sees all to guide our actions; instead I will speak the words my heart gives. Stay here in the town of your parting, for it is there your brother would look for you.'

'But how is he to know I am here, that I have returned from India?'

Glancing at the kettle, its lid jigging noisily with the pressure of boiling water, Rani moved to swing it free of the fire. 'I too have made prayer for answer to the problems of earning money.' She turned back to the table. 'I have asked of the gentle goddess Sita and she has whispered in my heart. Take that which you make from the gifts of heaven and share it with others.'

'The gifts of heaven?' Amber frowned.

'I see you are not understanding.' Touching a hand to the mortar in which she had ground fennel seed, Rani continued. 'Does man make what is in this bowl, is it a product of his hand? No, it is the gift of heaven as are the flowers and plants from which we make oils. Have you not said that women often comment upon the sweetness of the perfume those oils lend to your body, do they not sometimes ask where they also may obtain it?'

'*I swears I ain't smelled naught so pleasant, not in many a long day . . .*'

From the deep reaches of memory the words spoken by the woman she had met in Bloxwich cemetery glowed like a torch in darkness.

'*I says could it be bottled then it would bring a pleasure to women no matter they be queens . . .*'

That was what Rani had meant by sharing the gift of heaven with others. If they could bottle and sell the oils that would be a way of keeping themselves but . . .

'Your eyes say you are not happy with my words.'

'If they show that then they show wrongly,' Amber returned quickly. 'What you have said would prove a perfect solution to the problem of finding employment by which we can live, but how would it help with finding Denny?'

Seeing the uncertainty cast a shadow over Amber's face Rani returned to her chair, taking her friend's hand across the table. 'That also was whispered.' She smiled. 'We shall put your name and the name of this town upon every bottle and every pot then leave it to the gods to bring one into the hands of your brother. He will read and he will know . . . in that you must place your faith.'

It was a hope she could hold onto. Lying awake in her bed Amber thought over the conversation she and Rani had shared. But hope faded with time and this was a particularly fragile hope. Denny had been all boy from the moment of his birth. He had preferred the brook to the bathtub and mud to soap. It had been a kindness of Rani's to say he would read a label on a perfume bottle or a jar of cream, but they were a woman's province, one in which her brother would never set foot and which would never see her hold her brother again in her arms.

14

'People that says they tell you summat for your own good never 'ave anythin' good to say!' Edward Elton's small eyes gleamed with sarcasm.

'An' I says advice comin' too late be like medicine after death, it don't be no help at all!' Uriah Buckley's retort rang with irritation. Couldn't Elton see the danger looming like a rock above them both!

Edward Elton settled his portly frame deeper into the leather armchair. Why the hell had Buckley brought the problem here of all places? The Goscote was a private club admitting members only but those members had ears like bats, they could hear a moth fart a mile off, and Buckley weren't exactly farting!

'So what be this advice you be so eager to give? And keep your voice down lessen it be advice meant for the whole o' the country.'

Waiting for the brandies he had ordered to be set before them and the waiter to glide away on silent feet, Uriah lifted his glass to his chin, using it to shield his words. 'It ain't so much advice, it be more of a warning. My lad Jervis be returnin' 'ome. That bein' the way o' it then it be to your benefit as well as mine for that Neale woman to be finished.'

'I don't follow. What does one thing 'ave to do with the other?'

A breath of exasperation snorted from Uriah's nose. 'You

don't follow . . . you don't bloody follow! Then let me spell it out for you. That woman be the wench went wi' my grand-daughter to India; her lived in the same house my son lived in. Mebbe he won't recognise the name but should he see the face . . .'

'What if he do, it be just the face of a servant like any other.'

'Like any other!' Uriah gurgled, a mouthful of brandy adding to the colour of anger flooding his face. 'You be forgettin', Elton, you be forgettin' that servant you talks so blithely of could put you in jail an' that 'alf-an'-'alf son o' yourn on the scaffold.'

Edward Elton's florid face contorted. 'Be careful what you says, Buckley,' he breathed, 'be careful what you says regardin' my boy.'

The brandy goblet was touching his lips but Uriah hesitated, then lowered it level with his throat. 'Careful?' he sneered. 'Where be the use of tekin' care not to say that which be already known to every man in Darlaston and for miles beyond its fringe; that whelp o' yourn be bent as a florin run over by a cartwheel. He likes a man in his bed as much as he likes a woman, it meks no odds to him who fondles atween his legs or whether he be the jockey or the 'orse!'

Small eyes receding behind folds of flesh glared at Uriah. 'You've said your piece Buckley an' that be all I'll listen to but you hear this: Edward Elton don't be a man to tek slander lightly an' he don't be one to forget neither!'

'Seems you forgot one thing, seems you forgot the Neale woman be sister to them little uns! Or be it you've 'ad a lapse o' memory regardin' them?'

It had been an admirable suggestion, using the oils to make perfumes. Amber surveyed the various bottle and jars Rani had lined up on the kitchen table. It would have been wonderful except there was just not enough and their tiny garden was being rapidly depleted of flowers. Come winter there would be none and the heath also would be empty of many of the plants and leaves of trees and bushes which provided them with materials with which to work.

'You have lost joy for the task?'

'No.' Amber shook her head as she looked at Rani. 'I have not lost my enthusiasm. It's . . . well, we have so little, how can we possibly survive on that, even supposing it sells?'

'We will cross that river when it is reached.'

'Bridge.' Amber smiled. 'We will cross that bridge when we come to it.'

Small shoulders shrugging, the Indian girl laughed, the sound light and musical. 'River or bridge, we will cross together. Now we must place a foot before us.'

Take the first step! Amber kept the second smile to herself. Rani had learned English marvellously while she had only a few words of that girl's language.

'So what is our first step?'

'We are soon to be needing that in which to put the scented waters. We must have small bottles and jars . . .'

'Scented waters?'

'Is that not saying right?' Rani cast an anxious glance at Amber. 'We do not use the oil on the body before first adding it to water in which to bathe or to smooth over the skin . . . and the perfume of those oils give scent to the water.'

Of course! That was the answer. Rani had seen that from the beginning. It would not be the oils themselves they would offer for sale but oils mixed with water; that way the amount they had now would last well into next year.

Catching the other girl about the waist Amber danced her around the kitchen, her delight obvious as she said, 'Rani, you are a genius.'

'A djinn!' Doe eyes widened. 'No, Rani is no djinn, I have not magic.'

Laughing again, Amber released her. 'Genius is not djinn, it does not mean some evil spirit nor does it mean a magician. Genius simply says you are extremely clever.'

'Rani is happy not to be djinn.' A smile showed relief as the girl turned again to the table. 'But she thinks maybe only djinn will provide the bottles we are to be needing.'

'Then it is time I became a djinn.'

'You must not say such words, always the bad spirits they listen, they are ever ready to snatch the soul of one who mocks.'

Immediately contrite, Amber caught her friend's trembling hands. Rani had left India but India with its customs and beliefs had not entirely left Rani. 'I'm sorry . . . I meant no mockery. It was thoughtless to speak as I did.'

Her face still showing concern, Rani shook her head. 'The words cannot be recalled, but others can be said to Sita. I shall ask the goddess to defend you, to breathe her sacred breath and blow all evil from you.'

'*Shukria.*' Touching palms together and holding them to her mouth, Amber gave thanks in Rani's own tongue. Then as the girl disappeared to offer her prayers before the tiny shrine she sat at the table. It was time to make her plans.

The journey from Darlaston to West Bromwich had been tedious. Though relatively short in miles it had taken over an hour, the tram trundling laboriously from one stopping point to the next; then on reaching Wednesbury a change of vehicle had to be made.

'The tram from Bromwich be at the White 'Orse,' a woman had told her as they both alighted at the High Bullen. 'You needs to go along of this street 'til you comes to the crossin's, that be the five ways, you goes straight across an' follows your nose along of Lower 'Igh Street an' that'll fetch you to the White 'Orse.'

She had followed the woman's directions, coming to a large imposing stone building bearing the title 'White Horse Hotel.' A uniformed conductor had touched his boater hat respectfully, guiding her to the tram standing a few yards off and saying it would be some minutes yet before they got underway but she was most welcome to take her seat while they waited.

She had been so sure she was doing the right thing. All during the tram rides she had been keyed up with nervous excitement. Now, approaching Ryders Green, the excitement slid away, leaving only tension which had her nerves tinkling like the tiny brass bells heard everywhere in Meerut.

But she must not think of Meerut; she must keep her mind on the business she had set herself to do.

The address she had read in the newspaper. 'Pearson's, Charles Street, Ryders Green, West Bromwich', the advertisement had said underneath the larger banner proclaiming, 'Glass Bottles of the Finest Quality'.

But how much would 'bottles of the finest quality' cost?

'We can mek bottles of any size to suit the customer.' Simeon Pearson eyed the young woman who had been shown into his office. 'An' that goes for numbers, you only 'as to say 'ow many you'll be requirin'.'

'Numbers will depend very much on cost, Mr Pearson,' Amber answered honestly.

Across from her white beetle brows lifted slightly but the stars of grey eyes remained steady. 'Ar, numbers be affected by cost but then so does shape. Understand, Mrs Neale, fancy bottles can mean fancy prices.'

Yes, she did understand, but she also understood the effect

of packaging. A pretty label, a colourful box, they drew a woman's eye; her bottles must do the same.

'I realise the more work involved, the more money must be paid for the finished article. However if you would look at the sketch I have made and be kind enough to tell me how much one hundred of them would be I would be most grateful.'

Taking a sheet of paper from her bag Amber placed it on the dusty desk.

'A 'undred, you says.' Simeon Pearson studied the pencil-drawn sketch. 'That don't be a great many.'

'I do not have a great deal of money, Mr Pearson.'

'Mmm.' The head streaked liberally with white did not lift. 'This be a fish of a different kind than the ones swims through my stream. This be a design more intricate than any I've 'ad afore.'

Did that mean he would not accept her commission, was her idea of a bottle too much of a frippery for the man to bother with? Amber waited as he pored over the paper.

'Well now.' He looked up at last, removing the spectacles he had balanced on his nose. 'It be fancy rightly enough and o' course it will be more expensive than a plain everyday bottle. Be you certain a plain one won't serve you as well?'

How could she make him understand? Amber clutched the bag in her lap. 'Mr Pearson,' she said quietly, 'may I ask you a personal question?'

The man's mouth tautened and the beetle brows came together in the ghost of a frown. 'You can ask, Mrs Neale, though if I thinks what it is you wants to know be an inter-ference then the answer you get will be the door . . . closin' after you.'

'I ask if you have a wife and perhaps a daughter. Does a gift presented to them in plain wrapping excite as much as one made the prettier by its container?'

The shadow of a frown disappearing from his brow, his taut mouth relaxing, the owner of the glassworks looked keenly at his would-be customer. 'I sees your meanin'.' He nodded, picking up the paper and studying the neat drawing again. 'A woman's eye be pleased by a fancy bottle and a man's pocket be opened by her smile. Clever thinkin', Mrs Neale, mighty clever thinkin', but one worm catches only one fish. What you puts in a package won't sell twice lessen it pleases more than does the package itself.'

That woman in Bloxwich and others beside had remarked upon the pleasant aroma as they had talked with her and they had seen no package to tempt them. 'I understand.' Amber nodded. 'But like anyone else hoping to sell a product I can only do my best and pray it is good enough.'

The woman's clothes were not fancy and like as not her speakin' were the same plain truth when her said her didn't 'ave a deal of money. Simeon Pearson's glance remained on the paper. But there was a cleanness of mind about her, an honesty which put a clear gleam to her eye and kept the trip of a lie from her tongue, and this sketch . . . A bottle so elegant yet pretty had appeal but more than her sketch he liked the woman, liked her openness.

'A 'undred, you says?' He pursed his lips as if in doubt though his mind was already made up. He would make her bottles, and do the job cheap as could be done.

Elton weren't as sightless as he pretended. Still furious as he had been the night they had talked at the Goscote Club, Uriah stared out over the busy yard of the New Hope mine. He knowed well the two faces of that son of his'n but turned a blind eye to his cavortin', to his lying with women then as blithely giving his bottom to a man; and Elton also knowed that should breath of that reach the right ears together with what had happened that night the bend would be stretched outta that bloody pervert by a rope set about his neck and an open trapdoor 'neath his feet.

But swatting one wasp didn't destroy the rest. To unmask Elton's son, to divulge his practices to the police, would be to open up a whole bloody wasps' nest and every sting would be painful. Edward Elton wouldn't sit with a quiet mouth, but then why should he? He would be finished not only in Darlaston but in any place where newspapers were to be had. A man, especially a man with money, could get away with rape but homosexual relationships, and sodomy, were anathema to society. That would stay with a man's name and Elton would make sure his name was not the only one to suffer.

Homosexuality had never been the game of Uriah Buckley and no man could call him a pansy: but rape? Maybe that mud would stick . . . and what effect would that have on Jervis, on a son who had led such an honest life? But Jervis must never know and nor must anyone else. Elton must be helped from this world! But how to do it? Uriah's glance followed the figure walking towards the entrance of the tunnel leading to the inner recesses of the mine. It couldn't be done the same way as Pickering nor could he trust the job to any other man. Elton and the Neale woman, he must kill them himself!

Easy to think but how easy to do? Turning away from the window Uriah returned to his desk. Somebody had grabbed Pickering before he could complete the task of seeing the woman into her grave, or had that been the excuse Pickering had dreamed up to cover the fact he had been too drunk to do the job properly? But if in truth somebody had intervened, had saved the Neale woman's life, then might that somebody still be keeping watch over her? It placed the problem of killing her in a new light altogether. He would need to tread softly. But Elton had not been attacked, there had been no attempt made on his life; and should that life be suddenly snuffed out, should some 'accident' see Elton gone from this world, there would be no reason to suspect any ulterior motive; except perhaps on the part of his son. But that one would institute no inquiry, he would dance cocks an' breeches, he'd rejoice at being free to indulge his filthy little pursuits with no eye to watch and no hand threatening to cut the purse strings.

Restless as the thoughts careering through his mind, Uriah rose from his chair to pace the small office.

If only Elton were a sick man . . . a sick man! Coming to an abrupt halt Uriah smiled to himself. That could well be the road to follow. All sickness did not show itself in marks of the pox or by a weakness which kept a man to his bed; there were other maladies, ones which were silent, which crept into the body like a shadow and which claimed the mind with a feeling of pleasure and ease, with a contentment which hid the danger, the lethal result of the very 'medicine' with which people dosed themselves.

Taking his hat from the stand in a corner of the room Uriah went down into the yard. Calling for his carriage he climbed into the driving seat, touching the whip to the flank of the horse.

The world did not see Edward Elton as a sick man but it would soon see him as a very dead one! He liked his tipple, half a bottle of brandy after a meal liberally accompanied by claret and port was quite usual, but perhaps one intake of brandy could prove a little – no, a lot – more potent than he expected.

Driving the carriage along King Street Uriah glanced ahead to where the Church of St Lawrence rose above the topsy-turvy roofs of smoke-blackened shops and houses all huddling together as if seeking protection from some soot-breathing monster preparing to swallow them. Just beyond the church was Charles Doughty's chemist's shop, he could call there, buy what he wanted. But Doughty was a shrewd man. He would wonder why after such a length of time should the medicine be required again: best not arouse curiosity.

Flicking the rein he guided the carriage to the right, following along Victoria Road, his mind still busy with questions. Should he go to Wednesbury? There were chemists in that town . . . but it were no more than a mile or two and news travelled! Birmingham then, or Wolverhampton? They were busier and larger towns than Darlaston and folk there were mebbe's more interested in making money than in asking questions. So it would be one of them he would go to to mek his purchase, and it wouldn't be in no silk hat or drivin' in a private carriage. But first he would check!

Arriving at Bescot Lodge he brushed aside his serving man's enquiry regarding lunch, going instead straight to his room.

Verity had lain in the room adjoining his. She had preferred her own room, her own bed, since the birth of their son. It was an arrangement suited them both. Her fires quenched by the ordeal of childbirth, she had wanted no chance of a repeat performance, and he . . . ? He liked diversity, what lay twixt one woman's legs lay twixt 'em all, and he had changed partners often; but that would no longer be the case when Jervis came home. He would bring a new bride to a house that bore no shadow of shame.

Verity! He stared at the wall that separated the bedrooms. Had she known . . . had she guessed? Had she any knowledge of what he had done? Ill with an incurable tumour, she had suffered pain for weeks, the prescribed laudanum having little effect. The doctor then suggested poppy juice; opium, he said, was a powerful drug, one which induced narcosis, a peaceful, tranquil state of mind which in turn would help with freedom

from pain, and the nurse hired to care for her had administered the prescribed dosage each night. But he had purchased
his own supply of the drug and nightly during the hour he had
suggested the nurse take her supper in the kitchen so she might
chat with the staff and enjoy a brief respite from the sick room,
he had given Verity a second dose, always taking care to wrap
bottle and spoon in a handkerchief and slipping it in his
pocket. Combined with laudanum for the pain it had not taken
many of those extra spoonsful to bring about the end. Why
had he done what he had? That question had come many
times. Verity's death had brought him nothing he did not
already have; property, freedom to act as he pleased was his
so why help end his wife's life? Pity! The answer slipped into
his mind, the salve to his conscience it had always been. He
had felt pity at her suffering, at seeing her thrash with pain,
and he had ended it: after all a man wouldn't see his dog writhe
in pain so why let a wife suffer the same?

It had been an act of mercy. Uriah crossed the room to a
bureau he kept locked. Opening it with a key that never left his
watch chain he touched a hidden spring releasing a drawer
which to anyone else's eyes would seem part of the ornate
banding. Reaching into the confined space, he withdrew a
small bottle. Holding it to the light streaming in through the
high windows, he saw in the deep blue glass a line of deeper
colour. It still contained liquid . . . but would the drug it held
have retained its potency?

Uriah put the bottle in his pocket and relocked the bureau.
There was one sure way to find out – and he would take that
way tonight.

15

'Don't try running afore you can walk . . .' Her mother's often-spoken warning to an eager young girl sounded now in Amber's mind.

Was she being impulsive, was she moving too quickly? Watching Rani take the two tiny waxed cardboard containers bought from the chemist shop, Amber felt misgivings twitch in her stomach. Would it not be better to wait, to see if their perfumed waters found favour before starting on another project? She had discussed this with Rani but the girl had smiled at her caution. 'What would it lose us?' she had said. 'A little purified fat, a few flowers and an hour or so of time, and why did God give time if not to use it, and using it to bring pleasure or help to others gives merit to the soul.'

Pleasure it must certainly bring. Amber breathed the delicate perfume of the cream being spooned into the circular pillboxes. And it did prevent hands from chapping and the skin becoming rough in colder weather but would it sell? Would women part with any of their hard-earned pennies for what would seem to them a luxury?

Rani had sounded like the old men of Meerut sat outside the grounds of Colonel Buckley's bungalow, chewing on leaves plucked from the many neem trees that fringed the roadsides, their heads moving side to side as they offered sage advice. But would they give the advice that girl had given? 'Question what you do not know, for such is the path of learning, but do not reject what is not yet understood, for that is the way of foolishness.'

Perhaps the old men of Meerut would have said the same. Perhaps it was foolish to dismiss a thing out of hand before even trying it . . . But to sell hand cream? Amber bit back the sigh of doubt.

Once the boxes' lids were securely in place, Rani spooned half of the remaining cream into a well-scalded pottery jar which had once held meat paste, and the other half into a small thoroughly washed jam jar, putting them aside.

'Take this with you.' Her smile white against a creamy coffee skin, Rani handed one of the boxes to Amber. 'Ask the maker of glass to accept it as gift to his wife or daughter.'

That was out of the question! She could not presume to offer Simeon Pearson . . . Amber hid the quick surge of embarrassment by turning to look at the clock on the mantel. Then, slipping the box into her bag, she smiled.

'I shall spend a few minutes with Bethany on my way back, but I promise to be home before dark.'

'Sita guard every step of my *behen*.'

'And every moment of my sister.'

Standing at the Bull Stake, waiting for the tram which would take her to Wednesbury, Amber smiled at the words still heard in her mind. When had she and Rani taken to calling each other sister? Had it been those times they had wept together following a beating Gopal's wife had administered for some trivial offence? Had it been after they had left the village of Kihar? Whispered as they huddled beneath the vast canopy of silver-starred sky covering a wilderness while around them the cries and calls of animals froze their blood with fear? She could not recall the exact time or place she had asked the meaning of that word, only the warmth that had filled her when Rani had told her. Now it passed between them naturally; the two of them were more than *dost*, more than friends; they did not share the same blood but to each other they would always be sister.

Seated aboard the tram Amber held out a coin to the conductor.

'Wednesbury.' The man smiled amiably. 'That be thrupppence return or three 'appence single.'

Opposite her a small girl dressed in blue coat and bonnet, her feet in side-button boots swinging back and forth, piped in a high voice: 'Return means you can ride the tram all the way back to 'ere and not 'ave to pay.'

Giving a quick wink to Amber, the conductor adopted a mock frown. 'Not 'ave to pay, not pay to come back on my tram . . . ! And what would 'appen to my wages if'n folk don't need to pay to ride back?'

'Oh you don't 'ave to worry about your wages.' Blue eyes filled with smiles lifted to the conductor. 'When someone buys a return ticket it means they've paid for their journey back afore they sets away.'

'Does it now, well bless me, if that don't beat all! I says that be a good idea.'

'That be enough, Evie.' The child's mother shook her head as the girl made to speak again, then with an apologetic look at the conductor added, 'Her be overexcited seein' it be her birthday.'

'I'm seven today, my daddy says that be quite grown up.'

A ripple of quiet laughs sounded from the other passengers.

'And your daddy be quite right.' The man smiled, lifting his straw hat. 'Allow me to wish a young lady a happy birthday.'

Slipping from the seat the child held the skirt of her coat in each hand, bobbing a curtsy. 'Thank you,' she piped soberly, 'that be very kind.'

The ripples of laughter turned to murmurs of approval as the child hitched herself back onto the high wooden seat while whispers of 'good manners' drifted along the aisle.

He replaced his hat but the mock seriousness remained as the conductor returned his attention to Amber. 'So mum, after 'earing the good advice of that grown-up young lady which ticket will you be after wantin'?'

Keeping her own mouth straight Amber offered the silver coin again. 'Why, a return of course.'

Handing her a pink ticket the man touched a finger to his hat before moving on, leaving Amber to her thoughts. The child was seven years old today. Not so very much younger than Bethany and almost the same age as Denny had been when she had left them. Why had she gone to India, why had she not taken her sister and brother and looked for employment away from Bescot Lodge? She might as well ask the number of stars in the sky!

'Do you be sad?'

Piping tones together with the touch of a small hand had Amber blink away the tears forming in her eyes.

'You can use all o' my 'ankies. They be new, I 'ad 'em for my birthday.'

'Evie!' Catching the girl's arm her mother drew her back, her cheeks colouring with embarrassment as she glanced apologetically at Amber. 'I be sorry 'er be pesterin', mum, 'er don't never be so forward. I swears I don't 'ave the knowin' of what's got into 'er.'

Bethany had always bubbled with excitement with the approach of her birthday and like this child her tongue had run away with her when the longed-for day finally arrived.

Amber smiled at the woman, then at the child. 'Thank you for offering me your handkerchief. It is very pretty, but I have one in my bag.'

The child breathed deeply, catching the delicate aroma drifting from Amber's bag as she withdrew the handkerchief.

'Oooh!' The small mouth murmured while the blue eyes widened with pleasure. 'that be a right pretty smell, do it be scent? We ain't never 'ad no scent but I smells it in flowers my granny 'as in her garden, but they don't all smell pretty.'

Assuring the harassed mother her daughter was causing no offence, Amber looked again to the girl. 'I agree not all flower scents are pleasant. The perfume you smell on my handkerchief is elderflower and violet, and I too think it is pretty.'

'Mmmm.' The girl breathed again; nostrils widening to the delicate fragrance. 'Me granny always gives me a sixpence for me birthday an' I would like some of that scent to put on my 'andkerchiefs . . . please will you tell me what it be called so I shall know what it is I needs to buy?'

They had not decided on a name for the cream they had made. It was simply a means whereby Simeon Pearson could be given a flavour of what they intended using those glass bottles to contain.

'It does not have a name and you cannot buy it.'

Across from her the blue eyes lost their look of delight, a shadow of disappointment replacing it. Bethany had sometimes had that same shadow in her eyes and her lips had twitched as she fought back tears when a thing had had to be denied her. But this child need not suffer that same disappointment; she need not necessarily be denied.

'You cannot buy it because it is not yet offered for sale and it does not have a name because I have not yet given it one . . . perhaps you might help me choose.'

Speaking quietly to the mother, Amber gave a brief explanation of the ingredients of the box she withdrew from her bag, asking at the end would she allow her daughter to accept what was a cream for helping alleviate rough skin on the hands and to keep the skin soft.

'Bullen!' The conductor's call sounded over the noise and rattle of the steam-driven tram. 'High Bullen, this be where I leaves you all.'

'Mother!' The child tugged at her mother's hand as passengers began to shuffle to their feet, the plea in her eyes saying she had heard Amber's request.

'You have my word there is nothing can harm her, the cream is made of the purest—'

' 'T'ain't that,' the woman broke in quickly. 'But fripperies, children 'as to learn there be more important things to life, things more necessary than scent or creams.'

'Is anything more important than the happiness of a child?' It was a whisper as the face of her sister rose in Amber's mind, Bethany trying so desperately to stem the tears. 'I'm sorry.' She heard the woman's sharp breath. 'I was thinking of my own sister. She also would have liked your daughter to have the cream.'

Understanding dawned on the other woman's face and there was no need of explanation. Instead she nodded, the look coming to her own eyes displaying sympathy while not hiding the pleasure of her child being given a gift.

'Happy birthday, Evie.' Amber smiled, placing the box in the child's hand.

'Thank you, oh thank you!' Holding her gift, the small girl followed her mother to the rear of the tram, thanking the conductor with the same grave good manners she had shown before as he helped her from the platform, and once on the ground turned again to Amber.

'My name don't really be Evie, though that be what everybody calls me 'cept my gran. My name be called after her'n, it be Eve.'

'Eve.' Amber glanced from child to mother. 'A pretty name for a pretty daughter and one, if you will agree, I would like to give to my cream.'

'You means you'll call your cream Eve?'

'I think it would be a wonderful name for it.'

'Oh yes, yes please . . .' The girl skipped with the excitement of it all but then that graveness she had shown toward the conductor seized her and she stood still. 'But I 'aves to bide by what Mother says.'

For a moment the older woman's face was solemn, then as she caught her daughter's expression she broke into a smile. 'Can't do no 'arm,' she said to Amber. 'If it please you then you names your cream Eve.'

Watching them move off, the girl dancing from the rapture of her unexpected gift, Amber knew each time she smelled the perfume of elderflower and violet she would think of a little girl she met on a tram – but she would see the face of Bethany.

'This is beautiful; I never expected anything so attractive.' Amber held a small glass bottle in her hand while across from her Simeon Pearson watched. Often customers would find some fault where there were none so as to haggle over price. This young woman showed her satisfaction with his work but the question of cost to her was yet to be posed.

'The mould were made by me, that way were it not acceptable for any reason then no man 'as works for me could be 'eld responsible.'

It was true. Simeon caught the sparkle of the glass held in Amber's fingers. Why had he done the work himself? It wasn't as if several of the men who worked the glass couldn't have done as well. But there had been something about this young woman, something which had caught at him. The clothes she wore? No, not that. The pretty face, the gold-flecked amber eyes with their shadow of sadness? No, not that either. It was the quiet dignity with which she held herself. Not pride . . . no, not pride, but a respect of self.

'I could not be more pleased, Mr Pearson.' Amber's smile cut across his thoughts. 'This really is all I could have hoped for.'

'I followed your sketch near as I could an' though I says it meself the result be favourable.'

'Very favourable,' Amber agreed.

That was no way to go about gettin' a price favourable to herself; showin' such satisfaction with any commissioned piece could push that price up should the work be done by any but Pearson Bottle and Glass, but he had told himself he would make them bottles cheap as he could and Simeon Pearson were a man of his word. Watching her now as she set the tiny bottle on the desk separating them, the turn of her head, the quick smile, Simeon recognised the feeling inside him. He had seen that same thing before, so many years ago, when courting a shy reserved young girl who had not spoken, only smiled her yes when he had asked would she be his wife.

'Then you'll be wantin' a quote for the rest of 'em.'

Anything as pretty as this bottle had to be expensive. Amber felt a twinge more of guilt than apprehension. She should have asked for a definite cost before commissioning the work. What if the expenditure exceeded her limit? She would have caused this man a lot of labour for nothing other than payment for the making of a mould he might never use again.

Her glance resting on the phial, Amber waited as the glass-maker fetched a dusty black-bound ledger from a room adjoining his office. It was all she wanted: the elegant planed body, the fluted foot and neck topped with a plain round glass stopper, was distinctive without being flamboyant. Any woman would surely be delighted to own such a lovely object.

But even could she afford to buy them, would her scented oils and perfumed waters live up to such craftsmanship?

'There be a record 'ere of the materials used.' Simeon placed the open ledger beside the bottle. 'There be flint batch, sand, lead, ash an' saltpetre—'

'Please,' Amber interrupted, 'there is no need for an itemised account. I don't understand anyway.'

'You should 'ave a care to what you be sayin' to a manufacturer, no matter who or what it is you be a'buyin' from 'im, for there be many a one will add pounds to the askin' should he 'ear such.'

Glancing up from the ledger, its words and figures written in a flowing copperplate hand, Amber looked into grey eyes serious beneath white beetle brows and the gold-flecked hazel which had earned her father's pet name of Amber held a measure of the same gravity as she answered. 'I know I am very naïve when it comes to business, Mr Pearson, but I think I know just a little of character and that tells me I will be treated justly here.'

Again that simple honesty, the same trust he had been given when his own Sarai had joined her life to his! He had been right in his judgement of this girl. Simeon hid the pleasure Amber's words had brought by touching a finger to a column of numbers. His description of her unassuming attitude and open honesty when talking to Sarai of a young woman who had come asking for a hundred self-designed bottles had not been misleading, nor had his wife's reply of ''*Er sounds to be a woman I'd be tekin' a liking to meself, one you can give credence to.*'

'Be best for customer as well as maker to 'ave knowledge of amounts of materials an' their costin's, that way a man can go to any other maker of the same thing and compare what their charges be against mine.'

'A man, yes, and even a woman; but not me. I trust your word, Mr Pearson, I shall need no comparison.'

A flush marked the gratification that answer gave yet instinctively Simeon felt it contained no artifice, no flattery, nor had it been said in hope of gaining a more favourable deal for herself.

'Then all that needs be pointed to be the final sum.' He traced the column to its base. 'The cost o' each bein' fourpence farthin' brings a total of thirty-five shillin' an' fivepence for a hundred.'

The cost of each bottle was fourpence farthing; add to that the money she and Rani would need to live the simplest of lives and the total would still be more than the women of Darlaston could pay for what Evie's mother had called fripperies. Perhaps the idea of selling perfumed waters had been a silly one, and as for scented hand cream, women working pit banks or slaving in nail shops to help feed their families would hardly spend their pennies on anything so unnecessary. She would tell Rani when she got home, tell her what had seemed such a fruitful project was after all not going to work.

Leaving the tram at the Bull Stake she took the quieter way of Victoria Road to lead her steps to St Lawrence Church. Kneeling beside the grave she kept free from weed, Amber felt the familiar choking rise of tears. 'You would have loved gathering flower petals,' she murmured, 'adding their fragrance to oils or to make creams and I know you would have wanted that child to have some as a birthday gift. Giving gifts to others always delighted you more than the receiving of one . . . that was a special quality in you, Bethany, that is what made people love you as I loved you. Oh, I would trade my life to have yours back! It is my fault you died, and my fault Denny ran away. I am to blame, me and no one else.'

Sobs catching one on another in her throat, Amber touched the ground covering her sister. 'Be with Mother,' she whispered, 'be together, my loved ones.'

Leaving the small cemetery she gave a final touch to tear-damp cheeks then replaced the handkerchief in her bag. Daylight was already fading; it would be dark by the time she got home. She had stayed longer at the glassworks than she had intended but Simeon Pearson had insisted she see exactly the process by which her bottles had been made and she had found it fascinating, so much so she would have stayed longer watching workmen in the yard mix what was termed a 'batch'. This consisted of silica, sodium oxide, calcium oxide and limestone ground to white powder added to small pieces of broken glass Simeon called cullet; then inside a large cone-shaped building, its narrow neck rising high above surrounding huddled houses, the heat and roar of half a dozen beehive-shaped furnaces clustered around a central fire seemed to knock her almost from her feet. The place was reminiscent of the hell her Sunday School teacher had been so fond of telling them waited for children who did not behave as they were instructed. But that memory had been forgotten as she had watched young lads, called 'bit carriers', running with blobs of molten glass from a glowing furnace, balanced on the end of a long hollow tube, handing them to a man who set the viscous orange-red mass into a mould placed on the ground, then took each tube to his lips and blew long and evenly down its length. The whole process took only minutes; then the mould was opened and one of her small elegant bottles was lifted out and taken this time by a 'carrier-in' to the lehr, a long slow-moving bench-like machine which carried the still red-hot glassware through the stages of its cooling. It had seemed like magic and she had watched enthralled, marvelling at the dexterity of men and boys moving rapidly from furnace to workplace. Their feet never slipped, though the setts of the floor were wet with water splashed from the tubs, by the glassblower, as he plunged flamed hot glass in them. Fascinating as all this was, it was the skills of a seated man that held her breathless. 'He be most skilled of all of 'em,' Simeon had shouted above the roar of the fire. 'He's called "the chair".' It had been easy to believe standing there in the gloom of a building through which crimson balls of molten glass darted like shooting stars. The seated man had looked at her for a moment before taking the tube from the bit gatherer then, blowing the blob into a hollow sphere, shaped it with hand-held tools into a long-stemmed vase. Then Simeon Pearson's hand on her arm had directed her from the cone.

Behind her the church clock struck six, breaking the rest of her memory. She had promised Rani she would be home by this time. Turning toward New Street she hesitated. To go that way meant crossing the heath. Thoughts of the time she had taken that route before, of the attack which had come out of the darkness, rose warningly. She must not give whoever had tried to harm her the chance to repeat the act. She must take the way of Wolverhampton Lane; it would add to her lateness getting back but the care taken to remain where houses and people shared her path would please Rani.

Quickening her steps she passed quickly along King Street and Pinfold Street to Katherine's Cross. There was still a lengthy distance to walk. Shivering a little, the lightweight russet suit Greville had had made for her to travel to England no real obstacle to the rising autumn evening breeze, she waited for a carriage to pass and as it drew close her glance lifted to the man driving, hearing his expletive as he cracked a thin plaited driving whip.

Perhaps he had expected her to step mindlessly in front of the trotting horse and had shouted for her to stay clear. Giving no more thought to the incident, Amber went on. A stitch was pulling at her side from hurrying and she felt relief sweep her as the cottage loomed from the rapidly fallen dusk. But why did no light gleam from its windows, why was it in darkness? The pain of her side forgotten, she ran, trying to stem the tide of fear threatening to erupt in a scream, a scream which found its way past her throat as she burst into the living room and saw in the soft glow of firelight the body of Rani lying across the hearth.

16

The draught from opening of the cottage door caught the fire, fanning flames into a brilliant surge, long searching fingers of bright death reaching for the figure lying motionless.

The pyre! In an instant Amber was back in Kihar watching the body of Gopal lying on a pile of logs, the cries and sobs of his womenfolk sounding in her ears; cries from all except his wife. She was smiling but her eyes were hard with hatred as she lifted a hand towards a watching girl. *'Come.'* Low and insistent the words seeped into Amber's stunned mind. *'We will accompany Gopal, travel with him into eternity.'*

The hand stretched out; it reached the silent girl, fastened like a claw about her arm. Watching the phantom scene Amber shuddered, her mouth opening in a soundless scream. The woman was grinning now and her eyes . . . her eyes were spitting venom as she drew the girl with her towards the pyre wreathed in smoke from torches set to the brushwood, thick grey curling smoke through which spears of red-gold flame stabbed into the darkness, flames which snaked towards the girl's dress as she was pulled onto the burning logs, drawn into the deep heart of the funeral fire.

'Come.' The voice rose over the crackle of flames, 'come *feringhee* . . . wife to Gopal, go with him.'

'No . . . o!' Her scream freeing her brain of its waking nightmare, Amber stared for a moment, accustoming her eyes to the gloom of the small room and her mind to the reality of the present.

When her senses had fully adjusted, though her voice trembled, she dropped to her knees, cradling the still figure in her arms. Rani must not be dead . . . she must not be dead, please. Oh please, God, don't let her be dead!

'Freddy.' Half whisper, half moan, the word was almost inaudible. 'Freddy . . . he came . . .'

She was alive, her friend was alive. Joy and relief had Amber laughing almost hysterically, then like a whiplash the thought struck. Freddy. Rani had said Freddy – was he responsible for what had happened, had he come to this house and suddenly attacked Rani? But for what reason?

The other girl's soft moan told her all questions must wait until she had seen to any injury Rani might have suffered. She rose to her feet, her nerves tightening as a sound outside disturbed the silence.

Freddy? Was he still here . . . had he perhaps waited for herself to return . . . did he intend to . . . ?

Hands shaking, Amber reached a spill to the fire carrying it to the lamp standing at the centre of the table.

There had been no mistaking the name Rani had murmured. 'Freddy,' she had said. 'Freddy . . . he came . . .' But the boy had been so friendly!

The lamp sent a welcome glow of light about the room as she returned the spill to the fireplace, tapping it out against the grate before replacing it in the pretty jug Rani had found to keep them in. As she straightened the next thought flashed across her mind. Daft Freddy! He had told them folk called him daft Freddy! They wouldn't do so without reason; perhaps it was she and Rani had been wrong, and the boy's mind was unhinged. There was no other possible explanation.

He was not fully in control of his senses and in consequence not in control of his actions. Had he come here today expressly to harm them or had what he had done been the result of some seizure of the brain?

Beyond the door the sound came again. Taut as bowstrings Amber's nerves screamed while her brain remained strangely calm as she fastened a hand on the iron poker. She had no desire to harm anyone, especially not a boy of deranged mind not responsible for his actions, but he could not be allowed to strike again.

At her feet Rani moaned softly but Amber kept her glance on the door, her breath catching in her throat at the knock resounding loudly through the quiet house. He had seen the glow of the lamp shining from the window; he knew she was home. Fingers painful from gripping the poker she raised it above her head as the door opened and Freddy stepped into the room.

It had been her! Pouring a large tot of brandy, Uriah Buckley swallowed it in one gulp. He was not mistaken, the woman he had passed, the woman at the corner of Wolverhampton Lane . . . it had been her . . . the Neale woman!

Refilling the glass, he carried it to the fireside of the large overfurnished sitting room, slumping into a generous armchair.

The bloody woman seemed to haunt him. Every day he thought of her! And the days were getting fewer. Soon now Jervis would be home; he would be here at Bescot Lodge, even at this moment he could be in England.

Jervis in this house, in the place he belonged. Uriah swallowed from his glass, the heat of alcohol burning past his throat. There must be nothing to upset their relationship this time, nothing to come between father and son. And there would be nothing: no enquiries, no questions, no bloody pack drill!

But what if Jervis reached home before all danger of questions being asked was eliminated, what if he were faced with that one question, 'Why did my brother run away?' But he wouldn't be! Tossing the remnant of brandy savagely into his mouth, Uriah swallowed behind clenched teeth. He wouldn't hear that question because the Neale woman would never speak it.

A tap to the door arrested the thought and he glanced at the manservant standing hesitantly at the threshold.

'Well!' Temper already irritated by the thoughts churning his mind, Uriah's bark was sharp and acerbic.

'Dinner is served, sir.'

The man's quiet reply, distinctly divergent from his own irateness, added to Uriah's growing vexation. Throwing the glass to the floor he rose, pushing the servant aside to stride from the room. 'Then bloody unserve it,' the bellow drifted behind him, 'throw it to the dogs, put it wi' the rest o' the pigswill that cook calls food!'

Temper no cooler than it had been an hour ago, Uriah drove his carriage; but his mind was not on the streets still busy with carters' wagons delivering goods. Dinner! He cracked the whip, the tip of it lancing out above the erect ears of the trotting horse. It 'ad always been supper 'til he married Verity Deinol. But the language of the ordinary folk of Darlaston were not good enough for 'er household, supper must now be dinner and the midday meal must be luncheon. What bloody difference did a name make – a meal was still a meal! But Verity's money 'ad to be lived up to and 'er fancy educated ways adopted, especially so in the case of their son. He had to be all his father weren't; Jervis must speak proper, there were to be none of the peculiar Black Country dialect trace in his speech, none of the rough manners of the workman allowed to rub off onto him; none of his father's manners!

Memories of quietly spoken requests to adjust his words, to speak the Queen's English, requests that had really been a correction of his Darlaston dialect, fuelled the irascibility more brandy had done nothing to curb. His dialect hadn't bothered her the afternoon of that picnic given from her father's colliers and her'd given no mind to a man's rough way of lifting 'er skirts or the hands which 'ad fondled 'er breasts; the so-posh Verity Deinol had 'ad no complaint to a workman's hard flesh bein' pushed inside 'er! But that had changed with marriage, as had her appetite for his body changed after the birth of Jervis. Yet lack of her presence in his bed had caused him no restless nights and calling dinner 'luncheon' and supper 'dinner' had been a small price to pay for the New Hope mine.

The New Hope! Uriah's fingers tightened on the rein. The deep seam, the thick layer of rich coal, was thinning. Did that foretell the seam was petering out, p'raps finishing altogether? But that couldn't be: the whole of the town sat on coal. No, the seam were not finished. A week or so of tunnelling would reveal another thick deposit, this thinning were no more than a pause in the work of nature and so naught to worry on. The thought was meant to be reassuring but as the carriage came to a halt at the steps of the Goscote Club a niggle of doubt still chewed at Uriah's confidence.

Inside the ornately decorated building crystal wall lamps shed discreet light, thick Turkish carpet subdued the sound of footsteps from uniformed waiters, while winged leather chairs cosseted men seated in them, smoke curling in a fine spiral from cigar and pipe.

Would he find Elton here? Acknowledging the deferential answer accorded his enquiry he followed to where his business partner already sat with glass in hand. Dismissing his guide with an order for brandy to be sent to him he lowered himself into one of the spacious chairs.

' 'Ow be things wi' you, be they all right?'

Uriah remained silent as he took the cut-glass goblet held out on a silver tray and lifted it in salute to the other man. No, not everything was yet as he wanted it, but it soon would be.

'Business be well enough,' he answered, 'but then you knows that for you sees the ledgers for yourself.'

'Ar.' Edward Elton drank noisily. 'That I does, Buckley, that I does.'

But you don't see all of them, you sees only what I want you to see. And there be a different set of ledgers, ones kept in the desk in my study. Only they tells the true story of the New Hope and its thinning coal seams. Uriah touched the goblet to his lips, allowing only the smallest sip of alcohol to enter his mouth. He had already drunk more than he should; he must need keep a clear head if the problems plaguing his mind were to be cleared from his path, and the first obstacle would be cleared tonight!

'Why?' Amber's query trembled on her tongue but the hand clasping the poker was steady. 'Why did you . . . ?' The accusation she had been about to voice halted as a second figure came into the room.

'The lad said as 'ow you was hurt . . . Oh Lord above!' Her own words halted, a woman holding a shawl tight about her head stared as her glance caught the figure lying on the floor.

'I told you, I told you 'er were hurt.'

'Outta the way, lad.' Whipping off the shawl and thrusting it at the boy the woman was instantly on her knees beside the still figure. Gently she brushed the dark hair aside, paying no attention to the gasp coming from Amber as a patch of congealed blood showed on Rani's temple.

'Freddy, you help me get this wench to 'er bed, an' you, mum, would be more use in getting' hot water an' a cloth than you be wavin' that there poker about.'

A whimper from Rani had the woman's sharp tone softer and the hand touching the girl's brow was gentle. 'Be still, now,' she soothed, 'Ain't nobody goin' to harm you none.'

How dare he come back to this house and who was this woman telling her to get water and a cloth? Amber thrust the poker at the boy moving closer to the hearth and he halted, a look of puzzlement bringing his brows together.

'I come . . .'

'I know you came!' Amber snapped, 'and I know what you did. You attacked Rani!'

The accusation had the older woman's head lift sharply. Lamp glow touching her face showed a mouth tight with sudden anger and her eyes glistened as if filled with the same disgust as coloured her quiet retort.

'You be no different from the rest an' the lad be truly daft to think other. 'E ought never to 'ave come to this place nor me neither; but it don't be my way to turn from a body needin' help so I'll be gone.'

'Amber . . .' Rani's eyes opened. 'Amber, he came . . . he . . .'

The poker clattered from her fingers as Amber dropped beside the girl. 'No more,' she said quietly. 'You need be frightened no more.'

'Words be fine but they'd sound better to the wench were 'er washed and in 'er bed.' The glance meeting Amber was caustic.

Relief that Rani was conscious drained some of the worry from her though the anger of a moment ago still sat hard in Amber's chest and questions burned in her mind. The woman was right, Rani must be attended to first; but she would ask those questions and simple-minded or not that boy would answer for what he had done.

'Go fetch that water an' if it be you 'ave a marigold in your garden set the flower 'ead in the basin an' pour the boilin' water onto it. Be a good way of cleanin' any poison from a wound . . .'

She knew the antiseptic properties of the flower; she had learned that long ago from her mother and since coming to live at Ley Cottage had kept a supply of dried petals. Offering no argument Amber touched a hand to her friend before rising to her feet but as she made to move towards the scullery Rani called weakly.

'Amber . . . it was Freddy . . .'

What more did she need to hear? Rani had named her attacker! The short glance she threw to the lad standing back now nearer the door held all of Amber's grievance.

'You betrayed our friendship! You could hurt a girl who has showed you nothing but kindness!'

Supporting Rani as she sat up did not prevent the woman looking again to Amber; this time, however, the glisten in her eyes was no threat of tears but the gleam of pure contempt.

'P'raps it don't be becomin' of me to speak this way but I be doin' it. If'n your brain were quick as your tongue you'd be askin' yourself 'ow come a lad who'd beaten a woman would show 'imself back at 'er house an' fetching another to help 'er.'

'Amber,' Rani interrupted. 'Amber, Freddy came to the waste heap, he . . . he was not the one struck me, he found me lying there and brought me home.'

The boy had not attacked Rani. Just the opposite: he had helped her! The horror at her behaviour, at the accusation she had flung and her failure to listen to any explanation, brought swift colour to Amber's cheeks but even as she tried to speak the woman dismissed it with a sharp reminder of the need to attend to the injured girl.

Rani could have lain on the waste heap over against Herbert's colliery all night had it not been for Freddy; she might even have died. The awfulness of the thought had Amber's hand tremble as she carried the basin down the narrow stairs and into the scullery. She would never have thought to search for her there.

'You 'ave my apologies for enterin' your house unbid but the lad 'ad no knowing you would be returned an' neither did I think on it. Seemed like that wench might 'ave recovered enough to light the lamp 'erself.'

Looking across to the woman who spoke as she emerged from the scullery, Amber felt a deep sense of shame. 'It is myself should apologise,' she replied, her cheeks colouring as they had earlier, 'and I do, deeply, as I thank you for the help you have given.'

'Be no need of either. I was led to believe a wench were in need o' me so I come, but that need be over. I've spoke my regrets for steppin' into this house but I speaks none for what I said to you as regardin' your tongue. My lad were not deservin' of the words you said to 'im.'

Taking the shawl from the boy's hand the woman threw it about her shoulders. 'Ar, my lad. Freddy be my son an' though folks calls 'im daft 'e shows a sight more sense than some.'

'Rani and I have never called him that.'

The woman's fingers stopped tying the ends of the shawl beneath her breasts and her keen stare softened. 'That be what 'e told. I was set to leather his back when I learned where it were he had took to bringing 'isself, and I still might when I gets 'im 'ome.'

'Please don't punish him. If any are to be blamed then it is Rani and I. I am sure Freddy would not have come had we told him not to.'

'Well, 'e won't come no more.'

Glancing from mother to son Amber saw the stricken look cloud eyes she had only seen in the gloom of evening. He was hurting and she had caused the pain. Her own heart twisting, she broke the glance to look again at his mother.

'If that is what you wish then of course Freddy must not come again, but I shall be sorry to lose a friend. Rani and myself enjoy his visits and will miss them.'

'You truly count my lad a friend?'

'Truly.' Amber smiled. 'And I would appreciate having his mother's friendship equally truly. Please forgive my bad manners.'

'It's been said already there be need of no apology. You spoke out of fear for that wench upstairs and Becky Worrall don't be a woman to 'old a grudge. My lad tells as you've treated 'im kind and I thanks you for that though I still says 'e never should 'ave been to this house nor any other 'cept his own an' the few that gives 'im work.'

'Then if I am forgiven will you take a cup of tea?'

'I will and gladly . . . and if you 'ave no objection this 'ere lad of mine can tell how it be 'e come to find that wench out there at a mine which ain't seen no workin' for a five-year.'

'There were no answer to my call. I waited, honest I did, but nobody come to the door so I . . . I looked through the window. I d'ain't come in, Mrs Amber, that be God's truth, I d'ain't never come inside, you knows I never does that!'

Soft grey eyes stared anxiously at her. 'I know that, Freddy.' She smiled. 'But how did you find where Rani was?'

Calmed by Amber's assurance she believed him the lad answered more steadily. 'I were set to come away but I wanted to leave what I brought . . . I wanted to put it in a spot where you an' Miss Rani might look. The 'edge which runs across the bottom of the garden be the place I always stands so . . . so it seemed likely you might find it there.'

'Find what there, what be you talkin' of?' His mother's voice held a note of impatience.

'The present . . . I brought a present but weren't not nobody to give it to. You says a body shouldn't never tek back a present once it be offered an' I did offer it but nobody took it.'

The boy was becoming flustered; perhaps they should not question him further. Passing tea across the table Amber turned to the cupboard in which she had placed freshly baked fruit scones before leaving for the glassworks. She handed one to where he sat beside his mother; her smile repeated her reassurance and the lad continued.

'It were when I set the present atop the 'edge. That were when I seen 'im, ridin' fast he were, settin' the whip to the horse 'til it ran like a bat out of hell.'

'Language!' His mother's hand shot out, catching him on the ear. 'I've told you afore about usin' words you hears along of them stables – one more speakin' such an' you'll go there no more, just you remember *that*, my lad! Now, who was it you seen? And you tell it without no profanity.'

Sheepish at his blunder, the lad lowered his gaze to the scone. 'He were far off, I couldn't see proper, but that d'ain't stop me wonderin' who it were about the mine so I ducked behind the 'edge to watch if anybody else come racin' away. But nobody did. I knowed I shouldn't go pokin' about for fear of shafts collapsin' beneath me . . .' He stopped speaking, a flush saying he expected another smack to the ear. When it didn't come he picked up the scone, biting eagerly into it while his mother shook her head at Amber.

' 'E knows what 'e shouldn't do then goes right on a'doin' of it, but this time I be glad 'e did.'

'I was careful to watch where I stepped.' The lad swallowed then immediately took a second bite.

'We sees that.' Becky Worrall took up her cup. 'Just you teks that same care not to talk while your mouth be full.'

'So you went across to the mine?' Amber waited for the scone to be finished.

Brushing a crumb from his mouth the lad nodded. 'I went right up to windin' shed and then across to where the tallies were hung on nails once them miners come up from bein' down under the earth. I thought p'raps I might see whatever that rider 'ad been messin' at; but there were nothing shifted as I could tell so I come away . . . that were when I 'eard a moan. Seemed it were comin' from the heaps where the waste coal and dirt was dumped so I crossed over to look an' that were when I found Miss Rani; 'er face were caked with blood an' her didn't answer to my speakin' so I picked 'er up an' I carried 'er, I 'ad to, I couldn't leave 'er lying there . . . same as I couldn't leave 'er lying outside in the yard so . . .' The anxiety returned to the grey eyes that flicked to Amber. 'So I 'ad to come into the house. I just 'ad to, weren't no other way as I could think, but I never touched nothing, I swears afore God I never touched nothing, nor did I touch Miss Rani after settin' 'er down by the hearth for I knowed that wouldn't be proper so . . . so I run to fetch my mother. Did I do wrong?'

'No Freddy, you did not do wrong, you acted very sensibly and I am grateful, but Rani – did she not wake at all?'

His eyes speaking volumes, Freddy nodded. 'Ar, her woke. Her said a man 'ad rode up to where 'er were pickin' coal from the pit bank, said he hit 'er with his whip.'

'The man you saw riding away! Oh, if only you had been closer, if only you had recognised who it was!'

'Oh, I knows who he were.' Freddy's smile was triumph itself. 'I seen his face as he passed by where I were hidin'. I knows well who he be.'

17

Elton had already had more than a sniff of the brewer's apron.

The reins loose in his hands, Uriah let his mind wander over the previous few hours.

Elton had been slightly tipsy before they had sat down to that meal and by the time they had said goodnight he was three sheets to the wind.

They had talked of business, Elton declaring there were no need of either of them worrying over the future. Swallowing another brandy, he had laughed loudly. 'Coal an' iron, they be the things the country be cryin' out for an' we 'as 'em, Buckley, we 'as 'em both.' He had let the man talk, talk and drink. Uriah smiled to himself. Neither had taken much doing; brandy was a generous loosener of the tongue. But he himself had been careful to avoid that enemy of a man's senses, merely touching the strong spirit to his lips while his companion gulped it past his throat like it was his last. And with a bit of luck it would be!

The conversation had been dominated by Elton. Uriah let the horse find its own way towards Bescot Lodge. That had been to his advantage; the more Elton talked the thirstier he got and the more he slaked his thirst the louder he talked and that had brought more than a few glances in their direction. But for all that he had ensured the man's glass was regularly filled, the wine waiter coming and going throughout the meal. But Elton had not drunk wine. 'Be naught but bloody maid's water,' he had laughed when Uriah's glass was filled with a Sauternes. 'Bring me a man's drink!'

The man's drink had been his usual brandy and Elton had ordered a bottle to be brought to the table, helping himself liberally with almost every bite of food. Halfway through the meal the man had risen unsteadily to his feet, announcing none too subtly a need to relieve himself. He had weaved past tables, his portly frame bumping first one and then another, all of which had kept diners' attention on him and away from Uriah Buckley. That had been his chance and he had taken it. It seemed to any who might have glanced his way that he had simply taken the watch from his waistcoat pocket to check the time but along with the gold hunter he had withdrawn a small phial. It had nestled neatly in the palm of his hand. But he had restrained the urge to tip the contents immediately into that half-filled glass. He would take no chance of being observed; he must wait for Elton's return.

And that had been the performance he had known it would be. Deep in his thoughts, Uriah was almost oblivious of the sound of a train's steam whistle piercing the night. Elton had swayed into the dining room knocking against chairs and tables, the irate recipients of his slurred apologies observing: 'The man should be put in his carriage and sent home!' The commotion had provided the cover Uriah had felt he needed. He had kept his own glance on the stumbling figure, and with his hand holding the phial half-covered by the large table napkin he had removed from his knee and placed beside his plate, he had released the tiny cork with the tip of a finger. Then, making pretence of preventing Elton's glass from being toppled as the man dropped heavily to his chair, he had emptied the contents of the phial into it.

It had all been so easy! Uriah felt a glow of satisfaction. Poppy juice was noted for relaxing the mind and Elton's had already been fast approaching languor. So much so the glass with its additional contents had been emptied in one throw, followed immediately by another, larger glass of the potent liquor. Potent! Uriah's brain relished the word. If his plan worked then Elton would have no more potent a drink; in fact he wouldn't ever drink again.

Had that extraction of poppy held any taste? If it had then Elton had been too drunk to notice. Smell, then? That had been obliterated from the man's breath by constant mouthfuls of brandy . . . and should by some remarkable chance any trace of odour other than that of alcohol remain in the well-used glass? Uriah Buckley had taken care of that. Making it seem Edward Elton's waving hands had caught the half-empty bottle he himself had sent it toppling, smashing the other man's glass in the process. Watching the remnants being washed by the liquid seeping rapidly from the fallen bottle he had taken several moments before summoning the hovering steward.

But fate's helping hand had not stopped there. He had spoken quietly to the man summoned to the table, asking his help with steering the complaining Elton, who had clutched the stiffly starched tablecloth, dragging it with him as he shoved the chair from the table. The remains of the broken glass had slid to the ground where three pairs of shuffling feet had ground it to powder.

Some half an hour later had seen Elton in his carriage, a further bottle of his favourite liquor in one hand. He needed nobody to drive him home! The roar which had greeted the suggestion rang again in Uriah's mind. The steward who had stood while the swaying figure had heaved itself into the carriage had maintained a diplomatic silence, only nodding his head as Uriah had voiced his own, well-acted concern. He had taken care to remain at the Goscote Club for a full hour after

Elton's loud departure. Should the result he hoped for be realised then he must be seen to be completely uninvolved.

She could not remember Freddy and his mother leaving; she could not remember any one of the hours of the night or the dawning of a new day. Only the name . . . the name the lad had spoken, the name which had given the identity of Rani's attacker. Uriah Buckley! It rang like a bell in Amber's brain. Uriah Buckley!

A quiet call went unheard as she stared at the grey ash of an almost dead fire, becoming conscious of Rani's presence only when the girl touched her shoulder.

'Amber.' Rani's voice was anxious. 'Why have you not slept in your bed? Are you not well?'

The touch shattering her almost hypnotic state, Amber shivered as recollection poured like a tide into her mind.

'What is wrong? You tremble.'

'I . . . I was just thinking. There is nothing wrong and I am certainly not ill.' Excuses rushing from her tongue, Amber was on her feet. 'You are the one who is ill. Why on earth have you left your bed?'

'I am not feeling illness.'

That could not be true. How could Rani not be feeling ill after her ordeal? Putting her thoughts into words Amber shook her head at the answer which said a whip was not as hard as Indian stones. There had certainly been enough of them, thrown by people chasing them from villages.

'Stones or whips,' she said, 'either could cause a bleeding inside the head.'

'Which in its turn must bring a hurting to that head and mine does not hurt.'

'Maybe not, but we are taking no chances.' Not to be argued with, Amber shooed the girl back to her bed, promising to bring tea once the fire could be coaxed into boiling the kettle.

She had wanted to have the doctor last night but Becky Worrall had thought a night's sleep might be all Rani needed. 'The skin was broken on her forehead but the wound was not deep,' she had said after bathing it, 'and marigold would stave off any infection.' And Rani did sound much better though a dark bruise showed on one cheek; but a few days' resting was a precaution which must be taken.

'The man riding the horse, he is the same who was carer for your brother and sister, is that not so?' Her eyes held a wisdom surpassing her years as the Indian girl accepted the tea brought to her, holding the cup between her hands, appreciating the warmth against her fingers.

Amber sat on the end of the girl's bed, her feet curled beneath her. She glanced quickly at the bruised face. How could she know that? Freddy had not told the name until after Rani was sleeping!

'Your tongue has no need of answer. Your eyes have spoken it.'

Staring a moment into her cup Amber searched again for answers to the questions which had rested unspoken on her lips throughout the night. Why . . . why Rani? What could Uriah Buckley possibly have against a girl he had never met?

'Now you ask yourself the reason. It is a simple one. The day was cold. Your country does not have the hot sun of India. I thought the night would be more cold and fuel for the fire would need to be gathered so I went to the place of that fuel—'

'I told you never to go there alone. It is a dangerous place!'

'The deserts and jungles of India are also full of danger but we had to face them, my sister.'

'But coal mines hold a different kind of danger. They leave tunnels and shafts; pits dug deep into the earth and overgrown with bracken are a trap those unused to the heath sometimes fall into.'

'Is life not full of pitfalls ready to catch the unwary? Do we not each day tread paths whose way we do not know?' Rani asked.

'But you did know of this hazard, I cautioned you.'

'As you were cautioned by the ayah, the nurse of the colonel sahib's granddaughter. Did she not tell that to go to the market place of Meerut was not suitable for a *feringhee*?'

Rani's interruption was quick and Amber closed her eyes against the sudden vivid flash of memory it brought. Pictures raced into each other: turbanned men on horseback thundering into the open square, the cloud of sand thrown up by hooves and people scattering for safety, the glittering of evening sun on the swords which rose and fell and the heads . . . Lord, those heads!

'I should have listened. I should . . .'

'The roads of each life are laid by the Almighty.' Rani took the cup from Amber's trembling hands, setting it beside her own on the small bedside table. 'He puts our feet upon them that we might learn. We must follow that which is ordained even though often it is painful.'

'God does not ordain cruelty!' Words forced themselves past the sickness risen to Amber's throat.

'How can we know the workings of the All Holy?' Rani asked gently. 'I was taught that the pattern of a child's life is set before the birth of that child and though he or she might try the pattern could not be altered. Your religion teaches that every person has a freedom of will, that the path of good or evil may be chosen. How can we know which is truth? We cannot, we can only trust.'

'As I should have trusted the judgement of Narinder. If I had then Joanna would still be alive.'

Taking Amber's hands in her own, Rani's look was full of sympathy. 'It is not easy to see our own mistakes before they are made. You did not know those dacoits, the bandits of the hills, would descend upon Meerut. Nor did the ayah or she would have told the colonel sahib and he would have forbidden you go listen to the storyteller; neither did I know of the danger awaiting me when I went to pick coals from the waste heap and that is as it should be for were the future mirrored for us to see might not we be too afraid to live the life we are given?'

As so many times before Rani could see beyond the moment. Amber squeezed the hands holding hers. She was too kind to say what was sauce for the goose was sauce for the gander, even had she understood the meaning. Drawing tighter the shawl she had thrown over her cotton nightgown, Amber resigned herself to making no further reprimand, saying instead she could not understand Uriah Buckley's reason for striking a girl he did not know.

Rani leaned back against the pillows, her dark hair spreading like a black veil over them. 'I said the reason held by the man was a simple one; also I said the day was cold, too cold for a body always warmed by the hot sun. So I exchanged my sari for the clothes you bought for me and the shawl which lies now about your shoulders I wrapped about my head. The one who struck me gave the blow from behind; he did not see my face.'

'He thought it was me! Uriah Buckley thought it was me he hit with that whip!'

'Yes, my sister.' Rani nodded. 'He thought it was you.'

She had not come to the cemetery. Zachary Hayden removed the wilted blooms from the grave of a woman he knew only through his mother. He had watched each woman walk through the lych gate hoping each time to see the rich copper-coloured hair, the small heart-shaped face, but each time he had been disappointed. After half filling the small pottery jar of bronze chrysanthemums, he paused. That was what he felt, disappointment. But he shouldn't; it was not as if she were a relative or a friend of long standing . . . there was no right or reason for him to feel any sort of dissatisfaction. Amber Neale was nothing to him.

Nothing: Zachary glanced across a churchyard empty of all but headstones. Then why did he look for her? Why such an empty feeling now she had not come? And what had induced him to catch her in his arms, to whisper those words against her hair?

If tears are all I can have of you then I will take them gladly.

Hearing them now in his mind he chided himself for being a fool. He was no moonstruck lad, he was a grown man, and knew not to hanker after something he could not have. But what his mind knew and his heart felt were two different things; one did not fit with the other. Somehow he must clear his mind of the picture of that slight figure, of gold-flecked eyes so like rich amber, of a smile which haunted him, and his heart must be emptied of the feeling which disturbed yet at the same time thrilled. Amber Neale was wife to another man; that fact should be enough to rule out any other thought – but it hadn't. It had not prevented the dreams which came as he worked or those which drifted in with sleep and it did not ease the pang of longing to be with her, to hear again the softness of her voice.

'Did Freddy not tell you?'

Rani's question was lost beneath the crackle of flame which grabbed at the sawdust, devouring it with gleaming jaws, while instantly the scene became one of a blazing funeral pyre, its red-gold touch grabbing at a young woman's skirt, licking at her arms and legs . . .

'Amber . . . did the boy not say what brought him to the house?'

Struggling with phantoms that reared from the grate Amber made no reply and only the other girl's shaking of her banished the horror.

'Your speaking of that night has not banished the nightmare; even now it comes.'

Breath trembling, her face suddenly pale, Amber was glad to sit in the chair the other girl helped her to. 'It . . . it doesn't come so often.'

'But still it brings fear.'

There was no denying that and Amber did not try. Instead she took a moment to steady fluttering nerves.

'So we will not speak of that which brings the terrors of yesterday. Instead we shall drink *chai* and you will tell me the answer to my question.'

Tea. That had been her mother's answer to any upsetting situation and it was welcome now. Fetching cups to the table as Rani scalded tea leaves she had spooned into the teapot, she asked instead: 'Question. What question is that?'

Pleased her change of subject appeared to have dissolved the fear which had so swiftly coiled itself about her friend, Rani smiled. 'I asked, did Freddy not say the reason that brought him to this house?'

She had forgotten about it. In the turmoil of last night she had forgotten all mention of a gift.

'A present,' she answered now. 'Freddy said he had brought a present.'

The other girl's face beamed pleasure. 'A present! What is it?'

'I don't know.' Amber looked up from watching her friend fill both cups with tea.

The other girl frowned as she returned the pot to its

accustomed place on the hob of the fireplace, blackleaded to a polish that shone almost silver in the daylight streaming from the window. 'You do not know! Is it something you cannot recognise? Or is there a reason other than that?'

'There is another reason. I don't know what Freddy brought because I haven't seen it.'

'You are brought a gift by a friend yet you do not look at it! What way is that? Is it not proper to accept the gift of a man who does not be husband?'

Her laugh tinkling, Amber shook her head. 'It's nothing like that. I haven't seen Freddy's gift because he did not give it to me.'

Dropping to her own chair Rani's small frown deepened. 'I am being confused. You are brought a gift yet it is not given to you!'

'I'm sorry, I should explain. Freddy said he placed whatever it was he wanted us to have out there on the hedge where we would be sure to see it. If he did not take it away with him when he and his mother left last night then it must still be there.'

Leaving the other girl stirring sugar into her cup Amber ran into the garden. Her glance was drawn compulsively to the winding wheel drawn stark against the sky and she halted. Rani could so easily have been killed, as it was only the doubled thickness of shawl draped about her head had saved her from a serious injury. But that blow had not been intended for the one it struck; it had been meant for her. Turning her head, Amber stared across the heath. The attack which had taken place out there, was Uriah Buckley responsible for that too? She could understand the grief he must have suffered – be suffering – at the death of a beloved granddaughter, but could he not also realise it was no fault of hers!

The harsh cry of a crow lifting from a wide-branched sycamore recalled her to the fetching of Freddy's gift and she walked to the hedge. Wrapped in a piece of cloth, damp still with morning dew, it lay where he had said. Taking it carefully in both hands she carried it into the house.

Rani leaned forward as the package was placed between them, her eyes wide with anticipation. Her own interest aroused Amber peeled back the cloth. Once the last of the covering was removed, Amber's breath caught in a loud gasp. As she stared at the revealed object her hand flew to her mouth while every semblance of colour drained from her face.

'Amber.' Rani was at her side almost instantly. 'Amber, what is it! What is wrong?'

But Amber was staring at the contents of the package.

18

'I've told you the all of it. We ate a meal together. We often do that, it gives more time to discuss business; Elton and me be partners.'

'Yes, sir, we 'ave that information already.' The dark-suited man consulted a small notebook then asked, 'At about what time would you say that meal were ate?'

'Time!' Uriah Buckley thumped the desk in the study his son had wanted yet had almost never used. 'I don't remember what time. If whatever hour Elton and me took that meal be important . . .'

'It is, sir, most important.'

'Then go ask at the bloody Goscote Club! Mayhap they'll know what time that meal were served.'

Consulting the book again, the man who had been introduced into the room as Police Inspector Checkett answered. 'We've done that, sir, but we need to corroborate if what we were told be correct.'

It had gone as he had hoped. Something had happened or the police wouldn't be here . . . but had that something been fatal or simply an accident? Hiding his eagerness to know the answer Uriah continued his pseudo-irritation.

'I don't go marking the time everything I does! I takes a meal when I feels the need, no matter what hour that be. Suppose you asks Elton, he'll likely remember better than I can.'

In the moment of silence following his irate outburst Uriah

could feel his heart beat. Had the police found trace of that poppy juice after all?

'We would like you to tell us, sir.' The inspector looked up. 'It need not be a positive to the minute time; an approximation will be sufficient.'

There had been a marked emphasis on the word 'you' and no reference to having spoken to Elton. Did that indicate a suspicion, did this inspector have reason to think he had a hand in whatever business was being investigated? Deciding annoyance was the best cover, Uriah sent a hiss of breath between closed teeth. 'I don't see what the 'ell it be to do with you nor nobody but near as I recall it were approaching eleven . . . now if that be all . . .'

Notebook disappearing into a pocket of his dark coat the inspector made no effort to leave. 'Not quite, sir,' he said quietly. 'Would you say Elton had been drinking?'

'That be a bloody daft thing to ask!' Uriah's loud exclamation had no marked effect, the policeman nodded twice.

'That may be, sir, but if you wouldn't mind answering.'

Uriah's irritation was slowly becoming real. Why couldn't the man get on with it, tell the reason of his coming to Bescot Lodge? Thin lips tightening, he barked. 'I does bloody mind, I be a busy man wi' a business to run. I don't 'ave time to listen to codswallop questions!'

'We are both busy men, sir,' the other man returned calmly, 'and rubbish as you might think it mine is the business of asking questions.'

Behind heavy-lidded eyes Uriah's brain worked quickly. Become too angry and the man might leave without saying any more. If that happened he would have the worry of not knowing whether or not they had found a finger to point at him. Trying to strike a balance between resentment and irascibility he leaned back in the leather chair, saying calmly.

'Then do your business, ask your questions an' then p'raps we can 'ave done.'

'It is the same as I asked a moment gone. Would you say Mr Edward Elton had been drinking?'

'Why else do you think a man goes to his club?'

'I wouldn't like to say, sir, me not being a member of one.'

Give the man his due, he were not to be shouted down. Uriah's glance rested on the whiskered face. This needed a deal of care if he were to come out smelling sweet!

'Then let me tell you,' he answered. 'A man goes to his club to enjoy both a glass and intelligent conversation, summat he can't always find in his own house . . . and yes, Elton had been drinking and I would say he'd been at it for some time when I joined him; in fact afore the meal ended he were well into a bottle of brandy and that after Lord knows how many tots he'd swallowed afore.'

'Six, sir, the steward at the Goscote tells Mr Elton had already taken six and was on a seventh when you arrived.'

He had never thought the staff at that club to be so meticulous. Uriah felt the first sting of doubt. They saw how many drinks a man took, that went without saying, but what else might one of them have seen?

'There you go then.' He hid his thoughts behind a quick answer. 'It bears out what I says; Elton were already half drunk and having a bottle brought to the table . . . well that seen him near enough incapable.'

'But not so much he couldn't drive a carriage.'

So this man knew about that too! Pulling himself upright to the desk Uriah rested both hands on the surface. 'Let me tell you one more thing about a gentleman's club, Inspector. The members do not relish drunkenness and they certainly do not approve of one of their number making a spectacle of himself. The steward and myself helped him to his carriage but when

I offered to drive him home he shouted he needed nobody to do that.'

He had listened without interruption; now the policeman asked, 'Was Mr Elton's behaviour last evening unusual?'

' ''T'weren't unusual. Elton liked his brandy and often had a little more than were good forrim but last evening he didn't stop at a little, he kept on swallowin' – in fact as I recall he took a bottle with him in his carriage.'

Watching the other man nod, Uriah's nerves twanged. He couldn't keep this going without losing what temper he had and that most definitely would do him no good. Drawing in a breath he hoped showed none of the agitation in his mind he looked squarely at his listener.

'You've asked your questions,' he said. 'Now answer one o' mine. What be all this to do with?'

Reaching for the black top hat he had laid aside on entering the study the policeman brushed a finger over its brim before looking again at Uriah and making his reply in the same calm even tone with which he had spoken since arriving at Bescot Lodge.

'It has to do with what appears to have been an accident . . . a decidedly fatal accident. Mr Edward Elton was discovered in the early hours of this morning beneath his overturned carriage.'

Beneath its dark bruising Rani's colouring paled. What could be wrong with the gift the boy had left; why did it affect her friend in this way? It seemed like she had seen a djinn. Reaching for the object she made to remove it but Amber caught at it.

'Bethany,' she murmured again.

'She who was *behen* to you?'

'Yes.' It was a sob choked from the throat. 'She who was

sister to me. I gave this to her before leaving for India, I begged her to keep it safe until I returned, so . . . so how did Freddy come by it?'

'Perhaps your sister too gave it as gift.'

'No.' Amber shook her head decisively. 'Bethany would never have given it away; she treasured it as much as I did.'

'Then it has been taken without being given.'

'Stolen! Not by Freddy. I won't believe that. The boy is no thief. The number of times he has been to this house, many possibly before we even knew he was there, and nothing taken proves he is not.'

'I am also believing he is not a thief.' Her colour returning, Rani's anxious look became one of relief.

Last night had been a sharp lesson. She had accused Freddy, accused a lad who had more than proved friendship was all he sought from Ley Cottage, and it was a mistake she would not make again. But believing his innocence did not rule out the question: where or how had he obtained the one thing she had left with her sister? Amber reached out a hand to the cloth, letting her fingers rest on what it held. It was a puzzle, one she must find an answer to.

'That is treasure to you like seeds and leaves from India are treasure to me.'

'It was the one possession I valued above any other and I taught Bethany and Denny to love it the same way.'

'They were not of many years, your *bhai* and *behen* . . . brother and sister.' Rani repeated the words, putting them into a language still stiff on her tongue. 'Perhaps like other children they took it to the fields and in their games forgot where they laid it.'

It was a possibility but not a very strong one. Bethany would not have used this as part of a game and she definitely would have forbidden Denny to do so.

The gift had brought sorrow where it was meant to bring joy. Years of being friends, of sharing so many dangers, helped Rani recognise the nuances of emotion thought painted clearly on Amber's face. The heart of the English girl cried as did her own when in the darkness of night the faces of her family returned to smile at her. But tears of the heart could not be swept away by the touch of a finger nor dried with linen, for only time and love eased such hurt. Yet those tears, that pain of the soul, might not lie so heavy were it shared with another.

Returning to the chair facing across the table she asked softly, 'Will you not speak to me of your treasure?'

Drawing the piece of soiled cloth closer to her Amber hesitated before removing its contents.

'This,' she caught the word between her teeth, fighting the difficulty of speaking, 'this was my mother's, it is all we had of her.'

'You can be so sure? Is one book not like another?'

Tears misted Amber's vision so that the bruised face watching her blurred. 'I am sure. The cover there –' she touched a finger to a deep crack running across one corner – 'that happened when Denny tried to snatch it from Bethany. I remember they both cried at what they had done for they knew how much our mother valued her Bible but she took them both in her arms saying the book would mend. I did not see it after that until she told me to reach it from a drawer in the chest in her bedroom. "Keep it safe," she said, "keep it safe, my dearest, the words it holds." That was the last thing she said. She . . . she just closed her eyes and left us. I could not bring myself to look at the book for a long time after her death but when I did I found the date of her marriage to my father followed by that of my birth. Below these were the date of her second marriage, together with the birth dates of both Bethany and Denny. If this Bible is truly the one given by my

mother then that record will be on the inside of the cover.'
Turning back the board-like gilt-lettered cover Amber felt the
pain of that night long gone when she had taken her dead
mother in her arms and cried for her to come back.

Touching the handwriting, it seemed for a moment her
mother's hand rested on hers, guiding her finger over the
names, her quiet voice whispering them, but as Rani asked her
question the dream was snatched away. Finding it hard to
speak against the tears in her throat Amber answered quietly.

'Bethany is my half-sister and Denny my half-brother.'

'Half!' Rani frowned, 'half is strange. Brother is brother and
sister is sister, that is so in India.'

Wrapping the Bible in its cloth, Amber replied. 'There are
many differences between our countries. Mine calls Bethany
and Denny half-brother and -sister but I have never thought
of them as such. The fact of their father being not my own has
never been of consequence between us and I could not love
them more were we born of the same man.'

'Those words will find favour with your God. He will listen
to the prayer you ask of Him and send your brother home to
you.'

Rani had so much faith, she truly believed. But the faith of
Amber Neale . . . was it a lack of devotion which kept her from
finding Denny?

'You will keep this gift.'

Amber, lost in her thoughts, carrying the book across the
room, pulling open a drawer of the dresser. Now she looked
at it held in her hands. 'Yes.' She nodded. 'I shall keep it . . .
but only until Freddy comes again.'

A decidedly fatal accident.

Uriah Buckley's sense of satisfaction grew each time the
police inspector's phrase returned. He had listened to

the man's questions and given him the answers. Uriah smiled to himself. Let Inspector bloody Checkett check them, he wouldn't find anything to hold against Uriah Buckley!

Fatal! He smiled again. He liked the sound of the word: it was so finished, so final. Well, it told the finish of Edward Elton; that particular shadow on the horizon of Jervis's return to Bescot Lodge was there no longer – but that accident had taken only the father. Elton's son were still living and what one had known the other still knew!

Why had he been such a fool? An irritated flick of the reins had the horse trotting quickly. Why had he let Elton bring his lad that night? It hadn't been lack of knowing that one's tendencies; his preferences had been shown often enough in the way he sniffed around the stable lads . . . around *any* lads! It were no use to say Elton hadn't known his son were a queer. True, it had to be kept in the dark, but a father would be blind not to have seen it and Edward Elton had sight in both eyes. But with those eyes closed for good, with no threat or danger to his inheritance, who could say how that lad might behave in the future . . . what he might whisper in the ear of one of his dirty little playmates or to some profligate degenerate like himself? Or then again, what he might intimate in order to gain a new lover? Uriah's hands tightened on the rein.

As boys Elton's lad had watched Jervis with a different look on his face. He had dismissed it then as a bit of hero-worship, his own boy being the better at sport. But he ought not to have dismissed what his own mind were saying, that it were no look of dog-like devotion followed Jervis but one of desire, and it were no face was the object of that desire and the games he wanted to play weren't those of the sports field! So what if that boyhood fancy should rear again? What if word of what had gone on one night at Bescot Lodge, of what his own father had been party to, should be offered to Jervis in exchange for satisfying . . .

But Jervis would never do that! Uriah smashed a mental fist into the thought. His lad had never been inclined . . . never shown no tendency! Hadn't he married, begotten a child? No, Jervis were no bloody pansy, he'd have no truck with Elton. But refusal could bring on a different yearning, one powerful and potent as sex: the longing for revenge, a revenge which could only turn Jervis away again, and should that happen he would never return; his son would be lost to him forever.

But that would not happen. It must not be allowed to happen – but how to prevent it? Poppy juice could not be the answer a second time.

'It is kind of you to call; my father valued your friendship.'

'And I his,' Uriah answered, his feelings for the son of Edward Elton masked beneath a brief smile. 'He were a fine man and an astute business partner. We had ourselves some disagreements on 'ow things should be wi' the coal and the iron but were naught we didn't come to sort in the end. He would 'ave his say an' me mine then we'd get to settling things, mebbe over a meal an' a glass or two. I hopes it can be that way atwixt you an' me.'

'I am sure we will have a most amicable association.'

And I be sure that association will always 'ave a table or a desk separatin' we. Uriah's thoughts ran behind eyes wary beneath heavy lids as he accepted the chair a limp hand pointed to. The man might as well wear a frock for it wouldn't speak any the less plain!

'I knows this be painful for you and it goes wi'out saying you 'ave my sympathies on your loss but I be finding what happened last night hard to come to terms with. Your father were in good health, we 'ad supper together; I even seen him away home in his carriage. Then naught but an hour gone I 'ave a police inspector at Bescot Lodge askin' all manner of questions. I tell you I finds that more'n I be happy with, it give me the feelin' it were thought I 'ad something to do wi' your father's death.'

'You have my apologies for that intrusion. I certainly did not know of such intention on the part of that policeman or I would have told him my father stood in no danger from you.'

'Do that mean they suspects foul play, be they thinking it be something other?'

Uriah watched the long-fingered hand wave a dismissal and this time his feelings were those of relief.

'No. They say it could be nothing but accidental. It appears my father had been drinking heavily . . . a brandy bottle was found in his hand . . . that combined with what he had already drunk whilst at his club had probably caused him to fall asleep. It is thought the horse was startled, possibly by the shriek of a train whistle; they somehow always seem to sound the louder at night. In any event it bolted off the road and onto the heath and the carriage wheel was caught in a hole and tipped the carriage over, crushing my father beneath it.'

No mention of poppy juice! Driving towards the New Hope mine Uriah thought back over the conversation. Mebbe it had induced the sleep which had likely cost the life of Edward Elton, mebbe it hadn't, but it not being mentioned by either the inquisitive Checkett or Elton's lad meant there were no sign of it being found and so no fear of any more questions as to the cause of that accident. Uriah Buckley were in the clear!

But the shifting of one problem had given rise to another. Leaving the horse and carriage to the care of an attentive foreman Uriah walked across the yard of the coal mine towards the building which held his small office.

Elton's lad must be dealt with! One way might be to expose his sordid ways now before Jervis reached home, the other to send him after his father. Choosing the latter could be awkward; opting for the first gave the chance for Elton junior to speak out about that night.

After closing the office door on the clerk who rose expectantly as he entered, Uriah walked to the window, his mind churning as he stared down on the pit head.

The choice weren't easy and neither were the way . . . but one way or the other that pretty little pervert must be dealt with.

19

She had not visited her mother's grave for two weeks. Amber gathered the last sprigs of lavender from the garden. Would the small patch of ground be left with a vase of dead flowers? Zachary Hayden had cared for it but that was before he knew she now came to that small cemetery. He had said he feared he was intruding and though she had told him otherwise would he now leave no more flowers for her mother?

He had been so kind and friendly. Hands filled with the fragrant-smelling blossom, she smiled at the face watching from her mind, that same face which sometimes smiled back at her as she fell asleep. She had tried to avoid such thought, telling herself it was not proper to think about a man she scarcely knew, but how could she prevent her mind returning to those afternoons? Seeming to look now into vividly blue eyes, to see the smile curving a strong mouth, Amber felt the warmth of a blush steal into her cheeks as the question came . . . did she want to ban that image from her mind? That was an impossible question, one she would never voice a reply to! But what the mind asks the mind also answers, and the answer whispering now turned the blush into fire.

'It is the day of offering.' Rani looked across at Amber entering the kitchen bright with later autumn sun.

Lowering her face to the delicately perfumed sprigs, Amber hid the moment of embarrassment the girl's words caused. Could Rani possibly have guessed at those secret thoughts, could she know? Depositing the lavender on the table she had prepared, she kept her eyes averted.

'Two times you have not made offering. This has caused you sadness, my sister, a sadness I see in your eyes.'

'Nonsense!' Amber gave a short laugh. 'I told you I will take flowers to my mother's grave when I feel you are completely recovered.'

'And I have said I am well. A little shock and a little bruising is all I suffered from that attack and they are nothing; did we not suffer worse in India?'

Stripping flowers and leaves from the fine twigs then dropping them into a large old kettle they had found in an outbuilding Amber admitted there was no denying what Rani said. They had been subjected to worse and more painful treatment during those years.

'What brings sadness to you brings sadness also to me,' Rani went on, 'you can take it away from my heart and yours by consenting to take offering as before.'

'But . . .'

'No.' Glossy as a raven's wing, black hair caught the light as Rani shook her head. 'No . . . I will hear no buts. If I am to remain sad then it must be so.'

'You are as devious as a djinn!' Amber's laugh rang around the small kitchen.

'Devious?' Brown eyes full of innocent query stared. 'What is this word meaning?'

Turning from her task, Amber's hands went to her hips while her own eyes held the laughter which rested on her lips. 'It means you are intent on getting what you want by whatever means.'

'Then if you make visit and place flowers to your mother's memory I am happy to be devious.'

The girl was incorrigible. Amber could not keep her smile

from spreading, but to say so would lead to more of her 'black-mail'. Instead she returned her attention once more to the stripped leaves and flowers. 'Maybe tomorrow,' she said, half-filling the kettle from a tall enamel jug, 'maybe I will go to Bloxwich tomorrow.'

'Is this day not as good as the one which will follow?'

Stirring the contents of the kettle Amber's mind was suddenly filled with a picture of two young women, one in western clothes so ragged and torn as to be almost un-recognisable while the other, drawing a faded dust-covered sari over her dark head, squinted over an unending plain empty of anything other than dried scrub. 'I will not let you sleep!' Angry as the stamp of her foot the dark-haired girl grabbed the wrist of her companion. 'I will not let the sun steal your brain or the hyena eat your flesh! You will walk as I will walk; we shall go on together until the Lord Rama decrees the time of our leaving, finding safety, or until his hand lifts us from this world.'

Rani had been as obstinate then as she was being now. The picture faded as Amber glanced at the familiar face, clear now of that awful bruising. She had been so right in insisting they move on when all she herself had desired was to lie on the warm dry ground and never move again. It had been the girl's obdurateness had saved them; perhaps it would not be so wrong to give in to it now.

'I will go,' she said, 'but only after we finish making the lavender water.'

'Then we shall work quickly.' Rani smiled, fetching a stool and setting it a short distance from the fire over which Amber hung the kettle; then, bringing a jar she had sterilised in boiling water, set it on the ground beside the stool while Amber placed a small butt of water, ice-cold from the pump in the yard, on its seat.

'There will be no *chai* until this is finished.'

'No tea!' Amber drew her mouth down in a mock-mournful expression. 'How will we manage without a cup of tea?'

Laughing, Rani brought a length of pipe the blacksmith had made to their design, fixing one end to the spout of the kettle and the other in the jar, ensuring the curved middle rested in the cold water.

'There is no more to do but wait,' she said. 'That one can do; there is no need for both to sit and watch steam pass from the kettle or the cold water to have it, as you say, condense, to drop clear liquid into the jar.'

'But the water in the butt, it has to be kept cold.'

'You think I cannot do this?' Rani answered the protest. 'You think I cannot draw a cork, let the warmed water run slowly from that hole while I pour fresh cold water to replace it!'

'That cork is called a bung,' Amber said, her eyes twinkling.

'Cork or bung, it is doing the one same thing, and Rani, she can pull it out and can push it again into its hole. She is not needing your help, so she asks once more you go make offering.'

She still did not feel comfortable leaving Rani alone in the house. As she walked the short distance from the railway station to the cemetery, Amber's conscience pricked still. She had tried to reason with the girl, tried explaining one day was no different from another, that it did not matter which was chosen to visit a grave; she had even asked they come here together but Rani's obstinacy had risen again, impenetrable as ever. She would remain to distil the lavender and Amber must come to Bloxwich. It had been almost like arguing with Denny. He had displayed that same trait even as a very young child and it had grown with him into boyhood, but like Rani his doggedness had always had a care for the wellbeing of his sisters beneath it. Denny, he had cried so when she had left.

Swallowing hard against the lump the thought of her brother formed in her throat she walked more rapidly, passing beneath the dark wooden arch of the ancient lych gate; her boots tapped on the path which led around the side of the church, echoing in the stillness of its churchyard.

The flowers were there. Pausing, she smiled at the erect spikes of deep pink amid a cloud of fragile white. Zachary Hayden still came, he had not neglected to care for that small plot of ground. The smile remained as she moved to the grave-side, dropping to her knees to place her own pale pink flowers.

'Feverfew.'

Startled by the voice so close beside her, Amber scrambled to her feet.

'Sorry, I thought you had heard me come.'

'No, no I was lost in what I was doing.' A glance at the face the night hours often brought to her mind made her pulse resume its earlier race.

'Next time I will remember to come by way of the path, crossing on grass muffles the sound of footsteps.'

Next time! Amber brushed self-consciously at her skirt, a ridiculous feeling of gladness at deciding to wear the neat suit Greville had purchased for her bringing a slight tinge of colour to her cheeks.

'We have chosen to bring the same colour flower; they go well together.'

Deep and musical, attractive as the strong-featured face, the voice brought a thrill of pleasure. Afraid it would show, Amber turned back to the flowers.

'Feverfew,' Zachary Hayden said again. 'I particularly like their foliage, it's so feathery, and the flower. No more than an extra-large daisy but somehow appealing in its demand to be more.'

'There was not a great deal of choice. My garden is not large and already it is almost bare of flowers, but those you have brought are lovely.'

'Gayfeather. The leaves are not as attractive as those of the feverfew but the close-packed spikes of flower make up for that.'

Why were her pulses behaving so madly . . . and why did her heart tilt when he spoke?

'Gayfeather.' Amber kept her glance on the tall pink spikes. 'A pretty name.'

'Not the botanical one but I prefer it to liatris, and I think feverfew much more suitable than pyrethrum: that is far too grand-sounding.'

'And the white, it looks like a cloud, so soft and billowy.'

'That is gypsophila or, as we in Bloxwich call it, baby's breath.'

'Of course! I had been trying to remember, but time did not allow me to see much of the garden while living in Bloxwich or in Darlaston, and in India.'

'India?' The tone held as much surprise as it did query. 'You have visited India?'

Pushing back the onrush of memories the name evoked made Amber's answer sound tight. 'I lived there for four years.'

He should not have asked, it must have sounded like he was prying! Zachary Hayden had caught the tensing of that slight figure. He had wanted so much to see her, to speak with her, should he offend her now she might ask him to leave.

'My question was not meant to carry offence, Mrs Neale,' he said quickly, 'it was one of interest. Since leaving the sea you are the first person I have met who, like myself, has visited that country.'

'You were in India?' It was Amber's turn to sound surprised, then, realising it, she turned to him with a shamefaced look. 'Oh dear, I'm so sorry.'

Zachary Hayden's laugh rang across the deserted cemetery. 'How about we put aside all apologies and start again. I am Zachary Hayden.'

Her own laugh joined with his the world seemed suddenly brighter. 'And I am Amber Neale who has not yet thanked you for putting flowers on her mother's grave; I am most grateful, Mr Hayden.'

'When you did not come I feared you were ill.'

Was that concern she heard in his voice? Glancing into those vividly blue eyes Amber saw the answer and with it her senses tripped.

Aware of the tremble of her nerves echoing in her reply her glance fell away. 'It was not myself but my friend, Rani, met with . . . she has been unwell.'

'Rani . . . an unusual name.'

'For Darlaston, yes.' Amber nodded. 'But not for a girl born in India. That was where we met and when I returned to England Rani came with me.'

A slight frown settled between his dark finely drawn brows and Zachary Hayden did not reply. Had he been wrong in his judgement of her? Had he made a mistake in thinking she was a simple working-class woman, when really she was someone wealthy enough to have brought servants home with her?

His silence bringing her glance back to his face, Amber read the uncertainty there and immediately recognised the root of it. She smiled and gave a slight shake of the head. 'Rani is my friend, Mr Hayden. There is no memsahib and *nokar* at Ley Cottage, no mistress and servant.'

'Rani is a fortunate girl.'

'Fortunate to have left one country for another, or to have no mistress?'

His frown cleared; Zachary Hayden's eyes took on a soft gleam. 'Neither,' he answered quietly. 'She is fortunate in having you for a friend, to be with you every day . . . I envy her, Mrs Neale, I envy her a great deal.'

What had he meant by that? She had mulled over the words all through the train journey back to Darlaston and taking the way of Wolverhampton Lane rather than cross the heath to reach the cottage that was once part of Herbert's Park colliery buildings gave them yet more time to plague her mind.

She had not asked for an explanation; the sudden jerk of her heart had said to hear more would be unwise. Feeling as she did it would be easy to read more into what he might reply than was intended. So she had bent to touch the ground, whispering her goodbye to her mother; then, explaining she did not wish to leave Rani for longer than was necessary, she had walked quickly out of the churchyard, pausing at the lych gate only long enough to wish Zachary Hayden good day.

He had offered to walk with her to the railway station at Elmore Green and though every part of her screamed 'yes' she had refused. Had that refusal disappointed him as it had herself? Certainly not! The idea of his caring one way or the other was totally ludicrous and she should have more sense than to even think such a thing! Reprimanding herself, she hurried on, passing Forge Road to the next left-hand turn, the now rarely used lane which would lead her to Ley Cottage.

The hour was not late but the coming of autumn had the sun disappear sooner. Glancing at the sky, heavy with purple-edged grey, she felt suddenly anxious. It had been foolish agreeing to leave Rani alone. Had she learned nothing from the attack made on the girl! Anxiety turning her walk into a run she burst into the house, only to stop suddenly at what she saw.

Lit by the oil lamp, the living room was neat and tidy as they always kept it. The blackness of the cast-iron fireplace gleamed silver, the pretty chintz covers and curtains they had made were smooth and colourful against the glow of regularly polished couch and chairs; even the clock ticked as normal. So what had stopped her dead in her tracks?

The book! Her mother's Bible – it was there on the table!

'I be sorry to be callin' wi'out invite, Mrs Neale, but I felt I 'ad to.'

Only with those agitated words did Amber realise the presence of Becky Worrall. Her spine stiffly held, the woman sat perched on the edge of a chair.

'It were my lad,' she went on rapidly, not waiting for Amber to speak, 'he's been so quiet these couple o' weeks I've been fair worried, I feared 'im to be goin' doing with something, them there meezles or that inflooenza, but when there were no spots showed nor no cough took 'im I began to think other. I asked what 'ad he been up to, was he in any trouble, but I got no answer bar silence. But my Freddy don't be a lad to 'old his tongue against his mother so then I knowed there were something amiss and threatened a lampin' should he not say. I never 'ave taken the strap to 'im for I ain't a woman to believe in beatin' a lad nor a wench neither so when I threatened it then he reckoned I'd reached the end of my tether and he told it all, told of bringing a present for you, that he 'ad left it resting on the hedge a-bordering your garden. He'd kept his silence for he'd knowed full well I 'ad forbidden him ever to touch or tell anyone what were in the house along of us. It be the first time he's gone against my rulin' and that be the reason of my comin' along of this place.'

Rani had not moved since Amber entered the house but now she rose to swing the bracket with its bubbling kettle away from the heat of the fire.

'Mrs Worrall came to see you. I asked her to wait until you returned. Now you are here I will go upstairs to my room.'

'No.' One hand lifting in a swift gesture, Amber glanced at the girl walking towards the stairs door. 'There is no reason for you to leave this room; whatever is to be said will be said to us both.'

'Then will we let it be said over *chai*? I offered it but Mrs Worrall refused, saying it was not fitting until you were present to offer it also.'

'Well, I am here now and I too ask will you take a cup of tea?'

The older woman's eyes held the anxiety her quickly spoken words had already portrayed, but beneath that lay something deeper. Regret? Was that the emotion she could see? Removing the coat of her suit Amber laid it aside then helped in the preparing of the tea she suddenly felt such a need for.

'Could be you'll reproach y'self for the offering of this.' Becky Worrall took the cup handed to her.

Seating herself beside Rani, Amber smiled briefly. 'My mother taught that good manners had no need of reproach.'

'That be a teachin' I tries to follow and tells my lad always to do the same.'

'Freddy has never been impolite . . . but he has not been here for some days now. I hope he is not ill.'

First sipping her drink, Becky Worrall shook her head. 'He be well enough, I thank you.'

Deciding that to question the woman as to why, if the lad was well, had he stayed so long from visiting Ley Cottage would amount to rudeness, Amber desisted but Rani had no such compunction.

'He ain't been 'cos I told 'im not to.' The reply came firmly as the woman replaced her cup on the table. 'I says as it don't be proper forrim to be visitin' a house where no man lives. I would want no slur laid against you two for you've been ever good to my lad, but tongues wag in Darlaston and could be they talks wicked even when folk don't truly know the top and bottom of what they be on about.'

That was unfair on Freddy! The thought sprang to her mind but Amber clamped her lips, preventing it being put into words, thankful that this time Rani did the same, even though her candid eyes showed she too had that thought.

'But that don't be what has me to this house though I be glad it be said for I wouldn't want either of you thinkin' my lad be keepin' from you on account of any other cause; I come to speak of that.'

The woman's glance had gone to the book resting still in its shroud of dusty linen. Had she come to demand it be returned to her, to say her son had no right to give away what did not belong to him? But it did not belong to her! Amber's fingers twined together, resisting the urge to grab the book. Trying to keep her voice steady she looked across the table, meeting the glance lifting to her own.

'Mrs Worrall,' she began quietly, 'your son should have asked permission before—'

'Before takin' what don't be his'n to take!' Becky Worrall's interruption was sharp and decisive, but not so decisive as her next words. 'It were wrong of 'im to go leavin' that as a present . . . and I be 'ere to right that wrong.'

20

She had come to take it back. Becky Worrall had come to claim the Bible as her property! Amber felt her nerves flare. How could she prove otherwise? The names inside could be the names of any other children and without Bethany or Denny to back her own claim then it was word against word, this woman's against her own.

'That there Bible were never truly mine.'

Amber gasped with relief so profound she almost sobbed. Grey eyes a perfect copy of her son's looked back at her from Becky Worrall's tired lined face.

'It be as I said, that Bible were not mine from the beginning but were brought to me some five year gone. It were long past the hour my lad should've been 'ome 'an in his bed. I were near frantic wi' thought of what might 'ave happened . . . I told you afore folk says he be daft in the 'ead an' there be them as don't hesitate to strike him. Then as it were breakin' dawn he come. I admits I'd reached for the belt which had belonged to his father and was ready to leather his hide, such was the worry built inside of me, but the Lord stayed my 'and, praise be to Him. It were then, after my tears were done, he put that there Bible in my 'ands and said how he had come by it.'

For a long moment only the slow tick of the clock on the mantel sounded in the silence. Then the woman spoke again.

'Tell me, Mrs Neale, an' tell me honest, do you trust the

word of my lad? Do you believe his tongue to be honest an' free from lies?'

'I have no reason for believing otherwise, and I am sure Rani has none either.'

'The words of your son have given no grief to this house; he has brought no dishonour to his *mai*, to you his mother.'

'I thanks you for them words.' Becky Worrall's eyes misted as she looked at Rani. Wiping the moisture from her lashes with one finger she sniffed before adding, 'If that be the way o' things wi' you both then p'raps you might let him tell what he seen and 'eard for 'imself.'

'But you said Freddy may not come here again!'

'I knows what I said.' The woman answered Amber with a trace of a smile. 'But for this day I lay aside my words. If you be agreeable I'll call him for he be out there hidin' in the yard.'

Tall and gangly with youth, the boy stayed close to his mother as she brought him into the room.

Asking might he be given a sultana cake, Rani was met with another shake of the head.

'He will say his piece first, then should it please you he will take the cake for it be a favourite with 'im.' She touched his hand reassuringly and smiled at the worried-looking boy. ''Ave no fears, son, they 'ave said they trusts what you 'as to tell; just speak it as you did to me the night you fetched in that book.'

'I . . . I . . .'

The explanation seemed about to fade before it began. Amber said gently, 'Your mother is right, Freddy, you need have no fear of Rani or myself. We are not angry for your bringing the Bible as a gift; we saw it only as generous on your part and, as for believing what you may wish to share with us now, why should we not trust it be the truth when you have never lied to us before.'

'It *do* be the truth!' Eyes bright with emphasis the words

burst out. 'It do be the truth, Mrs Amber, I'll put my 'and to that Bible an' say it again.' Reaching to where the book lay he pressed a hand to the cover, repeating the words before drawing back. 'I . . . I were in the stables along of Bescot Lodge. I knowed I shouldn't 'ave been there an' should I be copped by one of the grooms I would get a hidin', same as I knowed it would be my own fault for they told me often enough to stay away; but I loves 'orses an' I wouldn't never 'urt not one of 'em. Them 'orses they knows that, they don't never kick nor buck when I stands beside 'em an' they always nuzzles my 'and after I gives 'em an apple, that be their way of sayin' thanks, don't it?'

'Animals also trust, they know truth of the heart just as we do.' Rani's answer, spoken softly, brought a smile to the boy's mouth and took the worry from his eyes.

'It were while I were there I 'eard this commotion in the yard. I thought it were a couple of the grooms 'avin' a set to, some of 'em don't get on well, so thinkin' what I did an' fearin' the loser might take his spite out on me I hid among the bales of straw. But it were no stable 'ands a-fighting, it were a young lad and a man. The man were dressed like a gentleman but not the lad. They come into the stables and the man sent the lad sprawling with a blow to the 'ead an' that book fell out of his 'ands. Then . . .'

'Go on, lad,' Becky prompted quietly, 'it needs be said.'

In the glow of the lamp Rani lit against the encroaching evening, Amber saw the colour race into the lad's cheeks.

Hands twisting together, he let his head droop to his chest. 'Then the older one closed the stable door an' set a bar across it. The lad were on his feet an' though he looked to be dazed he tried for the door but were grabbed again an' when he cried out to be let go the other one laughed and said he wouldn't ever let him go, said the master of the Lodge had given him away, had made a present of him, that he liked bein' given presents . . . especially this sort. The young 'un kicked out, sayin' he were going nowheres, but it were no use, he were no match against the strength of the other one, who laughed and said, "Oh you are going somewhere, my little playfellow, somewhere we will play a lot of games together . . . games like this one."'

'You needs tell the all of it.' Becky Worrall touched her son's hand. 'I knows it be against your nature for such to come from your tongue but heaven won't hold the tellin' against you so speak the rest of it.'

Had Freddy witnessed a beating, had he seen one of the stable boys being whipped? Seeing the disturbed twist of his fingers Amber felt sorry for him; she should tell his mother there was no need for him to say more yet something stronger than herself kept the words in her mouth.

Colour deepening yet further in his cheeks, his head remaining downcast, he made several attempts to do as his mother bid before the words finally came. 'The . . . the one who looked like a gent, he . . . he grabbed the lad when he tried to kick again an' fetched him a fair wallop to the 'ead. The little 'un was spun round by the force o' the blow and fell face down on the ground. Seemed he were either knocked out or dead for he made no move. I thought then the man would leave but I were wrong. He bent over the lad and pulled away his breeches then . . .'

Freddy paused once more, embarrassment at what he had said burning his face and pinning his tongue, so it took several gentle urgings from his mother to get him to speak again; when he did, Amber could hear the distress in his voice.

'He pulled them breeches clear, then he spread that little lad's legs, then he removed his own trousers and . . . I seen him, it were gloomy in the stable but my eyes be used to the dark, I sees good where others don't be able lessen they 'ave a candle or a lantern, and I seen that man kneel across the boy an' I seen . . .'

Lips pressed hard together, Becky Worrall's son fought against the teaching of a lifetime, a teaching which said neither look nor speak evil, but again the gentle pressure of his mother's hand granted temporary remission.

'I seen . . .' he said whisperingly, 'I seen his flesh hard an' . . . an' then it touched that bare bottom. I knowed that were wrong, I knowed it, so I throwed that empty water bucket. That were wrong an' all . . .' Clutching his mother's hand he lifted his head as he dropped to his knees beside her chair, his eyes on her face. 'I knowed I shouldn't never 'urt nobody but what that man were about, it . . . it were not right. I be sorry to 'ave gone against what you've always said not to do, sorry to 'ave brought you sorrow, but I ain't sorry I throwed that bucket nor will I ever say other!'

'I wouldn't want you to, son.' Becky stroked the tousled head. 'I be proud . . . proud to know you 'as the sense to recognise true evil. What you done was protection o' that lad and will be seen and judged that way by the Lord. Now tell the endin'.'

Anxiety lifted from his face, Freddy stood up and when he spoke the whisper of guilt was gone.

'The bucket caught against his back and he dropped forward, the weight of him banging the young un's 'ead again hard on the stone floor, but the man were not knocked out, he groaned, an' I were feared of him getting' to his feet an' findin' me; thought of being given the whip or p'raps passed over to the bobbies took my senses an' afore I were aware I 'ad grabbed a shovel an' hit the handle of it over his 'ead. He were breathin' when I rolled him off the lad an' I knowed he would wake soon. I were flummoxed as to what to do but I knowed I couldn't run away an' leave that young 'un, same as I knowed the lad were too 'eavy to be carried far, that way we would both be catched; then it come to me to take the bar from the doors an' set them wide then hide the lad along of me in the straw; that way it would seem he had run. I done all my mind telled to me 'cept though I grabbed the lad's breeches I forgot the thing he'd carried with him. The lad woke afore the man, he wanted to leg it outta the barn, but I telled him he would like be run down an' then he'd be back where he started so we both lay silent, the straw covered over us. We 'eard the man wake, 'eard him swear an' kick the door. I prayed in my 'eart he wouldn't search the barn, that he would think not only had the lad run but that bucket and shovel had fallen from the stable loft strikin' him accidental like. I squeezed the lad's 'and, giving him warnin' not to cry out . . . seemed an age afore a horse were ridden away but at last all were silent. But I 'ad sense enough to think that could be a trick so we lay not movin'.

'It must 'ave been hours we spent too feared to sit up; the sky beyond the open doors were dark an' no moon shone. I said for the lad to come 'ome wi' me, I telled him my mother would look after him, but he were afraid of being seen, of that man gettin' to know where it was he'd got to so being dressed once more in his breeches he took off. That were when I seen that book still lyin' where it 'ad dropped. Chances were he would come for it once he felt it safe but to leave it lying would be to 'ave it taken by one of the stable 'ands, so I carried it 'ome to keep it against his coming. But I ain't never seen hide nor hair of him from that day. That be the truth, Mrs Neale, I've done as Mother said I must, I've telled it all 'cept . . .'

He paused and as he looked at Amber his grey eyes held a slight bewilderment.

''Cept that since you come to live in this 'ouse, an' specially so after you an' Miss Rani said I was friend to you, I 'ad the same dream. More'n once it come but always it were showing me 'anding you the book I took from the stable along of Bescot Lodge. I dreamed it more an' more 'til in the end I fetched it 'ere; I hopes that don't go against me, I hopes you don't be thinking what I done be wrong.'

'No.' Amber's answer reflected respect as well as tenderness. 'No, Freddy, it will not go against you. All that you have told us has served only to deepen the regard Rani and myself have for you. You showed wisdom many a man might envy, as you showed a great deal of courage in staying to help a boy when you could have escaped. Your mother has every reason to be proud.'

She had forced herself to speak and though she meant every word her brain was screaming. Bescot Lodge . . . a boy . . . a boy who had run away! In an effort to hold those screams, to prevent the fear building in her brain from taking over her mind, Amber screwed her fingers into her palms until her fingernails bit into the soft flesh.

'Freddy,' she said tightly, 'the . . . the boy, had you seen him before, do . . . do you perhaps know his name?'

Freddy's quick smile showed appreciation of her praise of him as he answered. 'Oh ar, I'd seen the lad often though I d'ain't never talk with him until that night. He lived along of Bescot Lodge, an' I knowed his name for I'd 'eard it called many times from the kitchen. I knowed the name of the other one an' all for I'd 'eard that spoke by the grooms who cared for his 'orse the times he come a'visitin' of the Lodge. His name be Elton, he be the son of Edward Elton who be partner in business to the master of Bescot Lodge, but the lad, I knowed his name only as Denny.'

Denny! The boy the man had been about to rape was her brother! Uriah Buckley had given him away as he would a dog . . . made a gift of him to another man, a man who could subject him to horror. Trembling, Amber stared, seeing nothing, hearing nothing but those words beating in her head until Rani touched her shoulder.

'You have heard and your heart aches but the boy, your brother, his body was not abused, we shall give thanks for so great a blessing.'

'The lad Freddy spoke of . . . he be your brother?' Becky Worrall's eyes gleamed a new concern. 'Then the little wench, the lad's sister, her be *your* sister!'

'Bethany?'

'That be the name I seen in the book.' Becky nodded. 'The same as were spoke to me by a kitchen maid along of the Lodge.'

Fingernails biting deeper, Amber felt every nerve jar.

'Her told of a wench of about ten years bein' sister to a lad of about eight. Seems they was left along of an older sister travellin' with Uriah Buckley's granddaughter abroad to join her parents . . . said it were India they went to but I don't 'ave the provin' of that.'

'India was the country and I am the one who left her brother and sister; it was that or lose my post and if that happened how could I keep my family from the poorhouse!'

'You don't 'ave to go explainin' the whys and wherefores of what you done, I knows well the threat of the workhouse for I come under its shadow when my man were killed in the mine. I knows a body has to take whatever straw be held to 'em if they be to avoid that place an' you had to take hold of your'n, be no disgrace in that,' Becky Worrall said, a wealth of understanding in her tone.

Uriah Buckley had said Denny had run away and he had, but Uriah Buckley had not said the reason. Was that because he himself did not know of it, did not know the type of man the son of Edward Elton was – or could it be he did know but didn't care? Questions rushed like storm winds through Amber's mind. But it seemed the man had visited Bescot Lodge more than once: the grooms knew his name. Did Uriah know his nature? And what of that man's nature? He had agreed to her brother and sister remaining in his house, there-fore in his care, but what care had he really taken?

'. . . *the master of the Lodge had given him away.*'

Freddy's words rang in her brain. What kind of man would do a thing like that? A cocktail of anger and revulsion swirled in her mind and she became suddenly, terrifyingly still. She did not want to think that! She did not want to countenance that! Filled with a dreadful fear Amber tried to block the newest thought, prevent it from entering her consciousness, yet still it came, the chill of it turning her veins to ice. Uriah Buckley had not told all he knew of Denny's disappearance from Bescot Lodge – had he also not told all he knew of Bethany's death? He had simply said the cause had been pneumonia but had it, or was that simply another fragment of the truth?

'I've said what I come to say so I'll be takin' my leave.' Already on her feet Becky Worrall adjusted her shawl about her shoulders. 'I thanks you both for listenin' to my lad an' for the trust you says you 'ave in him. As to the bringin' of that Bible, I 'ad no way of knowin' it to belong of you or it would 'ave been brought to this 'ouse the first day of your comin'.'

Bethany . . . this woman had spoken of Bethany . . . no one other than Uriah Buckley seemed to have known of her existence. But that in most instances could be accounted for by fear of that man. With a word he could end a man's employ-ment, take his home, leaving his family on the streets; with that threat ever-present it was no wonder that neither man nor woman admitted to knowing of those children. But Becky

Worrall had heard of both. She had insisted on her son telling all he knew of Denny; had she told all she could of Bethany?

This might be the only chance she might ever have of finding out more about her sister . . . but was it fair to ask? The woman had already taken a risk in doing what she had; should it come to Uriah Buckley's ears that she and Freddy had been to Ley Cottage, wouldn't he demand to know why and should he even suspect Freddy knew of what had taken place in that stable . . . ! An inward shudder rippled through Amber. If a man could give away a boy, make a gift of a child to a man he must surely have known was of perverted nature, then what might he do to Freddy and his mother?

Watching conflicting emotions chase like shadows across the face of her friend, the avalanche of thought behind them was no mystery to Rani nor was the consequence of those thoughts being given voice. Amber's tongue might remain silent but her heart would weep her whole lifetime.

'Freddy's *mai*.' She spoke directly to Becky. 'You helped me when I needed it, though we were not *dost* . . . not friends . . . and though danger lay at your feet as you crossed the heath in darkness yet you came.'

'My son said you was a-needin' of help an' that were all what mattered. I would give help to anybody, friend or no.'

'Then I ask it of you once more. Give your help to one who is friend to me, one whose heart holds friendship for your son and for you.'

Fingers resting on the knot of the shawl tied beneath her breasts, Becky Worrall frowned but there was no annoyance on her face, simply a question, a question she voiced. 'Who be this friend and what be it you would 'ave me do?'

Behind his mother, Freddy shifted from foot to foot, light of the lamp catching the quick gleam in grey eyes so like hers, a gleam which revealed that the brain people held was slow had immediately realised the answer. 'It be Mrs Amber,' he said quickly. 'It be Mrs Amber, that be it, don't it, Miss Rani?'

At the nod of the sable head Becky Worrall glanced at the figure at the table. The wench were white as snow-bleached linen and it were more than sight of that Bible had sucked the colour from her!

'I don't keep my 'and from any who needs it.' Becky's fingers tightened on the knotted ends of her shawl. 'But I ain't seeing what more use I can be 'ere; the book be returned and my lad has spoken of how it come to be wi' us, ain't no more I can add.'

'It is not the book I ask you to speak of but the child,' Rani persisted, 'the girl you called Bethany.'

Striking the woman could not have produced a more dramatic effect. Although she did not move her whole body seemed to withdraw into itself, while above a mouth tight and closed her eyes became veiled. For seconds which seemed to Amber to dance into eternity she stared . . . then without a word turned for the door.

21

Colonel Jervis Buckley stared at the drink Ram Dutt had served him, gin with freshly squeezed lime juice. That man was an excellent *nokar*, a servant of the highest integrity who deserved more than to be just that, a servant of the white Raj. But if Ram did not work here in the bungalow he would need to work in the fields, battling the dry earth to grow enough to feed his family . . . although at least the field he tilled would be his own!

The thought had come often to Jervis when, his day over, he sat alone on his veranda and it came again now. He sipped the cool refreshing drink. Perfectly to his taste as always, but then Ram Dutt performed each of his duties well.

Duty! Jervis's head rested against the high back of his rattan chair. Just what did that word mean? A soldier did his duty when fighting for his country, a man did his duty by caring for wife and children but a job – any job – could that be called duty, and could one man's being at the beck and call of another be termed the same or was that a more acceptable title for servitude? True, those who served on the Army post were not shackled, they were not locked in some prison block at nightfall and each knew they were free to leave whenever they pleased; but free to return to what? To pay half of what they earned to some nawab, nizam or potentate and more recently to have all of what they had seized by dacoits, bandits who swooped down from the hills robbing and sometimes killing those who tried to oppose them . . . but his daughter had not opposed them!

His fingers tightened about the glass and he closed his eyes against the picture instantly invading his mind. Joanna, her white gown streaked scarlet, her arms and hands slashed with sword cuts, her head . . . no! He sat forward sharply, liquid from the glass spilling over his robe. He must not think any more – but how did he stop a nightmare?

'I am being sad to disturb the colonel sahib.'

Taking several moments to still the hands shaking from the horror which had invaded him, Jervis laid his glass aside then turned to the servant whose immaculate white dhoti and turban gleamed in the purple-gold of evening.

Unable to hide the last trace of the emotion which peeled his heart with every onslaught he asked quietly, 'What is it, Ram?'

'It is being an officer, Colonel Sahib, he is saying to see you.'

'Did he say what he wanted?'

'He says only that he is needing to be seeing the colonel sahib.'

'Did he give his name?'

His head tilting side to side, the servant answered. 'No, Sahib, no name and when Ram Dutt was asking to be told the officer shouted I was to stop wasting bloody time.'

One of his officers had spoken that way! Jervis's anger kindled as rapidly as had the memories moments ago. That Ram Dutt had repeated only what had been said to him was beyond question; the man was honest as the day was long. Rising to his feet, he beckoned for the manservant to follow.

Entering a sitting room he felt the gentle brush of air from a large carpet-like fan suspended from the ceiling. Woven of dried grass and operated by a man squatting outside pulling on a thin rope of twine it rustled the still hot air of late summer.

A smartly uniformed young man, moustache neatly

trimmed stood waiting. He saluted quickly but his words came even more quickly, the intervening minutes having left time for him to remember the warning about this commanding officer's ruling of politeness to the natives at all times. 'Colonel Buckley, sir, allow my apologies for my speaking as I have.'

The man had made a mistake and in his own eyes he was paying dearly for it. Having to apologise to a *nokar* was not something he relished nor something approved of by others of Jervis's own seniority; but while he was commander here then the rule would be obeyed. Jervis glanced at the manservant, who gave a slight bow before leaving the room. Ram Dutt had understood; compelling the lieutenant to add more would serve only to sour the situation.

'So . . . what is of so much importance it could not be dealt with by the duty officer?'

'Captain Mason thought it quicker should I deliver my message personally, sir.'

Nerves quickening, Jervis's attention came wholly to the young man, his breathing still heavy enough to denote a ride taken at the gallop. Captain Mason would not have sent him unless the matter demanded immediate action. Already loosening the tie of the robe he donned each evening he was alone, Jervis spoke one word. 'Report.'

'The patrol sent north to investigate the disturbance at Najibabad was ambushed. A few men only escaped back to Chandpur, the rest . . .' The officer broke off.

'The men who reached Chandpur, did they say who was responsible for the attack?'

'They said bandits, sir, but . . .'

But it would take more than a band of dacoits to wipe out a company of trained riflemen. Jervis finished the sentence for himself, only saying aloud, 'Do we know where these bandits are headed or did they scuttle back into the hills?'

'I do not have that information, sir, I was despatched with only the message I have related to you, but before I rode away from Chandpur the garrison there were preparing to march.'

Dismissing the lieutenant, Jervis rang the small silver hand bell that would summon Ram Dutt in order to ask for his uniform to be made ready. There were less than a hundred men at Chandpur and most of them sepoys; should they be kinsmen of those bandits would they fight against them or would they turn on their English officers?

Leaving the bungalow his eye caught the two low rectangular structures set deep in the garden; the rising moon played over the pale marble and for a moment he seemed to see again the mutilated bodies taken from the market place of Meerut. Catching his breath, holding it in his throat, he prayed silently. 'Not again . . . dear Lord, not again!'

The Bible which had belonged to her mother had been returned. Amber watched the shawl-draped figure reach for the handle of the door. The story of its being left behind when Denny ran from that barn had been told, yet there was more . . . something Becky Worrall had not disclosed. But she could not ask the woman to speak when the tightening of her features and the quick veiling of her eyes had said she had no wish to . . . she knew though, she knew more of Bethany!

Emotions pulling in both directions at once Amber could find no words; only her eyes as they followed Becky cried the plea: tell me, please tell me!

Rani too watched and as the handle turned beneath the woman's hand said quietly, '*Mai* to Freddy, your heart has felt the knife of sorrow, you know its pain. Will you not lift that knife from the heart of another?'

Fingers still on the handle Becky Worrall paused. Yes, she knowed the knife this foreign wench spoke of, had felt its stab so often after being widowed and felt it yet when folk called her lad daft. It were pain her would have no other woman feel.

'The strike of the knife is sharp and its bite is deep.'

Softly spoken, hardly louder than the tick of the mantel clock, Rani's words appeared to have no effect. Becky Worrall's fingers turned the door handle then dropped away.

'Ar!' She breathed, not turning her head. 'Ar, I've felt the bite, I knows the scars it leaves and I says a woman be better off not bringin' that where it ain't needed.'

Gentle as summer rain, Rani's reply fell into the quiet room. 'Only wounds which have healed leave scars, but those which remain open fester. The poison of them spreads until the body is sick; it is the same with the heart, stab it and it bleeds, wound it and it aches, but to let the sorrow of the knife remain allow it to twist and turn, to slash and slash again and heart and soul are sliced away by its blows. You say you will give your help to any woman – then give it now, give it to my friend.'

'Her be wise not to ask . . .' Turning to face Amber, Becky Worrall's intended refusal died on her lips. It were true what the other one said: Amber Neale's very soul were suffering. Telling her son to wait outside she moved back to the table, the lamp at its centre catching the glint of tears as she sat. 'I were along of Bescot Lodge . . . look, Mrs Neale, be you sure you wants to hear! I means . . .'

The woman's obvious concern breaking through the torpor which had gripped her, Amber nodded once. 'I know what you mean, Mrs Worrall, and I know your reticence to speak of my sister is because you wish to save me from further pain, but sharp as the stab you have spoken of may be the sting of it will heal with time, while not knowing all there is to know of Bethany holds a lifetime of wounds that can never heal.'

'I knowed the way of my man dyin'.' The woman's head

moved up and down in slow rhythm. 'I knowed he died 'neath a caving-in of that mine shaft and I knowed he d'ain't die alone. It be strange to them as ain't never lived through such but the knowin' of the way of his bein' took . . . that were a sort of comfort, had it been I 'adn't been given the knowin' then my mind could never 'ave rested and I sees it be that way wi' you so I'll speak what I ain't never spoken on from the day it were told to me.'

Light as a feather, the scent of jasmine wafting in the warm room as she moved, Rani went to stand beside Amber. She rested a hand on her shoulder and her dark eyes gleamed their thanks at the woman who glanced across at her.

'I were along of Bescot Lodge,' Becky Worrall began again. 'I goes there twice each week for to do the laundry, one day to do the washin' and another for the ironin' of it. There be a scullery maid who always be set to workin' along of me; her were not one as I'd choose to 'ave the workin' with but then paid help don't be given no choosin'. Seems this day her 'ad felt the weight of Fanny Saunders' tongue, her be cook 'ouse-keeper to Uriah Buckley, and her 'usband be manservant. Atwixt the two of 'em they sees to the running of the place . . . but like I says, the scullery woman had been given the rough edge of Fanny's temper and that loosened her own tongue. P'raps it was as her d'ain't mean for me to hear, for her mumbled over the washtub, but as we pounded the linen with the wooden maid anger lifted her words so every one come clear. "They think as nobody knows." Her words followed the thump of that wash stick. "They thinks there be nobody as knows barrin' them Saunders, but they thinks wrong, for Nellie Potts knows; I knows what they kept hid, the carryin's-on in that room. No doubt Uriah Buckley paid extra in their wages that week . . . paid for them to keep a still tongue, but his sovereigns were wasted 'cos I knows and mebbe one day

I'll tell it. One day Nellie Potts might take the comfort o' Bescot Lodge from Fanny Saunders, ar, and her man an' all!'"

Becky's fingers fiddled with the knot of her shawl and it seemed for a moment she would say no more, but then she went on.

'It be 'eavy lifting sheets from washtub to boiler and with the doing of it the woman kept her silence, but once back to the tub with the lift and drop of the maid then her started again. "Buckley knowed the tastes of Elton and that lad of 'is, and that taste don't be just for fancy food and bottles of wine each of which would pay Nellie Potts' wage for a two-year, no, they be different tastes, they be dirty buggers do Elton and his son, they 'as filthy ways and Buckley knowed it. He knowed when he sent for them babbies, knowed the reason, and so did the Saunders, my God let 'em both rot in hell for the goin' along of it. But Fanny and the one her be married to, they was takin' no chance of bein' sacked, drunk as they knowed Uriah to be they still danced to his biddin' and sent them two little 'uns along of that sitting room. A few minutes later Elton's son left by way of the kitchen no doubt wantin' none but the Saunders to see the child he dragged along of him, one who grabbed a book from the table as they passed, a lad of a few years but one as struggled like a fiend 'til a blow to the 'ead knocked 'im half daft. But what them Saunders forgot were Nellie Potts, they forgot her were in the scullery, an' I seen, I seen that yellow-haired little lad 'auled off by that dirty swine an' I 'eard the screams of that little wench, screams fit to turn a decent woman's blood to ice in her veins but not that of Fanny Saunders, it don't be blood flows in 'er veins, it be acid. Her can pour it out on women the like of Nellie Potts, them as be like to lose their livin' should they answer back, but when it come to that babby a'screamin' an' them men a'laughin' Fanny Saunders' tongue lost its use. They sat, the two of 'em, while it went on, the sound of fallin' china, the shouts of Buckley and Elton and that little wench's cries tellin' of her fears. Then there were the bang, that of a poker hittin' against summat, an' that wench flyin' through the kitchen . . . gold were 'er hair, gold as summer sun . . . streamed out it did, streamed behind 'er, but it were 'er little face told Nellie Potts the all of it, that terror-stricken face and little body stripped of every stitch, told clear what Buckley an' Elton 'ad been about. Pleasurin' theirselves, that be what they done, an' it sent a child racin' in mortal fear, racin' to 'er end in the brook—"'

Amber's agonised cry halted the quiet words and as she buried her face against Rani's middle Becky Worrall rose from her chair, her own face showing the stress of the past minutes.

'I said it were better for 'er not to ever be told an' it pained me to be the one to 'ave the doin' of it. Now it be done an' may God in His mercy help 'er to live with it.'

'Wait, Freddy's mother . . .'

Amber sobbed quietly against her as Rani called to the departing Becky.

'Bethany died of a noo . . . Noo . . . sickness.'

'Pneumonia?'

'Yes, that is the word, but the girl you speak of . . . you say her life ended in a brook. What please is brook?'

Once more stood holding the handle of the door Becky Worrall frowned, her mind searching for an easy explanation.

'A brook? It be like a stream . . . a small channel of water . . . a tiny river.'

'Ahh, a river.' Rani nodded her understanding. 'But river is not pneumonia.'

'Nor it ain't, nor did that little 'un die of that disease of the lungs though it be written on the stone which covers 'er. Nellie Potts d'ain't leave off 'er mumblings where I left off speakin', her said more: said as Fanny Saunders' man brought that little wench back, but it were a corpse he carried into Bescot Lodge, a child dead of drownin'.'

Removing the lid of a pot she had carried from the cupboard set in the wall to one side of the fireplace, Rani breathed in the delicious scent of roses. She and Amber had collected the petals from the garden and crushed them with a little olive oil. That had been a day so different from the hours which had passed since the visit of Freddy and his *mai*, the day of the making of rose oil had been a happy one! She had told Amber the legend related in India of how the fragrant perfume first came to be made. Long ago a Mogul emperor took himself a new bride. She was young and beautiful, with eyes the colour of a field blessed with rain, while her hair glowed with the fire of the setting sun. Because of his love for his new wife, the emperor had a channel built in the garden of his marble palace and when it was filled with water had a thousand buckets of rose petals tipped into it. Many days passed in happiness and then in the cool of evening while he walked in the garden he noticed the channel of water built for the delight of the empress had an oily surface; the heat of the sun had drawn the oil from the rose petals. Delighting in the heady fragrance, the emperor had the oil collected and presented it to his bride saying its beauty was such only his queen should ever use it and its name would be called attar of roses. But though the new wife was yet young she was not without wisdom; her husband must be thanked with more than a smile. Dropping to her knees in the garden, her lovely hair falling from beneath its veil as she bent her head, she lifted her hands in supplication, asking he grant her the favour of naming the perfume not attar of roses but attarjehanghiri, the perfume of Jehangir . . . in honour of her husband.

'The empress was wise.' Amber had smiled as the story

ended. 'I hope she lived many years enjoying her attarje-hanghiri, and I hope too the rose petals we are pounding will give us at least a little of the same.'

Emptying the contents of the pot into an enamelled pan and adding a further quantity of olive oil, Rani stirred the mixture, glancing at the figure huddled beneath the window as she did so.

Perhaps the mother of Freddy had been correct in her judgement; maybe it would have been better had Amber not heard how her sister had come to hear death, for from that moment those gold-flecked eyes had held no light nor that gentle mouth a smile. Rani carried the pan to the fire and hung it on the bracket, then continued to stir, allowing the mixture to heat slowly while her glance stayed with Amber. She had done her share with the house, with the cooking and with the preparing of the perfumed waters, but there had been no joy in the work, no interest; it seemed the very soul of her friend had died within her.

She had prayed to Sita. Returning the pot to the table Rani tipped the heated mixture into a clean bowl. She had begged the goddess to help her friend, to return life to her soul, but the prayers had not been answered.

'You should have said the oil was ready.' The clink of the pan being set aside in the hearth penetrated the silence Amber had drawn about herself. Coming to the table, she held a fine muslin bag over a jug while Rani, ladling the delicately scented mixture into it, prayed once more for guidance; but the still-ness in her heart remained unbroken.

22

There had been no further enquiry regarding Edward Elton's death. His newspaper lay unread across his knees while Uriah Buckley let his mind play over that event. The fact that Elton had been well under the influence of alcohol before he himself arrived at the Goscote Club, then had drunk more with his meal, couldn't have been more propitious. It had provided a perfect opportunity for the adding of that poppy juice to his glass and Elton had been so drunk he had noticed no difference as he downed the brandy in one gulp. Yes, it had all gone well, so well even that smart-arsed police Inspector Checkett had found no evidence of anything other than an accident.

Death by misadventure . . .

Uriah laughed low and deep in his throat. The newspaper had reported the findings of the coroner's court, but there had been no misadventure. Brandy and opium was a lethal mixture and he had poured both into Elton; but the man's departure from the world – and from the business – had not solved all of Uriah Buckley's problems: there still remained that of Elton's son. True, the man had not yet enquired into the business he now was part-owner of, but that could not be taken to mean he had no interest. Sooner or later he was bound to turn up at the mine or at the iron foundry; he might prove a sight more interested in both than ever his father had been, wanting to see the books . . .

The comfort of those earlier thoughts, of his self-congratulations, left Uriah with the swiftness of a passing breeze. If Elton's lad should have a mind for more than his dallying with his pansy boyfriends, if the brain in his head were acute as his appetite for other men's bodies, then the altering of the figures in them books wouldn't pass him by!

His head sagging against the back of the chair, Uriah closed his eyes. Having a new partner was a nuisance, an irritation; it placed an obstacle in his path, one which he had recognised could jeopardise any reunion with Jervis. Uriah drew air deep into his lungs, holding it several seconds before letting it out in a low slow stream. Yes, Elton's lad were an obstacle . . . but not one Uriah Buckley couldn't move!

It were one thing to think but it were something altogether different to act. Putting the newspaper aside he rose from the chair to stand looking over the garden Jervis had had laid out. Plants and nature! Uriah felt the tinge of old anger rise in his chest. That had been all Jervis had displayed a liking for; he had showed no interest in coal or iron. Where had he thought the money that kept him in comfort come from!

But that was in the past. Uriah fought off the feeling. Jervis would have had enough of nature and of the Army by this time; soon he would be taking his place here and there would be a new generation, a grandson, a new Uriah Buckley.

Nothing must stand in the way of that! Uriah stared unseeing into the garden, his hands curled into fists. Nothing must be allowed to threaten that dream – not a business partner and certainly no bloody upstart housemaid!

'It is well you bought more bottles.' Rani smiled as the last one was filled with rose oil and tightly stoppered. 'I just hope we can sell them all; I didn't expect so much oil.'

The barrier of silence which had encompassed Amber

showed no sign of breaking so Rani tried again brightly. 'The gift of a Mogul emperor – who could resist?'

Carrying the small glass containers to a cupboard in the cool of the scullery, Amber placed them neatly inside.

'The people of Darlaston are not knowing Mogul emperors,' Rani said as Amber returned to the kitchen, 'the story told in India is a lovely one so we shall let the perfume speak so in its name. We must give it a name which will do that, also a name which speak what a shy tongue stumbles on.'

A name is just a name, was that what her friend thought beneath her silence? Helping to clear the pots and bowls they had used in making the scented oil, Rani hid her anxiety. 'A name given to a child is more than a word; it is a piece of the heart, a gift of love, and that is what each bottle contains . . . a gift of love, and that is the name we should give to the perfume.'

As she took the kettle of boiling water into the scullery and emptied it into the washing-up bowl, the grief which had stayed with Amber through the long night welled so high she hurried into the yard where Rani would not see the blinding tears.

A gift of love!

Working the handle of the water pump she held the kettle beneath the silver stream.

A gift of love!

That was her mother's Bible. She had cherished the book, holding it to her breast long after she thought the three of them asleep, but the tears on that beloved face, the murmurs quietly sobbed, had not escaped Amber. She had seen and heard, yet something felt deep inside had kept her from asking why. And her mother had never told her the cause of those tears or shared with her the whispered words; whatever the source of her grief it had gone with her from the world. But she had left them her Bible, a gift of love to her children, a piece of her heart.

Water pouring from the overfilled kettle splashing over her hand brought Amber back to the present. She must not let Rani see her tears; she had seen too many already and though her words were always of sympathy and comfort a shadow of unhappiness was visible beneath them.

Taking time to shake the water from her hand, pretending the same had splashed her face, she brushed away the tears. Her silence was unfair. Her friend had her own memories of pain and misery but she did not hide away behind a barrier. Indoors again, she forced herself to speak. 'I like the name; as you said, it would help a young man tell a girl what his tongue cannot.'

Plunging the pots one by one into the hot soapy water, Amber tried to keep her conversation light though the unhappiness of the past night lay like a stone crushing her beneath it.

'Leave them, leave the pots and come with me.'

Surprised, Amber turned from the sink, soapy droplets of water dripping from her fingers as she looked at Rani. This was unusual; it was the girl's way to have utensils washed immediately they were finished with, whether they be ones used to make their perfumes or those employed in preparing a meal, yet now she was saying to leave them.

Alarm shot through Amber. Rani had sat with her until after the night sky had turned to pink pearl and that so soon after that attack upon her . . . it was too much! Anxiety showing clear on her face, she asked worriedly. 'Are you feeling unwell? A headache?'

'I have not a sickness nor pain of the head.' Rani smiled. 'I want only you come.'

'But the pots!'

'They do not have legs to be running away nor wings with which to fly.'

'The water . . . it will get cold.'

'Then I will boil more.' Rani dismissed the protest with a shrug of her small shoulders. 'You come, please.'

Rubbing her hands with a towel then laying it aside Amber followed the girl already out of the door. What on earth had gotten into her? Why the sudden need to be in the garden?

Rani had walked beyond the garden to where the out-buildings stood grouped together. Rounding the corner of one she halted. Beside her, Amber caught her breath.

'I . . . I didn't know this was here!'

'I did not tell,' Rani answered simply.

'But how . . . I mean who . . . ?'

'Who can tell where the Lord of the Universe will shed his gifts? We must only be thankful for them. It pleases you?'

'Oh, yes! It's beautiful, but why haven't you shown me this before?'

The girl smiled before answering. 'Rani has not the jewels of a Mogul emperor, the gold of a maharajah is not hers to make as gift; she has only the friendship of her heart. But how to show without making gift? I ask the great God this and he led me here. I heard His voice in my heart and I listened to His wisdom. Now I offer my secret to you . . . my gift of friend-ship.'

At the moment of those last words the sun threw off a covering of cloud, the brilliance of its rays bestowing an aura of gold on petals which might have been fashioned of purest ivory.

'I needed no gift to tell me of your friendship.' Amber pushed the words past the emotion blocking her throat. 'You have shown me that from our first meeting; as for a Mogul's treasure . . . he could have none would surpass such beauty.'

'Then you will take it?'

'No.' Amber shook her head as Rani made to break off an exquisite white rose. 'They are too lovely to sit in a vase; we should let them remain on the bush. They will live longer that way and we will have the added pleasure of looking at them, of enjoying their wonderful scent. Thank you, Rani, thank you for a most beautiful gift.'

Touching one perfect petal, Amber felt the velvet softness beneath her finger, breathed the delicious scent into her nostrils, then, smiling with the delight of it, turned to the other girl. But what she saw snatched the smile from her lips. The gentle doe-soft eyes were filled with a look she could only interpret as uncertainty. Had her refusal to have the roses picked hurt her friend's feelings? Did she think the blooms, lovely as they were, an unsuitable gift? Inwardly berating her own thoughtlessness, Amber bent over the flowers again. How could she explain, how could she convince Rani it was the sheer beauty of the blossoms so white against the deep green of their foliage had caused her to say they should not be cut? How to express the joy of them, of the gift which had eased the sadness of her heart?

'Rani,' she began, turning again to face the other girl. 'Rani, I . . .'

The other girl smiled, removing the uncertainty from her eyes, and shook her raven-dark head. 'Your heart is open to me,' she said gently. 'I read the words upon it so it is not needful they be spoken; I say only that the One who created all things is given happiness by our sharing those we find pleasing.' Breaking off, she walked to the flower-filled bush, cupping a full-blown rose between her palms. 'Please Him a little more,' she said quietly. 'Please Him and honour my so poor a gift by sharing it with your mother and your sister.'

*   *   *

They had clung together beside that lovely bush, Rani half
supporting her while emotion she could no longer hold at bay
poured out in tears. Amber saw the scene again in her mind.
Two young women holding on to each other while one of them
cried. Heavens, anyone passing – what might they have
thought!

The tears spent, she had cut just two of those wonderful
roses, each half-opened, their beauty as yet only a promise to
the world. Tall and graceful on their long elegant stems,
leaves gleaming like fabulous dark-eyed emeralds, she had
brought them towards her face the deeper to breathe the
exotic scent. When a fragile petal touched her cheek she had
felt a tremor rush through her, a slight trembling along her
veins, and then with a crash that might have been a thunder
clap the invisible wall which had enclosed her mind since
hearing Becky Worrall's words shattered and fell away.
Shudders still rippling, she had carried the blooms indoors to
wrap them carefully in paper to protect them against any
hazard of breeze or coat-sleeve brushing against them. Then
she had changed her everyday clothes for the suit Greville had
bought her.

The numbness had faded but in its place had come something which bound her every bit as tightly. It beat in her mind,
throbbed in her heart; it clutched her very soul and Amber had
recognised the face of it. Revenge! Uriah Buckley and the
Eltons would pay for what they had done to her family. After
securing the small green bonnet to her head with a hatpin she
had stared at the pale face looking back from the mirror,
features which, as she watched, had become those of a child.
Her own rich copper-coloured hair had faded to pale gold
falling each side of a small frightened face and blue eyes filled
with shining tears seemed to try to speak.

'Bethany!' Amber had reached a hand towards the mirror,

her sister's name a cry on her lips. 'Bethany.' But even as she touched the cool glass the image was gone and she was staring at her own face.

I know. The thought had followed the shade of her sister back into the silence of some unseen world.

Staring from the window of the train carrying her to Bloxwich, she emphasised it now in her mind. She *knew* the horror which had sent her sister running in fear to her death, she *knew* the men responsible and though it took her own life she would see them damned.

She returned the pleasant greeting of the stationmaster and with a few other passengers left the station, walking quickly to the small cemetery of All Saints.

The flowers she had left a week ago were still pretty, though they drooped in their vase, but the ones placed beside them were fresh and colourful. It could have been minutes ago they had been set there. Amber glanced about the churchyard, experiencing a sting of disappointment at seeing no tall dark-haired figure adding to the turmoil of emotion which already had her heart sore. She would not see Zachary Hayden today: the freshness of the blossoms on her mother's grave said he had already visited the cemetery.

Having put the spent flowers in the bin provided for them and refilled the vase with fresh water from the large rain barrel beside it, she placed the single white rose beneath the crude wooden cross.

Was it possible? Standing in the quiet of the afternoon, Amber stared at the painted name. The teachings of that long-ago Sunday school, the sermons preached in church, the Bible lessons taught by the headteacher of that small two-classroom school, his whiskered face and sharp all-seeing eye adding to the trembling of small children as he thundered the message of fire awaiting the sinful, had ended with the promise of resurrection, of a beneficent loving God who rewarded the good with a life in heaven. Did life in heaven permit the saved to see what happened to loved ones left behind on earth? Could it be her mother knew as she herself did . . . knew what had happened to Bethany and Denny?

'Oh Mother, how can you ever forgive me!' Bubbling up from the deepest parts of her the cry rushed past fingers clenched against her lips. 'How can you forgive!'

The feeling of guilt for leaving her brother and sister had brought that cry, but beneath it Amber knew another equally strong condemnation. Her mother might forgive the first for it was done in all innocence, done so Bethany and Denny would have a home and food, but the other she would not forgive: the hatred that flamed like fire in the heart of her eldest child.

It was a fire only revenge could quench. With her glance on the immaculate flower, the memory of the one she had placed at her sister's grave took its place in her mind. She had taken the rose from its wrapping and as she placed it in the small vase a thorn had pricked her finger and a spot of blood had fallen on one virgin petal. A tiny spot of crimson staining its purity and on the instant it had become a small body, its white flesh stained with blood. That had been when hatred in all its strength had risen in her breast. Her sister had been like that flower, pure and innocent, free of any blemish of sin until the evil of Uriah Buckley and Edward Elton had stained her body with the blood of lust.

Crouching to touch the cross, Amber ran her fingers over the lettering a man her mother had never met kept clear with paint. 'I know you cannot forgive me,' she whispered, 'so I shall not ask. I love you, my darling mother, I love you.'

The walk back along Elmore Green Road and Station Street, which she had learned on a previous visit had once been a lane leading to Sots Hole, a coal-mining and metal-working area now gone, though brisk, brought no colour to cheeks pale almost as the flowers she had laid on those two graves; but the fires of loathing burned hot in her heart.

Nearing the entrance to the station she opened her bag, checking her return ticket was inside, then as she refastened it heard her name spoken.

'Mrs Neale.' It came again and Amber looked up, wondering who it was addressed her. No one in Bloxwich knew her name except . . . a faint tinge of colour at last creeping into the pallor of her face, Amber felt her insides tremble. The dark-haired figure she had looked for in the churchyard, the tall muscular frame, the handsome face and vividly blue eyes . . . Zachary Hayden stood smiling.

'Mr Hayden, I . . .' The words stuck to her tongue and she felt the warmth flush further into her cheeks. 'I had not hop— thought . . . to see you.' The swift correction added embarrassment to that conjured by what Amber knew was a lie. In truth, though in the turbulence of the emotions swirling in her she had not recognised it, she *had* hoped to see him. Afraid the admission would show in her eyes, she fumbled again with her bag.

Zachary Hayden saw the bloom rising in the heart-shaped face. Was it that she did not wish to be spoken to in the street? Was it that she did not wish to be spoken to by *him*? But he had waited so long, had hunted the churchyard 'til folk must think him a ghost; he had wanted this moment so badly he could not let it pass now, let her go from him, have nothing of her save those few words. Searching for something to say which could give no offence, pushing away that which beat with every stroke of his heart, he recovered the smile his thoughts had snatched away.

'I saw from your flowers you had not visited the cemetery.'

It was said quickly, afraid any interim might see her saying goodbye.

Still not collected enough to meet those eyes, Amber continued fumbling with her bag as she answered. 'The flowers you put there are beautiful. It is very kind of you to take the time and trouble, Mr Hayden.'

'Time is nothing but moments of day and night, of light or darkness, pleasures and sorrows. Placing flowers on the grave of a woman who showed kindness to my mother is no sorrow while meeting with that woman's daughter is a true pleasure, one I had not expected to be given today but one which I hoped for every day.'

Hoped for! The words collided with Amber's tumbling senses, sending them turning and rolling all over again. Had he caught the word she had stumbled over, had he used it deliberately to add to the embarrassment flying now like flags in her cheeks? That was a shameful thought! Amber scolded herself. This man would not be so unkind as to take advantage of a slip of the tongue; she might not know him well but that was something her own feelings told her he would never do.

'I had not thought to come myself,' she said, aware of his eyes upon her, 'but with Rani being so kind . . .'

She had not meant to tell him of the rose or of Rani's asking she placed one on the grave of her mother and sister, but once started she could not stop. He had not once interrupted but those vivid eyes had darkened at mention of Rani's brush with an unknown assailant. At least her rambling had not included mention of Uriah Buckley's name; but to have told anything at all and to a man she had spoken with so rarely – how could she have been so thoughtless!

'That was unforgivable,' she said, wishing she had passed straight on into the railway station with just a polite nod to the man whose gaze seemed to take away her common sense.

'I should not have presumed upon so much of your time.'

Blue eyes intense and deep, his fine mouth wearing no smile, Zachary Hayden answered quietly. 'I will never think it a presumption, Mrs Neale, only a pleasure, one maybe I will be privileged to enjoy again in the future.'

The hiss of rushing steam and the shrill toot-toot of a whistle announced the imminent departure of her train. Amber felt relief and regret course side by side. Relief that she did not have to find words to answer those she had imagined held a depth of feeling and regret at her leaving him.

Once seated in a compartment she silently thanked heaven was empty, she glanced through the window and her heart somersaulted. Zachary Hayden stood on the platform and his eyes watched only her.

23

Regret? Fields of stubble, dry and yellow after their reaping, went by unseen, Amber's inner vision blocking them with pictures of the man she had minutes ago said goodbye to. How could the emotion playing so strongly in her stomach be regret? Why would she feel so personal a response? Zachary Hayden was merely being polite in staying to speak with her. But was it politeness that made him follow her into the station, to stand watching until the train had pulled out? There she went again – giving mind to silly fantasy, fabricating the real for the unreal, imagining what could not after all be fact! Yes, Zachary Hayden had stood on that platform; yes, he had glanced at the train but that did not imply he was there merely to watch her until the last moment: that was her own imagining.

Pull yourself together and stop behaving like a love-struck girl not yet out of puberty! Amber gave herself a sharp rebuke. Like the vast majority of people Zachary Hayden had a living to earn and that being so would not moon about a railway station simply to watch a woman he barely knew. He would have had business there; he was probably waiting to get a train himself.

It had been trickery of the mind. Eyelids pressed hard down, Amber tried to force her brain to clear. She had not really seen those eyes darken as he listened, she had not seen the fine mouth harden or the hands tighten at his sides, nor had he come to the platform only to watch her to the last moment. All of that was illusion dreamed up out of . . . out of what? Hopelessness, despondency, despair for a life gone so terribly awry, for the wrongs she could never put right? Was that what she was doing? Was her mind attempting to create something to replace the wretchedness which ever lay heavy on her heart?

Castles in the air were useless as they were insubstantial. Amber's eyelids lifted sharply. Figments of imagination, daydreams, inventions built out of misery, give them what name she would, they were all a dupe, a deceit intended to fool her into believing the impossible. But what pulled at her now was no delusion, no ruse or trick of the brain, no fraudulence of the mind; what she felt was real as it was painful and that pain was born of yearning for the impossible, of wanting what could never be . . . and of wanting to remain longer in the company of Zachary Hayden.

That final admission was a wind that blew everything else from her mind. She wanted to be with Zachary Hayden! But of all her longings that was the most impossible. Greville had married her out of pity, married her in order to give her back respect in the eyes of the English in India; and Greville had not needed physical love. Zachary Hayden might also pity her but . . . Amber clutched her bag, modesty bringing colour rushing back into her cheeks. She did not want another marriage such as her first!

Still pink with the brazenness of what had sprung into her mind she alighted from the train, passing with other passengers quickly into the street. She would think no more of Zachary Hayden.

'You are not being wise.'

'Perhaps not.' Amber's glance met that of the other girl and saw the concern in her eyes. She felt an immediate guilt for bringing yet more worry to her friend. Rani was afraid for her, yet even so what had been decided was what she must do.

'What can come from going there?' Rani's dark head swung slowly from side to side. 'The page is written and the words will not be being erased, you cannot undo that which already is done. You cannot be bringing life to your sister.'

'I know that.'

Sharper than usual, Amber's swift interruption sounded loud in the quiet of Ley Cottage.

'Then why be going when it is known in your heart it can bring no good!'

Fastening the last button of her suit, Amber paused. There were many things in her heart, some of which would never know peace, and others maybe time would heal; but one she had to deal with herself. That much she owed to her family. Looking again at her anxious friend she smiled gently. 'I go because I have to. Try to understand: only that way will I feel Bethany can truly be at rest.'

The words of the tongue were not the words of the heart. That held only one, revenge; her friend wanted revenge and who could blame her – but should not revenge be left to the hand of the gods? Rani's thoughts showed in her eyes, the hint of them plain in her next words.

'Only the foolish direct their feet to where they know danger waits and only a foolish woman thinks she can stand against a man.'

'But it is a coward takes the easy way. Is that not a saying of your people?'

'It is their saying.' The small shoulders slumped in defeat, the dark eyes glistening with the unhappiness of it. 'You are not a coward, my sister,' Rani answered softly. 'Love for your lost ones has the strength of the tiger, it flows with the blood in your veins; may Sita smile her own gracious love upon you and Rama guard you with his hand.'

It was the strongest wish the girl could make for her protection and deep inside Amber prayed her own Christian deity bless and keep her friend in safety. Shaking her head at the plea repeated once more that they do this thing together, she went quickly from the house.

She had not gone to the rear of the house, to the tradesman's entrance, but to the imposing front door, its polished brass knocker gleaming bright against the dark wood. Her hand half lifted, Amber paused. She had never once come to the front of Bescot Lodge; servants and people of the lower class would never dream of doing so. But she was no longer a servant! The thought added a firmness to the resolution she had made when placing the lovely white rose on Bethany's grave, and which she had repeated over the resting place of her mother. Amber grasped the knocker, sounding it against the door before that firmness could desert her.

'I wish to speak with Uriah Buckley.' She had expected the request to tremble in the asking but each word followed the other in steady rhythm.

As he held open the door Alfred Saunders stared first in surprise and then disdain. It was several years since this woman had been a servant serving under him but her leaving this house had changed nothing. She was not gentry; she had no right to expect the front entrance to be opened to her.

Breath singing through pinched nostrils, the door already beginning to glide shut, he answered imperiously: 'The servants' entrance is to the rear.'

The arrogant scorn, the dictatorial scowl had ever been the rods, with which he had ruled the staff of this house but with herself it had become a parade of power, an ostentation behind which to hide his wrongdoing, a shield to cover the smarting cut of rejection, her rejection! Time and again his hands had tried to fondle her, always seeing to it she was given tasks where he could follow, where unseen by his wife he could press his body against hers. Then one day while Fanny Saunders had been taking her afternoon nap he had sent her to the cellar. Moments later he had been there with her, his breath hot on her face, his frame pinioning her to the wall while he snatched frantically at her blouse, ripping it away, bringing his mouth to her breast. She had tried forcing him away but lust had too strong a hold; panting with desire he felt for her, gasping with the delight it would give both of them, he had half dragged her to the stone floor when she had grabbed the metal candle-holder kept in place on a barrel. It had hit him on the side of the head and she had darted up the steps of the cellar and up the back stairs to her own room. He had not tried his filthy tricks again but then neither had he forgotten; the look now on his face spoke the fact with a clarity needing no word. That same aversion that had so many times choked her rose again but this time her throat remained clear as the ice of her reply.

'Unlike yourself, Mr Saunders, I am no servant.'

Alfred Saunders inhaled sharply through pinched nostrils and glared at the woman who had dared set her hand to the door.

'The master is not at home!' he snarled as Amber rested her hand on the closing door.

'*Your* master, not mine!'

Firm, without the slightest quiver, the words brushed past and into the hall. Had they been heard by anyone other than himself, had someone overheard this woman, this dismissed housemaid speaking to him as she had? Anger fumed on the sharp foxlike features of the butler. Drawing himself to what proved an overwhelming stance with those in service beneath him Alfred Saunders cast a pretentious supercilious glance the full length of Amber before announcing in a voice meant to be heard below stairs: 'Mr Buckley does not receive persons of your kind.'

She had expected no less, but in that expectation was preparation. Keeping her hand to the door, making no pretence of disguising her loathing for the man watching her with smug self-satisfaction, Amber answered every syllable cold as arctic snows.

'But he employs those of *yours*, the sort who prey on young girls.' Dropping her hand from the door Amber gave a frigid smile. 'But perhaps I should go to the servants' entrance, tell your wife of the things you did and probably still do, tell her of the time you followed me into the cellar, yes . . . the servants' entrance is much the better way.'

'Wait!' The hiss slid toward her while Alfred Saunders shot a quick glance at the hall behind him. Then drawing the door back on its hinges he said more loudly: 'The master is in the sitting room. If you would be kind enough to wait here I will enquire if he will see you.'

While everything in her world had changed Bescot Lodge remained the same. The smell of wood polished with beeswax, the softness of carpet thick beneath the feet and the glitter of crystal hanging from an ornately plastered ceiling. She had scrubbed and cleaned every inch of this hall and every other room in Uriah Buckley's house, washed every ornament, made every bed and helped prepare every meal. She knew this place better than any other. The small house at Bloxwich, the bungalow at Meerut, the mud brick one-roomed houses of Kihar and the home of Greville Neale, all were stored in her memory but Bescot Lodge was engraved deep in her soul. This was the house of her brother's terror and of her sister's abusing. Now it would be the house of her vengeance!

The last word was hardly free of Alfred Saunders' lips before Amber walked determinedly across the spacious hall. She knew which room he had spoken of; she needed no guidance and this man's master was having no opportunity of refusing to see her.

'What the bloody hell . . . !' Uriah snapped at his suddenly being disturbed then, as his glance rested on Amber, he growled, 'Nobody sent for you!'

The collected coolness she had shown when answering the manservant stayed with Amber now she answered the master.

'Forgive my not waiting for an invitation but my business could not wait forever.'

'Business!' Uriah barked. 'I does no business wi' females.'

'Not the acceptable kind, I agree,' Amber returned scathingly. 'It is your way to strike a woman from behind and for your dealings with young boys and ten-year-old girls to take place behind closed doors.'

The silence which followed seemed to fill the room with a roar. Standing a few feet from her, backed by the elegant surround of a mock-Adam fireplace, Uriah Buckley's eyes glinted alarm and a balled fist rose as if to strike.

'Get out!' Breath like cracking ice snapped each word. 'Get out afore I 'as you thrown out.'

'Are you sure that would be a wise course of action?' Amber wondered where her courage came from but as long as it stayed she would face this man.

'I don't needs be bloody wise to 'ave you chucked into the streets along wi' the rest o' the shit in this town!'

'Nor to have your own name paraded along with the garbage printed in every newspaper in the country. News of doings such as yours does, I believe, make what is popularly known as "the headlines", and they are certain to live up to those descriptions.'

Faced with the cold aloofness in that voice, the detestation gleaming unrelentingly in eyes of iced fire, Uriah's closed fist dropped to his side. A sharp flick of the head, an unspoken bark to Saunders, had the manservant leave the room but knowing him as she had Amber harboured no doubts as to his standing at the other side of the door, one ear pressed close to its panelling.

'Now then!' Uriah snarled as the door clicked into place. 'I warns you the law comes down 'ard on a woman mekin' accusations 'er can't put substance to!

'A woman making any accusation or a woman accusing a man, especially one of such influential standing in the town?' Amber smiled coldly. 'But I do have the substance you speak of: you were seen riding away from the waste heap of Herbert's Park colliery, seen and recognised; you thought it was me you struck about the head, me you had left for dead, but as you see you were mistaken.'

'Mistakes can be rectified!'

The sheer savagery in the throw of words, the menace in iron-grey eyes, was unmistakable but the long worry-filled days and even longer heartbroken nights spent wondering about her brother and grieving for her sister, compounded by Becky Worrall's statement, was stronger in Amber than any fear.

Quiet with its own threat, her reply was clear. 'Rectified . . . yes, some might be but not those made by you; neither can they be forgiven, but they can be paid for.'

A sneering laugh gurgling in his throat Uriah Buckley glared at the slip of a woman facing him. So that was 'er game, money! 'Er thought to blackmail him. Well, that was another mistake, only this time it were not made by him. Contempt obvious, he laughed again. 'So it be money you wants but it won't be money you'll be gettin'. I told you that

first time you called at this 'ouse. Now I warns you for the last
time . . .'

'Or you will do what!' Amber snapped. 'Give me away,
make a present of me to the son of Edward Elton as you did
my brother, or abuse me as you did my sister until I run naked
to drown in the brook? And before you try any denial I have
proof of that also. There are witnesses to what happened that
night here at Bescot Lodge just as there is a witness to your
assault on a woman at Herbert's Park colliery. No, Mr
Buckley, it is not money I want; it is revenge.'

As if washed away by a flannel the contempt disappeared
from Uriah's mouth, leaving it a thin tight line, the menace
vivid in his eyes becoming a look of alarm before heavy lids
half closed over them.

'Witnesses!' he demanded hoarsely. 'What bloody
witnesses? Tell me who they be!'

'So you can make sure they will give no testimony?' Amber
shook her head briefly but the defiance embraced in the movement was steadfast. 'No, I will not give you their names.'

'Hah!' Loud and triumphant the laugh echoed in the taste-
fully furnished room. 'It be as I thought. There don't be no
witness, there be nobody to raise voice nor finger against Uriah
Buckley.'

'In that case you will have nothing to fear when called to
appear in court. I hope Mr Elton has the same confidence.'

'Edward Elton be dead!'

It was meant to stop Amber, to put a swift halt to anything
else she might say. Uriah gleamed with new-found assurance.

Calm as before, Amber inclined her head once, the simple
nod emphasising the tenacity burning inside her. 'Mr Edward
Elton is. He will be called to answer by his Maker, but his son
is not dead and he will pay in the same coin as yourself.'

Cold and hooded, the grey eyes glinted while taut lips parted just the fraction needed for the serpent hiss to slither through. 'Take care, woman . . . waggin' tongues 'ave a way o' bein' silenced.'

Immediate as it was undaunted, Amber's response was almost tranquil. 'I have no doubt of that,' she said, smooth as syrup dripping from a spoon. 'You cannot have the name of Buckley dragged through the mud. To prevent that you would not hesitate at murder. It is for that reason I have taken the precaution of placing a letter with my solicitor, a letter containing the names of the witnesses to your filthy deed and instructions for your indictment in the case of my death.'

There was no such letter. Amber felt the first tremor of nerves. Nor was it probable the maid Nellie Potts would repeat what she had seen; and Freddy? Any evidence he might give would be dismissed as the ramblings of an unsound mind, while any of Becky's that of a woman defending her son. Beneath their covering of gloves her hands felt suddenly cold and her mouth seemed instantly dry. Would Uriah Buckley believe her lie or would he challenge it, tell her to bring her case before the justices?

In his turn Uriah too was weighing the for and against of any action he could take. He could call her bluff and take the risk of it being a lie, in which case she could go right from this house to a lawyer and lay everything before him now. Should that be so and them witnesses turn out to be real then how would his own word be taken? Either way would be of no benefit to his name. And then there were Jervis, he'd be like to turn around and take himself straight back to India. So there was only one way. The woman had said her wanted no money, but offer enough and there'd be no refusin' of it. Reaching into his pocket he withdrew a wad of banknotes. 'You've made your threats and though there be no truth in them I be tired of runnin' around the Wrekin you sayin' your piece an' me mine so let's get down to the real reason of your bein' 'ere. How much?'

Glancing momentarily at the five-pound notes riffling between stubby fingers, then at the contempt once more evident on that sneering face, Amber's stomach was suddenly a bottomless pit of blazing white-hot anger.

'I have told you what I want from you and from the son of Edward Elton,' she flared, 'but from you most of all. It was you killed my sister, you who gave my brother to be bestialised, giving him over to God knows what perversion, you who are responsible. When I agreed to go with your granddaughter to India you gave your word they would be safe in this house, safe under your protection; but your word, your promise was like chaff in the wind, blown away and forgotten. But mine is not. Listen to it now, listen to a promise I make. I swear on God's Holy Book I will destroy those who took my brother, and as for Bethany, the child you and Edward Elton treated worse than a street whore, the child you drove terrified into her grave, I make this sacred vow. Though it cost my own life I will see you, Uriah Buckley, in hell!'

24

'I threatened I would see him in hell . . .'

Reaction still holding tight to every nerve, Amber recounted her meeting with Uriah Buckley.

'I told him I knew what had happened to Bethany, that his saying she had died of pneumonia was a lie and that Denny had been given away by him to a man who wanted him only for one purpose, a purpose no decent man would ever dream of . . .'

'You said the name of those who brought this news to you?' Rani's eyes were full of apprehension as she turned from scalding tea in the pot.

'No.' Amber shook her head. 'I spoke no name other than that of the Eltons. I said the son of Edward Elton also would be made to pay for what they did to my family.'

Stirring the contents of the teapot, Rani hid the alarm pricking her stomach. Her friend had made a bad mistake in going to that house, in telling the Buckley all she too had been told; he would not sit quietly under such a threat, he would not lose face before the world. He had already harmed a woman he had thought to be Amber and there could be no doubting he would do so again.

'Did the man not ask from where you heard of the things you accused him of?'

It was a question quietly put as Rani filled cups with hot tea but it had the effect of a slap, bringing Amber up sharply. She had not thought of that but now she did it brought a cold touch in its wake. Uriah Buckley had not pressed her into revealing where or from whom her information had come; was it that he had not needed to . . . that he had already known?

'It is not to be thought such knowledge was in the man's keeping.' Rani answered the new concerns trembling on her friend's white lips. 'Had it been he knew there were others with the same knowing would he not have silenced them?'

Consideration of others found no favour with Uriah Buckley, had he not already proved that? Amber stared at the tea she no longer had a taste for. His own welfare, the name he was so proud of, were what he held to be of supreme importance in his life. The name of Uriah Buckley must carry no slur, no shadow of shame must be cast upon it, and if deaths of innocent people were the way of ensuring that then he would suffer no qualm of conscience.

'You must have no fears for Freddy and his *mai* . . .'

'But I have.' Amber blurted her feelings. 'I do have fears for them. Uriah Buckley would never have allowed me to leave Bescot Lodge without giving the names of my informants, he wouldn't have let that pass. How could he? Having others privy to his doings is something he would not live with – will not live with!'

The last few words trickled out, sounding in Amber's ears a testimony to her own thoughtlessness. She should not have gone to Bescot Lodge while revenge was a furnace blasting its fire in her heart. She should have waited, taken more time. Time would not have quenched the agony of what she had learned from Becky and her son! The thought screeched in her mind, providing a cover for the soreness arising out of her hastiness, but was as soon ripped away by the cry of the one following. She had placed those two in danger!

Uriah Buckley had an astute brain. Even if, as yet, it were

unknown to him who had talked of that night, how long would he remain in ignorance? How long before he put the facts together? He would realise only those working in his house could possibly be responsible for relating such as she had thrown at him, that it was gossip from the mouths of those employed in the running of his household. But Freddy was not employed there! It brought a momentary relief to the anxiety rocketing in Amber's mind but in seconds the blaze of it died beneath a newer fear. Freddy was no servant at Bescot Lodge but his mother: she was laundrywoman! Two days of every week, sometimes more often if entertaining had required the use of extra linen, Becky Worrall worked at that house. She would be questioned as would every other employee and though common sense would guide her answers could the same be said of Nellie Potts, the scullery maid who worked alongside her in the wash-house and laundry room? Should that woman babble all she had seen and heard would it not be logical to presume she had babbled it all before? Logic was something Uriah Buckley had in plenty – and it would lead him to Becky Worrall.

'We can be having no certainty of that.' Rani tried to still the fears she heard trembling in every word as Amber spoke the thoughts that had flashed in her head.

Eyes glued to the snow-white cloth covering the table, Amber held the scream inside herself. That was the one thing they could be certain of!

'The seam be almost thinned out, another week or two of diggin' will see the coal finished.'

'How much were brought up last week?' Uriah Buckley tried to keep his mind on the man facing him in the office of the New Hope colliery and the report he was making.

'Like I told Mr Elton's lad, 'twere no more than fifteen tons and three parts o' that good for no more than chuckin' on the waste heaps.'

The half of Uriah's mind still wondering over the visit of Amber Neale snapped rigidly into place. Attention now fully on the yard foreman of the mine, his grey eyes glinting with sudden wariness, he snapped: 'Elton's lad . . . he's been here?'

The prominent Adam's apple bobbed nervously in the other man's neck, his hands torturing the flat cap he had removed on entering the room.

'Day afore yesterday, he come with another man; asked the tonnage and quality an' I . . . well, I had to tell 'im seein' as he be the new part-owner.'

So Elton's lad were not all of the fool he thought him to be. Uriah's brain worked rapidly. He had been here asking questions and he had asked them not of his partner but of a man who could furnish him with the truth as to the output of the New Hope. That truth would illustrate another; this source of his livelihood was all but done, something Elton Junior would not have enjoyed the hearing of. But what would he do about it and why had he brought someone else with him?

'This man with Elton, who was he?'

The whites of his eyes emphasised by the coal dust streaking his face, the foreman looked at the man who could take away his living with a word. Buckley were not pleased and that displeasure were not all to do with the drop in tonnage.

'Can't put no name to him, Mr Buckley, sir, seein' as how none were given me but if you'll forgive the sayin' he . . . well, he were different.'

'Different?'

Uriah's increasing irritation, partially concealed by the seeming indifference of his question, was nevertheless not lost on the man who had seen the same on so many occasions when all had not pleased his employer. Fingers throttling the cap, he answered cautiously.

'The manner of him, his clothes . . .' The foreman hesitated. How could he put it? How could he say one were dressed like a dandy while the other were dressed as Buckley himself.

'Clothes!' Uriah repeated the word, the razor edge of warning cutting it from his tongue.

Swallowing hard, the bob of Adam's apple sliding up and down his thin neck, the workman dropped his glance. 'They . . . they was different to Mr Elton's. His were more . . . more fancy like but his companion wore a dark suit and tie rather like yourself and his way o' speakin', well, I can only say he were a man who knowed what he were talkin' of.'

'Explain!'

It was a cannon shot, loud and lethal, and it had the foreman jump in his boots.

'He . . . he asked how long the coal seam were like to last and when I told him he asked about the quality of the stuff comin' to the surface. Then he said they should look to the books an' they went across to the office. That be all I knows 'cept the clerk were sent packin', sacked on the spot by Mr Elton.'

Elton had sacked the clerk! Dismissing his workman, Uriah strode to the window but the busy scene spread before him made no impact on a brain seething with anger. That little pile of shit had sacked the office clerk without consulting him! And the books, he had looked at the books; so let him, he would find nothing, at least not in the set kept here. But that were not the wasp buzzing in his mind right now. There were another and that one were set to sting.

Who was it had come with Elton? Driving home, Uriah continued to be plagued by questions. Why had they come to the New Hope – why had he himself not been approached? But he had not, not even on the matter of sacking the clerk.

Worrying as summer gadflies, questions to which he had no answers flitted in and out of Uriah's brain. Why now were Edward Elton's son, that bloody little shirt-lifter, taking an interest in the business he couldn't suffer even to talk of while his father were alive?

The grind and screech of a steam tram setting away from the Bull Stake had his horse backing into the shafts. Snatched from his thoughts, Uriah wrestled the frightened animal, taking several minutes to calm it, then swore loudly, giving vent to his dislike of newfangled transport. Folk who couldn't afford the keeping of a horse and carriage should use their feet!

Feet! Uriah's face was grim as he set the horse to a steady walk. Young Elton were feeling his feet . . . or were it the man feeling the little tart's arse whose feet were on the ground? Whichever, it were New Hope ground they trod on, Uriah Buckley's ground! Teeth clamped hard together, Uriah flicked the rein. They were feet which must needs be shifted!

The day's work finished, Amber tried to relax but her body refused. Taut with anxiety the busy day had not vanquished, she sat upright in the chair she and Rani had covered with pretty flower-strewn cloth. 'I acted without thinking,' she said, the worry in her mind clear on her face. 'Now Freddy and his mother are in danger.'

'You think the *pita*, the father of the Colonel Buckley, would truly revenge himself upon them?'

'I am absolutely positive and you would be too had you seen the look in his eyes. They held more than hate or fear; they held what I could only call desperation.'

'It can be understanding.'

'Yes, of course it can be understood,' Amber returned. 'He has so much to protect; but understanding is not a reason for allowing him to harm others.'

'Then others must be warned.'

Amber's hands moved restlessly in her lap. That was the obvious thing to do, the practical thing. But how?

'Neither of us know where the Worralls live and there can be no telling when or even if Freddy will come here again, so how can we warn them?'

'They can be known in the village.'

Despite the tension stringing her nerves, Amber's mouth curved to the fleeting touch of a smile. Rani's acquiring of the English language was to be applauded but it was not yet completely mastered. Darlaston could hardly be called a village.

'It is quite likely people in the town will know where the Worralls live,' she answered, 'but should word of our enquiry reach Uriah Buckley's ears, he will have little doubt it was Freddy and his mother who told us of what was done to Bethany and Denny; and knowing that he will most certainly strike at them.'

'You are speaking wisdom I did not have.' Rani's head swung gently from side to side in the manner of so many of her own people. 'Evil is not governed by the place of being born; the *pita* of the Colonel Buckley is as wicked as the man who took my body and his heart is black like the heart of the wife of Gopal.'

Amber closed her eyes against the truth of her friend's words and leaned at last into her chair, weariness weighing each limb. Yes, Uriah Buckley was evil, his heart was filled with it. He would do his utmost to prevent the Worralls speaking again of that night, then he would turn his malice against herself and Rani also; and this time there was no Jaspal to defend them, no Greville to rescue them.

'The darkness of fear is keeping light from your mind. Let your heart speak, let it banish the shadows.'

Amber opened her eyes and looked at the girl whose own chair was drawn against the fireplace. Rani should not have to be part of all of this. She should be in her own country, safe with her own people. She had done nothing to deserve being cast out to be abandoned by her family as she had done nothing to Uriah Buckley. He would turn his hand against her but maybe he would not leave her to wander the country, maybe he would see her also dead! That too would be the fault of Amber Neale; she could have refused to have the girl come to England. Greville would have agreed had she pointed out how lonely the world is when none of your own people share it with you. But she had not refused and now Rani too was in danger.

'I have tried to think clearly.' She sighed heavily. 'But I can't rid myself of the thought of what could happen to the Worralls and . . . and to you.'

'Do not be sad for me.'

'How can I not be!' Amber's cry, filled with the stress of the day, rang round the quiet room. 'Were it not for my selfishness you would not be here, Uriah Buckley would never have known you.'

'And Rani would have no *dost* and no *behen*. You are my *dost*, my friend, you are my *behen*, the sister of my heart. Your grief is my grief, your pain my pain. We have journeyed far together and always it was because I wished it so. Do you truly think I could not have left you in those desert wastes, slipped from your side in the forest thickness or hidden from you in those mountain foothills? No, Amber my sister, it is not your selfishness causes me to be here, it is mine.'

'Oh Rani . . .' A sob bubbling in her throat, Amber reached out her hands to the other girl, who smiled as she took them in her own.

'Now,' Rani said when both of them had calmed their

emotions. 'We must find a way of removing the worry which keeps the smile from your face.'

'There is no way. I've thought and thought until my brain is turning somersaults.'

'Summer salts?' Rising to her feet, the Indian girl frowned. 'What is being these summer salts?'

Despite the millstone of dejection pressing heavily on her, Amber smiled.

'Ahhh! Now I am knowing.' Rani's light laugh following Amber's explanation was like a ray of sunshine after rain. 'The brain it often jumps about like the cricket in the grass, and though *chai* will not quieten the cricket it will help quieten the brain.'

The tea, hot and sweet as Rani preferred, was welcome but while it soothed it did not provide any lasting solutions. If only Freddy would come she could explain, tell him that for his safety and that of his mother they must leave Darlaston. But hoping and wishing were useless. Returning her empty cup to the tray set on the table, Amber's shoulders slumped.

'Your brain is still as the cricket?' Rani caught the droop of the shoulders.

'I can't help it. I've thought of everything but nothing offers a way out.'

Placing her cup too on the tray Rani swung her head gently. 'The frog in the lily pond jumps from one pad to the next and then to the next until he finds the way to leave the water; he does not give up. You must be as the frog, you must go on trying until you also find the way.'

Hazel eyes reflecting despair lifted to Rani. 'It's no use. I have made promises I cannot keep. Money is power in this country; Uriah Buckley and the son of Edward Elton both have money and I have none except what we have made from selling our perfumed waters. Therefore I haven't strength enough to keep the vow I made to avenge my sister and brother.'

Soft as summer breezes Rani's murmured reply brushed the silence of the pretty living room while her face radiated the measure of some inner conviction. 'Turn to Him who is All Powerful,' she whispered, smiling. 'He will hear the sorrows of your heart and His face will not turn from you. Speak to Him of that which is deep within your soul and He will send His help to you.'

25

Let your heart speak, let it banish the shadows.

Preparing for bed, Amber heard the words again in her mind. Rani usually gave such sound advice but this – she pulled the brush through a tumble of rich red-gold hair – how was her heart to speak, how could it banish the shadows? But in the other thing she had said Rani had been right. There was a darkness in her mind, one so dense it blotted out everything other than her fears for the safety of that young lad and his mother.

Laying the hairbrush aside she turned towards her bed. There had to be a way, a way of alerting Freddy and Becky, but that way was hidden from her.

Ending prayers she had not thoroughly concentrated on, prayers she had made to the Almighty yet in her heart knew He could not grant, she blew out the bedside candle, a whisper on her lips as she settled on the pillow.

'Help me, mother. I'm so lost, show me what to do, show me the way.'

Beyond the window a streak of silver moonlight slipped between storm-grey clouds and in its gleam the tears on Amber's cheeks glittered like crystals.

How long had she slept?

Eyes wide, brain perfectly clear, Amber stared at a sky paling with the first flush of dawn.

Before sleeping she had prayed; she had asked God was it wrong to want to bring Uriah Buckley down. She had asked it over and over, listening in her heart for an answer, then when it hadn't come had added: If it is not wrong let me be given the way; and in the hours of her sleeping the answer had been given. But it had been no whisper of her mother's, that beloved face had not smiled back at her from the dreams. The figure which had filled her sleeping world had been tall, the hair tipped with grey and the clothes a scarlet uniform; Greville, holding out a velvet-covered box . . . Greville had shown her the way.

Slipping from the bed and lighting the candle, she carried it to where a travelling trunk stood against a wall. Setting the candlestick beside it, she lifted the curved lid. She had not touched the contents since packing them in Greville's house on that Army compound in India. Fine cottons gleamed their colours, pinks and blues, soft cream tinted gold by the sprinkling of candlelight; these were the dresses Greville had purchased for her to wear those weeks before leaving India, dresses that gave her back her identity but yet did not make her acceptable company to some officers' wives. But that had not altered Greville's acceptance of her and his kindness had never faltered. Then on the eve of their wedding day he had given her his marriage gift.

She reached between the folds of the gowns she had not worn since leaving India until her fingers fastened on the box secreted low in the chest, the box Greville had held out to her in her dream.

Carrying it along with the candlestick back to bed she let it lie a moment on the covers. This was Greville's gift to her, the one thing of value he had owned, yet he had given it to her.

Opening the velvet-covered case she blinked against the flash of green fire.

'*It was a kind of medal, I suppose . . .*'

In the silence of memory Greville's voice spoke.

The regiment was preparing the ceremony with which it honoured the Queen's birthday. The Rajah of Fathepur always attended. It was seen as an exhibition of his friendship but we soldiers knew it was simply an exercise undertaken to keep the British Raj from delving too deeply into his affairs or his territory. Usually he was not accompanied by any member of his family but that year he brought his son. The crown prince had begged to be allowed to attend and once at the camp asked if he could watch the final rehearsal. He made a fine picture in his gold brocade tunic and turban covered with jewels and you could be forgiven for thinking him already rajah, he stood so straight and proud. The first ranks marched by rifles at the slope, feet and hands moving in perfect rhythm as they followed behind the regimental band. From where I stood I could see the lad on the podium, the flash of gems as his hand rose to his brow copying the salute of the colonel, but it was not the flash of rubies or diamonds that gave the warning suddenly thick in my chest, it was the dull shine of steel. A sepoy we found afterwards was in fact a dacoit, a rebel from a band recently operating from the hills. He had strangled one of the men, taking his uniform, rifle and a couple of rounds of ammunition; then taking the soldier's place in the parade, broke ranks. The flash I had seen was his moving his rifle to the firing position. I remember the strange feeling; it seemed the world was suddenly devoid of sound. The smell of horses, of polished leather and metal, of the men's uniforms and arms, the dry dust thick in the throat, the regulated march of feet; everything was as it should be yet everything was wrong. I remember looking again towards the podium. The boy, so small beside the colonel, still had his hand raised to his brow in salute. The gold of his splendid costume, the scarlet of officers' uniforms bathed in the brilliance of the morning sun, seemed unreal, a picture in a book; they seemed to hold the senses, to hold the brain in invisible bonds, and in this unreality every-thing moved slowly, so slowly it could have been the earth had stopped revolving. Then in the miasma of heat and silence the rifle barrel moved again and the glint acted like cannon fire, shattering that strange enveloping silence; and in the instant I realised what was truly happening. The sepoy was no soldier but an assassin bent on murdering the prince. There was no way of giving warning, the band or shouts of command would have drowned a cry and no one could have reached that boy before a bullet; so I did the only thing left for me to do: I stepped in line of the rifle.

Deep in the memory Amber saw the hand touch a shoulder, saw Greville's smile as he looked at her, then the soundless words went on.

The maharajah came to my bedside after the bullet was removed from my shoulder. He thanked me for saving the life of his son, then took the jewel from the front of his turban and pinned it to the bandages swathing my chest. It was a paltry reward for such bravery, he said, and though it could not be so precious to me as would be a medal given by my own great queen he hoped I would accept. Now I offer it to you . . . a gift for the woman who is to be my wife. Use it as you will, my dear.

Use it as she would! Propped against the pillow Amber looked at the jewel in its box, beams of light flashing from its green heart, brilliant spurts sparkling like a thousand stars from its surround of diamonds.

Yes, Greville had shown the way.

'You were correctly informed, Mr Buckley, I did visit the mine and yes, I did dismiss that clerk.'

Look at the simpering clown! Uriah's thoughts burned like acid as he watched the younger man, a lace-edged handker-chief dangling from long elegant fingers. A bloody pansy who had never done a day's work in his life! A useless lump of—

'Why . . . why did I give the man his tin, that is what you are about to ask, is it not?'

The high-pitched voice broke across Uriah's mental outburst but the vehemence of it resounded in the sharp, 'Yes it bloody well were! What the hell gives you the right to go sackin' anybody at that mine?'

An affected turn of the hand, a smile which hid none of its smugness, accompanied the answer.

'Not hell. Hell did not give me that right; that was part of my father's gift, the gift of love to his son.'

'Love, pah!' Uriah spat his temper. 'Edward Elton 'ad love for none but himself and a brandy bottle.'

'Mmm!' Expertly trimmed and laced with macassar oil the small head nodded, no hair moving out of place. 'Maybe you are right but that does not alter the fact he was part-owner of the New Hope and that he *did* give to me. I am now your partner; I have as much jurisdiction over that coal mine as you do. Therefore if I wish to give any man his tin I shall proceed so to do.'

'You'll do no such bloody thing!' Uriah's fist banged hard on a delicate rosewood sofa table standing against the matching blue silk striped Regency-style settee, its brass mounts and claw feet glinting in the daylight streaming from tall beautifully draped windows.

For a moment the lace-trimmed handkerchief hung in the air, the smug smile static on the too-feminine mouth, then with a trace of perfume following it waved again.

'Really?' The smile stretched a fraction but the eyes above it gleamed a satisfied 'remember who you are speaking to'. The look, not lost on Uriah, kindled a fresh surge of anger, bringing his fist crashing again.

'Yes, really!' he snarled. 'You'll do nothing wi'out asking me first.'

'As you of course always consulted my father, as you always asked his consent in any aspect of management of the New Hope.'

'We had an agreement. The running of the mine would be left to me; Elton trusted my judgement.'

'But his son does not.'

Across from the languid smiling figure Uriah Buckley's face purpled while his fist closed in a hard ball.

'Please!' A carefully defined eyebrow rose. 'If you are going to display the temper of a schoolboy denied his pocket money then might I ask you do it on something other than a perfectly exquisite table.'

This wasn't the lad he'd known before! Some of the wind had been taken out of his sails; Uriah's fist lowered to his side. He was every bit the nancy boy, more in fact than he had seemed those few times he had visited Bescot Lodge, but behind the foppery and the overdone mannerisms there was what he might almost call a tenacity, a strength of purpose. But whose tenacity and what purpose?

The hairs on the back of Uriah's neck, that silent warning that told him when something was not as it should be, rose now. The one who had accompanied this lecherous excuse of a man! The companion who had gone with him to the mine, was he the driving force behind this new behaviour? The influence at the back of all of this self-assurance?

'You had an agreement with my father.' The handkerchief flicked an immaculately creased trouser leg as the womanly tones broke the sudden hush. 'But I am not my father and his agreement is not mine. From now on you will do nothing concerning the New Hope without first consulting me. I intend to be a fully active partner, Uriah, but of course should that not be to your liking then you can buy me out.'

This dirty little toerag, this filthy cocksucker, was

challenging him: the emphasis as he spoke the name Uriah had made that eminently clear. Throat blocked with rage, Uriah watched the tug of a bell pull, the entry of a manservant into the room, then as he rose the wider smile of Elton's son as he said:

'Do give my regards to Jervis; my father told me he was expected home quite soon. We really must get together.'

Had he imagined an undertone to the 'get together', was it a figment of his own creating, an illusion born of the dislike he had for Elton's son?

Driving away from a house whose elegant trappings displayed no sign of Edward Elton's hand, Uriah clamped his jaws hard together.

Figment or fact, it didn't matter. There would be no meeting between his son and that of Edward Elton!

'You be sure o' that, Mrs Neale?'

'Yes, I am perfectly sure. Thank you for your help and advice.'

'You be welcome. I just 'opes things go well for you.'

Had she done the right thing? Leaving the glass bottle works, Amber felt the apprehension she had fought for the past few days rear yet again. Simeon Pearson had been in no doubt he could produce her designs in glass and, he had assured her, could supply the amounts she required. But was it wise to do as she suggested? The beetle brows had climbed up his forehead like white caterpillars and the grey eyes had shown the doubt he held. He had spoken like a businessman and advised like a father and she had listened but remained of positive mind. Now, making her way home, that sureness was beginning to falter.

The dream had shown a way of solving the problem of Freddy and his mother, but the method? Choosing a seat toward the rear of the tram she took the return ticket she had purchased at the start of her journey, holding it between gloved fingers.

'Be a nice day.'

'Yes, very nice,' Amber answered the conductor as he clipped her ticket.

'Won't go on much longer, though, I reckons we be in for a hard winter.'

'The oracle be at it again . . . Lord, missis, you don't want to go takin' notice of what old moanin' Morris tells you.' A woman's laugh echoed the length of the clanking tram.

'That you don't.' Another took up the call. 'Why, if I had the number of sovereigns to match the number of dire 'appenings he's predicted then I'd be riding like the Queen in my own coach.'

'Now that makes a picture no artist could paint, Maisie in a tarara.'

Amid the burst of laughter the woman Maisie piped loudly, 'Ain't meself that there artist would find impossible to paint, it would be my old man with a sceptre in his 'and.'

'The dropsy is it, Maisie?'

'Dropsy my arse! 'E ain't never dropped a pint glass in his life!'

Maisie's reply set the women giggling again, the rest of their banter drowned beneath Amber's returning thoughts. Rani had listened in silence as the dream had been reconstructed and had caught her breath at the beauty of the jewel but had offered neither help or criticism when asked if the conclusion reached was the right one.

Her gaze on the window, Amber saw nothing of the passing landscape, the workshops and factories, the tightly packed houses lining each narrow street, each coated in soot from the thick cloud of smoke which hid the blue of the sky. It was so different from Meerut; there the sky was an almost perpetual azure that gleamed with the gold of the sun. But not all of India was so different from West Bromwich and Darlaston; the poverty seen here in the Black Country was found there also, people there struggled to find the means to live and here the same. Work and hardship were too often their only gift in life.

'High Bullen, all change lessen you wants to do the trip again.'

The shout of the conductor mingled with the hiss of steam as the vehicle drew to a halt.

'Mind 'ow you goes, we don't want none o' you ladies a-fallin' off the step.'

A chorus of rejoinders answered the man, who managed a smile as he handed Amber to the roadside. Thanking him, she crossed to the other side. Seated on the tram which would take her from Wednesbury back to Darlaston, she glanced at a high wall. Running several yards along the curve of the street, the bright red lettering announced the building it enclosed as The Crown Iron Works, prop. Uriah Buckley. The making of iron had been among the items Simeon Pearson had mentioned as being the main industries of the area. Amber glanced again at the lettering, then with the passing of the tram allowed it to slip away from her thoughts.

For once Rani had made no positive reply. Amber's mind returned to the morning when she had told her friend of the dream in which Greville had appeared to hold out the velvet-covered box. She had made no comment as to the right or wrong of the notion put to her, but the common sense so inherent in that small figure had shown itself clear as it always had.

'The jewel it was being a gift of love,' she had answered quietly. *'It was given with the words "use it as you will" and that is how it must be. Only you can choose.'*

She left the tram, boots tapping on the setts as she crossed the Bull Stake to walk quickly along Pinfold Street with its bevy of carts and wagons carrying a bevy of goods to and from the town.

Only you can choose . . . only you can choose.

The words in her mind beat in rhythm with her feet.

Only you can choose.

Reaching the turning for Wolverhampton Lane she paused. Was what she had done been wrong? The emerald pin given Greville in honour of his bravery, the jewel he had presented to her on the eve of their wedding, had she been wrong to sell it, had that in some way dishonoured the man who had done so much for her?

'. . . it was being a gift of love . . .'

Words spoken so quietly now seemed to shout in her mind. Greville had given her everything. He had allowed her the use of his bungalow, moving himself into other quarters, calling only to enquire after her welfare; he had befriended her in the face of the opposition of officers' wives and shielded her from any abuse the soldiers might have offered. Then he had given her his name, he had married her, and the rajah's gift to him had become a marriage gift to her.

A gift of love and she had sold it! A pang like the stab of a knife shot through Amber's heart. She had meant no dishonour of Greville . . .

A sob choking in her throat, she crumpled against the wall of a greengrocer's shop.

God knows she had never meant that!

One hand pressed to the wall preventing her falling, the other pressed against her mouth, it seemed the pain of the thought would cut her in two. Then of a sudden it was gone and in its place a quiet voice spoke, a voice she had at first respected then had come to love.

'Courage, girl.' Greville's words crossed the divide of death to sound gently in her swirling mind and with it came the same comfort it had brought the many times the regimental wives snubbed her. 'Courage, girl . . . use it as you will.'

Drawing herself upright Amber smiled against the haze of tears collected in her eyes. There had been her answer.

Greville's greatest gift had been the wisdom of his heart. He had seen beyond the adornment of a lovely jewel; he had seen the enrichment it might one day make to her life and through her to the life of others.

A smile touched her lips, and Amber's silent 'Thank you, my dear' floated into that great chasm of silence only love could cross.

26

Simeon Pearson had been so helpful. He had introduced her to a jeweller working in Birmingham's gold quarter, the area of that town housing the trade of goldsmith, and the man had quoted what he thought the emerald worth, which had staggered her.

Fastening an apron about her waist Amber glanced over the collection of utensils that would be needed for the morning's work. Many years of labour by herself and Rani producing flower oils would in no way come within a wide margin of the money she had got for the turban pin but money – like perfume – did not last forever, so work must go on.

'The flowers are being ended.' Rani looked up from the batch of geranium petals and leaves she had fetched in from the garden.

The last – and winter was a long time in passing. Taking the large bowl from Rani she deposited it firmly on the table, then grasping the hand of the surprised Rani said quietly, firmly: 'Leave it!'

'Leave?' The other girl frowned. 'To leave is to be losing . . .'

'Never mind.' Pushing her friend into a chair, Amber shook her head. 'I have been thinking,' she said, seating herself opposite. 'The perfumed waters we have made . . . they are not enough.'

'We use all from the garden, we cannot be making that which does not grow.'

'I did not mean we are not producing enough; I meant the returns.' Seeing the frown deepen, Amber went on. 'The returns means the profit, the money we have left from the work we do after everything involved in producing and marketing goods has been paid for.'

'You will sit in market like in India?'

'No.' Amber smiled. 'Not like in India.'

'Then how do you call market?'

This was going to take some explaining. She had spent half of the night thinking how to say it so her friend would understand, but putting thought to word was not always so easy.

'Rani,' she began. 'Putting the scented water in pretty glass bottles with nicely drawn labels is the way we market our product, the way we present it to the public.'

'Bottles and labels is market?'

'I know it's difficult to understand but that is the way of things in England. It is the wrapping which helps a thing to catch the eye. It entices people to buy.'

She could see the doubt in those liquid brown eyes, read the thought behind it. A woman could not sprinkle wrapping on her sari or touch it to her body!

Deciding explanations were too greedy of time, Amber ignored what she saw. The bottled waters had sold but the profit they brought was not enough to provide a living and she had only a few pounds of the four hundred Greville had left her. That, together with what she had been paid for the emerald, must be put to better use.

'Bottles and labels are one way, advertising is another.' Amber pressed on before the puzzled frown became a question. 'Remember how we found the maker of our glass bottles?

We read his advertisement in a newspaper. That is what we shall do; but not yet, not until everything is ready; until then we shall sell no more perfumed waters.'

It had been difficult for Rani to grasp.

'It is being like house of maharajah!' she gasped, her dark head bobbing from side to side. 'Will women want to be concubine?'

'It will not be like that.'

'But you say house of beauty.'

'Yes.' Amber smiled. 'That will be the name given but it will not imply a harem; it will be a place where women can come to be pampered and their bodies cared for, like in the stories Joanna's ayah used to tell.'

With the speed of a lightning flash Amber was back in the gardens of the bungalow at Meerut, twisting a spray of what Narinder had called 'moonlight of the grove' because of the plant's habit of opening its exquisite flowers at night releasing their heady fragrance. 'For the pleasure of lovers,' the ayah had added, a look in her faded eyes speaking of memories forbidden to the tongue while her charges waited enthralled to hear more of her imagined accounts of life for women enclosed behind the walls of one man's house.

'If it is not being harem then why such name as house of beauty?' Rani recognised the swift passage to the past and intervened before the coming of the pain which followed at its heels.

'What?' Amber blinked, her fingers still moving over the imagined blossom, the remembered fragrance seeming to linger in her nostrils.

A part of her still remained in gardens the scent of whose exotic flowers lay over the hot stillness like some precious perfumed veil, the song of tinkling fountains playing in her ears; she took a moment to answer and when she did her voice held a trace of enchantment those memories always cast over her.

'Because it will be that for any woman who comes, it will be a house devoted to making them beautiful.' The charm of remembered gardens not quite gone, Amber spoke quietly as if words might shatter their splendour. 'Each woman will be treated like those in Narinder's stories, each must be treated as a maharani.'

'But how to do? This house is being not big, it has not many rooms as harem is having.'

'Then we shall not use Ley Cottage.' Amber smiled, her dreams of yesterday faded. She would use the money from the emerald to create her own dream, her own house of beauty.

Eight hundred pounds. Amber looked again at the receipt the bank had given for her money. Eight hundred pounds: it was twice the life savings of Greville Neale. She must use it wisely.

'Mrs Neale?'

Turning at the sound of her name, Amber smiled. 'Mrs Worrall, we were hoping Freddy might come visit, and you also you are both welcome.'

'It don't be safe.' Becky Worrall flashed a quick glance along King Street. It seemed normal as ever with its black-garbed women coming and going from the shops, scurrying here and there like so many ants. But normal was no longer normal; who was to tell who watched!

'What do you mean, not safe?' Amber frowned.

With a second darting look taking in the street, Becky Worrall drew her shawl low over her brow before answering.

'Uriah Buckley be like a bear with a boil on its ars— its backside. I got it from Nellie Potts, 'er says 'e has been rantin' and ravin' like a lunatic these past days . . . but it don't be wise to be seen talkin'. Buckley's money can buy a hundred pairs of eyes.'

'But I . . . Mrs Worrall, I have to ask—'

'No!' Becky's shawl came across her mouth and nose, leaving only eyes stark with worry peering over its edge. 'Like I says, it don't be safe.'

The final words drifted back from the figure already hurrying away. It was not safe to be seen talking. Amber frowned more deeply as she resumed her own journey. And Uriah Buckley was raving like a lunatic – what was the reason? It could only be the fact he was searching for the person who had told her what had happened to Denny and Bethany, and it could not be long before he found out! The woman had placed herself and her son in danger telling her what they had; somehow she must protect them.

But what to do? The problem plagued her the whole of the way to Bloxwich and it still scratched at her mind as she placed flowers on her mother's grave.

'An excellent choice as always.'

Submerged in thoughts of Uriah and his anger, Amber was startled.

'There I go again, startling you. It seems I always do; my mother often told me I was all brawn and no brain.'

A sweep of pleasure adding fresh discomposure to her already turbulent mind, Amber blushed deeply. She so often nursed her few memories of this man, reliving their conversations, her inner vision going over every angle of his face, and now suddenly confronted by him her nerves shook as if she had been caught in some crime.

'Asters . . . they . . . they were the best the florist had, he . . . he said there was not a deal of choice this time of the year.'

'Not in the gardens.' Zachary Hayden smiled easily, though like the woman he had waited each day hoping to see he felt his tongue stick to the roof of his mouth. 'Anything still blooming will soon be killed by frosts.'

'That will be a double problem for me.'

'A double problem?' Zachary Hayden's smile evaporated.

How could she have let those words slip from her tongue? Bending to arrange a delicate lavender-coloured flower which was already perfectly in place she tried to hide her confusion, but when she straightened the bloom of it was still in her cheeks.

'Flowers for my mother and sister – I shall not be able to obtain them so easily during winter months.'

'Your sister, she is also here in this churchyard?'

What was the matter with her? Amber screwed her fingers inside her gloves. That was the second blunder; her brain and her tongue seemed to be independent of each other. Not wanting to answer yet knowing not to do so would be a rudeness, she said quickly, 'No, my sister is buried in Darlaston.'

'Well, flowers are no difficulty. My glasshouse can provide enough for all three. But that solves only one problem and you said you had two.'

'It . . . it's nothing.'

'Problems might be small but they can never be said to be nothing.'

Were they the blue of the gentians which grew wild behind the outbuildings of Ley Cottage, were they the colour of the bluebells which swept the heath in summer, the deep rich blue of forget-me-nots? Being caught by the intense colour of those penetrating eyes was like drowning in a soft gentle sea and Amber could make no move to keep herself afloat.

'Won't you tell me your other problem? Maybe it is as easily solved as that of flowers for your mother and sister.'

It was something she had never felt before; like hauling herself back from some blue wonderland. A long breath blocked in her throat and Amber struggled to overcome the feeling of never wanting to leave it.

'Flowers.' It came on the rush of released breath. 'One problem is the same as the other.'

The return of a frown to those dark brows was the herald of more questions, questions she might once more answer without due caution. Turning towards the church she explained briefly about the making and selling of perfumed waters; finishing as they reached the lych gate with 'it is not very exotic, just a light fragrance to finish a woman's toilette, but now the flowers are finished I'm afraid there will be no more.'

She had not told him all, that should her dream of a beauty salon become reality this problem of flowers, small as it might be now, could become very large indeed; for the garden of Ley Cottage could provide nowhere near enough the amount which would be needed.

'From what you tell me it seems your toilette water sold well. It would be a pity not to make more if it is so enjoyed.'

'Rani and I can only use what we have; the garden is not large.'

They had reached the railway station. She had not noticed he had walked all the way with her and now stood beside her on the platform. As she turned to say goodbye his gaze made her pulse race and the soft tinge of colour flare once more in her cheeks.

'Could your husband not buy extra land? I think he could find more than a few men willing to work it.'

Offering her hand, Amber withdrew it after the briefest of shakes. 'That would not be possible, Mr Hayden. My husband is dead.'

'You can always buy me out.'

Uriah shoved his untouched meal savagely, sending the

plate halfway the length of the long Georgian dining table to crash against a tall crystal centrepiece.

'Get out!'

The snarl directed at his manservant had the man withdraw quickly.

Buy him out. Snatching his wine glass with equal savagery, Uriah swallowed the contents in one gulp. Elton's pup weren't interested in the mine, that much he was certain of, it were the money he could get for his half. Kicking away from the table he grasped the brandy decanter from a sideboard perfectly matched to the table. Pouring a hefty measure he swallowed half before resuming his seat.

Money! Fingers tightening about the cut glass tumbler, he stared at the smug face smiling in his memory. How much of that had Edward Elton left? Was it enough to continue to give his son the lifestyle he was accustomed to having? Was there enough to pay his playmates or was he already feeling the pinch?

Another swallow of brandy burned in his throat; Uriah set the glass slowly on the table, another question entering his mind. Was it one playmate behind all this – the man who had been at the New Hope – was he doing more at Elton's back than simply buggering him?

How to find out? They were hardly likely to go trumpeting their affairs about the town. Uriah nursed the glass. He could go see Edward's lawyer, ask outright what was given to the son apart from a house filled with fancy furniture and a half share in a worked-out mine; no, he rejected the idea. Chances were the lawyer would show him the door. But there were other ways: a paid man perhaps? That idea was shaky as the other; look what had become of using Pickering to see off the Neale woman. No, this was something he needed to think about. Pickering's death beneath a fall of coal had been accepted as an accident, as had Edward Elton's death in a turned-over carriage, but too many accidents could arouse suspicion.

Yet he must know. Leaving the half-full brandy glass he left the dining room, his only reply to the hovering manservant being to demand his carriage.

He could think better away from the house. His hand easy on the rein, Uriah guided the animal toward the Goscote Club. Bescot Lodge with its memories, its miseries and failures seemed to stifle him more each day. Once it had been his pride, it had shone in his eyes, the crown of his achievement, the culmination of his scheming; yet now it seemed more like a tomb, a tomb filled with the comforts of life yet totally empty of it. He had not realised how much Jervis's leaving would affect his days . . . or his nights. Verity he had not truly missed, a retinue of mistresses had replaced her in his bed, but his son, Jervis, his departure had punched a hole that nothing had filled. Prostitutes at night, business of mine and iron during the day; he drank fully of both yet always the emptiness remained. But that would soon end. Jervis would return; yes, he would return and all the old quarrels would be forgiven, the past would be laid to rest, there would be a new beginning.

Bowed into the club by the uniformed doorman, his hat taken by the cloakroom attendant, Uriah entered the smoking room. Choosing one of the few empty seats he ordered a cigar. Selecting the same from a humidor brought to him, he snipped one and then lit it with the match also brought to him. Blowing a stream of lavender-grey smoke from pursed lips, he settled for a glass of claret. More brandy would inhibit his mind and that he must keep clear.

'I see there is some unrest in India, brigands coming down from the hills.' A face bedecked with a beard trimmed and pointed in the style of the Prince of Wales, horn-rimmed spectacles perched on the large nose above it, peered over a lowered newspaper. 'Your lad, has he mentioned anything of it in his letters?'

He had hoped to be left in peace; conversation was the last thing he wanted. Taking a sip of his wine Uriah hid his irritation. To say he had no letters was to illustrate a rift with Jervis, something he had kept hidden even from Edward Elton, but not to say anything at all . . . that would set minds thinking and tongues wagging.

'Some,' he answered, inspecting the ash gathering on the tip of the cigar. 'But nothing near to his post. Seems it is concentrated further to the north.'

'Damned blighters!' The beard bobbed. 'I say give 'em a lesson they won't forget in a hurry, send a force to wipe 'em out, get rid of the lot once and for all.'

'Not so easy to do.' Uriah forced a smile. 'India is a vast country and according to my son a group of bandits can lose itself for months in the mountains with no way of tracking them.'

'Damned ungrateful – the whole population be damned ungrateful!' The newspaper rustled. 'Don't these Indian lackeys realise how fortunate they be having the British run the place, making a civilised people out of a rabble! The Government be too soft on 'em, be my opinion.'

It was an opinion he could do without hearing. Uriah made no answer as the page turned. With luck it was already forgotten. But luck seemed unready to smile.

'I see the price of coal be up by ten shilling a ton.' The paper lowered again. 'Be fortunate for some, Edward Elton's lad being one.'

Halfway to Uriah's lips, the cigar paused. The price of coal had risen. Elton knew the production of the New Hope had fallen but no one else did. If he could sell his share he would do it now before anyone had the chance to find out.

'Elton's lad?' The enquiry, so casual-sounding, had to be forced past the acute tightening of Uriah's throat.

Folding his newspaper with a satisfaction at having an interested listener, the man laid it aside. 'That be who I said, young Elton. He be letting it be known he wants a buyer for his half of the New Hope, but then you knowed that already, you being his partner. Not like his father, that one, he has no time for business.'

No time for anything but his nancy boys! Uriah felt the crab of anger sink its claws deep into his chest. But those words, *you can always buy me out*, had been a taunt with background. There had been a meaning to them: the scab of a man truly intended to sell.

'I suppose you'll be after taking it off his hands, eh, Buckley? Can't see you wanting anybody else having fingers in your pie; best kept to the family, I agree, pass it clean to your son and then to his. Business be a strong chain, it binds a family together.'

. . . your son and then to his . . .

Cigar smoke drifting before his face hid the look darkening Uriah's hard eyes. Jervis had no son nor had he ever shown any inclination towards or even an interest in the New Hope or the Crown iron works; in the instant of its birth Uriah killed the thought. All of that was in the past. Jervis was coming home. He would have sons, sons whose hearts would be in coal and iron, grandchildren Uriah Buckley would be proud of.

'The house be going as well, the lad's father wouldn't have wanted that I don't suppose, but then that young no-good don't give a farthing for feelings other than his own; I reckon it were a mistake giving him everything he asked, letting a son play at life instead of putting him to the grindstone be a wrong thing . . . a wrong thing altogether: Edward worked from a lad same as we all done, pulled himself up by the bootstrings until he were his own master and what for, what for, eh, Buckley? So his son could sell the lot to go live abroad.'

Beech House also to be sold! Uriah held a sip of wine on his tongue, afraid the swallowing would choke him.

'Be enough to have Edward turn in his grave . . .'

The voice droned on like a bee in Uriah's ear.

'. . . a lifetime's labour and that lad of his gives it all up so he can keep his pretty lover in his bed.

'A man can have a mistress but he don't sell up on account of her.'

Removing the spectacles, the talkative man breathed first on the lenses, then rubbed each vigorously with a handkerchief.

'A mistress, yes, but not the sort that be the taste of young Elton. He prefers to play with them as have a tail on the end of their belly.' Holding the spectacles to the light of an over-head gasolière the man inspected them, adding, 'It were obvious enough while his father lived, the fancy clothes an' all, but since that one's laying to rest there be no reserve; walking about dressed like a peacock an' not caring who sees him being handed in and out of a carriage by one bent as himself.'

Replacing the spectacles, nodding as a silent-footed waiter informed him his table was ready, the man rose.

'Can't have a wife of the same gender as yourself, not in this country; that be the reason of Elton's son ridding himself of any possessions. The only one he wants to keep be the man he be taking with him. I can only say he best skedaddle soon afore a few men in Darlaston decide to see him off – and that won't be nowheres on the Continent.'

Yes, young Elton's health would be safer should he leave soon. Uriah agreed silently. People knew his sort of behaviour went on but they would not tolerate it under their noses. It had been a fear of getting their tins had held men back, fear of

Edward Elton's reprisal should his son be harmed, but now Edward was gone and so probably was that reluctance.

Nodding to his departing informant Uriah drew long and slow on his cigar. Elton would know the climate of opinion in Darlaston, he would know flaunting a male lover would not be tolerated, and that would have the dirty little sod running for foreign shores and he would make his move quickly.

Finishing his wine, Uriah sent for the supper menu. He too must make his move quickly, but not so quick as to draw attention to himself.

27

They had laughed and talked, planned and schemed, filling the hours of evenings, with ideas for their house of beauty salon notion becoming wilder and more fanciful until they had reached the totally ridiculous. Palaces of ever more exotic proportions, silk-draped rooms opening into beautiful flower-filled gardens, each with gentle rippling fountains or canals strewn with rose petals; they had meandered through realms of fantasy both had enjoyed but now it was time to return to reality, to plan not the dream but the real thing . . . and to do it sensibly.

'The first thing is to decide on a house. We will need one with several rooms,' Amber said, dusting away the layer of fine grey dust arisen from clearing the grate of ashes.

'How many is being several?' Rani entered the living room with a tray of freshly washed dishes in her hands.

'One for storage and preparation.' Amber's hand paused from dusting the oil lamp. 'But how many for treatment is more difficult to decide.'

'But one only is needed, women are being together like in harem.'

Positioned once more in the centre of the table the rose-coloured glass of the lamp reflected daylight in a spray of shimmering ruby points.

'English ladies are not like those of India,' Amber said with a smile as she crossed to dust the chairs. 'Their toilette is something done in private, not in the presence of others.'

Returning dishes to the dresser, Rani shook her head in a gentle 'it is too silly' movement as she answered. 'English ladies I am not understanding.'

Sometimes she hadn't either. The dusting finished, Amber took the cloth, shaking it in the yard. When she had first been taken into service at Bescot Lodge she had been unable to understand why the housemaid disagreed with the kitchen maid who decried the work of the hard-pressed scullery maid, who then sniffed haughtily at the efforts of the laundrywoman while all of them laboured under the critical eye of the house-keeper. It was like being caught in a vicious circle of jealousy, making life harder than it already was, so it had seemed like a miracle when Joanna Buckley had chosen her to be her personal maid. Jealousy of position was a dangerous emotion; it had driven Gopal's wife, eaten away at her mind until she had demanded another lie beside her on the funeral pyre, hate-ridden jealousy lending strength enough to drag the despised *feringhee* with her into the flames.

That could not happen here but Darlaston, as did the Indian village of Kihar, had its boundaries, areas which could not be crossed and secrets not to be disclosed. Many of the most closely guarded secrets were those of a woman's beauty: the aids employed to disguise the effect of time on face and hair, none of which the wealthy would admit to using.

Watching motes of dust float away on the air, Amber stood a moment before turning indoors. Privacy must override all else in her house of beauty.

They had gone together to see the house, Rani's expression revealing she understood little of what the agent had told them as he moved rapidly from room to room. The clothes had highlighted the fact that this property was far beyond their means. A coffee-skinned foreigner dressed in Western coat and bonnet, and an Englishwoman in an outmoded green suit! Who did they think they were fooling?

Thoughts she guessed had tripped through the brain of the dapper little man showing them the property had been clear to Amber as if they had been spoken, but she had listened and borne the underlying disparagement with patience, hiding her own smile as a disdainful one met her cool. 'We will give you an answer in a day or so.'

Walking now through one of the four upstairs rooms Amber smiled, remembering the look of astonishment crossing the small ferret-sharp features of the agent when she had called asking a contract of sale be drawn up. It had taken a savage bite out of her finances and the niggle of doubt she had felt on paying the required price pressed again in her chest. That had been only part of the expenditure; the rooms had needed to be furnished and women of the sort she hoped to attract would not be impressed by shoddy surroundings. She and Rani had toured the second-hand salerooms of Walsall and even Wolverhampton, choosing the most tasteful pieces, yet haggling interminably over prices; the same with the colourful satins and shimmering gauzes which swathed windows. Every penny spent was a penny less to fall back on should the project be unsuccessful. She must not harbour such thoughts, must not give way to doubt, for that invited failure! But the mental encouragement did not dispel the doubt; it flitted along every nerve as Amber finished her inspection and returned downstairs to what had been a drawing room but was now the reception room. This would be where clients would be shown on first arriving at the salon.

Mr Pearson had been aghast hearing her requests the last time of visiting his glass bottle works. 'Figurines made outta glass!' He had stared at first, not believing his own ears, then at her assurance he had indeed heard correctly, had said, 'Ar, wench, it can be done but do you be thinkin' that the safest way o' spending your money?'

It might not have been the safest but it was the best way she could think of. She looked at them now, arranged in niches black-draped with gold satin overlaid with the sheerest amber silk gauze which, catching the changing light, cast nuances of copper, bronze or gold. This caused each lovely figure to appear as if made of gleaming coloured crystal which played its beautiful beams over chairs and couches upholstered in blue and cream striped silk. She and Rani had scrubbed these until the cloth was clean as new and the legs looked polished as the day they had first left the workshop. Now, their reflection shining from a floor worked on equally hard, they spoke of a refined elegance. The sitting room, now the room where clients would be introduced to the treatments and products from which to make their choice, had been decorated with the same care and thought, the figurines being repeated on perfume bottles and jars of scented creams while the dining room had become the office and the kitchen given mainly to preparation. But preparation of what? Amber's nerves twittered again. The garden was empty; it would be that way for months. Not until late spring would there be the first flowers she and Rani could use, but even given those flowers how would they find the time to distil the oils from them? She had done exactly the thing her mother had so many times warned against: she had jumped into the water without knowing its depth!

But it was done and there was no going back. Walking away from the house set amid an acre of lawns and bushes she drew a long breath. Here was another concern. How were they to keep these approaches to the house neat and tidy? First impressions! She released the breath. They could make – or they could break. If the outside displeased then clients would not wait to find what the inside held.

Young Elton had offered his half of the New Hope for sale! Uriah's fingers drummed the surface of the large desk dominating the study of Bescot Lodge. Tittle-tattle had it Beech House were already sold to some buyer or other but then gossip in this town were as sturdy as butter placed in the sun: it had melted away when questioned by himself. But the selling of Elton's share of the mine, that were as near the truth as a tanner was to a sixpence, they were both the same. It were no idle chatter going around Darlaston, it were the truth, and should it be sold . . . !

Unlocking the lowest draw of the desk, he withdrew a large book. This were the true record of the money made out of the product of that mine. He fingered the black cover. Only this book had account of the profit made and the share given Edward Elton, the share that nowhere approached the fifty per cent the man had believed he was getting. Should this volume ever leave this room he, Uriah Buckley, would be known as a thief, a man who had for years robbed his partner, but with this evidence burned any finger raised could be pointed in the direction of the clerk young Elton had dismissed.

Taking the ledger to the fire, Uriah fed each page separately to the flames before placing the stiffer cover on the coals and watching it become slowly devoured; then relocking the desk drawer and pocketing the key left the house.

The New Hope was worked out, the last of the coal once rich in its seams wasn't worth the hauling up. Should Elton be lucky enough to offload his share then the buyer would soon learn his money had drained into empty ground. That would mean his own share, being about as much use as a tinker's cuss, was worth not a penny. But put his half to that of Elton's half, sell the mine as one piece . . . that way he could get as much as Elton did. It might not be a great amount but it would be more than he could wring out of a mine without coal. The New Hope would be a millstone about the neck of any owner and that necklace must not adorn the throat of Jervis Buckley. Get half the mine sold and there wouldn't be another fool found to buy the rest. But any move must be well thought out; it wouldn't do to go off half cocked. Leaving the house, Uriah drove on towards the mine. The money a sale made he would invest in iron, expand the works, make it the biggest in the Black Country.

'You chose well the name, it truly is a house of beauty.'

'I must admit it does look much better than ever I hoped, seeing everything in it is second-hand.'

Looking up from the pan she had lifted from the oven Rani frowned.

'What is being two-hand?'

Setting knives and forks beside both plates Amber reached for the mint she had chopped and mixed with vinegar to which she had added a teaspoon of sugar dissolved with hot water. Placing the small jug on the table she replied: 'It isn't two-hand. It means something which belonged to someone before it belonged to you.'

'Your voice it was saying this second-hand is being not good . . . why?'

Placing a small spoon beside the jug of mint sauce Amber admitted there was no denying the tone of her voice had carried that meaning. 'The women that I hope will come they . . .' She paused. Why was explaining the ways and customs of this country sometimes so difficult? 'The women,' she tried again, 'those with money to spend on beauty products, they . . . they will expect everything around them to be new and beautiful.'

Spooning potatoes onto plates, Rani thought a moment before saying. 'Those who think only new is beautiful are having great sadness for their eyes know only blindness and their soul is empty. Is not gift, this second-hand? Did it not first belong to one who bought it to give to a loved one?'

Logical as it was sensible, Rani's question provided its own answer. Her friend would have made a very good prime minister. Lifting lamb chops from the oven Amber smiled to herself . . . now that *would* be something new! She concealed her smile at such an incredible notion and took her place at the table.

'So what names will we give to our products?' She asked the question quickly, changing the subject before Rani asked more questions on the subject of second-hand. 'I think each cream and lotion in which the same oils are used should form one range, all have the same name, do you agree?'

'The flower which gives its oils could give also its name.'

'Mmmm.' Amber nodded, chewing on a potato.

'But flower name is being second-hand?'

Oh Lord! Amber swallowed the food in her mouth. This was going to be difficult.

'No.' She shook her head, her own glance meeting the gentle brown one. 'Flower names are good, it's only that they are not . . . not . . .'

'New?'

Rani's smile hidden from her lips played in the depths of her velvet eyes and seeing it Amber laughed. 'For that bit of teasing, miss, you can wash the dishes all by yourself.'

'Then I will be giving the name of dishwater to one of the perfumes.'

'It will sell like crazy and we will both be rich as maharajahs.'

'We will bathe morning and evening in the deliciously scented dishwater and be the envy of every maharani.' Rani's laugh joined to that of Amber and for several minutes the banter flowed back and forth, each idea bringing fresh giggles until both of them were gasping for breath.

'Come on,' Amber said finally, 'let us both try the so-fragrant dishwater and get these dishes washed.'

Later, dishes put back in place on the dresser, the fire banked for the night, Amber looked at the glass containers she had brought in from the scullery which now stood on the table, the light of the lamp striking a rainbow of colours from their depths. Simeon Pearson had created more than a mere jar or bottle. Each was a thing of beauty; the lines of a gown flowing like ripples of water over a body the shape of which might have been a painting on canvas, the delicate features of a face caught in a half smile could have been the work of Michelangelo; but it was the hand of Simeon Pearson had crafted them, the hand of an artist in glass.

'Yes, they have great beauty.' Replying to the remark Amber had not realised she had breathed Rani took one of the bottles, holding it on the palm of her hand, watching the lamplight dance across the facets of its surface.

Too beautiful for dishwater, maybe even too beautiful for the perfumes they were intended to hold. Amber watched the spears of colour lance from the glass. How could they hope to find names fit for such works of art, how not to mar the beauty Simeon Pearson had achieved?

'She is like Sita rising from the sacred Ganga Mai.'

It was a whisper but the awe registered in it echoed that of Amber's own feelings. The tiny figure which was the stopper did indeed appear to be rising from a river, the disturbance of its waters seeming to give birth to a slim form standing in a seashell while trickles of itself ran from waist-length hair over graceful limbs to rejoin the spouting turbulence beneath the feet. It was a miniature version of one of the figurines she had placed in niches when decorating the house they were turning into a salon; in fact each of those glass statues was echoed either as a raised relief around the body of a jar or as the stopper of an equally lovely bottle, each a thing to be treasured, each an inspiration.

'Venus! Of course – that is Venus!'

Returning the small bottle to stand with the rest Rani cast a puzzled glance at the smiling Amber. 'What is being Venus?'

'Not what: who.' Amber's eyes glistened bright as the light-enhanced glass. 'It was a painting in the drawing room of Bescot Lodge, a woman standing on a great shell which floated on the sea. She was so beautiful, long golden hair falling down over her body. Whenever I got the opportunity I would stand and stare at that picture. Then one day Joanna saw me and told me it was a copy of a painting by an artist called Botticelli. It was his study of the Roman goddess Venus, who was reckoned to have been born fully grown to womanhood out of the Mediterranean Sea off the island of Cyprus.'

'Born already being woman?'

'It is just a legend.' Amber smiled again. 'A story told by people who lived hundreds of years ago. They believed in the reality of gods and goddesses.'

'As I know Rama and the blessed Sita?'

Her glance still on the lovely liquid figure, Amber nodded. Rani clung to the religion of her people. It was one bit of India she could have with her always and one Amber would never attempt to take away.

'She is being beautiful, this Venus of Romans, so the perfume she holds must be beautiful also, maybe violet.'

'No, not violet.' Amber shook her head. 'Venus was thought to be the goddess of love, a perfume named for her should be voluptuous, sensual . . . it should breathe the passion of a lover.'

'As the petals of the rose strewn on water spoke the love of a maharajah for his Persian bride.'

'That is it exactly,' Amber said, touching the tiny exquisite glass figure.

'Then would not the rose perfume be good choosing for the Venus to hold?'

Pausing briefly, her glance caressing the pretty container, Amber replied. 'Rose will be perfect and the name Rose of Persia, do you like that?'

'I think it is being a good name.'

'Then what about this one?' Amber took another of the bottles, holding it, as Rani had, balanced on the palm of her hand. Rectangular in shape, the corners of its sides planed along its length, the front of the body encompassed a large oval within which, chased on the glass, spirals of air fanned outward and upward, curving about a figure which appeared to rise from them, the arms held as though reaching out towards a lover while the head, slightly uplifted on a slender neck, seemed to be welcoming a kiss.

'She also is being beautiful.'

'But not a Venus,' Amber said softly. 'She is more like a spirit of the air, she enchants . . . captivates, she creates desire. The perfume she holds should be an elusive fragrance, one which whispers of shadowed gardens, of arbours where only the murmurs of lovers are heard above the sighing of the stars. It should be the essence of desire yet seductive as silver moonlight.'

Those were the thoughts and words of a woman in love. Rani held the thought close in her mind. They were words she had never heard Amber speak before. Could it be they did not arise from memories of the man who had been husband to her friend but were words that whispered of another! The man who had brought flowers to the resting place of her mother, the man she had named Zachary Hayden. Was Amber in love with Zachary Hayden? Watching the face intent upon the glassmaker's lovely creation, Rani felt the cold tip of apprehension touch her heart. Should it be as the thought said and should Amber become wife to the man, where would be a place for Rani? She could not live here in a land of strangers; but would the land of India be any more happy for her? Was she not an outcast, despised and wanted by none?

'It must call to the senses . . .'

Amber spoke again and Rani pushed her thoughts aside, but she knew they would remain waiting in the shadows to plague her heart in the hours the sun was gone from the sky and the darkness of night stalked her room.

'. . . play on the heart like the spell of a full moon.'

'Your words are those the people of my country say when they speak of the jasmine, when they call it moonlight of the grove.'

Returning the bottle to the table, Amber smiled a moment. 'Jasmine is a delicate flower and the name your people give it is the same. It is delicate as the kiss of moonlight and that is what we will call the perfume: Moonlight Kiss.'

They had at last thought of names for the remaining bottles, matching each to a pot which would hold cream that had the same aroma. They had giggled at the more outrageous, hummed and aahed over the more sensible, choosing and discarding until finally both were satisfied. Dressed in her cotton nightgown, rich copper hair plaited and tied with white ribbons, Amber drew back the covers of her bed. She blew out the candle on the small bedside table; instantly the room was filled with silver radiance. The full moon. Amber stared at the small-paned window. The kiss of moonlight! Smiling as the words returned to her mind, she crossed barefoot to the window. Drawing back the curtains, she lifted her face to the lambent glow. The kiss of moonlight! But that was not the touch she imagined now against her lips. It was no beam of the moon but the brush of a man's mouth, the kiss of Zachary Hayden.

28

'You can always buy me out.'

Uriah whispered savagely beneath his breath. That no-good bloody fairy, that nancy boy Elton had called a son, had dared to laugh at *him*, at Uriah Buckley! 'Well, you little arsehole lover,' he muttered, opening a drawer of his desk, 'you are in for a big surprise . . . a very unpleasant big surprise!'

'Did he say what he wants?' Irritated at being interrupted, Uriah barked the question.

Standing a few feet from the door of the comfortable study the manservant answered hurriedly. 'He gave only his name sir, Detective Inspector Checkett.'

'Bloody nuisance!' Anger served as a cover for the quick tightening of Uriah's nerves. Why had this man called again? Had they come up with something that could link him to Edward Elton's death?

'Will I tell him you are not at home, sir?'

'What? No, no, that'll just have him back here tomorrow.' Uriah emphasised his irritability with a scowl that hid the flicker of alarm shooting along his veins. 'Best show him in . . . and Saunders.' The manservant turned. 'If the man don't be gone in five minutes then I have a previous and important appointment.'

'I understand, sir.' Beyond the door Alfred Saunders smiled to himself. He understood very well. Uriah Buckley had a touch of the jitters and well he might have; there was a lot had

gone on in this house he wouldn't want the bobbies ferret-
ing into.

Dressed in the same black suit, the same notebook in hand,
Detective Inspector Charles Checkett glanced at the man who
had not invited him to sit. But that was not new; he hadn't been
offered a chair during his last visit to Bescot Lodge; and
neither was Uriah Buckley's behaviour anything new. There
was the same underlying hint of nervousness the loud voice of
irritation couldn't quite hide, the same guarded look he had
seen when enquiring into the death of Edward Elton: but why?
The inspector's mental nose twitched.

'So why be you here again? I've told you all I knows about
the night Elton died.'

All . . . I doubt it! Touching the tip of a well-sharpened
pencil to his tongue, the inspector kept the thought to himself
while answering blandly. 'The information you supplied was
most appreciated, sir.'

'Then why bother me again!' Uriah snapped. 'I thought that
whole business were over and done.'

'Quite.'

Quite . . . quite! What the bloody hell did that mean? Uriah's
nerves sparked afresh as the pencil was licked again.

'Tell me, Mr Buckley, am I correct in the assumption you
were at the Goscote Club on the evening of Wednesday last?'

Wednesday last? Brain working like quicksilver Uriah
flashed over the couple of hours or so he had stayed in that
club.

'Can you confirm that, sir?'

Watched by the detective Uriah knew he must answer. To
refuse might awaken old interests . . . but suspicion of what?
He'd done nothing but talk and that not more than half a dozen
sentences.

'Yes, I confirms it, but what be the reason of your asking?'

'Did you speak to anyone while you were there?'

'Well o' course I spoke to somebody! That be the idea of going to a club, to socialise with folk, an' you can't do that unless you talks . . . but then I forgot you don't belong to a club!'

The snide ending to the eruption showed no sign of being recognised by the policeman, who calmly proceeded to write in his notebook, at the same time asking, 'Would you care to give me the names of the people you *talked* with?'

His face reddening as he caught the intonation, Uriah's irritation deepened. 'I don't bloody care to!' he barked. 'Take your questions to the Goscote – ask 'em there!'

Pencil hovering, the detective inspector glanced at the flushed features, his own mouth smiling slightly between mutton-chop whiskers. 'I have already taken them to the Goscote Club and now I have brought them to you.'

He could tell him to go to hell, have Saunders throw him and his questions into the street! Uriah's eyes gleamed fury but his brain told him to stay calm. Answer what was asked, give this man no ground for suspicion. 'See here,' he began, his tone several shades more even. 'The case of Elton's death be done and done with, the coroner brought in a verdict of accidental death, and that don't go to say men can't have no discussing it.'

'That is correct.' The inspector nodded.

'Then what—'

'My enquiries have nothing to do with that accident,' the policeman interrupted, noting the quick flicker in the hard grey eyes, a flicker he recognised as relief! Making a mental note of it he went on. 'I ask you again, sir, would you care to tell me just who you talked with at the Goscote Club on the evening of Wednesday last?'

Nerves calmed by the news that Elton's death were not the

reason of the inspector's coming to the house, Uriah's answer almost held a trace of cordiality. 'Apart from ordering a glass of wine and a cigar from a waiter I spoke only to Edgar Bull. He be the owner of the *Star*.'

The local newspaper was only one of that fellow's holdings. The inspector wrote the name in tight neat script.

'We talked of news of the minor uprisings in India . . . that sort of thing; we spoke only a few minutes then Bull went into the dining room.'

'You spoke of nothing else?' The pencil hovered.

What the hell was Checkett after? Uriah caught the snap behind his teeth.

'There were a few words. Bull said as how Elton's lad were sellin' up, said summat of his leaving the country.'

'Did you know of this?'

A trick question? Uriah smiled inwardly. It would take more than a bloody half-baked bobby to trip him up.

'I don't be privy to any decision Elton's lad makes an' I don't hold it to be any business o' mine to go poking into his or any other man's affairs.'

'But as part-owner of the New Hope colliery you must surely have been aware that Elton's share had been put up for sale.'

Eyes hard as grey rock, Uriah stared at the policeman. 'Elton's share? Elton has no share in the New Hope. That coal mine belongs to me alone; yes, Edward Elton liked to have it known he owned half and as the man's good friend I let the impression stand – after all it were doing me no harm; but the truth of the matter is as I've said. That mine is the sole property of Uriah Buckley.'

'And Beech House?'

'That were Elton's, so far as I knows it were bought and paid for by him, so if his lad chooses to sell then it be his right to do so.'

A quiet knock to the door halted the conversation, the inspector returning notebook and pencil to the pocket of his dark coat as Uriah's manservant entered the room.

'Yes . . . yes, I'd forgotten.' He nodded a reply to the prearranged interruption then glanced at his visitor. 'You can check with Edgar Bull . . .'

'No need.' Inspector Charles Checkett met the grey eyes with a look of granite. 'I have already spoken with Mr Bull.'

There was summat in the wind, summat had that bobby nosing around! But if it weren't that accident then what were it? Waiting several minutes, giving the policeman time to be clear of the house, he rang the bell, summoning Saunders.

'You knows the staff over at Beech House?' He jabbed the question as the man stepped into the room and receiving a nod growled on. 'Get you across to there, find out what be going on. And Saunders, you say naught of that policeman 'aving been here.'

There had never been any contract drawn atwixt Edward Elton and himself. After Saunders left, Uriah pulled open the drawer he had pushed shut before the inspector had been shown into the room. They had pooled money to revive the business, flagging from Uriah's excessive spending, and as it recovered Elton had taken what he thought were fifty per cent of the profits; but as for signed papers he had never mentioned that and Uriah had never raised the subject. No papers, no partnership! It had been a lie he had told Checkett, but a lie nobody could prove. From this moment the New Hope was indeed the sole property of Uriah Buckley!

The salon was ready. Amber had walked through each of the rooms in turn. The foyer where patrons would be received had glowed with colour reflecting from crystal figurines to sparkle over couches and fiendishly polished wood; the two treatment rooms were elegant with silk-draped chairs and chaises longues. She smiled to herself. Who would guess them to be 'two-hands'.

Rani had worked hard and long as herself scrubbing, polishing and then making creams and lotions.

'All of the body must be welcoming to a lover,' she had said. *'Did not the ayah of the daughter of the colonel sahib teach this, did she not tell what daughters in the lowliest of villages in all India are told, that the limbs which entwine must breathe the perfume of love?'*

Thinking now of those words Amber blushed as she had when first hearing them. Rani had smiled, seeing the rise of colour in her cheeks, then had shaken her head, perplexed. The English customs were strange indeed and none more so than daughters not being guided in the art of love. The thought had shown clearly on her face as Amber had explained.

But the face creams and body lotions they had made together held within them the essence of all that Rani had spoken of; their perfumes ranged from delicate scent of lily of the valley to the deeply sensuous, exotically heady Rose of Persia. But how to set that lovely allure to words? How to present it to the public? The small handwritten labels which had gone onto those earlier bottles of toilet water would not serve for the beautiful containers ranged along the shelves in the salon storeroom.

She had hoped for so much from those labels, from the name and place written upon them. Amber Neale: she had prayed it would be seen by Denny, that it would have him return to Darlaston, but the prayers had gone unanswered and the dream remained empty.

'Your heart is being heavy, my sister.' Returning from the scullery Rani caught the heavy sigh. 'Is it fear brings sorrow to your lips?'

'No.' Amber looked at the other girl. 'I was just thinking . . .'

'Thinking your perfumes will not be that which is hoped.'

Would not be successful, was what Rani had meant to say. Amber smiled but did not correct her for in an obscure way she had chosen exactly the right words; the toilette waters had sold well but they had not brought her what she longed for, they had not brought the return of her brother.

'I was thinking about the wording of the labels and that of the advertisements. We have to advertise if we wish to reach further than Darlaston.'

'Words.' Rani nodded solemnly. 'They are being of importance, but Rani is not of help, her tongue is clumsy.'

'That is not true!' Sharper than intended, Amber's reply resounded in the cosy kitchen. 'You are more help than you can know. Who else could have told me of moonlight of the grove or of a Persian bride whose maharajah husband created for her a whole canal of rosewater? I could never have come up with anything like that for myself.'

'If my words were pleasing then my heart sings.'

Amber watched the girl, her movements graceful as she moved about the small room. There was nothing clumsy about her, especially not her tongue. Born, as she had related, of peasant parents and reared in a poor mud-brick house in a village whose inhabitants were equally poor, Rani had an innate elegance, a natural poise and beauty of nature many a princess might envy. As for being of help, how could those days in the village of Kihar and those of wandering over empty barren land have been possible without Rani to pull her through them? She was in truth as much a sister as one born of the same mother.

'Speaking words of such beauty as is in the glass of the sahib Pearson will be a hard task.'

'And quite beyond me, I feel.' Amber glanced at those she

had left remaining in Ley Cottage. They were of loveliness which caught at the soul.

'No paper should touch them,' Rani went on as she took a chair at the table.

'Maybe not.' Amber smiled. 'But they have to be labelled, otherwise how will they be recognised?'

'The perfume of each will speak its own words.' Taking a bottle in her hands, Rani held it gently. 'Does not the beautiful figure speak . . . does she not promise the gift of love? And the woman who lifts the stopper, will she not recognise the promise of its perfume, a promise that needs no words to convey? It will whisper to her each time her eyes rest upon the bottle, she will feel again the desire in the touch of her lover, his kiss upon her lips. The word of the tongue is not needed when the heart speaks.'

How could *that* tongue ever be spoken of as clumsy! Amber smiled again. It was not merely extracting oils from flowers her friend could do; she could speak what was deep within every delicate blossom, speak the very language of flowers.

But that language had not come easily to a tongue restricted by the niceties of English society. To write exactly some of the phrases Rani used would be to shock more than to entice. It had been difficult to reconcile the two but at last it had been done. Hair braided for bed, Amber felt a glow of contentment inside. Different worlds yet so alike. Settled beneath the covers, she blew out the candle. Both held luxury and poverty, both knew kindness and cruelty and both could destroy a life without raising a hand. Rani had been turned from her home, disowned by her father and chased from the village. Though no fault rested with her she had been ostracised, banished by her own people, her life brutalised by the very ones she loved most. And her own life, the life of Amber Neale, that also had been made desolate, ravaged by the action of a man she had once taken to be a friend – a man to whom she had entrusted the care of a brother and a sister, two young children whose safety and welfare had proved of no consequence to him. Amber felt the scorpion sting of bitterness stab in her chest. Uriah Buckley had caused the death of Bethany, he had given Denny into the hands of a man depraved beyond belief and by doing these things had ruined her life also; but her family would be avenged . . . if it took every day of this existence left to her she would see that same ruin visited upon Uriah Buckley!

Edward Elton had never clapped eyes on this. The door of the study closed behind the departing Saunders. Uriah pulled open the drawer he had slammed shut before that police inspector had come in. Withdrawing a single sheet of heavy cream paper, he smiled at the writing covering it. Clear and neat. He laid it on the desk. The words were written clear and neat – but not so clear as the message they conveyed.

'All Deeds and Title . . .'

Black and bold, the letters danced across the page.

'All Deeds and Title of the property hereto being known as the New Hope colliery . . .'

No, Elton had never seen this document. Uriah touched the stiff parchment, a glow of satisfaction warming his veins. The registering of the partnership had been left to him. *'You be the businessman, you be best to sort that out, I don't have the brain for dealing along o' lawyers.'*

As the careless dismissal returned to his mind, Uriah smiled. Edward Elton had been interested in nothing but that which swung between his legs. On the rare occasions he had raised a question concerning the mine it had easily been diverted by the introduction of his real interest: that of young flesh! Giving Edward Elton the chance of satisfying his particular fancy drove all else from his mind as it had the evening that young girl had been brought into the sitting room. That had been a brilliant move. The glow of satisfaction deepened under self-congratulation. Elton had brought his son along of him to Bescot Lodge; no doubt it was his urging had given his father reason to ask of the profitability of the coal mine and its prospects as an ongoing venture.

Ongoing venture! Uriah swallowed the acid of contempt. 'Twere a question if Edward Elton even understood them words. But his smart-mouthed son might well have done! He might have gone on to ask to see the document naming his father as part-owner of the New Hope; that fancy schooling p'raps could have given him more than a taste for men's arses . . . like the taste for a lad! It had been a flash of inspiration. What had brought to mind the idea of sending for them young 'uns, of having them perform a few songs, a few tricks to add amusement to the evening, Uriah could not recall but the flash of those greedy little eyes, the tongue passing wetly over the lips of not only father but son, came clearly from the depths of memory. To watch children singing had not been the amusement the Eltons wanted, no party tricks; but the promise of something else had their mouths watering and their minds empty of the question of the New Hope colliery and the names on the certificate of ownership.

Setting the paper back into the drawer and locking it, Uriah leaned back in his chair. There could be no arguing with that. It was a legal document drawn up by a solicitor and it said the New Hope mine had one master: himself.

'You should 'ave been more careful, Elton,' he breathed. 'You should 'ave been a whole lot more careful!'

29

She had been told to wait until enquiries could be made, advised against acting rashly.

Not quite believing what she had done, Amber walked along Wolverhampton Lane, its sounds lost among the accusations shouting in her brain.

Why had she done what she had . . . and why that way?

Hadn't she and Rani always decided things together; hadn't they always talked over any proposition before acting upon it. So why now had she acted alone, saying nothing of her intentions to the other girl?

That would have been to dissuade her. Amber crossed the street, passing the noisy Victoria iron works adding its sound to the cacophony of a forge and the rattle of the new workshops producing nuts and bolts. Discussing what she had in mind would have had Rani urge caution as it had been urged an hour ago and the girl's down-to-earth logic and common sense could well have won where others had failed.

Leaving the road for the track which led across the heath towards Ley Cottage she let her thoughts play on, freeing those until now imprisoned at the back of her mind. She had not wanted Rani to know what she planned, had not wanted to hear her words of caution, had not wanted to be told to wait.

It had been the behaviour of a child. Amber slowed, a flush of guilt tingling her cheeks. She had deliberately kept today's happenings from Rani; like a child not wishing to share a toy with someone else she had hidden it away, hiding one truth beneath another. She had told the girl she was going to Pearson's glass bottle works, going to inspect the samples before the main order was made up. It was the visit which had followed that she had made no mention of. Would she mention it on reaching the house, admit to her friend what was already an accomplished fact?

How would Rani take such news? Would she be hurt, feel betrayed? Of course she would! After the years they had shared each other's doubts, comforted each other's fears, what else could Rani be expected to feel? And she, Amber, had known.

Yet still she had acted alone, kept her purpose a close-held secret, and now that secret burned like a brand on her conscience.

Amber sat in the cosy living room redolent with the fragrance of flower oils. The gleam of fire and lamp spread a silvery shine over the iron grate, blackleaded religiously twice a week; over cupboard and chairs, and glinted on the assortment of crockery adorning the pine dresser. She tried to find the words to tell what she had done. She had meant to do so as soon as she entered the house but somehow each time she tried courage had deserted her.

Rani had kept her own secret, wanting the meal she had cooked to be eaten in peace of mind. Now with the last of the dishes washed and returned to their places, she turned to look at the woman sunk in her own thoughts. The heart of her friend knew a sadness she was not yet ready to share. What must be told would bring only more grievance, yet it must be said. Taking a chair drawn to the side of the fireplace she drew a short breath, holding it behind small white teeth. Would it be so harmful to keep within her that which could only arouse a fresh serpent to bite, bring another tiger to claw at the heart?

I would shield you from hurt, keep soreness from placing its mark upon you. The thought rose as Rani looked at the face slightly turned from her. But a shield warding off one blow could be the weapon of another – and did wanting to protect carry with it the right to keep secret that which was meant for the ears of a friend? Releasing the pent-up breath she spoke quietly.

'Freddy was being in the garden.'

Quiet as it was, it pierced the barrier of thought and Amber looked up.

'He asked if his *mai* could speak with you.'

Her wandering attention arrested, Amber centred it firmly on Rani. 'His mother! I spoke with her in the town before taking the tram to West Bromwich last week.'

'It don't be safe to be seen speaking . . .'

A coldness suddenly grasped her insides as she asked: 'Did Freddy say what it was she wished to speak about?'

'He came only to the garden, to where the bushes would cover him. I saw his face only for the time of blinking but the moment was enough. It showed the fear his lips did not speak, they said only that his *mai* would come.'

'It don't be safe to be seen speaking . . .'

Amber's hands twisted together in her lap, the words ringing in her head loud and slow as the passing bell. Becky had been afraid when she had said that, so afraid she had covered her face with her shawl. Had any of those eyes she had spoken of watched as they had talked together, had someone eager to gain Uriah Buckley's favour and perhaps a sovereign informed him of that brief meeting? Or could it be he had attacked Becky, striking her down as he had struck Rani? Anxiety rising fast, Amber's next words were tight.

'Did Freddy say when . . . did he say what time his mother would call?'

Lampglow bouncing blue arrows from hair darker than the feathers of a blackbird darted in all directions as Rani shook her head.

'The hour was not spoken . . . only words being of her coming.'

Why had she not come with her son, why send him alone?

The chill in Amber's stomach became ice, thickening with each new thought. Had it been because she was injured? Rani said there was fear on Freddy's face; was an attack upon his mother the reason behind it? She tried to dismiss the question, striving to hold her agitation, but the leash snapped. Freddy had shown his bravery on several occasions; had his mother been harmed in any way he would have gone after the one who had done it. Had he done that very thing? No. Amber's troubled mind rejected the thought. Freddy would not have escaped such an encounter without mark of it showing but Rani had said he showed only fear, not injury.

But what had he found when he returned home – his mother beaten as a result of Uriah Buckley's vengeance? Had the boy himself become a victim of it? Could they both be dead!

Each consideration seemed more dreadful than that preceding it. Amber rose from her chair, moving restlessly about the room. She must not let her fears run riot, panicking would do no good. Striving to remain calm, she went over in her mind the conversation she had held with Freddy's mother, checking and rechecking each word that had passed between them, but the result always came out the same: Becky Worrall had most definitely been afraid – and now she was too.

'Did Freddy look all right?' She had already asked herself the question and given it answer but twanging nerves had her ask again and this time aloud.

'Fear should not be the hand that wipes a smile from the face of a child or sits as a stone in his belly,' Rani answered quietly as before, 'yet it stared from the eyes of him who came. He seemed as one threatened by the great djinn.'

The great djinn! Amber's nails dug into her palms. An apt description for a man as evil as Uriah Buckley!

No sound had come to Amber's ears but the quick stiffening of Rani's slight figure showed she had caught some movement from beyond the closed door. Amber turned to glance at the window but it showed only blackness. Uriah Buckley . . . a hired assassin . . . or did both stand somewhere out there? Nerves twittering like angry birds, she felt her fingernails bite deeper. Maybe if they screamed; but that would be of no use. There was no house within a quarter of a mile! The poker and the carving knife, they could defend themselves . . .

'Shh!' Rani's lips pursed on the soft sound and her hand closed over Amber's wrist, holding her as she made to move.

There could be no reason for the girl's warning other than that someone moved in the garden. Trained from earliest childhood to listen for sounds of animals other than those of cattle or goats, warned to stay alert for movements in the long grass of a faint rustle that might be tiger or leopard, Rani's senses were honed to a degree; and those senses were now saying they were not alone! Hardly breathing, Amber watched the other girl's face, saw the tightness often painted across it during those days in India. Rani too was afraid.

'The poker—'

The whisper, half formed, broke off with the swift shake of Rani's head but the tension holding the girl's features had relaxed.

'They are come. The footsteps of two people only, they are not being more.'

But who were the two people? Amber's hands remained clenched.

'Amber . . .'

A soft, almost inaudible voice answered her question, releasing the tension which had kept her limbs taut as iron. Amber felt suddenly weak.

'. . . Amber, it be me, Freddy.'

Opening the door on the last word Rani placed both her palms together in traditional welcome as Freddy and his mother stepped inside.

'I be apologising for comin' here after dark.' Becky Worrall nodded to the woman who took her shawl before ushering her to the fire. 'But me and Freddy, we couldn't take the risk of being seen.'

'Seen by whom?' What an insane question! Amber chided herself. Who would the woman be afraid of other than Uriah Buckley!

'It be Buckley.' Becky confirmed the thought already in Amber's mind. 'Like I said to you a week gone when we spoke along of King Street, the man were full o' temper then but this mornin' it were worse. Nellie Potts said he were like a demon fuming and storming at Saunders, then kicking and slashing at everythin' he passed as he slammed out of the 'ouse. I were feared at what Nellie told, feared it had been found out what my lad has known these years through. I thought Buckley might have gone to find him so I left them sheets half washed and I run, run all the way to our lodgings praying I might see my lad on the way, and I did. Going to Buckley's stables he were . . . thank God I were in time to stop him.'

'But what makes you so certain it is the knowledge Freddy has . . .'

'What else be like to have Uriah Buckley raging like the devil when locked out of 'eaven?' Becky's eyes glistened with her fears. 'What went on that night along of Bescot Lodge were a work o' such evil as only Satan himself could smile on; I says it be memories o' them doings and the fears o' their being found out has Buckley acting like a madman. It don't be safe for my lad no more . . . Darlaston don't be safe for any Uriah Buckley might suspect knows of what were done to them poor babbies – God rest 'em. That be why I sent Freddy along of asking could I pass words with yourself, it were to warn you best leave this town same as we be doin'.'

Rani had said nothing but Amber had seen her push the iron bolt into place across the door before proceeding to brew tea. She also, it seemed, harboured worry that Uriah Buckley might come to this house. But to leave! Where would they go? How would they live? Especially now she had done what she had!

Her smile brief but grateful as she took the cup of steaming hot tea held out to her by Rani, Becky Worrall went on in words quietly rushed. 'We could have gone no sooner I met up with my lad for there be nothin' in them lodgings as we can't live without. Me and Freddy could have been miles away by now but after the kindness you two showed him and the understanding you had concerning my keeping o' that Bible . . . well, I just couldn't leave afore tellin' you and I do be tellin' you, Mrs Neale, Uriah Buckley don't be a man to stay his hand when he feels himself threatened. One whiff of me or my lad bein' seen at this house and he'll be on you like a ton o' bricks, and if it's mercy you expects of him then I answers you be sadly mistook.'

Her brother and sister had found no mercy at the hands of Uriah Buckley and she knew the same treatment would be handed to herself. To do what he had, to sit by while two children were treated as Bethany and Denny had been treated, spoke of a strain of evil difficult to comprehend and one he would not hesitate to use again. That much was proven by his attack on Rani – an attack on a woman he no doubt believed to be Amber Neale.

'I've had the saying o' what I come for so now I'll be goin'.

Think on what it be you've had the listening of and get yourselves away.'

Her tea quickly drunk, the woman set the cup on the table.
Rising from the chair she reached for the faded shawl which
was her only protection against the night air. Setting it about
her shoulders, fingers drawing the corners beneath her breasts,
she threw a glance to Rani. 'Take heed of what has been said,
wench,' she said, tying the ends of her shawl into a knot,
'gather what it be you needs can't leave without and get the
both of you away from Darlaston.'

'Your visit is born of kindness.' Rani's answer was softly
made. 'Rani says thank you for the goodness of heart which
brought your feet to this door; the great god of the Universe
walk always at the side of Freddy and his *mai* as you journey.'

Journey where? Amber's mind snapped to the moment,
leaving the thoughts which seconds ago had filled it.

'You can't leave.' As she stood up she saw Becky frown.
'The heath is too dangerous to cross in the dark.'

'I be knowing the heath, Mrs Neale. I can find the way.'

Lips set determinedly Amber looked at the lad who answered
for his mother. 'I have no doubt of that, Freddy, but your
mother is tired and to feel so is not beneficial to safety when
crossing the heath at any time. To do it at night when there is
not even a moon to light the way is a danger best avoided.'

'But we has to cross it, we can't go back—'

'And you won't,' Amber interrupted. 'You and Freddy will
stay the night here and tomorrow . . . well, we will let tomorrow
decide for itself.'

'But what if Buckley should come?'

'Then there are four of us to face him.'

It had been said out of sheer bravado, of a confidence she had
not felt. Sleep evading her, Amber watched the flecks of dawn

prick the dark sky. She had insisted the boy and his mother pass the night in Ley Cottage, Rani and herself bringing blankets and pillows for makeshift beds in the warmth of the living room. But what of the morning, what if Uriah Buckley came looking for them? Or for her! He would know there was no man at Ley Cottage, that she and Rani had no one to protect them; his money could buy him all the information he required. Maybe he had bought it already. Dark on dark, dawn-cast shadows leapt into her room, looming on walls, looking down from the ceiling. Closing her eyes against them was easy but shutting her mind to the thoughts plaguing it was not. On and on they came, each trailing a fresh band of worries.

Buying that house, attempting to set up in a business totally foreign to Darlaston, maybe foreign to the whole country, for she had never heard of any other house of beauty, no salon where women could be introduced to methods of caring for their skin, methods she herself had learned from Joanna's ayah and more recently from Rani. But would the women want a house of beauty, would they want the perfumed creams and lotions? Had the whole thing been a waste of time? Had she thrown away all that Greville Neale had left her on an empty dream?

Maybe that was heaven's way of repaying her selfishness. Turning her face into the pillow she let the thought run unchecked. She had vowed vengeance on Uriah Buckley. It was for that reason only she had sold the emerald, for that reason she had bought and furnished a house, had beautiful creations of glass made to decorate its rooms and miniature replicas to contain perfumes and cosmetics. But the teaching of her childhood, priest and Sunday-school teacher had stressed that vengeance was not given man to take but was the prerogative of the Lord. She had vowed to see Uriah

Buckley in hell. But in trying, was she preparing a hell for herself?

'*Amber . . .*'

Standing in the centre of a garden, the scent of its flowers a delight in her nostrils, Amber smiled at the sound of her name drifting on the warm air.

'*Look, Amber . . .*'

Turning towards the call, her smile deepened at sight of a young boy laughing as he chased a girl, her fair hair loose and streaming behind like a golden cloud.

'*Help me . . .*'

Blue eyes gleaming like precious stones, the girl called again and Amber threw her arms wide to catch the flying figure but as she grasped it to her the pretty face no longer smiled, the sparkling eyes were closed and the mouth which a moment before had called her name was filled with slime and mud and the lovely golden hair streaked with river weed.

'*Bethany!*'

Horror caught in her throat as she glanced at the smaller figure which had followed but it was no longer that of a young boy but of a man – a man who laughed viciously, a man she knew as Uriah Buckley. Reaching out, he caught her hair, twisting it savagely, pushing her to her knees, but the face glaring down at her had changed.

'Feringhee *bitch!*'

Her head was snatched back on her neck. Amber stared at a face whose skin was now lined, its colour that of old leather; the grey eyes were gone and in their place were twin studs hard and black as ebony while above them the head was swathed in coils of cloth wrapped about in a turban.

'Feringhee *droppings of a she-camel would dare to answer . . .*'

A stinging blow to the side of her face made Amber cry out,

then hauled to her feet, she was pushed into the centre of a ring of jeering turbaned men, each grabbing and pulling at her while she screamed in fear. A sword rose above her; she closed her eyes, waiting for the touch of steel, but it was Rani's hand that touched her shoulder, Rani's voice which whispered to her. Overhead the sun blazed, a great orb in a golden sky, the heat that of a furnace beating down on her head, the earth a relentless fire beneath her feet; and all around on every side men with swords at their hip laughed and pointed, ignoring her plea for water.

'Foreign dogs deserve no water!'

Amber cringed beneath a threatening fist, yellowed teeth and sour breath turning her stomach as a leering face came close to her own.

'*We did not take the* feringhee *for your sport!*'

One face melted into another and a different hand placed a goatskin water bag in hers. The trickle of cool liquid soothed her parched throat, a few precious drops tipped into her palms eased her dry dust-covered face. Amber lifted her eyes on a different scene. The men still surrounded her but now they squatted on the earth, their turbans moving and bobbing like the heads of so many flowers, and behind them spread a wonderland. Buildings of dull red sandstone, graceful and beautiful, glowed a deeper carmine as the rays of a lowering sun blessed their walls with its red-gold touch. But it was an empty wonderland; no people other than the band of men who had swooped upon herself and Rani as they scooped water from a river were to be seen in its vast courtyard or walking beneath the delicately fluted arches of its colonnades. Caught by the beauty of cupolas, great white marble domes gilded by sunlight lancing over the tiered façades of exquisite buildings, their windows promising a haven of shaded rest free from the burning brazier of the sun, Amber rose; but at her first step towards that beckoning sanctuary the fist shot out, knocking her almost senseless to the ground, her cry for Rani a half-sob.

'*Cries are useless!*' The words, ground between the same yellowed teeth, were accompanied by a throaty laugh. '*There is no one to hear, the city of Fatepuhr Sikri is deserted; it knows no life other than pariah, the wild dog which eats all it finds . . . even a* feringhee *bitch!*'

Curled into herself, the heat of a merciless sun scorching through the thin cotton of a sari grudgingly given by the wife of Gopal and now torn and smeared with the stains of river mud and dried earth, she trembled as her captives fell to arguing among themselves.

'*Up!*' She was jerked to her feet and pushed in the direction of a square two-storeyed structure smaller and set a little apart from the rest. Even as she stumbled beneath the rough shove of several hands the grandeur of it stole what breath she had. Rectangular window spaces and a tall curving archway open to the air bisected the lower level of its red stone body while around the centre ran a wide balcony. Supported on a series of intricately carved buttresses, it enhanced the graceful window apertures of the upper level. These were crowned by a sloping overhang roof, each of its four corners topped by large cupolas standing on platforms balanced on slender columns.

'*On!*' A jab to her back sent her staggering and she was inside the graceful building, the shelter of its walls seeming a blessing; please God they would leave her here! But the prayer whispered in her heart found no ear in heaven. The ring of grinning men surrounding parted and another came to stand in front of her. A sharp word made every other man turn his back; this one, in an embroidered blue silk coat reaching to the knees of matching silk trousers, stared openly.

'*Hmm.*' Faint, the sound issued from unmoving lips while

black eyes, brilliant in the shaded coolness, travelled the length of her; then with one swift movement a jewelled hand reached out, snatching the covering from her head and the sari from her body, leaving her naked.

The sound which before had been faint became a hiss and beneath an elegantly wound turban the black eyes took on the hungry look of a vulture. Again! It was happening again! Her helpless cry mixed with the shouts of remembered horsemen, swords gleaming as they bore down on the market place of Meerut. The cool tiled floor of the building became the hard stony earth of mountain foothills and the vulture eyes those of the dacoit as he lowered himself over her. Then the whole of it whirled and danced in the flames of the funeral pyre that licked along her body while the laughter of Kewal sang its madness in her ears.

A cry bubbling fresh in her throat, every inch of her trembling like wind-tossed leaves, Amber woke. Turning her eyes to the window and a dawn fully broken she let the tears flow. It had been a dream, fleeting pictures of the past; but as she stared at a sky dull with the promise of rain the pain of that past was a reality which stabbed, the pain of a past she knew she would never forget.

30

The nightmare had shaken her; she knew it was in the past, that the danger of being sold by those brigands and taken into the harem of some rich man was long over, yet still her nerves quivered. Having washed in cold water from the jug kept on the washstand in her room, Amber dressed with shaking hands. It was silly, her feeling this way, common sense told her; but common sense held little sway in face of the fears that dream had reawakened. In fact it had deserted her, leaving her whimpering even as she had realised she was safe in her own bed.

Moving quietly as she could she smoothed the covers of the bed before folding them across its foot, opening it to the air after the fashion taught by her mother. Her mother! Pausing in her task Amber stared, seeing nothing. She would be able to make one last visit to that churchyard in Bloxwich, to whisper to her mother of what she had done and the result of that action – a result which meant she would be unable to continue to visit as she had. If only she had given herself time to think on the advice Simeon Pearson had given her, discussed the proposition with Rani; but she had done neither of those things but instead had gone blindly on; only now were the consequences beginning to seep through.

She heard a sound from downstairs and drew a deep breath. This worry must be kept to herself.

'Oh there you be, Mrs Neale,' Becky Worrall said as Amber

entered the kitchen. 'Me an' Freddy be off now but I'm glad the chance were given to thank you once again afore we goes. It were kind of you, offering the shelter of your roof.'

Coming from the yard, a bucket of coal in one hand, Freddie apologised for his appearance his likeable face blushing as he stammered. 'Me mam said to wash me hands and face under the pump but it seemed daft to do that afore bringing coals to the fire, I'd only 'ave to wash all over again.'

'And that would pain you, wouldn't it, Freddy Worrall!' Becky answered her son tartly but beneath the sharpness was a thick layer of tenderness.

'It seems to be the sensible thing to do.' Amber smiled, her eyes asking Becky's forgiveness for going against her judgement.

Pleasure spread the boy's mouth wide as he emptied the coal onto the fire awakened from its slumber by the poker.

'He don't be a bad lad.' Becky's glance followed the gangly figure. 'Nor he don't be weak in the 'ead though folk calls him daft, my only sorrow be I couldn't do more forrim, seen to it he had a better start in life.'

'Freddy is most certainly not stupid.' Amber comforted a woman whose eyes portrayed an old sadness. 'And you have given him the best start any child could be given, that of a mother's love. The knowledge that he has that will stand him in good stead Mrs Worrall; believe me, holding that truth in his heart, life will never truly defeat him.'

As Rani emerged from the scullery she threw Amber a quick look, and the bond the years spent together had built between them seemed to strengthen. As with herself, Amber knew it was Rani's memory of her mother's love that had been the one thing that had helped her live through those months in the village of Kihar, and to survive the horrors which went before and followed after.

'Them be kind words and I be grateful for the hearing.' Becky's eyes misted. 'Ain't been no other time since my lad were a babby I've heard such 'cept from the lips of you two . . . you don't know the feelin' it gives me.'

Glancing beyond Amber and Rani the woman nodded to her son as he came back to the kitchen. 'That be better. I can see your face now and not just coal dust. Now give your thanks to Mrs Neale and Miss Rani and we'll be on our way.'

'Calling me Amber and not Mrs Neale is all the thanking I need and Rani, I am sure, feels the same.'

'To speak only Rani makes us *dost*, that is friend. Be friend would give great pleasure.'

A smile quivering against the emotion held inside her, Becky Worrall could only nod as she reached for her shawl.

'In the villages of India friends do not part before they have shared in a meal.'

'And it is the same in Ley Cottage,' Amber supported. 'You and Freddy must have breakfast.'

Once the meal of porridge sweetened with honey followed by a slice of bacon topped with an egg was finished, Becky Worrall would not be put off washing the dishes and ordering her son chop sticks in the yard. 'He's had the teaching of showin' appreciation best as I could give, it be right and proper he show it now by cutting a supply of firewood, and Mrs— Amber, be there anything I can do for you, anything at all, then you would please me greatly by the asking.'

Draping the cloth on which she had dried the breakfast dishes over her arm, Amber picked up the tray on which she had stacked them. 'There is one thing,' she said, then immediately wished she had not. She had placed herself and Rani in danger by returning to Darlaston and facing Uriah Buckley. She could not compound that by placing others in the same danger.

Having waited until plates and cups had been replaced on the dresser while still not hearing what the request was, Becky Worrall asked firmly, 'What do that one thing be?'

'Nothing.' Amber tried to answer flippantly but a quick stain of colour in her cheeks evidenced the lie.

'Won't do no good.' Becky's hands caught together across her stomach. 'You be forgettin' I've had the rearin' of a lad and there be none better at sayin' there be nothing when all the time there be summat and I can see you don't be one as glib at telling an untruth as some I've met with; so you'll ease us both by asking what it is you be keeping back.'

'I will be seeing Freddy.'

'No!' Amber's exclamation halted the girl she knew was leaving the room to afford privacy for what must now be said. 'What I wish to ask involves you.' Amber went on quickly. 'I wanted to go to Bloxwich today but . . . but I am afraid to leave you here alone. There in the scullery I had thought to ask Becky to remain at this house until I returned but now I realise the selfishness of such a request.' Glancing at the older woman, still standing with hands clasped across her middle, Amber continued. 'Rani and I will pack some food for you and Freddy . . .'

'Be no need.' The woman's hands dropped to her sides. 'Freddy and me won't be leaving just yet.'

'But Uriah Buckley— Oh Lord, why did I have to say anything!'

'Mebbe that be the Lord's way. Folk do say He has some strange choices when it comes to workin' things according to His will.'

'No.' Amber shook her head. 'It is not God's choice nor His will to have you place yourself in danger.'

'Then it be mine!' Becky's mouth tightened and her faded blue eyes found new light. 'Mine be the will and mine the

choosin' – and I chooses to be right here while you have the
doin' of the business takes you along of Bloxwich.'

Wearing a smile of satisfaction which widened with reading
Uriah read through the letter again. The mine was sold and
the money it had realised was every penny his. There had been
no argument, no threat of a legal action brought by Elton's
son; in fact the little pansy had said nothing . . . and never
would say anything!

But that bloody police inspector had had plenty to say. How
long had the mine been put up for sale? Were he and Elton in
agreement over the disposing of the property?

The look on the man's face when being told no part of the
New Hope belonged to young Elton or indeed had ever
belonged to his father, that the mine had come to Uriah
Buckley on the death of his wife's father! What Uriah had not
revealed was that the mine had long ago needed capital he
himself did not have, that Edward Elton had supplied the
investment needed to keep the place a going concern. Now
nobody would ever know!

The police inspector had been so certain, confidence had
oozed like syrup in his words. *'Would there be proof of that?'*

There had been proof all right. Uriah's smile folded into an
expression of contempt. When the policeman had been shown
the document taken from the desk drawer the syrupy confidence had suddenly become tart, the mouth tightening as if
the bitterness of aloes spread across the tongue; and Inspector
Charles Checkett had closed his notebook.

'We had to ask, sir.' Uriah was remembering the clipped
explanation of another police visit to Bescot Lodge. *'What
with it being commonly thought that yourself and Mr Edward
Elton were partners in the business of that coal mine . . .'*

'What be common knowledge be often wrong knowledge,' he had

intervened, taking pleasure in the other man's discomfort.

The notebook stored away, the inspector had reached for the hat he had kept with him. *'Just so,'* he had replied acidly, *'but the slightest whiff of smoke has the making of a fire beneath it . . . and I mean to put the fire out.'*

Had it been meant to worry him? Uriah placed the letter he had read yet again in the drawer beside the document Edward Elton had never seen. Had those words been a threat, did the policeman believe him involved with that business up at Beech House? He had pretended shock at being told, had given a laudable display of horror, of being stunned by the disclosure, but that was all it had been: a performance.

He had known well in advance of Checkett's revelation. Leaning back in his wide leather chair, Uriah wallowed in the warmth of self-satisfaction. He had been informed before the smart-arsed policeman had called. Hadn't he sent Saunders to Beech House following that previous visit, told him to find out what were going on while keeping his own mouth shut? And what had Saunders found out?

Leaving the study Uriah walked slowly to a sitting room which had never held real warmth and comfort for him; no rooms of the house marriage had brought him held those feelings, not even the bedroom shared for those few short months prior to the birth of his son. What satisfaction that would have brought to Samuel Deinol's heart, what pleasure it would have given to the man who had not wanted his daughter wed to a 'common bloody foundryhand' – to know the house he had inherited knew no love. But it would. When Jervis returned it would be filled with the sounds of children's laughter.

Pouring a measure of brandy into a heavy cut glass goblet and carrying it to a chair Uriah sat with it in hand. Yes, *his* son were no pervert, *his* son took his pleasures as God meant them to be took, as Uriah Buckley had always taken his own: with a woman. There would be no scandal attached to the name of Buckley, no dirty carryings-on like them along of Beech House.

Sipping a little of the brandy, the blaze of it hot against his throat, Uriah's thoughts flipped back to the study and the words of his visitor. *'The slightest whiff of smoke has the making of a fire beneath it . . .'*

Had the inspector hoped to see a blaze caused by those words? Had he thought to discover the fire he talked of here at Bescot Lodge, hoped his next words might set those flames leaping? Had the intention of catching him unawares renewed a little of that former assurance, the not-too-well hidden belief that Uriah Buckley was more involved in the death of Edward Elton than enquiries had disclosed? Was it that he had heard in the policeman's parting words when, already at the door of the study, he had turned to say: *'We may need to speak with you again before the investigation of the death of Edward Elton's son is brought to a close.'*

The death of Edward Elton's son.

Uriah sipped again at his drink but not all the warmth flowing inside him was due to the effects of the brandy. The Fates were batting on his side. No question could now be raised as to Edward Elton's part-ownership of the New Hope; the only men who could ever have accused him of deceit were both dead. One secret was safe and the other, shared by the Neale woman, would be too before Jervis's return.

It had been a mistake letting the father strip and fondle that young girl, but it had been a bigger mistake giving the son an even younger child to take with him as a playmate in his filthy games. He should have found another way of turning aside any possible enquiry the Eltons might have come up with. But he had no need of worrying about that now; the

Eltons, father and son, were dead as both of them young 'uns were dead and despite any suspicion on the part of that policeman, no incrimination could be thrown at Uriah Buckley's head, no charge of corruption or reprehensible practice laid against him. No taint of evil would touch the name of Uriah Buckley and no baseness or degradation would attach to him because of any action of his son's, as had happened to Edward Elton.

And what shame that son had brought, what disgrace! No father's name should be blighted with the stigma that would be attached to Edward Elton's, the tarnish imposed upon it by an obscenity that was his only child! The whispers and behind-the-doors gossip no doubt already taking place in Darlaston would be talked of for many years to come.

"'T'were the way o' findin' 'im.'" Saunders had repeated the words of Elton's own manservant. *"'Fair turned my stomach, blood all over the pillow.'"*

It appeared Elton's lad had been called upon by a man who had elbowed aside the servant who had said he would ascertain whether the master were at home. He had known Elton were home, had been the rough reply, and he would show himself upstairs.

'There 'ad been no sound o' voices,' Saunders had been told, *'nothin' 'cepting the bang of a gun goin' off. I were in the kitchen when I 'eard, echoed through the 'ouse like a thunderclap; well, I run up them stairs like the hounds of hell were snapping my heels but when I went into that room I seen it were not me them hounds were a-chasin' but young Elton, and they 'ad caught 'im. He were spreadeagled, naked wi' not a stitch a-coverin' 'im. I seen his eyes, wide open they was, a look of surprise shinin' from 'em like he could still see the man who had put a bullet clean through his forehead before blowin' his brains out. But that weren't the all o' what these eyes o' mine seen. There were another in that room,*

a man naked as Elton 'imself were lying with his 'ead atwixt them spread legs, lying with Elton's private part in his mouth as he were a suckin' of it when they was busted in on; as he were when I run outta the room, for the back of his head had been blown away by a bullet!'

Caught in the act! Uriah stared into the rich depth of colour half filling his glass. The lecher caught in his own carnality, one pervert murdered by another. The jealous lover! Lifting his goblet to his lips he swallowed a mouthful of the fiery liquid. Inspector Charles Checkett had said nothing of any of this; but then the inspector was a disappointed man. The murderer of young Elton had been there in the room, the gun he had used to kill two men and then himself still in his hand, and any case he might have hoped to build against Uriah Buckley was so much spit in the wind!

She had been reluctant to have Becky and her son stay the extra hours her journey to and from Bloxwich would take but there had been no arguing with the woman. It was the least they could do, Becky Worrall had insisted; Freddy were sharp-eyed, he would keep watch against anyone coming in the direction of Ley Cottage. As she sat in the empty compartment waiting for the guard to signal the departure of the train, Amber still felt the press of nerves that had stayed with her on the outward journey and had preyed on her mind even as she knelt by her mother's grave. It was the last visit she would be able to make. She had whispered the reason over that small patch of earth, whispered what she had not yet divulged to Rani. But the murmured confession had been followed by a promise. Her throat choking, she repeated it now in her mind. *'I will not forget, I will visit Bethany every week and if heaven wills I will kneel here again some day.'* Fumbling in her purse for the ticket the conductor would need to punch she could not close out the thought which followed, one which voiced a hope she had nursed since arriving in Bloxwich: the hope of seeing Zachary Hayden. But she had not seen him, and now she probably never would.

That too had been with her as she had placed her flowers next to those already there beneath that plain wooden cross and the hurt of it stung sharp now as then. Zachary Hayden had kept his word, but how long could he be expected to take flowers to the grave of a woman he had not known, a grave her own daughter no longer visited? What connotation would be put on that? Would he brand her thoughtless, uncaring – a woman of little loyalty to whom a mother's memory meant nothing? Whatever he thought, he would never know the truth.

Great hiccups of steam belching in loud spurts from the engine trailed over the platform, tendrils of mist curling like fog, touching the window like some unearthly phantom seeking a way inside. A shout from somewhere beyond the veil of cloaking greyness, warning of departure, was followed seconds later by a deep-throated groan and it seemed the world lurched, pitching her forward as the heavy iron wheels began to turn. The grinding noise of the train moving drowned the sound of the carriage door opening then snapping shut so the gasped apology had Amber straighten quickly.

'Sorry to jump in on you like this. The train was moving by the time I reached the platform and there won't be another one for several hours so I risked the guard's anger by sprinting – and my neck by throwing myself into this carriage.'

The sound was rich and deep, a hint of laughter bubbling beneath the words tumbling quickly from the tall figure brushing a hand over the jacket of a dark suit.

'But I will have to face the music when I get back, Tom Berry isn't a man to allow jumping his train go by without the culprit getting a tongue lashing and I . . .'

Was it all astonishment she heard in that last word, had there been a trace of pleasure or was it something else? Her back once more resting against her seat, the stricture which had earlier held her throat thickened and the nerves of her body twanged like the strings of a bow as the masculine figure turned and two vivid blue eyes rested on her face.

31

Eyes closed, weariness wrapping his body like a pall, Colonel Jervis Buckley dropped heavily into the rattan chair. The past days had been a nightmare of blood and death. He had personally led a detachment of sepoys, trained Indian soldiers. Together with a couple of officers they had marched hard and long, taking little rest as they headed for the town of Chandpur. It had been his intention to join with the troops stationed there; together they would head north and clear Najibabad of the nest of vipers which attacked not only the military but any of the local people who happened in their way. But press on as they had they had come too late for the men of Chandpur. *'We expected no attack.'* A seriously wounded sergeant major had tried to rise from his bed to make the report. *'It was thought them blighters would 'ave made for the hills, that they would hide out like the dogs they be. But we was wrong, Colonel, sir, they didn't scuttle off but followed a few hours behind. Took the post by surprise they did. They knowed as most of the men had been sent on that patrol and that them who'd been lucky enough to make it back were too done in to make a fight of it; and they was right, swarmed right over the camp like a plague of locust but the crop they ravaged were not rice or corn , it were men and their families. Everyone and anyone thought to be linked to the Army slashed and sliced like so much mutton!'*

So it had proved. The wailing of women, the keening shriek of their mourning, had reached the column before they had entered the outskirts of Chandpur and the thick oily smoke of funeral pyres rising from the ghats, the low hills which encircled the town like a necklace of green gems, rolled in dark clouds across the brilliant sky. And everywhere had been the evidence of slaughter: the stench of congealing blood, the buzzing of flies massing to feed at its pools, the slinking shapes of pariah dogs drawn by the scent of decomposing flesh, and the few sepoys who had been thought already dead.

Drawing a deep breath, holding it against the sickness riding his throat, Jervis saw again the devastation in that which had been the garrison station of Chandpur. Men with arms sliced from their bodies, heads and faces lost in a sea of blood, legs chopped at knee or hip, and worse . . . much, much worse. The bodies of women and children, blood dried black on throats slit from ear to ear. It had not been retribution, it had not been vengeance, it had been annihilation!

So much death, so many wasted lives! Breath easing from him, eyes opening, he rose from the chair and walked the length of a garden that was now drawing the cloak of evening about its flower beds and walkways. Soon only the tinkling of fountains would tell of the beauty hidden by the dark velvet of night.

So many wasted lives! Jervis found the object of his journey. Resting his hand on marble gleaming rose-gold in the setting sun, he felt the arrowhead of regret pierce his heart.

Helen! He stroked the tomb with a gentle loving hand. Her life had been given to him, given in a love which had never asked why . . . why she had not had such a love given in return. Had she known his deceit, known the secret kept inside him? If she had then it had remained hidden with her as with himself. Helen, the quiet graceful girl he had married in the church of St Lawrence in the smoke-choked town of Darlaston. Helen, the woman who had come with him to the heat-oppressed India, the woman who had died here without ever being told!

Grief lay heavy and binding on his heart. Fatigue restricting his limbs, Jervis felt the warmth of tears collect in his eyes as they switched to the second edifice, a perfect match to the first.

'Joanna!' Unobtrusive as a falling petal, the whisper drifted on the settling night. 'My dearest child. Your life gone before it could begin . . .'

From the veranda circling the low-slung bungalow, the manservant Ram Dutt picked up the tray on which he had served the *chai* requested. The tea was cold, untouched as had been much of the food and drink served since his master's return. Glancing at the figure standing between the two tombs, his head tipped slowly side to side. The colonel sahib was filled with a sorrow too big for the heart of a man; soon that heart would break.

'. . . your life also was wasted.'

Oblivious of a pale shadow in the purple-grey gliding into the deeper shadow of the house, Jervis continued to murmur.

'I could have prevented your death. I should have refused permission for you to visit the market place but I did not. I destroyed you as surely as I destroyed your mother. I will not ask the forgiveness of heaven as I have so often asked it of you both. Your deaths are my purgatory; I must live it in this life as I will live it in the next . . .'

Sliding to his knees, a hand placed on each smooth marble structure, the warm silk of tears slipping down his face, Jervis bent his head.

'Helen.' Gentle as the fading light, the whisper made no sound beyond his lips. 'Helen, I have come to a decision. I . . . I have decided to return to England.'

Engrossed in the pain of that decision, Jervis was unaware of a muteness dropping swiftly over the garden; a stifled gagging halting the calls of roosting birds; a silence suspending the sounds of crickets in the grass.

'I know I said I never would but . . . but what is left for me here?'

Cloaked by the night-time's murder of the sun, one with the gathering shadows, a shape moved furtively.

'I have come to realise Father is right after all.'

No sound disturbed the soft whisper, sinuous and silent as the creeping dusk, the shape moved closer.

'I should go home, take up the reins of business, make a new life . . .'

From the distant hills the first cool breath of night drifted over the garden, robing itself in the perfume of flowers as it wafted towards the kneeling figure and the shape advancing, slow and insidious, every movement a mere flicker rapidly lost amid the encroaching gloom.

'I cannot give either of you back the life you have lost.'

Resting his forehead on the hand touching the marble covering his wife's grave, Jervis's whisper became a sob. 'But I can give something to Father, and I must . . . believe me, Helen, I *must*.'

The increased volume of the murmured words halted the progress of the shadow-enshrouded shape, hooded eyes never leaving the kneeling man. A moment, two, shade on shade the watching shape waited; then slowly as before, no rustle of grass betraying its presence, no muffled tread evidencing its existence, it moved on.

'I have ruined too many lives.' A tremor on the silence, Jervis whispered on. 'But one at least I can restore, I can give back to my father that which I robbed him of: a grandchild; I must marry again.'

Fluid as grey vapour, silent as descending mist, the inaudible threat slid closer.

'I must marry and give my father an heir to carry on his business after me. I have already written to tell him of my return; now, my dear, I must tell you what it is has lain secret for too long. It is not easy . . .'

Drawing a deep breath, Jervis lifted his head. Even now it would not be easy! Silvered fingers of the rising moon filtered through the swooping branches of the neem trees set each side of the softly gleaming vaults as, the breath becoming a captured sigh in his throat, the warm tears blinked from his eyes, Colonel Jervis Buckley stared into the face of death.

'Mr Hayden!' Smoke from the train engine cleared from the window; Amber looked into eyes the vivid blue so familiar of her daydreams.

'Zachary.' The tall figure smiled, showing even, well-scrubbed teeth. 'Can't we make it first-name terms . . . we are friends, are we not?'

'Yes, yes, friends.' Amber blushed.

'Then I can call you Amber?'

Settled on the seat opposite, Zachary Hayden's handsome mouth smiled again. 'Such a pretty name, but then amber is a beautiful stone.'

'Amber is not my given name.' Embarrassment brought the quick explanation. 'I was christened Emma after my grandmother.'

'So how come Amber?'

She had so wanted him to come, to have him stand beside her in that churchyard, to talk with him one last time; she had wanted it so much it had been an almost physical pain in her chest, a throbbing pulsating pain she could not ease. Now Zachary Hayden was here with her in this carriage but the pain had not diminished, it had simply moved to hold her throat in what had become a pincer grip of shyness as the memory of those thoughts, of that longing, rushed in on her.

It was the voice she heard as sleep carried her into its own hidden realms, a gentleness overlying strength, a softness beneath which stirred the waves of passion.

'Are we not friends enough for an answer?'

Startled as though shaken by a rough hand, Amber's blush deepened. Had her thoughts been spoken aloud?

'It . . . Amber . . .' She struggled to control the turbulence running inside her. 'It is a name my father gave me, he . . . he said my eyes were the exact colour of the stone. He called me by it and so did everyone else.'

'Your grandmother's name, Emma.' Holding it on his tongue, Zachary's blue eyes seemed to stroke the pink of her face. 'It is also pretty, but I agree with your father, Amber is the better choice; it carries within it the whisper of eternity, the promise of love which once given can never be withdrawn but like the gem will outlive time.'

The stifling hold on her throat keeping breath from her lungs, blood pounding her temples, Amber snatched herself free of that stroking, drowning blue. He had meant to be complimentary but his words, his gaze . . . they threatened her, not with any danger from him but from that of her own emotions.

'My . . . my sister.' She locked her own gaze on the window but saw nothing of the fields slipping past. 'She was named Bethany and my brother was Denny.'

Allowing the moment he himself needed, Zachary Hayden watched the shadows, which spoke of heartbreak chase across that lovely face. She had said *was*. Did that mean her brother and sister too were dead?

'My sister and brother . . .'

Uninterrupting, Zachary listened to the answer he had not asked for.

'They stayed behind when I left for India. Those at Bescot Lodge promised they would be well cared for; but my sister drowned and Denny ran away. I have not been able to find him though I hope he will one day see my advertisement and come home.'

How had a young girl come to drown, and why would her brother run away? Questions pricked Zachary's mind but, pushing them aside, he said, 'An advertisement in a newspaper, asking information, is a good way of searching for your brother. Newspapers have a wide circulation.'

Amber broke her gaze from the window but still did not meet the eyes she felt still watched her. 'It does not ask information, nor is it actually a newspaper, not any more.'

'It does not ask information and it is not a newspaper!' Zachary Hayden frowned. 'I'm afraid you've lost me.'

Waiting until the ticket inspector had punched her ticket and left the compartment, Amber explained Rani's idea of putting the name Amber and the town name of Darlaston on each bottle of toilette water; how they had decided not to advertise their beauty products in newspapers as these might not be of great interest to women at home; the advertisements would not be read by a lad but every package would have the same information and maybe somewhere he would see one of them.

Rani is no nokar . . . *there is no servant and mistress . . .*

Zachary felt his insides tighten as the remembered words sprang to his mind. Amber Neale might have no servant but she had property and business. A house of beauty! There was no place in such a life for a plain everyday workman.

'But even should he see he might still be too afraid to come back.'

'*Still* too afraid?' Attention immediately back with what was being said, Zachary caught the flicker of anxiety. 'Amber, you have already told me your brother ran away, now you say he might be too afraid to return. Why . . . who is he so afraid of?'

She had not meant to speak of that; it had slipped from her tongue. Catching her bottom lip between her teeth Amber stared mutely at hands now twisting in her lap. What must he think of her? A woman hawking not only her own but her brother's private affairs!

Leaning forward, Zachary reached for the hands worrying together but withdrew quickly. She had given him permission to use her name; it did not include permission to touch her. But none was needed in order to offer help.

'Amber,' he said, 'I know something is wrong. It isn't only what you have told me makes me certain of that, it is what I've seen in your eyes. Tell me what is bothering you. Who is it has your brother afraid?'

Head bent so she did not have to meet his gaze, Amber remained silent. There was nothing he could do; to involve him would have Uriah Buckley direct his venom towards yet another innocent person.

The clickety-click of the train wheels passing over the points provided the only sound as Amber tried to sort the scramble of thoughts crowding her brain. She could not reveal the truth of Bethany's dying, she could not disclose that of Denny's humiliation, yet to say nothing . . . !

Catching a breath, holding it, then releasing it she lifted her head. She would answer and if it meant lying to protect Zachary Hayden then she would lie.

'When I returned from India,' she began quietly, 'I was told of my sister. She had gone beyond her depth and had drowned; as for Denny, he got into an argument with the older stable boys at Bescot Lodge: he was barely twelve years old and the threat of a beating had him scared, so he ran away.'

And that was supposed to be the truth! Zachary's inner

smile was grim. Showing none of his disbelief on his face nor allowing it to colour his voice he asked, 'Who told you all of this?'

She must not make another slip! Teeth clipping again at her lower lip her reply was almost lost beneath the repetitive click of wheels and points.

'The housekeeper, Mrs Saunders.'

'Mmmm.' Zachary nodded. 'And was Mrs Saunders in the stable, was she present when the other lads threatened your brother?'

'No, it was Freddy.'

'Another stable hand?'

The words were asking more than the question they formed; they were asking for the truth. But that she would not give. Shutting away the disquiet lying always brought, forcing herself to meet those intense blue eyes, she shook her head.

'Freddy was not supposed to be in the stables, to be caught there would mean a beating for himself. You see, he is supposed to be weak in the head but he is sane as you or I. He saw what happened to Denny; he was hiding in the loft. Somehow the others now know of what he saw and heard; they fear the results of Freddy sharing that knowledge with me and as a consequence his mother is fearful for his safety. They spent last night with Rani and myself but Becky insists they leave Darlaston altogether. But to go where? They haven't the means to rent and Becky Worrall will not accept charity.'

There was more than he was being told, much more. Zachary glanced at the lip bitten sore. A young brother running away . . . yes, that was problem enough but it was a darker grief than that weighed on Amber Neale's shoulders.

'Does this Becky Worrall have a special town she wishes to go and live in?'

'I don't think she would mind as long as it is away from Bes— from Darlaston.'

The pause, the slight pull of her mouth before correcting her reply: it had shouted volumes. She had almost said Bescot Lodge. That house had been the origin of the sadness always present in those soft golden eyes and it held problems for her still. So who owned Bescot Lodge – and what taint of evil touched it?

32

He had not been wrong to trust to his convictions; they had not proved false.

A gleam of triumph lighting iron-hard eyes, Uriah Buckley slapped the letter he had just read onto the couch beside him. Jervis was coming home, his son was returning to England! Satisfaction swelling inside him, Uriah rose to stride to the window. All of this, the house, the land, the iron foundry, everything would pass to him. But not only to him, not only to Jervis. A short laugh sounding this triumph he stared out over neat well-tended grounds. Jervis would marry again. Oh, the letter hadn't said as much but some things had no need of being said. Jervis were a man still in middle years, he would beget children, an heir . . . a son to inherit after himself, a grandchild to carry the name of Uriah Buckley on into the future.

And it would be a future to be proud of! Swivelling to face into the room, Uriah smiled. He would teach the lad every trick of the trade, every last way of finishing on top; he would not be the namby-pamby his father had been. It would not be nature would fill the boy's mind, not bloody arty-farty statues and paintings: his mind would be kept on the producing of iron, his soul would be gifted to the building of the business. That would be his love, his passion, and Uriah Buckley would be his mentor.

Everything had turned out well! The smile became one of smug contentment. Edward Elton had passed no share of the

New Hope to his son, and that dirty lecher had met his come-uppance before he could contest the document which left him with nothing. Shot by another of his own sort, a man not given to the love of women. Perverts! The thought spat in Uriah's brain. They deserved to be dead, all three of 'em, the world were well rid of that kind!

The New Hope! The smile fading, Uriah felt a tinge of doubt. Ought he to have sold the mine, should he not have waited, discussed the proposition first with Jervis? 'But then I hadn't knowed Elton's lad would be murdered,' he muttered aloud. 'I 'ad no knowing he would be put outta the way afore he could lay claim.'

Taking up the letter he glanced again at the words scrawled across the page, words telling him Jervis was coming home. Yes, he had done the right thing getting rid of a worthless coal mine. Jervis might have dilly-dallied over the rights and wrongs of selling, knowing it was worked out, and that would have proved too late; the hope of offloading onto some fool would have been dashed. Whoever had been daft enough to purchase the New Hope had done him a service – as had the love-crazed shirt-lifter who had shot the brain from Elton.

But who now owned a mine with no coal? The smile eased back over Uriah's mouth. He hadn't bothered to ask; but he might. Yes, he might.

She had told more than intended, one lie had tumbled into another. Alone in her room, Amber at last gave way to the tears which had threatened all day. Zachary Hayden had recognised she was not telling the whole of the truth; she had seen proof of that in his eyes, yet he had not probed but only listened. But how could she tell what had really happened? The stripping and pawing and possible rape of a girl hardly out of childhood, the near-rape of an even younger boy . . . and the attacks upon herself, how could she tell of them without giving the name Uriah Buckley? So she had let the lies stand. And he had left with them undenied.

Tears warm and wet on her cheeks, she climbed into bed. Zachary Hayden could not solve her problems but he had solved that of Becky.

He could attend to his business in Birmingham another day, he had told her when she had protested against his idea; the market which took his produce would not become insolvent for waiting a while. So he had come with her to Ley Cottage and there had offered his own home to Becky. *'It has an outbuilding warm and dry enough for a bed.'* The quiet even tones seemed to bite into her mind but it was the rest that stabbed into her heart.

He had turned to Freddy then, the boy's face lighting up with pleasure as he was offered a chance of work and of responsibility. He would show him what was needed, Zachary had told him quietly, he would teach him how to regulate the heating of the glasshouses, how to sow, how to plant seedlings and the care necessary for raising of vegetables.

'But you'll be there yourself,' Becky had said. *'You'll be there to see everything be done proper . . . and speaking of proper, it don't be right you turning your 'ome over to others while you be sleeping in an outhouse. You can't not never expect a body to go along of that.'*

Then had come the blow that had rocked her on her heels, the stab that had pierced her to the quick, the words which had snatched at her soul.

'I shall not be sleeping there long, Mrs Worrall. I am leaving Bloxwich . . . I am going back to sea.'

Going back to sea.

Four short words yet they rocked her world. Eyes wide, Amber stared into the darkness.

He was leaving Bloxwich – going out of her life! She had known today's trip to her mother's grave was the last she could afford to make; she had reconciled herself to the fact she would likely not meet with him again but behind that had been the comfort of hope, hope that if finances should permit then there was a chance, a slim chance, of their meeting once more. But with his return to the sea that hope was dead inside her.

She had never thought to feel like this, to experience such emptiness, such devastation. Bethany . . . Denny . . . the loss of them had left her heartbroken, but the loss of Zachary Hayden, the knowledge of not seeing, not speaking with him again went deeper. It seemed something within her had withered.

Becky had promised her mother's grave would be cared for. Turning her face to a moon-chased sky, Amber tried to end the thoughts of Zachary Hayden, but as often as racing clouds flipped the great silver-white orb from sight they returned.

He would stay until Freddy was comfortable with the work of the smallholding. Stress of the day pressed on eyes smarting with tiredness and little by little they began to close. But what if Uriah Buckley found out where Becky and Freddy had gone? Eyelids drooped lower. What if he learned they were at Bloxwich? Obstinately her eyes jerked open. It was not beyond his powers; Bloxwich was not a world away. Suppose he did trace Becky and her son . . . suppose he waited until they were alone, would he go after them? Would he send men to . . . ? Eyelids lowered, shutting out shadows creeping towards the bed, lids that did not lift as an owl hooted from the heath.

The men hired by Uriah inched slowly towards two figures. Nearer they came and on a signal formed a circle about Becky and Freddy and as the couple lifted their heads, spotting them, they sprang.

Behind sleep-closed lids Amber saw the figures change, saw

the hands reach out, watched them haul two frightened people to their feet, drag them away by the hair. But the attackers were not wearing soot-blackened trousers and jackets, no flat caps, and their faces were not smeared with smoke; they were robed in thigh-length kaftan type tops over wide-legged cotton trousers and their heads were swathed in bright coloured turbans and the frightened figures they hauled away were not Becky Worrall and her son, they were Rani and herself.

Feringhee!

The word hissed in her dream-filled mind, spat at a thin terrified girl being pushed and dragged, while all around buildings of unspeakable grace and beauty seemed to float upwards from dust-dry earth.

Then the hot brilliant light was gone. Like a spectator at a play, Amber watched the pictures her tired brain resurrected, watched the past play vivid and stark. The light was softer now, the heat subdued by the stone of a great pillared hall, the girl huddled where she had been thrown amid a circle of men.

In the moon-filled bedroom, Amber's body crouched beneath covers her clutching fingers had caught against her mouth.

'Please,' she sobbed, 'please!'

But the murmur did not penetrate the dark vaults of subconsciousness, did not pass the doors of sleep to recall her to wakefulness.

Somewhere from the shadows came a sound and like clockwork toys the grinning men turned their backs, the circle now enfolding another, dressed in gleaming blue silk, jewels glittering at his throat. Strands of them wound about his turban while others gleamed on the hand reaching for the girl.

'No!' Caught by the sheet crumpled against her lips, Amber's cry made little sound in the silent, night-shrouded cottage, but a jerk of her head on the pillow mimicked the action that dragged the covering from the head of a trembling girl, her sari ripped from her body while eyes, black and devouring, burned down at her.

Chained by sleep, Amber watched, her whimpers becoming a cry as the jewelled hand reached toward soft white breasts, the stone-hard eyes gleaming . . . gleaming down at *her.*

But even as the dream showed her own face it showed another; another hand gave back the flimsy cotton of the sari; other, more gentle, eyes looked into the stricken face, the eyes of a man dressed in scarlet uniform. But those eyes were vivid blue, and the face was that of Zachary Hayden.

A gasp breaking from her, Amber was suddenly awake. Trembling as shadows of the past seemed to flit about her bed, she lit the candle.

Greville! Afraid to close her eyes, afraid the nightmare would return, she leaned against the pillows. Greville Neale had handed the sari to her then covered her with his own coat. The Army had been informed a group of bandits roamed the hills terrorising local villages, that they used the deserted city of Fatehpur Sikri as a meeting place. Greville and a troop of soldiers had lain in wait there. The flash of her hair had alerted him to her presence; closed in by that ring of men he would not have seen her in time had not the rich copper of it caught his eye.

. . . would not have seen her in time . . .

Remembering the later explanation of those words, Amber felt her whole self tremble.

'They would not have let you live. The abduction of a European woman would have meant death for each and every one of those men. They would have taken their revenge first, those swords would have left little of you.'

Sergeant Major Greville Neale: the man who had taken her from that awful life, the man who had married her. But his were not the eyes had looked at her; his not the face she had seen in her dream, not the one which stayed with her now. Zachary! She drew the sheet up to her mouth, stilling the name which trembled on her lips. The face had been that of Zachary Hayden!

It was wrong – wrong to think like that! Guilt ran a warm flood swiftly along her veins. Greville was her husband, the kindest of men, it was him she should see, him she should love!

'I heard the cries of your fear.' Gilded by the touch of candlelight, Rani's black hair gleamed as she came quickly to the bedside. 'Is it sickness of body ails you?'

Above the sheet still clutched to her mouth, Amber's eyes reflected the golden flame; but behind it glittered a deeper flame: the fear Rani had seen so many times.

'The night has sent its demons to plague you once more,' she said, sitting on the side of Amber's bed. 'They are there still in your mind; but they are only the mist of sleep. Touch them with your waking and they will melt away.'

'I . . . I'm sorry I disturbed you, it was . . .'

'The dream,' Rani answered. 'They come not at our bidding but at the will of the Dark One; but they cannot harm unless we allow; you must not allow, my sister, do not let old fears take on new life.'

Was that what was happening? Was the fear she had felt at the hands of those bandits becoming a different fear? Fear that the love which should be given only to Greville Neale was being given to Zachary Hayden!

Gently pulling the sheet free of Amber's convulsive grip, Rani took both hands between her own. 'Share the dream with me,' she said gently, 'let us touch the mist together.'

Haltingly, fright not yet completely eclipsed, Amber related the terrors that had filled her sleep, pausing when the face of her rescuer took on the features of Zachary Hayden.

'The haze of mist is not yet gone.' Rani met the hesitation with understanding. 'Drifts of it linger and will stay to form new clouds should you not clear them with words.'

Words! To put words to the picture which had formed part of that dream would only add to the guilt burning inside her; it would compound the treachery.

'Fight the Dark One, speak of the fears he has placed in your heart, let the light of truth chase the shadows of his coming.'

'It . . . the uniform.' Amber's fingers twined with those of her friend. 'It was Greville's, but the face . . . the face was Zachary's.'

There was new love in the woman she called sister. Rani felt the trip of apprehension she had felt on that first realisation, but this time no thought of herself, of the place she might no longer have in the life of Amber Neale, followed it. A smile gentle on her mouth, she said; 'The man whose face took that of your husband, was he not always kind to you? Why now does your heart feel fear of him?'

'Not him.' Amber shook her head. 'It isn't him I am afraid of, it's myself!'

'You are in fear of your love for him, this is the mist, the tendril which remains. But why does it linger?'

'Because . . . Greville, he gave me love, he married me, gave me his name when others would turn their back on me! He does not deserve to be forgotten.'

Turning her face towards the window, Rani's stare passed beyond reality to gaze at moon shadows, the shadows of her own past; figures of a man and a woman, her parents smiling in the silvered moment, children laughing as they caught her hand, drawing her into a game . . . a man grabbing a young girl who walked with a water pot balanced on her head.

'The paths of memory wind through many gardens.' A sheen of moisture glistened like dark gems in her eyes as she turned again to the girl propped against pillows. 'Some are strewn with the blossoms of happiness, their walkways bordered with flowers of content, and all is cooled with the sweet air of pleasure; but there are paths lead other ways: their gardens are grey with melancholy and their trees bear bitter fruits of regret and sadness. To follow either can seem to give what it is the heart desires, but to let the feet rest too long upon them is unwise, for they can become a place of refuge. In them we can hide from the world of reality. That would not be the wish of the sergeant major sahib; do not bind him with chains he cannot break but let him wander freely in the garden of your memory. Do not use his love as a barrier against a love your heart cries for.'

Releasing the hands she held, Rani rose to her feet, but as Amber made to speak, shook her head, saying softly, 'The hours day brings will be many, they can be filled with our speaking, but those left of night are few and need to be given to sleep; rest now, my sister, the peace of the Almighty hold you in its embrace.'

. . . do not use his love as a barrier against a love your heart cries for . . .

The words had come too late! Amber turned her face into the pillow. Zachary Hayden was gone from her life. He had returned to the sea!

She had hidden it too long. Amber watched the sari-clad figure checking jars and bottles in the storeroom of the house they had turned into a salon. She had acted without consulting the girl who had done as much as herself to launch the business. Without the skills learned in her childhood, the flower oils and leaves she called her treasure, there would be no house of beauty.

'There is little of this, it has proved the most wished for.'

Rani turned, a small carton in her hand emblazoned with the logo the girl herself had insisted become the trademark of the range of cosmetics after hearing the term Joanna Buckley had used to describe Amber's neatly kept room. 'Salon d'Ambre', that girl had laughed, whirling happily round and round the room. 'I shall call this the Salon d'Ambre.'

'We will need to make more.'

Rani's words brought her back to the present. Amber took the carton. Withdrawing the crystal bottle she gazed at the beauty of it. Moulded into the figure of a woman, a leaf-filled branch of a tree draped across the thighs, tresses of softly waving hair covering one breast, the lovely enticing face smiled.

Eve. The perfume named for a child she had once met on a tram. Staring at it now, Amber was caught again by the beauty of its lines, the sparkling clarity of its crystal. Like all the rest of the bottles and jars Simeon Pearson created for her, this was a thing of beauty in itself.

But she, Amber Neale, had not the unblemished honesty of that child on the tram. She had deceived as had that very first Eve, she had lied to Zachary Hayden and kept a truth from Rani. Setting the perfume bottle again in its carton she looked at the girl who had turned back to the shelves.

'Rani,' she said quietly, 'there will be no more of this . . . no more of anything. The dream is ended. The salon must close.'

33

'I am not understanding.' Leaving the checking of stock Rani stood, her gentle features registering surprise.

'How could you without knowing the stupid thing I have done. I meant to tell you, really I did but . . . but . . .'

That had been at the salon. Rani had seen at once the emotion playing behind the words she had stammered and had asked no more be said until they were in the homely comfort of Ley Cottage. Now sitting with the tea the other girl had hurried to make, Amber tried to find a way of telling how she had excluded her from that one decision.

'It,' she breathed deeply, 'it was the time I visited the glass works. I heard two women talking . . .'

'You do not have to be telling what it is you have done. It is not to be needed—'

'But it is!' Amber rushed in. 'I need it. Oh, if only I had waited! I've been so selfish. I thought only of myself.'

'The action of the mind is sometimes too strong, it pulls where we would not go.'

'But I was told not to go there, advised as to the risk, but I would not listen. The women on the tram, I could not help but overhear their conversation. They said the New Hope colliery had been put up for sale; one of them said her son had heard it from the clerk of the solicitor who handled the affairs of Uriah Buckley.'

That man! Rani felt the ripple of a shiver. Had her friend

not yet realised the danger he posed, had the lesson not been learned? Knowing that to interrupt might be to have Amber turn from her decision to speak of what it was troubled her, and that such a decision would serve only to prolong and maybe deepen the worry that was so obvious in the twisting fingers, Rani stayed silent.

'The words kept running through my mind.' Amber's voice dropped to a murmur as though the explanation were for herself. 'I could not rid myself of them or the ones which followed, words my own brain added. Simeon Pearson saw the agitation of them and when he heard he advised I return home and think things over clearly.'

'You spoke of your worry to the maker of glass?'

The hint of sadness in Rani's question was echoed in the look that met Amber's own.

'I should have followed his advice, I should have put the proposition to you, but I did not. Instead I bought the New Hope colliery.'

Smiling faintly, Rani shook her head. 'You are mistress of yourself, my sister. Only to husband or father do you speak of your actions, and you have no husband and no father.'

'But I have a friend!' Amber cried. 'A very good friend. I showed disrespect in not asking your opinion, Rani. What saddens me most is the fact that the coal is exhausted.'

'The coal, it is weary?'

Despite her feeling of shame, Amber laughed. 'No, it does not mean the coal is tired. Exhausted is used to say there is no more left, the mine is empty of coal.'

'You were not knowing this when you purchased the mine?'

The laugh dead in her throat, Amber replied, self-condemnation thick in every word. 'No, I did not know, nor did I follow Simeon Pearson's caution of taking the advice of someone who probably would have known. He said Uriah

Buckley must have a reason for selling, that a profitable business was not sold without one. But all the way back to Darlaston, like a hammer driving nails into my head, were the words 'buy it', echoed over and over without stopping, just those two words. They seemed to paralyse all other thought, to hold my brain insensible to any but themselves, and like someone trapped in a dream I did what they said. Now it's too late. I cannot wipe my name from the document I signed, I cannot take back the money I paid. That is the reason the salon must close. The money meant to pay its upkeep until it would pay for itself . . . I threw it away on a spent-out coal mine!'

Filling cups with tea, Rani added milk and sugar before placing one in Amber's hands. Then, gazing into her own cup, said quietly, 'The words driven like nails, they could not have such strength unless driven by the gods; there is purpose not yet revealed to you, a guidance that drew your steps, that put your hand to sign, a design heaven will show only in its time. Put sadness from your heart, for fate chooses its own path while we must follow after.'

'I can't blame fate for what was nothing but irresponsibility. I acted without thinking and as a result I have left us virtually penniless.'

Touching Amber's hand, urging she drink the hot sweet liquid, Rani smiled again. 'Have we not been without an anna before? Has there been no time when a single rupee seemed the wealth of a maharajah? The money that comes from the selling of creams and perfumes will not buy rubies and diamonds such as his, but it will pay for food; with care it will keep the house of beauty open.'

'No, no, it will not.' Placing the cup on its saucer, Amber met the liquid brown gaze. 'I visited the New Hope mine. I talked with the few men whom Uriah Buckley had not given their tin . . . who had not yet been sent away.' Amber explained away the quick frown of confusion settling on the other girl's brow. 'They told me there was very little coal remaining, that in weeks there would be none at all. I saw the worry in their eyes, heard the fear behind their words. They were men with families, with children to feed. How could I deprive them of the means by which to do that? How could I take away all that they had to keep open a salon whose purpose is simply to flatter women's vanity, to pamper those who already have so much they will never know the pain of hunger or the misery of poverty? Truth is I could not. I could not bring more suffering where the traces of it already showed deep in the faces of those men so . . . so I told them to carry on with working the mine.'

'You listened to your heart.' Rani smiled. 'You heard the word put there by the Lord of heaven and you obeyed. There is no wrong in that.'

It was meant to console, to alleviate the sense of guilt, and Amber's glance carried her gratitude, but worry remained clear in her answer. 'But there is wrong in taking from you. The salon was intended to provide you with comfort, a life that would never again be burdened by want; I have ruined any chance of that.'

'My want is satisfied by your friendship and there is no need of anything but the returning of peace to your mind. The names written in the book, they will be honoured, but no others will be placed there.'

Yes, the appointments already accepted would be kept but no more would be made. Confession had lifted the weight that had pressed so heavily; Amber collected the cups, making to follow Rani to the scullery, but a sound from outside had her suddenly still, only her nerves jumping at the calling of her name.

*　　*　　*

'I 'ad to come, it don't be in my nature to take a body's 'ospitality only to turn my back and forget all about them.'

'But you could have been seen.' Amber looked anxiously at the woman sitting in her kitchen. Becky Worrall had declined the living room, saying, 'I be more rested in the kitchen.' Now, settled with hot tea and a fresh-baked scone, she beamed at Rani. 'These be good, I could make no better meself.'

The compliment bringing a smile, Rani enquired of Freddy.

Brushing away a crumb of pastry from her mouth, Becky Worrall shook her head. 'Be like Amber said about bein' seen. A woman wi' a shawl over her head and a basket on her arm don't go drawing attention walking along of Wolver'ampton Lane, they be two a penny; but a lad, especially one old enough to be at work a-getting' of a livin', well, that be different. My Freddy be tall for his years and his body be near that of a man growed. Notice would 'ave been taken and mebbe word could reach Buckley's ears. Least that were what I told him to keep him from coming to visit, but how much longer he will heed me be anybody's guess.'

'Freddy is good behaved, he listens to the counsel of his *mai*.'

'For the time he do,' Becky replied, sipping her tea. 'But for how much longer? He be a changed lad since we went along of Bloxwich.'

'He is not in any trouble?'

'Lor' bless you, no, he be in no trouble.' Becky smiled at Amber's question. 'I was meaning only that he be so confident, so sure in what he does. The slowness be going from his tongue and he don't think himself daft Freddy no more, an' that be due to Zachary.' The pride that had glistened in her eyes as she spoke of her son became a gleam of gratitude and her voice held a quiet salutation as she went on. 'Eh, he's been so good, has Zachary Hayden, so patient with the lad. Firm, yes he were firm but never angry, though sometimes I asked meself how he kept from it, the blunders Freddy made. But he kept on showing what needed to be learned, showed how to use one plant to give a dozen, what to set in the open and the month of that setting, explaining and showing over again 'til it were strong in the lad's brain; then he did the same with the instructing of how to care for them there glasshouses, need almost the looking after of a babby they does, and my Freddy weren't of the mind he had sense enough for the doing of it, but Zachary Hayden were of another mind altogether. Looked at my lad, he did, and smiled . . . you know, that quick smile that fills his eyes . . . well, he smiled and said, "Fred, if I thought you could not do what is necessary then I would not ask, and I certainly would not leave my land to any but a man capable of looking after it. You are that man, Fred, you are the one I can trust."'

Yes, she remembered that quick smile that filled his eyes. Amber glanced away, fearful her own eyes might betray the disturbance thought of Zachary Hayden caused inside her.

'He ain't never used the name Freddy to my lad, not once since the knowin' of him.' Becky talked on, not noticing the bloom of colour risen to Amber's cheeks. 'Speaks to him like he was already a man, does Zachary, and a man with all his senses. That be appreciated more'n all the rest of his kindness; Zachary Hayden might not have the wealth of some but he do have the heart many a man could wish for. But there I goes a prattling on when I should be telling what it is I was asked to say. Zachary said to ask what flowers you would want growed and Freddy . . . Fred would see they was planted right and proper; but I'll ask you be good enough to set the names on paper lessen I forgets. Flowers don't be summat a washer-woman often has the dealing of.'

'I don't understand.'

Seeing Amber's perplexed frown, Becky Worrall chuckled

softly. 'He said as that would be the case. Said he knowed nothing of the making of perfumes and the like, but a business such as the one you talked of on the train would have need of more flowers than you could grow in your garden. That being so he said Fred were to keep a vegetable plot and the rest of the ground be given to growing whatever it was you asked for.'

More than a little dazed by what she heard, Amber tried to collect her thoughts. Zachary Hayden had offered to supply her with flowers, to grow them specifically for her use! Glancing at Rani, her eyes asked what she should reply but for once the other girl knew she must decide for herself.

To refuse would appear a snub; to accept knowing she could not pay . . . There was only one way. Glancing once more at Rani, then to the woman enjoying a second cup of tea, she said: 'Please thank Mr Hayden for his offer but we will not be needing any more flowers. The salon is to be closed.'

'Closed!' Becky lowered her cup. 'Eh, that be a shame. The both of you worked so hard, and God knows the women of Darlaston deserved summat pleasant, a change from the stink of factory smoke and coal dust. But you knows your own way best, no doubt there be a reason. As for that there basket of blossoms my lad picked from them glasshouses, I reckon I best throw them on the waste heap.'

'No.' Rani smiled, taking the basket the woman reached for. 'The gift of Zachary and the kindness of your son is received with gladness; please tell them *shukria*.'

'Shuk . . . shuk . . . ?' Becky Worrall reached for her shawl, not trying the strange-sounding word again. 'I'll tell Freddy, though it won't sound nowheres near the same coming from my tongue; but as for telling it to Zachary, that I can't do for he be gone from Bloxwich.'

He had kept to his decision. What he had said at that last meeting had not been just words – Zachary Hayden was gone from Bloxwich! An emptiness she could not describe left Amber trembling as she followed Becky from the cottage.

'Your mother's resting place be neat as I promised. I takes flowers every week as you would want.' With the basket Rani had emptied and returned to her slung on her arm, the woman paused. 'I speaks to her each time I goes. I tells her that soon, God willing, you'll be taking flowers to her yourself.'

Edged with silver tears, Amber's reply came quietly. 'Thank you for coming, I hope we can meet again soon.'

I hope we can meet again soon.

Returning to the living room the words she had said sounded again in Amber's heart, but she knew they were meant for Zachary Hayden.

Mrs Greville Neale . . . Mrs Greville Neale had bought his coal mine! Driving his carriage across the Bull Stake and onto the Darlaston Road, Uriah laughed aloud. The stupid woman had bought the New Hope! What had her used for brains? But then women had no brain for aught but the running of a house, and quite a few of 'em 'adn't the brain for that! Her had had money, money enough to pay the price asked. However, the money handed across the desk of his solicitor wouldn't be the total of all that mine would cost her. Mrs Greville Neale had bought herself a millstone, may it hang heavy and the neck it adorned break beneath it!

Part-way up the steep rise that was King's Hill he pulled at the rein, guiding the horse left into the yard of the iron foundry.

Buckley Iron. He read the words worked in metal and set above the curve of the wide double gates. Soon he would have the pleasure of driving through them with Jervis at his side. Together they would build a foundry bigger than any this Black Country had ever seen, together they would build that empire he had dreamed of so long ago, an empire which would pass to grandsons and then to their grandsons; Buckley would become the name this town were built on.

But should Jervis prove to have any of the dreamer left in him, any of the daft ideas of moral virtue, then any suspicion of what had passed in this house, even a mere suggestion of what had happened between the Eltons and that pair of young 'uns, any mention, any insinuation and Jervis might be like to turn tail.

The balloon of satisfaction burst at the thought. Uriah's face was grim as he strode through the bedlam that was the foundry, the clang of iron rods being pushed through the rings attached to the sides of crucibles, the sparks from white-hot metal showering like stars as it was tipped into moulds, all going unheeded as he pushed past sweating men.

Edward Elton and his son were dead! Uriah slammed the door of his office behind him. That left only one avenue by way of which any disclosure, any denunciation of those activities might come. Servants, any in his direct employ or those his money could destroy? They would hold any inklings they might have to themselves; but there was one who held no fear of Uriah Buckley, one who would not hesitate to lay her accusations before Jervis. The Neale woman! Uriah's mouth compressed hard against his teeth. He had told himself that bitch should be destroyed; now he told himself again.

. . . I will see you in hell . . .

Eyes narrowing, Uriah recalled the words thrown at him. Maybe that were true, but her would be there afore him – he would see to that himself!

The flower heads Becky had brought had not been wasted. Rani had suggested they be used as women in her own village had often used flowers. Together they had carefully plucked and separated each petal laying them in neat precise lines on shallow trays of purified fat. 'The fragrance of the petals will be given to the fat.' Rani had smiled at Amber's obvious doubt. 'It will become scented cream same as others.' Now the whole cottage had the fragrance of summer once more. Zachary Hayden had instructed those flowers, so tenderly nurtured in special buildings of glass, be brought to her, that almost his whole grounds be given to growing more. Why should he do that? Life in Bloxwich no longer suited him, it was not what he wanted. But why not sell his property, why hold onto it if all he desired was a life at sea? Thoughts sharp as arrows stabbed at Amber, the sharpest of all, the one she tried so hard to depress, bringing a stifled sob to her throat. Zachary Hayden had not looked at her as he had left with Becky and her son, he had said no word meant only for her; she had no place in his heart.

'The shadow of sadness lies over you, my sister. The sorrow of closing your house of beauty is hard for you to bear.'

Deep in the misery that had closed over her at Becky's disclosure and had held her from that moment, Amber had not heard the soft tread of Rani returning from placing the last tray in the scullery. Now as she turned she saw the concern etched across the other girl's face.

'Your heart carries much grief,' Rani said, her eyes showing sympathy, 'but the cause it comes from was for the welfare of others. You have taken from yourself to give to men digging coal; the great God sees this and will return the blessing.'

It isn't the salon's closing has my heart sore! Amber wanted to cry; instead she forced a pale smile.

'You reminded me we managed during the bleak days in India. I'm sure this can be no worse for us; but the men working the coal mine, what of them once the last of our money is gone?'

'Many women came to the salon. They bought perfumes and creams; they will come again when more is made.'

'England is not like India,' Amber returned ruefully. 'The sun does not shine here every day of the year. Winter is cold, we have snow which you have not yet seen. Those months are too cold for the growing of many flowers and plants we need to use. I should have realised this before ever we started.'

'It is not given for us to see all that is planned.'

'Maybe not, but I should have seen that. I ought to have realised this garden is far too small to have supported such an undertaking; I have wasted all that Greville left to me! I'm ashamed of my stupidity!'

'The sergeant major sahib would not call you foolish, nor would he say you had wasted what he gave. He would be only proud that you help those men and the families they are feeding.'

How could he have been proud of what she was doing? He would have seen no sense in buying a coal mine without first having a thorough check made of its past and present capacity. Greville Neale had been a kind but practical man; he would never have approved of the rashness she had shown.

The salon would have to close, the coal mine she had purchased would drain the very last of her finances but neither of those things fed the feeling Rani had called the shadow of sadness; the weight she could not lift was that of Zachary Hayden's returning to the sea. The thought had plagued the rest of the evening and hours later it plagued yet. Sleep still far away, Amber lay staring at the night. To feel this way was to dishonour the memory of Greville Neale; it was a betrayal of the hospitality he had shown her after the rescue from the deserted city, a violation of the love she had known he had come to feel for her in the days which had followed.

He had loved her, it had shown in his eyes the rare moments his guard had dropped. And she had returned that love! But it had been a love born of gratitude, the love she might have felt for a brother; it had held none of the emotion, the nerve-quivering trepidation, the fire that ran through every fibre, the fervour that flamed with the presence of Zachary Hayden. It had held none of the desire thoughts of him aroused.

Yet the time spent with Greville had been happy. He had taken pleasure in showing her a little of the beauty of India's great past, the legacy of some of its rulers.

Eyes closing against the darkness of her room, Amber allowed the warm light of memory to flow over her. They had visited the huge Red Fort set in the heart of Delhi, its high sandstone walls rimmed with close-packed tessellated arches, the broad Lahore Gate with cupolas seeming to challenge their approach. But the magnificence of those walls had hidden a splendour to rob the onlooker of breath. Fluted and carved, stone walls were cut into patterns of intricate design, cool passages led to inner chambers, the loveliest of which were the once-royal apartments whose rooms were set with fountains playing in shallow basins cut to represent wide-petalled blossoms festooned with tracings of flowering vines, the whole inlaid with semi-precious stones.

Greville had smiled at the delight which had grown with each place they visited; the beautiful Jama Masjid mosque with its marble inlaid walls and massive domes, the serene beauty of the Humayun's tomb. She had thought nothing could possibly compare with the grandeur of such buildings, but she had been wrong.

Eyes opening, she turned her glance to the window and at that moment a high moon broke from behind the clouds and the night turned to silver.

That was how it had been on the last night of their brief tour.

There was something he wanted her to see. Greville had smiled, refusing to say more. As they rode in a tonga, a small two-wheeled horse-drawn carriage, he had resisted all attempts at trying to get him to reveal their destination. Then the tonga had halted and he had helped her alight. Why had they needed to return to Agra, a place he had brought her to earlier in their short holiday?

The Taj Mahal had held her breathless. Greville had stood beside her as she had drunk in the unbelievable majesty of the building reflected perfectly in the brilliant sun-touched waterway that formed part of the approach to the gleaming white tomb. Flanked by needle-slim minarets and topped by a great dome it had seemed to gaze serenely into eternity while she had felt she could remain forever, lost in its timeless beauty. Greville had not spoken; understanding the emotion inside her he had let her take her fill of the magnificent entrance and symmetrical archways built into its perfect white walls. They had spent a whole afternoon there, her throat tight with tears as she gazed at the nearly transparent alabaster twin sarcophagi set with flowers and vines worked from semi-precious stones, and which covered the bodies of the great Shah Jahan and Mumtaz Mahal, the wife for whom he had raised the wonderful edifice.

But why come here again, and in the darkness of night? Greville had smiled, reading the spoken query showing plainly on her face lit then by the brilliance of a great sky-filling moon, and answered he could not take her from Agra before showing her its secret.

And it was a secret she would thank him for in her heart for sharing. She would remember that evening for the rest of her life. Climbing the few wide steps leading to towering solid wood doors opened for them by a turbanned watchman she had stepped into a silvered dream. The gardens, which during their daytime visit had been peopled with others wishing to see the beautiful building, now lay silent and empty except for the myriad fireflies twinkling like tiny golden stars among the dark-leafed branches of trees; the watercourse which had glittered gold in the blazing sun now glistened a ribbon of silver and above it, set on marble platforms whose grandeur challenged the superb gardens, the exquisite monument seemed almost to float in mid-air.

The cry that had tumbled from her on stepping through those doors had sounded across the spacious grounds. It had been as if she could not breathe, that the heart of her had gone out to the two people for whom life had ended but whose love never would. It was not simply a tomb she had looked at. Amber stared into the moonlit darkness of her room. Not simply a building; elegant and graceful as it was, there was more, a soundless chord that struck deep to the heart. The Taj Mahal was more than a tribute to a beloved wife: it was the soul of a grieving man; cast in marble, it whispered across the span of centuries, a love song in stone.

That was the kind of love she should have felt for Greville, deep and abiding, a love beyond passion; but she had not. Her eyes closing on the thought, Amber felt the warm line of tears rest on her lashes. Tears of Guilt? Yes. But not the guilt of feeling as she had for Greville, but the guilt of the love she carried for Zachary Hayden.

34

The night had been long, her dreams peopled by shadows of the past. Her parents, the man who had become her stepfather yet seen by her so very rarely his face remained elusive, hidden by the wake of time. But Bethany, her sweet face had been clear, the tears of parting brilliant in her eyes; and Denny, his eyes too had brimmed their sadness and the pressure of his arms as he clung to her in dreams seemed still to press about her as she had awakened.

Movements tired and listless as they had been all day, Amber repressed a sigh of relief as she parcelled perfume and matching scented creams for the woman draped in elegant furs. Word of the salon had spread, bringing clients from Wolverhampton, Birmingham and beyond. All had expressed delight in the facial treatments she and Rani had given and each had voiced the desire she open a salon in their home town. It would have become a business which would have supported both of them had it been able to continue.

'You may renew my appointment for this day next week.' The woman took her parcel, a fatuous smile becoming a glare of resentment when Amber answered that would not be possible.

'Not possible!' Resentment flashed to anger. 'Can I have heard wrongly, do you realise to whom you are saying a further appointment would not be possible?'

Were this woman the Queen herself the answer would be no

different. Politely she explained flower oils could not be obtained during winter, therefore the salon could not operate for those months.

Clearly disapproving, the woman snatched up her purchases and stormed from the salon.

'She is being not happy,' Rani said, coming into the reception room as the door banged behind the departing client.

'That makes two of us.' Amber's shoulders sagged. 'Why couldn't I have given more thought . . . I should have waited until we had built a larger stock before opening a salon.'

'If we listen only to words telling what we should have done the life becomes a burden too heavy to carry,' Rani answered quietly. 'Problems are the stepping stones which form the path of learning; unless we tread upon them we remain as children.'

'Sometimes there are two many stones and the path is far too long.'

'The gods place the stones and they put only those they know we can pass.' Rani smiled. 'Always it seems the way is too difficult, that we cannot continue; but always the gods are watching and if we trust they will not let us fall.'

Everything was so simple in Rani's philosophy! Amber slipped into the coat the girl held for her. Trust the gods, they will take care of everything! But Rani's gods were not hers, and the heaven she prayed to every night did not listen.

Could heaven be blamed for that? Had not help been offered through the advice of Simeon Pearson, had he not told her to think carefully before purchasing that coal mine? No, she could not accuse heaven of not listening when she herself had done the self-same thing. It was she and no one else had brought this present problem, she alone had placed this stone in her path – and it was one she could not surmount!

Anxiety for the welfare of others, Rani and those miners

whose living she had assumed responsibility for, weighed heavy in Amber's heart as together she and Rani walked the distance to Ley Cottage, keeping her silent while they shared the chore of making the evening meal.

Dishes washed and returned to the dresser, Rani stood beside it, her glance full of sympathy for the girl she had come to love as a sister, and her voice carried every atom of it as she said gently, 'Your heart cries tears I cannot dry, your soul sinks beneath the weight of a sadness it is not given to me to lift or I would take it gladly, but there is the book of your *mai*, it helps bring comfort when you read . . . will you not read from it now?'

Her mother's Bible! Rani was right, reading a little of it or simply holding it seemed to bring her mother close. Nodding assent, she whispered in her heart as the other girl handed her the book, 'Help me, Mother . . . help me.'

It had slipped from her hands. Amber stared at the Bible, the cover of it twisted as it lay on the floor. She had taken it from Rani and in that moment it seemed it had been caught away from her, snatched from her hands.

'Amber!' Rani's distraught cry rang loud in the following silence. 'I am being so sorry, my hands they are without care . . . the book of your *mai*, it is being broken.'

The sharp anxiety in the other girl's exclamation brought Amber's glance from the book. 'You are not careless,' she said quickly, 'and books do not break.'

She had been clumsy, her mind had been far away instead of on taking the book from Rani and as a consequence it had dropped from her fingers. Saying as much, she retrieved it but as she laid it on the table Rani's distress was obvious.

'It is as I say . . . the book, it is being broken.'

Hiding her own anxiety Amber tried to make her smile

reassuring, though looking at the twisted way the Bible lay the smile was merely a charade. The book her mother had cherished, the one thing she had left to her children, was damaged. Keeping the smile she met the dismay vivid in large brown eyes. 'There is no real harm done, the cover is simply twisted, it can easily be put into place.'

But the cover did not slip into place. Manipulating it carefully, wanting to avoid further damage, Amber smoothed the bent pages then closed the Bible. Several times she repeated the process yet the book somehow remained misshapen.

'It will not be as it was.'

'It is not torn!' Amber answered Rani with a firmness she knew she had to keep if the girl was not to break into tears. 'It can be read and that is all that matters.'

Giving credence to her words she lifted the cover, turning to the page which bore her mother's handwriting. A forefinger touching lovingly over each in turn, she murmured the names inscribed there. Almost every evening her father would open this book and with his own finger would point out the letters of her name, teaching first the individual sound and then the complete whole, Emma Ann Neale; then, laughing at her objection that her name was Amber, he would swing her up above his head saying she was right, she was Amber – his own precious amber, his lovely gem.

Tears thickening in her throat as she closed the cover, feeling the awkwardness of the shape beneath her hand. But the front of it lay almost square as it had always done; perhaps the back was not level. Turning the book over she inspected the back. The brunt of its fall must have been taken by the top edge, twisting it slightly from the spine. Turning back the heavy cover she saw the thick vellum that was its lining had somehow peeled away and now lay folded back on itself.

'There.' She smiled at the watching Rani. 'That is the reason the book does not lie flat, but a little flour paste will have it stuck down and it will be exactly as it was before; so you see, you have worried over nothing.'

With a smile of relief, Rani turned to the dishes on the dresser, reaching for a shallow bowl in which to mix a spoonful of flour with a few drops of water.

'I will be making—'

The words fell away, Amber's gasp ending the sentence before it could be finished.

Each sheet of paper had been folded to fit exactly between the cover of the Bible and its facing.

The jacket of her green suit buttoned to the throat, her bonnet pinned to hair glowing copper, Amber glanced at a frowning sky. Jagged-edged clouds like great daubs of dark mud thrown against the grey streaked to the horizon. The rain Rani had warned of began to fall in slow heavy drops but thoughts of the previous evening kept Amber oblivious to its threat.

So precisely had those papers been folded she had not at first been aware of them, but as she attempted to press the vellum back a little further she had disclosed what had been hidden for years.

Was it something had been put there during the book's making – blank sheets of paper to provide a padding for the cover? Or was it something else?

Fingers shaking slightly from the effort of preventing serious damage she had withdrawn first one, then two, then one more. Three sheets in all, three documents. With Rani at her elbow she had smoothed each one flat, questions rattling through her mind as she read the words written in ink, their copperplate form flowing elegantly in neatly sectioned spaces.

Ann Elizabeth. The name had smiled up from the first paper she looked at, a certificate of marriage. The next, written in the same hand, had read, Verity Bethany Vachel and the third Deinol Vachel; names which for the most part she had not seen or ever heard spoken.

But her mother's name had appeared on each. Confused, she had read the documents again, paying closer attention to the words recorded on them. Apart from her mother's given names, and that of Bethany, the others had conveyed nothing to her until . . .

Rain splattering against her face, Amber's fingers tightened on the small bag clutched close against her.

The names had conveyed nothing until her eyes had rested on the surname, then the truth of what she looked at had exploded in her brain.

Buckley! The groom's name on the marriage certificate had read Buckley: Jervis Deinol Vachel Buckley! The sections apportioned to recording the father of the groom bore the title Uriah Buckley, and written beneath, the words 'not present'.

Uriah Buckley! Her breath had been snatched from her chest as the implication had rushed in on her. The certificate of marriage was between her mother and the son of Uriah Buckley – the man who was Joanna's father!

She had checked and rechecked. The groom's place of residence – it had read Bescot Lodge in the parish of Darlaston. At first she had grasped the one straw available to her, the one which said there might be two Jervis Buckleys, even two houses of the name Bescot Lodge but not in Darlaston! She had been forced to accept what was written was truth. Jervis Buckley was the man her mother had taken as her second husband and the two remaining documents were the birth certificates of the children of that marriage.

But Joanna had been near enough the same age as herself!

She had stared at the date written on the first of those certificates. A gap of some seven years separated her sister from Uriah Buckley's granddaughter. Joanna could not have been born out of wedlock; Uriah would never have acknowledged a child begotten in sin, which left only one explanation. She had closed her eyes, shutting out the words, but the consequence of them danced in her brain. Jervis Buckley had been already married when he had gone through that ceremony with her mother!

Had her mother known? Could she possibly have known? Questions had plagued the whole night through and with the coming of morning she had accepted the answer. Her mother had known: that and only that could have been her reason for hiding those documents in her Bible. But why marry a man you knew had a wife already? Love! The answer had whispered in her mind, love was the reason. But the whisper which should have eased the torment, should have ended the questions, instead opened the way for others. Had it been a one-sided affair? The love being her mother's? If not, why had Jervis Buckley deserted her? And why had he gone to India?

A passing carriage travelling too fast threw a spray of muddied rainwater, the dark stain of it patterning the green skirt of her suit, but Amber paid no heed. Her mind was alive only to the questions revolving in it.

Why had Jervis Buckley deserted her mother, turned his back on the children – *his* children? That could have only one answer. Bigamy was illegal, the proof of his committing that was in those documents, and even with all his father's money he would have been jailed.

Perhaps he had not known of her mother's death. Perhaps that was the reason he had not returned to England. Passing along Katherine's Cross, her footsteps automatic, Amber turned along Pinfold Street. Oblivious of hurrying women, children clutching at dark skirts, babies fastened securely inside shawls drawn tight against the rain, she walked on seeing nothing of the busy King Street, hearing none of the carts trundling up and down Church Street, and even on entering the small low-windowed building in Walsall Street the chaos of thoughts still raged.

Why had she herself not recognised Jervis Buckley as the man her mother had married? Why on arriving at that Army post, while living in that bungalow, had she had not recognised who he really was? She had stood in that church while he had made his vows, she had seen the smile, watched him take her mother's hand to lead her out into the quiet churchyard.

The quiet churchyard! Only now did the reality register. As a young child she had not understood the strangeness of a wedding without guests, with no family of the groom present; and after that day, in the years which followed, the visits had been rare: mostly coming after she had been put to bed, leaving before she had wakened, Jervis Buckley had remained a shadowy figure, a face time had erased from her memory.

Standing on the quayside of one of London's docks, Zachary Hayden stared at the clipper newly arrived from India. Allow time to take on fresh cargo, maybe pick up a few new crew members, revictual, the whole operation would take no more than ten days and the ship would sail again for countries far from this one.

From his position beside a stack of crates and barrels he watched men scurry like so many rats about her deck. He had vowed he had finished with that life, finished with standing watch in driving rain, finished with praying howling gales would not blow him overboard, and finished fighting waves threatening to scoop him into themselves then drop him into the ocean. He had done with the sailor's life, of seeing men work themselves half to death only to be ordered to do more or feel the bite of the lash across their backs; yet all of that was preferable to a life in Bloxwich longing for a woman he could never have.

But he would take a little of her with him. Maybe it was no more than an empty box, but it had her name on it, Amber Neale's name.

He had seen the small carton at the shop of a Birmingham florist to whom he supplied a regular order of flowers. It had taken no effort of mind to realise what the elegantly illustrated container held. Seeing him stare at it the florist's wife had handed it to him. It was empty, she had said, but it was so pretty she was reluctant to throw it out. He had taken it in his hand, the name dancing up at him recalling a face with smiling eyes, a head whose red-gold hair caught the light to shimmer like beaten copper. 'Maybe you should buy some of that perfume for your wife.' The woman had smiled. 'Her would love such a gift I be sure, but lessen you takes that box along of you I be just as sure you'll go forgettin' the name of the scent along with that of its maker.'

The name of the scent . . . yes, he might forget that, but the name of its maker? Never. His hand going to the pocket which had held the box since it was given to him, Zachary Hayden's breath stalled. Then he swore loud and hard.

The box was gone. He had been robbed!

'It will take several days to complete. Mr Mills advised I see him again a week from today, he said—'

Amber got no further in recounting her visit to Walsall Street; the sentence hanging in mid-air, she reached for Rani's hand as a second thump sounded at the door.

For what seemed hours their frightened glances locked but

it could only have been seconds before a fist knocked again followed by an urgent calling of her name.

It was not Freddy's voice nor that of his mother! Relief that was twofold ran through Amber as she realised neither was it the voice of Uriah Buckley.

'Mrs Neale,' the shout came again, 'Mrs Neale, be you to home? I've come from the New Hope.'

The New Hope! Amber released her fingers from Rani's grip. The coal mine? What could be so urgent a man needed to hammer on her door?

Mrs Neale . . .'

A lad stood there wearing trousers tied about the ankles with string, jacket, open-neck shirt, sweatcloth tied about his throat black with the thick coal dust that covered his face, his hair and flat cap indistinguishable one from the other, his words tumbled breathlessly.

'Mrs Neale . . . Will Nichols sent me, said to tell you should oughtta come to the yard straight away.'

William Nicholls, the man she had left in charge at the mine. Why should he send for her?

'He says you should come!' Almost startlingly bright the whites of the lad's eyes contrasted against the black dust coating his face, agitation working his mouth even when his words ceased.

'Did he give a reason?'

'There be reason all right!' He moved restlessly, heavy boots marking a step which Rani kept immaculately, scrubbing it daily before adding a fresh coating of whitening. 'The reason be a cave-in, the old number one seam, roof be down!'

A cave-in! Amber felt the cold tide of fear sweep along her veins. She remembered the phrase. The years of her childhood at Bloxwich, and those spent in service at Bescot Lodge, all had been interspersed with words telling of mine accidents of one sort or another, and all had been witness to the agony on faces of women whose men had been killed or crippled in the disaster.

'A doctor?' She was already reaching for the jacket Rani had taken from her less than an hour before.

'Will Nicholls sent a lad for Dr Magrane, he be certifyin' doctor for factories an' the likes; he be the one attendin' to any accidents 'appens in any o' them or in any coal mine. It has to be 'oped he be to 'ome!'

Was anyone hurt . . . killed? Rani beside her, Amber kept pace with the young lad leading the way to the mine. Please God, let the answer be no. Please let it be no!

35

Nothing appeared amiss. Amber sent a swift glance over the colliery yard. The small brick-built office with its dust-caked windows, the winding house, its huge wheel outlined against a still sky, the tubs, no longer needed to transport coal, the last seam having given up its all, stood lined on the metal track which once ran them from the yard to be emptied into carts ready for transporting to the railway freight depot.

But the very stillness, the silence which hung so heavy it could almost be felt, told that something was very much amiss.

'Is anyone in there?'

White-faced with anxiety, Amber shot the question at the man she had placed in charge of the New Hope, repeating it heatedly as he stared open-mouthed at Rani, her eyes wide and dark seeming huge against pale coffee skin, a shawl thrown about her shoulders concealing little of the flimsy sari she preferred to wear when indoors.

'There . . . there be three of 'em. The last bogey were fetched up this mornin'.' He pulled his stare away, directing it to where the line of tubs stood black and empty. 'Were no use tryin' to fetch more out, all we be getting were dirt. So I thought to have the men do a thorough check of the tunnels, mek sure all were safe afore closin' down for good. I—'

'The men, are they still down there?' Explanations would keep for later. Amber started for the winding house but the man's answer had her turn quickly about.

'No. We got 'em out, meself and a couple of others went down. Lucky the collapse didn't trap the three behind it or they'd be there still. They be in the office, I thought seein' as how it be warmer in there, with 'aving a stove.'

She had heard the hint of apprehension; having men filthy with coal dust taken into the office! It could rebound badly on him; but Amber had no time right now to calm such fears. Skirts held clear of dust earlier rain had turned into thick black mud, she ran towards the low building.

Following the way to the small office, Amber's stomach jolted with fear as she stepped inside. Eyes closed, his body unmoving, a man lay on the door which had been used to carry him from the winding house; his leg, twisted at a sickening angle, rested awkwardly against the other, while one arm dripped soot-darkened blood from beneath the sleeve of a torn shirt.

A shuffle of boots sounding from the open doorway was followed by a breathless, 'The doctor . . . he weren't to home.' The young lad his face red with the effort of running, broke off, gawping open-mouthed at the pretty dark haired girl who had turned to look at him.

'But didn't his housekeeper say where he could be found?'

Silence greeting Amber's enquiry, the chargehand shook the lad by the shoulder. 'Use your tongue lad, 'tain't like you've never seen a woman afore.'

'I ain't never seen one pretty as that,' the lad breathed. ' 'Er be like one o' them fairies you sees in little 'uns' books.'

'Ain't fairies you'll be a-seein' my lad, it'll be stars lessen you answers Mrs Neale – an' right sharpish!'

'They said . . . they said he were gone to the iron foundry, the one up along of King's 'Ill.' Red cheeks became deep carmine, embarrassment adding on exertion as he caught Rani's smile.

'You weren't there? You ain't come back 'ere afore going to that foundry?'

'Course I ain't.' The lad glanced indignantly at his superior. 'I don't be daft! I run all the way, seein' how bad Mr Turner looked when you fetched 'im up outta the pit. I knowed the doctor 'ad to be fetched.'

'Is he come with you?' Amber glanced beyond the two stood just inside the room. What was keeping the man?

'No, missis.' Uneasy at being faced by two women, one of them he still wondered at, the young lad squirmed as the older man's hand tightened painfully on his shoulder.

'What do you be meanin'? You says you went along o' that iron foundry an' now you be sayin' no, the doctor don't be along of you.'

'Yes . . . 'e ain't.' His tongue twisting like the body he tried to twist from that iron grip, the lad stuttered. 'I means yes, I went to the foundry, and yes, doctor ain't be come wi' me.'

'But you told 'im!' The face of the chargehand glowered a dire threat. The lad's arse would smart for a week should he 'ave got things wrong.

'I d'ain't get to talk to 'im.' Almost lifted off his feet, the lad struggled to answer. 'I seen the watchman along of the gate, he were about to go tell the doctor when the gaffer come into the yard; told me to bugger off, 'e did, said the doctor were busy, and when I told 'im men were bad hurt in a cave-in at the New 'Ope 'e said again to bugger off, that they could wait.'

'Who told you this?'

'Who?' Bright eyes swung to Amber. 'Like I told, it were the gaffer 'imself. It were Uriah Buckley.'

Stunned by what she heard, Amber stared. How could one man behave so thoughtlessly?

'I couldn't go sayin' owt else to 'im, not with 'im bein' the gaffer 'ere.'

'Buckley don't be gaffer 'ere no more, but I sees what you means, lad. It don't do for the likes o' we to go answering back to gaffers, no matter what.'

It seemed to Amber the voices came from far off, that she was not part of the scene in this room.

'Amber.' Her mind now so preoccupied Rani's voice made no impact, the contemptuous eyes and hard mouth of Uriah Buckley pushing all else from her brain.

'We are needing hot water and cloths, you bring these?' Rani had turned her full attention on the man still standing in the office doorway. 'These men are needing help, the wounds must be washed if poison is to be kept from their blood.'

The woman were a foreigner; he couldn't go lettin' 'er wash his workmates. He shook his head, the rejection in his glance needing no words.

She had seen that look so many times in India: From the women of villages she had been driven from, sticks and stones adding emphasis to cries of 'unclean'; at the camp of the Army, the wives of the white Raj, their faces had shouted what their minds held and what was muttered behind their hands: now it was here, in the eyes of this man. But this time she must not run from it.

Removing the shawl she said quietly, 'Poison of the blood kills where wounds might not. Your friends must be washed if death is not to come.'

'The doctor be the one to say what be best, there'll be no meddlin' afore 'e gets . . .'

The slight raising of the voice, the disparaging edge to the tone, brought Amber snapping back to reality. Looking directly at the chargehand, she said with quiet authority: 'The doctor is not here, Mr Nicholls, therefore *I* will be the one to say what is best. We will need hot water, soap, towels and the medical box.'

The gaffer of the New 'Ope were no longer Uriah Buckley, but this one, albeit a woman, would tek no back answerin', and though this job couldn't be carried on more'n the time it took to seal off the mine he didn't want to be given his tin afore it had to be given. The thought flashing through his mind, William Nicholls' answer was polite. 'There be soap an' towel. Uriah Buckley never used either but they were kept in the clerk's room against being called for; but a medical box . . . there ain't never been no such to my knowin'.'

No medical box! A helplessness rushed in on Amber. They needed ointment, bandages . . .

'Hot water . . . please, you must bring.'

'Do it, quickly!' Amber ordered the man who still looked distrustingly at Rani.

Pushing the lad before him, instructing him to go fetch the injured men's womenfolk, the chargehand did as he was bid.

'This one, his brain is sleeping. To straighten his leg will cause much pain.'

Understanding that Rani was advising they do what they could for the injured man while he was unconscious, Amber nodded. But they needed splints to keep the leg secure, and bandages to hold them in place. The chair in the outer office! It was not leather-padded, as was the one behind the desk here; it was a simple wooden chair with strong straight legs. They would be her splints and a petticoat would make good bandages.

Ordering a bewildered Nicholls to slit the dust-encrusted trouser then to kick the legs from the clerk's chair, Amber removed her jacket while reassuring the two other men their own wounds would be tended.

Returning with legs from the chair he had kicked apart, William Nicholls glanced to where Rani was gently washing coal dust from the twisted leg. A foreigner her were, but the touch of her were no less gentle than that of his own wife tending their child.

'Best let me do that, mum.' He glanced to Amber, struggling to tear the petticoat she had slipped out of. ''Ands that 'ave 'ad the wielding of pick and hammer for years be stronger than your own.'

'It must be now, before his brain it is waking.'

She knew what Rani said was common sense. While unconscious the man would not feel the agony of a broken leg being moved, but without a doctor . . .

'It is now,' Rani urged, 'we should do it now.'

Stomach lurching, doubt a sickness thick in her throat, Amber stared at a face pale beneath its film of black. He had already suffered great pain and there would be more in the days ahead; but a little could be avoided if she could bring herself to do it. Sucking in a deep breath, she nodded to Rani.

It was done! The grating of bone against bone as they had lifted the broken leg, straightening it ready for the makeshift splints, had left Amber trembling. But the work of tending the man was not finished. Asking the watching Nicholls to tear away the shirtsleeve she caught her breath at sight of the jagged cut running from shoulder to elbow.

'Fallin' coal be the culprit.' Nicholls glanced at the gaping wound. 'Edges can be sharper than a surgeon's knife and they cuts clear to the bone.'

'Clean water, bring it quickly please.' Amber forced the words to come calmly but worry gleamed dark in the eyes which lifted to Rani's. 'Water and soap is not enough,' she murmured, 'we need an antiseptic. I'm as guilty as Uriah Buckley; I should have made certain a medical box was kept here!'

'Blame does not heal wounds whether they be of heart or body so we will not give breath to it. We have no box of which you speak but we have this. I am thinking it will be of help until the doctor he comes.'

While speaking, Rani's hand had dipped into the folds of her sari and now held a bottle Amber recognised. She had not noticed the girl take it from a shelf as they had hurried from the cottage but she had blessed the sense which had her do so.

Tincture of marigold! Made from the flush of summer flowers it was a strong ally against infection of cuts. Looking again at the closed eyes, purple shadows lining the lids, Amber prayed it would work for this man. Dropping a strip of folded cloth from her petticoat into the bowl to which Rani had added a measure of the tincture, she placed it tenderly over the freshly washed wound, binding it with another strip of cloth.

The two men who were also injured, one with a deep gash to the hand, the other clutching a forearm, had remained silent but now, when Amber asked did they prefer to await the arrival of the doctor, they answered quickly.

'Not me, mum.' The bleeding hand lifted. 'Seein' as how you've tended Joe Turner, I reckons I'll get no better from a doctor; it would please me greatly to 'ave yourself and . . .' He paused but only for a second before he smiled. 'And the lady along of you, see to the dressing of this 'ere hand.'

'That be my choosin' an' all.' The man clutching a forearm smiled but his eyes showed the pain he was in. 'If you would be so good, mum.'

Taking the shawl she had put to one side, Rani draped it over the still-unconscious man. Then, approaching one of the others she pointed to the injury and then to herself before asking quietly, 'It is permitted?'

'There be tea fresh made, Mrs Neale, mum.' The basin emptied, soiled cloths disposed of, the chargehand carried a plain wooden tray with a variety of chipped enamel mugs, setting it down on the desk. 'We, the man an' meself, likes a cup o' tea if time allows, but time or not I thinks we all be deservin' o' this one, though I understands if yourselves don't be given the fancy to drink from no enamel mug.'

If only he knew some of the things they had drunk from: leaves broken from trees, hands brushing insects away before they scooped water from mud-filled pools, heads bent over rivers praying crocodiles did not lurk there.

'A cup of tea is most welcome.' She smiled, taking one and handing it to Rani before accepting another for herself.

'Might I have a cup also – seeing my assistance is no longer called for!'

They had done well. The doctor had approved their strapping of the broken leg and had nodded enthusiastically on hearing of the use of tincture of marigold. 'They could have used nothing better,' he had said, smiling over a steaming mug of tea, 'the injured men had much to thank them for.'

But why had he not come sooner? Had the accident at the iron foundry been so very bad?

'I knew nothing of a cave-in at the mine.' He had answered as if hearing her question spoken aloud. 'If I had then of course I would have come as soon as possible instead of talking to the manager of the iron foundry; but I only heard of what had happened here when my housekeeper said a young lad had been sent to the house asking could I come.'

Uriah Buckley had said nothing of the boy! Had left the foundry without sending word of the mining accident to the doctor! Remembering the rest of the conversation, Amber felt the same rush of anger she had felt while listening to the explanation. Uriah Buckley was callous as he was cruel! But just how cruel, just how far his callousness had gone, he was yet to find out.

'Come to bleat about that mine have you, want me to buy it back?' Uriah Buckley laughed at the young woman standing in his study. 'Found out business be too much for your brain - but I could have told you that much, could have told you women have no brain!'

She had expected no courtesy from this man, no politeness. Looking directly into eyes of grey ice beneath their heavy lids, Amber's response was calm.

'It is not the mine I have called to discuss . . .'

'Discuss – discuss!' Uriah's laugh rang around the book-lined walls. 'I wants no discussion wi' a bloody serving wench!'

'Then perhaps you will speak with the stepdaughter of your son.'

The hooded lids lowered, leaving a slit through which his gaze glittered threateningly. This man had shown how dangerous he could be: he would not hesitate to show it again. But she was here now; against all of Rani's pleading she should not do so, she had come to Bescot Lodge alone. Feeling the venom of the stare which had not once left her face, Amber forced her own to remain unflinching.

'That be a good one. Yes, I admits it be a good one!' The heavy lids lifted as Uriah Buckley laughed aloud. 'Trust a woman to come up wi' something like that. But it don't be good enough. My son has no stepdaughter. His wife Helen were a maid still when Jervis wed her, and their daughter Joanna were my only grandchild.'

The laugh died as rapidly as it had come, leaving despisal to draw the thin lips to a snarl.

My *only* grandchild,' he hissed, 'the girl you led to her death!'

His son must have written telling the true facts of that massacre, of Joanna's death, but written on his mouth, gleaming from his cold eyes, came the fact that Uriah Buckley preferred his own definition of the cause. Amber watched the face lean towards her across the wide desk.

'You come to this house once afore tellin' a cock-an'-bull story, that didn't work. You thought to live off my charity but when you got nothing you slunk away to think up another. Well, my not-so-clever Mrs Neale, you can bugger off back to where you come from. You'll get nothing from Uriah Buckley save a prison sentence should you try again!'

Waiting for the tirade to cease, Amber gave a slight shake of the head. 'You are as wrong about my wanting your charity as you were in thinking I came to ask would you buy the New Hope back from me—'

'That be fortunate.' The thin lips spread to a smile. 'For the answer be no to both.'

'As you are wrong on yet one more thing.' Amber went on as if no interruption had come. 'I grant that Jervis had but one child from his marriage with Helen, but the woman he took in a second marriage already had a daughter.'

'Tek care what you be saying!' Leaning further across the desk, Uriah's face darkened. 'That be slander of a man's name.'

'It is the truth!' Amber snapped. 'Your son, Jervis Buckley, took a woman who had a child not yet seven years old.'

'The truth!' Uriah smiled cunningly. 'And this child, this be the stepdaughter you say exists? Then bring her here, produce her so I can speak to her myself.'

'You are speaking to her now – *I* am that stepdaughter.' She had not known how those words would be received but the howl of laughter was surprising.

'It gets funnier.' He straightened, a chuckle rumbling in his throat though none of the ice had gone from his eyes. 'It be finer than a play at the theatre. You missed your vocation, you

would have made a better actress than you did a chamber
maid, and certainly more convincing a liar!'

'I am not lying; I have proof of what I have said.' The very
quietness of speech, the clear look that met him, threw the
laugh back into Uriah's throat, instincts which had helped him
rob and lie his way through life suddenly pricking his veins.
This woman were not feared of him, hadn't that been shown
already? And as for brain, though he held that women were
not blessed with such this one were an exception; her
were smart – too smart to come to Bescot Lodge stating things
of which her had no certainty. Proof, her had said, but what
proof? Where? And what would it take to destroy? Taking a
moment, forcing the sudden churning of his mind to order, he
stared at the slender woman who was speaking again.

'I have the proof of a form of marriage taking place
between—'

'Form!' Uriah interrupted again. 'A *form* of marriage! There
can be only one, it be made afore God and witnesses; that be
the only bloody form my son ever made!'

'No,' Amber spoke with the same quiet calm. 'There is
another, one that was made before God but without a witness
from Jervis Buckley's family. Your son made a bigamous
marriage.'

'That be a lie, and by God it be one you'll pay for!'

Meeting the blaze full on, Amber smiled briefly. 'Of that I
have no doubt, neither do I suspect payment will be taken by
any but yourself . . . in your own sly underhand way.'

'You've made a grave mistake in coming here.' The glare of
anger becoming the rabid fire of hate, Uriah Buckley placed
himself between Amber and the door.

'A very grave mistake – but I promise you there will be no
more!'

36

His pocket had been picked! Zachary Hayden swore again, this time softly and beneath his breath. After all his years at sea, after the repeated warnings of his father that he 'watch out for his pockets' at each port where they docked, he had been 'lifted' by a wharf rat. Silent, stealthy as the vermin they were called after, pickpockets infested every dockyard, watching for the unwary, relieving them of anything they could steal before disappearing as silently as they came. But he should not have been unwary. He knew the docklands of this world and should have had his wits about him!

Condemning himself every bit as much as the thief who had robbed him he had glanced about. It was an empty box, of no use to any thief, nobody would give them a penny for it; that being so it had probably been thrown away somewhere in the close vicinity. But he had found no box. That had been the day before yesterday, yet the hours had not eased the sense of loss. It had been all he had of Amber Neale, a box and a few memories.

Memories! No one could rob him of those, but neither could memories ease the ache constantly with him. Both were empty, one as useless as the other. So why add to them? The question challenged his mind. Why subject himself to a situation whose only reward would be more heartache?

Yet that was what he was doing. He could have despatched that purchase, sent it by carrier to Bloxwich. Yes, he could have done that, he *should* have done that, but he had not. Deep inside he smiled, a cynical self-reproaching smile. Was there a bigger fool anywhere on God's earth than a man in love?

'James Bridge.'

From the seat opposite the only other passenger in the train compartment looked enquiringly at Zachary as the conductor came along the corridor announcing the next stop.

'I had thought to travel to Darlaston, but the man is saying "James Bridge".'

'The town is Darlaston,' Zachary explained, smiling, 'but the station is at James Bridge, a little way out of the centre; but it will be no trouble getting there, a hansom cab will take you where it is you are wanting to go.'

'Thank you.' The passenger glanced through the window as the train began to slow. Taking an envelope from the pocket of his heavy coat he leaned forwards, holding the paper for Zachary to see. 'Where I am wanting to go, could you perhaps give me directions?'

Bescot Lodge! The letters danced, merging and parting as he looked at them. Bescot Lodge . . . just a couple of miles from Ley Cottage!

'No, you'll mek no other mistake,' Uriah Buckley's breath hissed past clenched teeth, 'and neither will I. Mine was to let you go on livin' after you coming here whining that I give your brother over to Elton's lad and—'

'Caused my sister, a child of ten, to drown in the brook running from the hands of a man old enough to be her grandfather while her true grandfather looked on.' Feeling repugnance, coiled tightly with anger, Amber disregarded the look that shouted danger. She had waited long enough to face this man with the truth and now he was going to hear it: every last syllable. 'Yes, your own granddaughter!' She hurled words one after the other. 'The child I left in this house, the young girl you promised would be well cared for, she was the daughter of Jervis Buckley, and the boy was his son – *your* grandson; and before you cry 'liar', there is the proof.'

Taking several sheets of paper from her bag, Amber threw them onto the desk.

'Read them' she said. 'Read for yourself what is written on those papers, see the dishonour your son brought to my mother. See how he wed one woman while married to another!'

Snatching up the documents, Uriah glanced at each in turn, his rapid breath becoming harsher as it was dragged into his throat. He had admitted to himself this woman were smarter of the mind than most but he had not reckoned on how devious that mind could be. True or false, in the wrong hands these papers could put a slur on Jervis's name, p'raps block any marriage of consequence. That was to be avoided no matter the cost . . . and that cost would not be paid by a Buckley, father or son.

Controlling the anger bubbling so close to the surface he turned it to derision as he lifted his glance. 'What did you think to gain from this?' he sneered. 'A place in this house as my son's stepdaughter? Then you have overestimated yourself. This is what I think of these! Crumpling the papers into a ball he hurled them towards the fireplace, his voice lowering. 'Again I tell you, this will be the last mistake you'll ever make. Your filthy lies will end here – and so will your life!'

He moved fast for so bulky a man. The words were hardly ended before his hands fastened on Amber's throat, his eyes gleaming hate as the grip tightened.

'Excuse me, sir, I thought you would want to see this immediately,'

Air flooding into her lungs, Amber staggered backwards against the desk as the manservant entered the room.

'I don't be finished with you,' he snarled, lips curling back like those of an enraged dog. 'Count the hours Mrs Neale, count what be left to you, for I promise they won't be many!'

He could have killed her, he would have killed her if that fool Saunders hadn't come into the study. The woman would have been dead by now, her lying tongue stilled forever; now she was gone. But a chance missed didn't mean another couldn't be found! He knew the road she must take to reach that cottage . . . and he knew the heath. Give her ten minutes. Glancing at the envelope he had snatched from the servant's hand he muttered, 'I said for you to count the hours, Mrs Neale. I've changed my mind, now you must count the minutes.'

Determination cooling the rage which had gripped him watching Amber Neale leave the study, he looked again at the envelope. A letter from Jervis, this would be to advise the day he would arrive at Bescot Lodge.

Sitting in the chair behind the desk he turned the envelope. Meerut. He read the address of the sender. Meerut was the place of Jervis' Army post, but the handwriting . . . that was not Jervis's. A frown settled between his brows as he tore open the envelope.

Dear Sir.

He read quickly.

It is my sad duty to inform you of the death of Colonel Jervis Buckley. He was a fine officer respected by his peers and the men under his command. His body is interred beside those of his wife and daughter. The regiment offers its most sincere condolence.

Signed . . . George Coleman-Harper. Major Acting Officer in Command.

My sad duty . . .

Uriah stared at the neatly written words.

. . . the death of Colonel Jervis Buckley.

This was wrong! Anger returning, he slammed the letter down onto the desk. Those bloody fools had it wrong! Jervis was on his way home, he would be here any moment. Hadn't the letter of a few weeks gone said as much?

He would write a letter to the War Office, set a bloody cannon 'neath the arse of the one who'd signed this stupid letter. George Coleman-Harper. Major! He'd be naught be a skivvy by the time Uriah Buckley were finished with him!

A tap at the door had him look up. Still wary from the previous disturbance, Saunders swallowed nervously.

'Well . . . what be it now?'

'A caller, sir.' The manservant answered the roar while remaining auspiciously close to the door.

'The woman?'

Saunders shook his head. 'No, sir.'

'Then I don't want to see . . .'

'He said he brings word of your son, sir.'

Some bloody Johnny had already got the wind up; that Major fellah had realised his own cock-up and nervous of the consequence he had despatched somebody with an apology. P'raps it were the man himself. Well, this visit would be one he wouldn't forget . . . not for a long while! The satisfaction of promised revenge coursed along his veins as Uriah nodded. 'Show him in.'

The soft closing of the door indicated his visitor had entered the study and the servant had withdrawn. Uriah kept his glance on the letter he had folded and which now lay beneath his hand. Let the bugger squirm, he deserved much more . . . and by God he would get it.

'You be here to apologise for your blunder.' He did not look up.

'Apologise?'

'Yes, apologise. You send a letter tellin' a man his son be dead, you write words fit to cause a seizure . . . what else would you follow such with except an apology? But I tells you this: major or no major I'll see you reduced to the ranks, I'll have your commission.'

'Sir, I am not major.'

'I don't bloody care what you be, I'll have—'

It stopped there. Surprise deepening the frown creasing his forehead, Uriah stared at the man standing at the opposite side of the desk, a man whose coffee-brown skin and dark eyes contrasted sharply with a snow-white collar showing beneath a dark suit.

'I am not major, I am Ram Dutt, *nokar* . . . servant . . . of the Colonel Buckley.'

'You are Jervis's houseboy? But why send you in advance of himself? Where the hell *is* he? When does my son intend getting home?'

Irritation rising fast, Uriah was oblivious of the quick compassion flitting across the dark eyes.

'The colonel sahib will not be returning to the home of his father.'

'Not returning – not bloody returning!' Uriah's fist clenched, his fingers crumpling the letter he had read moments before. 'Changed his mind, has he, gone back on his word but be too cowardly to tell me himself, sent you to do it while he be off somewhere moonin' over art and nature. Or do it be a woman? Has he brought himself a woman back with him and be afraid I'll tek against her – do that be it?'

Across from Uriah, coal-black hair gleamed a halo of blue as light from the window glanced over it and Ram Dutt answered quietly, 'The colonel sahib is in Meerut. He lies beside his wife and his daughter.'

The world went suddenly silent. Uriah listened to it in his mind. A muteness, a stillness that stifled the breath, a hush that muffled thought; but then thought returned, coming with the force of gunfire.

'. . . *his body is interred* . . .'

Uriah's head snapped back on his neck.

'. . . *beside those of his wife and daughter* . . .'

Vacant, unbelieving, grey eyes fastened on black ones.

'I am sorry to be bringing sadness to the home of the colonel. Perhaps tomorrow the time it will be better.'

Somehow the words reached into the pit that had swallowed Uriah, reached into the infinite depths to drag him back to the surface.

'No.' Half plea, half command, the word halted the departing Ram. 'How? When? Was it during that expedition to quell an uprising?'

His head moved several times from side to side before Ram Dutt spoke. 'It was not happening on that expedition. The colonel sahib returned in safety. He was all prepared to leave for England. The evening before his leaving I served him tea on the veranda. A little while later I saw him beside the tombs of his wife and the Miss Joanna. It was his practice to go there to speak with them. Later still he knelt with hand on each tomb; Ram did not have heart enough to make the disturbing, but when the shadows of night they thickened I went to him. He did not answer when I called, he did not move. But the darkness of night is not always friend, Ram knew this, knew the colonel sahib should not stay longer. Begging his pardon I touched his shoulder, then as he fell I saw the mark upon his brow. Two tiny circles showing in the moonlight, the kiss of the cobra.'

It was her doing! The Neale woman had brought this disaster on his home. If she hadn't come seeking his charity, bringing two brats along of her, if she had gone to some place other than Bescot Lodge asking for work then none of this would ever have happened. His granddaughter, his son . . . they would still be alive; but instead they lay dead, buried in some God-forsaken village in a country far from their own, and all of it the fault of Amber Neale.

Amber Neale, the woman who had tried to inveigle her way into Jervis's life by producing fake marriage lines and equally fake birth certificates, a woman who still lived while his son was in his grave.

Grasping the shotgun he had grabbed from a cabinet minutes after the Indian had left, Uriah's face was a mask of hatred. Yes, Amber Neale lived now – but soon she would be dead.

Hidden by a bush of thick gorse, a tall figure watched the slim shape of a woman leave the road to cross the heath.

Hair, piled now beneath a small bonnet, gleamed in the pale afternoon light, rich red-gold hair . . . hair he remembered so well. She would come this way, pass within yards of where he stood; but she must not see him. Slowly as dissolving mist the figure lowered to a crouching position. Obscured from view, yet with a line of sight clear between the stubby leaves of the bush, the figure smiled. She would not know anyone was there.

I know that of which you never spoke. Unaware of the presence on the heath, Amber's thoughts spoke in her mind. I found the papers you hid in the Bible, I know of the marriage between you and Jervis Buckley and I understand, Mother, I understand the love you felt for him; I shall never truly know if you had been told he already had a wife, but you gave your vow before God and my heart tells me you would not have done so had you known.

From the shelter of the bush the crouching figure watched a gloved hand raise a scrap of linen to the face, touching each eye. Tears! The mouth tightened.

I have told Bethany her true identity . . . Unconscious of all but her thoughts, Amber walked on. Told her of her father, but Denny . . . I have not found him, but I will go on trying. I promise he also will be told of his father even though his grandfather thinks the certificates I showed him were something I had dreamed up; he threw them from him but that will not affect the truth for the originals are in the safe keeping of a solicitor. Uriah Buckley may deny Denny's heritage, but one day Denny will know, he will know all of the truth.

She was close now, close enough for her face to be seen clearly; a few minutes and she would be level with the bush. Eyes quick and sharp as a hunting hawk scanned the expanse of heath then became still, focused on a second figure. Some distance behind the woman a man walked quickly, a man who used the bushes for cover, a man with a shotgun in his hands.

Tense, watchful, silent as a wraith, the crouching figure remained still; only his eyes moved as they followed the man.

Carrying a gun, using the gorse to conceal himself, his movements stealthy: the man was on the hunt and the only game on the heath was . . . the woman!

With his breath a soft hiss caught in his throat the figure sank lower. The man with the gun was stalking the woman!

I bought the coal mine for Denny. In her mind Amber talked

softly with her mother. I thought to make him independent, for him to have the means of looking Uriah Buckley in the face as equals in business, to show he neither needed nor wanted that man's recognition; but I was foolish, I bought a mine which no longer had coal.

Watching the slender figure, green costume and bonnet marking it clear against the grey sky, Uriah Buckley's eyes held pure poison. That woman had come to his house, defiled the name of his son with her filthy lies. She had caused Jervis's death then tried to take his inheritence, but all she would have was a bullet in the head; and the consequence of what he was about to do? Who was to say it was not simply another hunting accident, a workman after rabbits for a dinner – and Uriah Buckley was not in need of rabbit stew!

From the vantage point affording a perfect view the secreted figure watched the gun being lifted to the shoulder. He intended to shoot; out in the open as she was the woman was a perfect target. To shout might give her warning, but even disturbed the man would have time to shoot, and no one could outrun a speeding bullet.

Even as the thoughts raced a hand brushed against a fist-sized lump of rock. Fingers curled about it; still with the silence of a shadow, the figure rose and, hardly pausing to take aim, threw. Straight as an arrow the missile headed for its target; but the pause, minute as it was, had been too long; even as the rock struck the side of the man's head his fingers pressed down on the gun's trigger.

Sound echoed into the distance, ricocheting off rock mounds, but the racing figure heard nothing but the cries in his own heart.

Coming to where Amber had fallen, the tall figure gathered her in strong arms, his words muffled as he pressed his face to hers.

'Don't be dead,' he sobbed brokenly. 'Please, Amber . . . don't be dead.'

Who had thrown that rock? In the comfort of his bed Uriah pushed the doctor's hand away.

'I be all right!' he snapped. 'A fall be all it were, a fall in which I catched my head against a stone.'

'Nevertheless, you need to rest. The fall caught you on the temple.'

Lord, would the man never go! Fighting the urge to throw the man from his room, Uriah closed his eyes pretending a need to sleep, but thoughts screamed in his mind.

There had been a second figure on the heath, one he had not seen but who had seen him; someone who had seen him raise the gun and fire. But who? And why had whoever it was not called the constabulary?

Inspector Charles Checkett! Uriah's eyelids lifted as the doctor left the bedroom. How he would love to have Uriah Buckley on a charge of murder.

But was it murder, had the bullet struck the Neale woman? Was she dead?

He could not send Saunders to find out: that would be tanta-mount to a confession. He must bide his time; if it were the first attempt brought him no joy then the next one would. Throwing the cover aside he rose from the bed; then stood with a hand to his brow while the room revolved. Should he discover who it was had hurled that rock then they wouldn't live to travel down the line!

Breath steadying him, thoughts came quickly as he dressed. What had that Indian fellow called himself . . . a *nokar*, a servant? But what was a bloody servant doing comin' all the way to England? A packet, the man had offered him some sort of packet! He had thrown it aside. Uriah fastened the buttons of his shirt. He had wanted no packet, he had wanted only news of his son, to hear that some bungler had made a mistake, that Jervis was alive. But that had not been the news he had heard.

'. . . *the kiss of the cobra* . . .'

Cold and deadly as the serpent itself, the words stung Uriah's brain.

He had gone into the garden, knelt between the graves of his wife and his child, and now his tomb lay beside theirs.

'*The colonel sahib entrusted this to Ram Dutt.*' Words spoken the previous day filtered through the clouds of anger and heartache dulling Uriah's brain.

'*It was given the day of his leaving to deal with the uprising at Najibabad. Should he not be making a return then Ram Dutt was to bring this package to the colonel sahib's father with his own personal hand. It was not to be shown to the other officer sahibs, not to be sent with his belongings, but brought by his friend, Ram Dutt.*'

Friend! Uriah reached for his jacket. How could a foreigner – and a servant at that – dare to call himself Jervis Buckley's friend? He should have booted the man's arse, kicked the bugger from Bescot Lodge. He still would, should he set eyes on the creature!

Crossing the hall to the study he waved away the hovering Saunders. The package was on the desk where he had left it. Tearing away the wrapping he stared at a tiny golden pool fallen on the dark wood. Verity's necklace, the gift of her parents on her wedding day. Taking it in his hand, the gleaming stones dripping between his fingers, Uriah seemed to see the tears which had often glittered in the eyes of a small boy: Jervis's tears, tears a father had never dried.

Letting the necklace slip away he took the sheet of paper

folded beneath it, his heart beating hard at sight of the flowing handwriting.

My dear father,

Dear father! Uriah's throat tightened, had he ever really been that to Jervis?

This letter is given into the keeping of my trusted servant and valued friend Ram Dutt. He is instructed, in the event of my death, to bring it to England and put it only into your hands. Regard him well, for he is a good man.

Tomorrow I lead a detachment to Najibabad to put down an uprising. Should I return in safety then a few weeks will see me in England; but Fate, as we all know, is a flighty lady, who can frown as easily as she might smile. That being so I briefly put into words that which has been kept secret so very long. Some seven years after my marriage to Helen, I fell in love with another woman. She had no knowledge of my background and in our years together made no demands upon me. She loved me for what I was. I know she no longer lives for the girl who came to India as companion to Joanna talked of her, yet I did not reveal the relationship – the bigamous marriage I had contracted with that same woman, Amber's mother, nor did I confess the children born of that liaison, children who, thank Almighty God, were left in the care and protection of Bescot Lodge. Cherish them, Father, for they are your grandchildren. Find it in your heart to give them the love you never gave your son.

Jervis.

37

'There be no more I can tell you 'cept I don't think he were a man growed. Tall he were, and strong lookin', but there were summat as said he were a lad yet.' William Nicholls had glanced from one woman to the other. 'I were comin' to this house to tell that in clearin' the fallen rubble from the tunnel we come upon a new seam. The New Hope be rich wi' coal, not half-formed sea coal but hard and black as the devil's tongue . . . beggin' your pardon.'

The New Hope mine was rich with coal. The man's face had shown delight, and though she was happy that miners who had been given their tins could now be reinstated, Amber's mind kept slipping to the part of the conversation that had told how he had seen Uriah Buckley leaving from the heath, a shotgun over his arm, and then what he had taken to be a man bending over a figure lying on the ground. He had shouted and the man had looked up, then seconds later was running away.

'It were then I seen he were not a man growed but a lad yet, despite his strength.'

Tall, strong, but still with characteristics that had marked him a lad. Freddy . . . it had to have been Freddy. Becky had said her son was sure to visit Ley Cottage again but if Uriah Buckley had seen him, recognised him!

'You should be taking rest.' Hearing the short intake of breath, Rani turned from her cooking.

'There is no need.' Glancing at a face which still showed

anxiety, Amber smiled. 'I wasn't looking where I was going and so caught my foot in a rabbit hole and fell, knocking myself out in the process; it was no more than that.'

'But the shooting of the gun . . .'

'It wasn't shooting at me.'

But had it been a bullet meant for her? Uriah Buckley had said she should count the hours left, they would be few.

About to challenge the denial, Rani hesitated, a knock to the door sharpening the anxiety still so prevalent.

'It will be Freddy come to assure himself and his mother I have taken no bad effect from my fall,' Amber said, but even as she moved Rani was opening the door. What was she doing? She never welcomed Freddy or any other with those words! Perplexed, Amber watched her friend, palms together, add a slight bow to the murmured '*Swagat dost.*'

Welcome friend, Rani had said welcome friend. But who beside the two of them would understand those words?

'*Shukria.*'

The softly spoken 'thank you' made Amber frown, then as their visitor stepped into the room, a delighted smile spread over her mouth.

'*Ram . . . Ram Dutt!*'

A bigamous marriage . . . children . . . what the Neale woman had claimed: it was all here written in Jervis's own hand. This was what he would not risk having seen by those responsible for shipping his personal effects home to England.

Shock holding him fast to his chair, Uriah gazed at the sheet of paper. He had read it over and over until letters and words blurred into one black mass and always with the one conclusion. This was the reason behind the running off to India, the shame, the disgrace. Jervis had ever been weak; he would not face up to the result of being found out. But Jervis was dead and so were the dreams of his fathering a son to carry the name and business of Buckley.

Anger flared like a torch burning along Uriah's veins. He needed a child with *his* blood, *Uriah Buckley's* blood! But there would be none, no more children born of his son for that son was dead. And the father? Fingers clutching the paper, Uriah felt the hate of his veins subside, leaving the anger cold. The father would beget no child; the ability to do that had died in him long ago.

A son, Jervis had written of a son. A bastard child, a child no one else must ever know of.

The documents he had thrown aside when Amber Neale had handed them to him, had they been removed by servants cleaning? Glancing to where he had thrown them, Uriah swore, then as his glance travelled to a side table he breathed slowly. The papers were there.

Spreading them on the desk, Uriah smiled grimly. He would see for himself, prove the lie and then destroy it. Jervis had played away, taken himself another woman and then hoped to pass her bastard off as his own, to have it take all that should have been given a true grandchild.

Marriage lines! Any name could be written on them. Tossing the paper contemptuously across the desk he glanced at the next. As he smoothed the creased paper he felt a finger of ice tracing his spine.

'Bethany Helen Gautier.'

Catching a breath, holding it behind compressed lips, Uriah smoothed the second birth certificate.

'Deinol Vachel Jervis.'

Each name came as a blow between the eyes and the pent-up air was snatched from his mouth.

Gautier, the name of Jervis's great-grandmother, Vachel the

name of his grandmother and Deinol the maiden name of his mother!

Gautier . . . Vachel . . . He stared at the papers. Neither were heard in Darlaston. Gautier was French and so was Vachel, while Deinol was Welsh; all names brought to the family by Verity's forebears taking wives from those countries. But who except Jervis would have known those names? Names followed by the proclamation: 'Father . . . Jervis Gautier Vachel Deinol Buckley.'

His son had been weak, a dreamer, even a fool, but fool enough to put his name to that of another man's children? For the first time doubt crept into Uriah's mind. No, Jervis was not such a fool! Staring at the papers, Uriah's world exploded. Jervis was not such a fool, those children had been born to him . . . the girl who had died in the brook, the boy he had given to Edward Elton's lecher of a son.

A cry erupting from his throat, Uriah crumpled the papers in hands suddenly devoid of feeling.

The Neale woman had said she would see him in hell. A moan the sound of a man in torment tore at his throat. The doors had already closed behind him!

Amber's thoughts were of the letter delivered to her by Ram Dutt, a letter written by Joanna's father before leaving on an expedition to Najibabad. Deinol: she seemed to see the neatly written name her mother must have shortened to Denny. She had read that letter many times in the week since its delivery. It supported the certificates she had found hidden in her mother's Bible, copies of which she had left with Uriah Buckley. Had that man also received such a letter?

'The boy on the heath, he told the place you could be found.'

Bringing her mind to order, Amber forced herself to

concentrate on Ram Dutt, though he himself seemed unable to keep his eyes from Rani.

'He told of an English woman and her—'

'Friend,' Amber said quickly. 'Rani is my friend, she is no servant in this house.'

Nor would she be servant in the house of Ram Dutt. Amber interpreted the look she had seen often in those deep brown eyes. This man loved Rani. She had said as much when she and Rani had sat together one evening, said that love should be accepted; but Rani had shaken her head, tears accompanying her answer. 'The red flower of womanhood blooms but what man can love where he was not the one to pick the first blossom?' She would hear no more, yet Amber knew that deep inside the girl nursed an equal love.

'Would you not like to be seeing India again?' The question was one her friend could refuse to answer but instead she looked openly at the man she had come to love during the time she had lived at that bungalow.

'It is not mattering what I would like.' Speaking softly she told of her rape, of her being cast out, finishing with, 'So to return is not possible, my family would not be accepting me. Rani would still be as the Untouchables, people would turn from her.'

'Not if you were to be returning as wife to Ram Dutt.' Hearing the girl's soft cry he smiled. 'The great god Rama does not place blame where there was only innocence. He sees no fault in the child who walked that path from the river and neither do I; so I ask, be my wife and by that make my home *bahut khubsurat ghar*, a house of beauty.'

Only later, when she had dried Rani's happy tears, did Amber recall the phrase Ram Dutt had used: *bahut khubsurat ghar*, house of beauty. Was it a coincidence he should choose those words?

★   ★   ★

It was a dream, a dream she did not want to end. Amber smiled at the figure sitting beside her, faint lines of worry still visible on the handsome features.

'I were so feared . . . feared that bullet had . . . so feared you were dead.'

A strong hand closed over her own; Amber stayed inside her warm, wonderful dream.

'I watched him come, come across the heath. I guessed he were up to no good the way he used the bushes for cover, but not 'til he raised that shotgun, not until he pointed it direct at you, not 'til then did I realise . . .'

Fingers covering hers tightened.

'But he'll pay, he'll pay for trying to kill you. If it takes my own life, I swear Buckley will pay.'

. . . takes my own life . . .

It seeped through the soft warm mists, each word an icicle stabbing and tearing its way to her brain.

He had recognised the man William Nicholls had also seen leaving the heath. He knew the immorality of Uriah Buckley, but not the vicious evil; the sinister mind that did not even stop at murder in order to satisfy its own wants.

'No!' Her cry as heartfelt as his words, she pressed her cheek to the hand still holding hers. 'You must not go near Bescot Lodge nor the man who owns it, promise me – promise me!'

In the tiny silence following Amber's plea, a pair of blue eyes looked tenderly at her, at red-gold hair a vivid splash against his dark sleeve. He had waited too long, prayed too hard to be with her again, to deny her now. Lifting her gently, drawing her into his arms, he smiled, 'If that is what you wish, sis, then I'll leave Buckley alone.'

★   ★   ★

The mine was already paying its way. In the empty compartment of the train, Amber allowed her thoughts to wander.
The surrounding land which had formed part of its purchase
was to be tilled and set to growing flowers for the making of
perfumes and cosmetics while the more exotic blooms, those
not able to grow in this colder climate, would be raised by
Rani and her husband and the oils shipped to England. He
was to be manager of an estate, Ram had explained, the
owner of which would not mind the growing of flowers on
land not used for tea bushes, an owner he confessed was
Zachary Hayden.

Rani and Ram Dutt . . . it had been some sort of miracle,
but an even greater miracle had been the return of her brother.
He had read the name on a cardboard carton he had found
lying about the dock. Denny had worn the same sheepish look
he had worn in childhood when something he said was not
quite the truth, but she had been so happy having him with
her she had not questioned.

He had not recognised the name Neale, but Amber, and
then the town Darlaston, had seemed too much of a coincidence so he had returned. Then had come the perfumed oils.
But there the miracles had ended.

Who apart from Rani and Becky knew of the need for those
oils, who but Zachary Hayden? But it had been Freddy had
delivered that box to Ley Cottage, explaining Zachary had had
it brought from India. He had not wanted to see her, otherwise he would have come to the cottage himself, but as Freddy
told her, Zachary Hayden was returning immediately to join
his ship.

That had been weeks ago, weeks when the joy of having
Denny returned, of seeing the happiness in Rani's eyes, had
been dulled by the ache in her heart. Zachary Hayden would

have brought the oils himself; but he had not. He had returned immediately to sea.

Leaving the train, walking quickly along well-remembered streets, she entered the tiny cemetery of All Saints church. It had been here in Bloxwich she had first met Zachary Hayden, first realised a love she would never know returned, yet herself would never lose.

As she knelt beside the neatly tended patch of earth, the spring flowers she had brought arranged beside others set beneath the wooden cross, she smiled. Becky Worrall was keeping the promise to care for her mother's grave.

'Denny is home, Mother.' Softly, its sound not disturbing the stillness of the churchyard, Amber whispered. 'He is safe back with me. You would be so proud of him, he has grown tall and strong . . . he will make a fine man. But I have not told him of the papers I found in the Bible you left to us, of his father, of his grandfather. That must wait until he is older, until the hastiness not yet grown out of him is gone. I fear the rashness of youth which he still has would lead him to act without thought of his own safety; but Denny will understand once he knows of what happened between yourself and Jervis Buckley, just as Bethany would understand, as I too understand. You loved Jervis as I love Zachary. It is a love which asks no questions, knows no boundary; it is a love given only once in a lifetime . . . Oh Mother, if only I could be given such love.'

A shadow fell across the patch of ground, stilling the sobbed words. Amber raised her head to look into a face drawn with tension.

'Zachary!' Her eyes sparkled with tears as the sob broke from her.

His vivid blue eyes dark with longing, gleaming with love he could no longer hide, Zachary Hayden reached out his hands, raising her to her feet.

'Amber,' he murmured, 'could you ever love me, could . . . could you be my wife?'

Going into his arms, raising her face to his kiss, to the love she had dreamed of, Amber knew that she could.

0800 గ్యాస్

08459665840